ACCLAIM FOR MAEVE HARAN

'I had to tear this novel from my flatmate's hands, so engrossed had she become' – *Daily Telegraph*

'An entertaining writer with a delicious lightness of touch' – *Sunday Times*

'Unputdownable holiday entertainment' – *Options*

'Realistic, compassionate but still as pacey as they come' – *Cosmopolitan*

'Maeve Haran has become required reading for modern romantics' – *The Times*

'Plenty to laugh at and a strong compelling plot' – *Independent*

'Maeve Haran writes as she is: warm, witty and wry' – *You Magazine*

D1372721

A Family Affair

Maeve Haran

LEIS
FIC
HARA
FAM

PENGUIN BOOKS

SIGNET

Published by the Penguin Group
Penguin Books Ltd, 27 Wrights Lane, London W8 5TZ, England
Penguin Books USA Inc., 375 Hudson Street, New York, New York 10014, USA
Penguin Books Australia Ltd, Ringwood, Victoria, Australia
Penguin Books Canada Ltd, 10 Alcorn Avenue, Toronto, Ontario, Canada M4V 3B2
Penguin Books (NZ) Ltd, 182–190 Wairau Road, Auckland 10, New Zealand

Penguin Books Ltd, Registered Offices: Harmondsworth, Middlesex, England

First published by Michael Joseph 1996
Published in Signet 1997
1 3 5 7 9 10 8 6 4 2

Printed in England by Clays Ltd, St Ives plc

For A. G. with love, as ever

Acknowledgements

With thanks to Susan Watt for being a continuing inspiration, my editor Richenda Todd for her endless patience, Carole Blake for being a good friend as well as unfailingly encouraging, Finn and Anne Kennedy, who founded Clothkits, for background on the ups and downs of running a highly successful mail-order business and, last of all, my family for their love and support and for constantly saying, 'Haven't you finished *yet*?'

Chapter 1

Lily Brandon let the applause wash over her, sweet as honey, and just as busily worked for. The cast had been called back on stage five times and the clapping showed no sign of waning. There was none of that half-hearted acknowledgement actors dread, knowing that for the last fifteen minutes the audience's mind has been not on the play's climax but on dinner and how soon they could get there. This audience had been in the palm of their hands. And sweetest of all, Lily had to admit, was that the loudest applause had been for her.

She waved at the audience, all signs of the intense and austere character she'd just played vanished, and bowed low. She'd put her heart and soul into this role and it had paid off.

'If this doesn't transfer,' hissed Ray, her leading man, when the clapping finally began to die down and the audience groped for their coats, 'I'll open an antiques stall in Brighton.'

Lily squeezed his hand. The rumour was that London's most influential theatre critic had been in the third row, clapping like a madman.

As they all knew, if the reviews were good enough and

there were enough bums on seats, the show might, just might, move on to the West End after its run here. Lily didn't let herself think about it. Whatever happened, this was the best night of her career. If only Ben could have been here it would have been perfect.

But Ben had been committed for months to giving out the awards after a drama school production, and hadn't been able to get out of it. Ben Winter was the London stage's most exciting actor, already in demand for television and teetering on the brink of a film career. At least he'd be at her first-night celebration in the Italian restaurant round the corner. As usual, Lily felt a leap of excitement at the thought of seeing Ben which six months of going out with him hadn't remotely dimmed. She still felt like the fat girl at the party, amazed when the local heart-throb asked her to dance.

Back in her dressing room – cubby hole might have been a more accurate description – Lily hugged her joy to her. If she could have danced around the tiny space, she would have, but there was no room to swing even a rat, let alone a cat, and the already limited inches were reduced by the armfuls of flowers and good-luck cards.

Ray popped his head round the door. 'See you there in ten minutes. If you're late I'll eat your antipasto. Is glamour boy coming?'

Everyone knew about Ben. She nodded.

'That'll annoy the director. He hates being upstaged. Goody. By the way, chook, you were brilliant.'

Lily slipped off her stage clothes and hung them up carefully, her emotions soaring like a skylark on a summer morning. She knew she'd been good, she'd felt it in her gut. Before today she hadn't dared think about her performance, it had seemed like tempting fate, but tonight everyone was acknowledging how terrific she'd been.

It felt gloriously, unashamedly wonderful.

2

Come on, she warned her naked reflection, don't turn into a complacent old cow after one good performance. You might be out of work in six weeks.

Pushing to one side the reality every actor had to live with, she took out a beautiful black dress, short and clingy, chosen to emphasize her endless legs, which men stared at in the street, and to draw attention away from her slightly heavy hips, which women enjoyed pointing out to each other. It had taken her entire first week's wages, but a first-night dinner called for a splash. Maybe in a few months, if they did transfer, she'd be wearing it again, this time to the Ivy, where the top drawer of actors had their first-night celebrations. But for tonight Romeo and Giulio's in Wingfield High Street couldn't be nicer.

Putting on the dress, she released her coils of hair from the elaborate 1940s arrangement the play had required. It fell in tumbling waves over her creamy shoulders. The pale stage make-up suited her, so she simply removed some of its thickness with a baby wipe. She might look a shade over the top, but this was *her* night and she was going to enjoy it. The final touch was a pair of bronze earrings that exactly matched her eyes.

She caught sight of the photo of Ben next to her make-up and kissed it. Ben's dark, intense eyes looked out at her, in the role he was best known for, a television drama about a politician trying to expose a nuclear cover-up. It had made such an impact that real political parties had fought to get Ben to join them, hoping to harness his amazing charisma. Ben had laughed and pointed out that it was only a role; but Lily knew better. One of the things she loved Ben for was how much trouble he took helping other people, especially young actors trying to get their first breaks. That was why, she reminded herself, squashing the sliver of resentment that kept trying to break through, he was at the Sanders School of Dramatic Art tonight, instead of being

3

here to witness her glory. She forced herself to regain her heady joy and set off for the restaurant.

Romeo, aptly named for his flamboyant style, stood in the doorway of the friendly neighbourhood trattoria waiting for her, a red rose in his teeth. Romeo saw himself as the joker of the two, always flashing his giant pepper pot suggestively at shy lady diners, and persuading them to order a 'special' which turned out to be a dessert made of two scoops of ice-cream propping up a large banana with an uncanny resemblance to an erect penis.

He handed the rose to Lily. 'Per la diva,' he announced as though she were Kiri Te Kanawa at Covent Garden rather than Lily Brandon at the Wingfield Theatre. Lily accepted it as if she were the former, hoping he wasn't about to carry her over the threshold.

Fortunately even Romeo knew his limitations and he simply scraped a bow. 'Your friends are inside.'

As Lily stepped into the restaurant the clapping started, this time from the rest of the cast, causing even the eyes of strangers to swivel in her direction. Lily drew herself up and sailed, bosoms thrust forward, past the crowded tables.

One of the waiters produced a camera, immortalizing her forever, with Romeo and Giulio's arms around her, Giulio peering down the front of her dress. Duly autographed, the photograph would be hung on the walls of the restaurant with all the other 'celebrities', so that future diners could peer at them and wonder who on earth they were.

Finally she made it to the crowded table and was enveloped by old friends congratulating her until she felt almost drunk with praise. As the last hug was administered her eyes raked the table for Ben and she had to bite back her disappointment when there was no sign of him. Lily sat down, telling herself he must have been detained at the awards ceremony, refusing to let it spoil things. Instead she selected her favourite tomato and mozzarella salad and, struggling with her conscience but ordering it anyway, some melt-in-your-mouth calf's liver.

By the time her main course arrived he still wasn't there. How long could an awards ceremony take? There are always a million excuses available to the lovelorn and Lily riffled through them for a suitable one. Maybe he'd been roped in by the organizers to have a quick drink afterwards and had been too polite to refuse. Mechanically she ate the delicious food, prepared with love by Giulio, then went to the loo to review the possible explanations and repair her make-up. He couldn't have got the night wrong, she'd talked to him only that morning.

Lily locked herself in a cubicle and willed herself not to cry. Outside she recognized the voices of two of the other actresses, both in minor roles. Neither of them had joined in the warm blanket of praise thrown over Lily. She wondered if she should warn them of her presence but their words cut her short.

'He's not here then?'

'Who?'

'Who do you think? The Olivier of our generation.'

'Probably doesn't know where Wingfield is. Or maybe he's like a cabbie. Won't go beyond the six-mile limit.' They both laughed.

'I bet she only got the part because of him. I mean, what's Lily Brandon ever done?'

It was too much for Lily. She'd worked long and hard to get this role, fighting to repress the bolshy nature that sometimes lost her work. She threw back her long hair and pushed open the door. 'Quite a lot, as a matter of fact,' she blazed. 'I'll get my agent to send your agent my CV, shall I? That's if you have an agent.'

She didn't wait for an answer, but enjoyed the sight of the woman's jaw dropping.

Back in the restaurant there was an unexpected hush at

her return. It didn't take long to see why. Ben Winter had finally arrived, but he was not alone. He was sitting at the far end of the long table and next to him, in the place just vacated by Lily, was the reason he had kept her waiting so long. She was about nineteen, coltishly beautiful, and hanging on his every word.

Ben stood up, his dark liquid eyes full of sincerest apology. 'Lily, love, sorry I'm so late. It was impossible to disentangle myself.' He ran a hand charmingly through his black hair. Lily, not normally either jealous or suspicious, could see from whom. Ben noticed her sceptical look. 'This is Lara, by the way, I've just been giving her some advice on how to get started.'

Lara gazed at him adoringly, reminding Lily of a deer with learning difficulties. Lily sat down in the space that Ray had made for her and tried to chat brightly with him. Three seats away the pink table-cloth lifted for an instant as someone reached down for a fallen napkin, revealing Ben's hand on Lara's nubile knee.

Fury fought with a sick, shaking feeling stronger even than she'd had before going on stage tonight. How could he do this to her? He knew that everyone would be watching. If he wanted to dump her, he could have done it in private, not with two dozen of London's prime gossips watching. He wasn't even showing basic courtesy, let alone love. Lily longed for the meal to be over so that she could escape to her flat and her private misery.

Finally Romeo arrived, grinning like a gargoyle, with a tray of coffees and distributed amaretti in tissue paper to each diner. With cries of childish delight the assembled cast rolled the wrappers into cylinders of tissue and began to light them, enchanted that they burned down almost to the end then, instead of igniting the table-cloth, sailed suddenly towards the ceiling, distributing their cobwebby embers over the other diners.

Lily knew she had to act. She couldn't let herself be walked over like this in front of all her fellow actors.

'Would the signore like a cappuccino?' Romeo asked her, indicating Ben.

Lily took the cup of frothy liquid and with an enchanting smile poured it into Ben's faithless lap. She said goodnight just as a camera flashed from a distant corner of the restaurant, capturing Ben's disbelieving outrage for all posterity.

When she woke the next morning and remembered what had happened, Lily wept. She'd burned her boats, not to mention a precious part of Ben's anatomy. To other people her act might have seemed uncalled for, deranged even, but Lily knew why she'd done it. If she hadn't taken drastic action, she might have let herself believe his lies. This was a statement to herself as much as anyone else that she was nobody's fool, not even Ben's.

The trouble was, it didn't stop her loving him.

Unable to resist the misery that lapped around her, she did what she always did and reached for the phone to call her sister Connie. As she waited for her sister's warm and sympathetic tones to come on the line, Lily wondered what it would be like to have a loving husband, kids, a tidy well-ordered home and some idea what you would be doing the week after next, like Connie had. The order and peace of Connie's life were so removed from her own unpredictable existence, however, that she might as well imagine being ET.

Over a hundred miles away in deepest Dorset Connie Brandon turned left off the main road towards Safeway's. She had been to Bidchester Safeway so often and was so familiar with its layout that she could, literally, do the shop with her eyes closed and end up with all the right products. Maybe she should suggest it as a gameshow idea. Blindfold Supermarket Sweep.

By the traffic lights a black and white poster of two gloriously attractive, apparently naked people licking ice-cream
off a spoon invited her to buy Häagen Dazs ice-cream. Why
did everyone else appear to be having exotic sex when she
got more of a thrill out of packing a nice neat dishwasher?
She made a mental note to buy Ben and Jerry's as a protest.
It wouldn't help her sex life, unless she liberally applied it to
her husband in the manner hinted at by the poster, but she
couldn't be bothered with any of that. Gavin would probably love it, but Connie couldn't be doing with dressing up
in a French maid's outfit or having gleesome threesomes
with the shower attachment. If you had to go to that much
trouble to spice up your love life, forget it. Sex would seem
another chore, less enjoyable than taking the lint out of the
tumble dryer and a lot more time consuming.

She repeated to herself, as she had done countless times
before, that it was the familiarity she liked about marriage,
its safety, the sense of living a sane and structured life. And
if the cost was a certain predictability, so be it. All the
same, she wondered how other people kept the passion in
their relationships. Maybe they didn't. Maybe they took up
gardening and transferred their lust and libido into growing things. There had to be some explanation for the British
obsession with producing outsize marrows.

She was about to pull into her usual parking space, which
she had ergonomically calculated as being the shortest distance between the trolley park and the supermarket entrance, when she had a sudden vision of her sister Lily,
single, independent and unencumbered by children or shopping lists, being tied to a bed by a nameless man with a
terrific torso and no small talk.

And she wished it were her.

'Here are the amended designs for the new collection you
asked for, Mrs Brandon.'

Charlotte Brandon, Lily and Connie's mother, jumped at the interruption and ran a hand through her neat grey hair, both uncharacteristic gestures. The young junior designer waited nervously to be ticked off for spoiling the great woman's train of thought. She'd heard about Charlotte Brandon's demanding standards and knew that she didn't suffer interruptions gladly.

Charlotte, however, simply thanked the girl graciously. She'd been sitting at her desk in Victoriana's offices, in their converted watermill high above the Dorset countryside she loved so much, looking out at the millstream in the afternoon sunshine, but noticing none of its familiar beauty. Instead she was thinking about her daughters and why neither of them had shown the slightest interest in the business. Perhaps with Lily it wasn't surprising. She'd always been a rebel, and though she had a strong style of her own, had never been even remotely interested in fashion. But she'd once had high hopes of Connie. Then Connie had suddenly settled down and thrown herself into homemaking and motherhood with an indecent passion that Charlotte took as a rebuke against her own haphazard ideas of childcare. Motherhood, Charlotte had found, was all very well, but deeply boring. She couldn't understand this crazy child-centred generation of Connie's who seemed to want to immolate themselves on the altar of maternity and run round after their offspring to endless classes and hobbies, half way between a governess and an unpaid chauffeur. Her own children had been expected to fit in with Victoriana's burgeoning needs.

In the beginning Charlotte had designed clothes because she was so angry at the greedy dictates of fashion which made women feel they couldn't wear a favourite garment if the hem was suddenly an inch too long, or the shade didn't conform to what some male fashion guru thought they should be wearing that year. She had simply wanted to design romantic and nostalgic clothes that reflected a long-gone and more peaceful time, and would last for years. The speed of the company's success had taken them all by surprise, blossoming within a few years from a tiny enterprise run by both of them to a venture with 150 employees. The press had loved them and Charlotte Brandon had become a sudden star in the clothing business. But for what, when, thirty years on, none of her three children wanted to take it on after her?

Just last night she'd asked Edward, her husband, if he thought that their son Jonathan or his wife might consider it. Edward had almost laughed. 'Jonathan doesn't even like to go south of the river,' he had retorted, 'and dirt is a four-letter word to Judith. She couldn't cope with country life.' She had to admit Edward had a point. Jonathan and Judith were confirmed townies. She couldn't see either of them moving here, where Victoriana's soul and inspiration were based.

The pain she'd been having in her chest tightened suddenly with the anxiety. If none of her children would take on the business what on earth were they going to do? The idea of strangers getting their hands on Victoriana horrified Charlotte. It would be like burglars blundering into her home and destroying everything because they had no sense of what was of value and what wasn't.

The rest of the conversation with Edward came back to her. Crazily, he had suggested they approach Lily again and when Charlotte had protested he'd accused her of never loving Lily because she'd been difficult and plain as a child. He'd even dragged up that ridiculous incident about not letting Lily pose for the catalogue when she was ten. Edward still insisted it was because Lily hadn't fitted her mother's notion of the Victoriana ideal like blonde and fragile Connie had.

Charlotte sighed. There was absolutely no point thinking about Lily running Victoriana. The idea was ridiculous.

Chapter 2

She wasn't going to think about him any more.

Lily kicked the pile of leaves with the toe of her tartan Doc Marten, watching them eddy up into the air of Hyde Park with satisfaction as if they were bits of Ben Winter's inflated ego. The trouble was, he kept sneaking back into her mind. Why, when a relationship folded, could you only remember the good things? The surprise lunches in dark bistros going on all afternoon because, unlike people in the real world, actors' days were free. The wonderful gossip. The sympathy when you were feeling neurotic. The cups of tea in bed. Having someone else to read your reviews and keep the worst from you, at least until after lunch. His wonderful, dark, brooding eyes that could nevertheless light up in fun, even if it was usually at someone else's expense.

You weren't going to think about him, she reminded herself severely. And why was she here at all? Hyde Park was miles from her home. As if she didn't know. It was round the corner from Ben's flat and he might just be out walking. Lily knew the absurdity of her logic. If she wanted to see him she could just ring him. Maybe he'd put the phone down, maybe he wouldn't. Ben liked drama, especially drama that starred him. But she couldn't do that. Somehow walking here on the offchance of meeting him was acceptable where phoning him was not. It wouldn't be a climbdown.

Sunset was approaching and the afternoon was getting colder. There seemed to be lovers everywhere: on benches, holding each other's hands, warming each other up, running and laughing, as if entry to the park were only permitted to people in pairs.

Lily turned for home, picking up an evening paper and a kingsize Mars bar for the tube home. Maybe he would have rung her to apologize and there would be a message on her machine. You weren't going to think about him, she repeated the mantra, grateful that from now on the day would be quite a rush. Getting home, grabbing a sandwich, changing, getting to the theatre.

It was crowded on the tube, and warm. Lily felt grateful for the crowds, especially since she had a seat. She unwrapped the Mars bar and settled down to read the paper.

It was there on page 18. Under the headline One Hump or Two? The story of how aspiring actress Lily Brandon had dumped her cappuccino in lover Ben Winter's lap because he turned up with a twenty-year-old at her first-night party. There was even a photograph.

He looked so ridiculous that Lily couldn't restrain a giggle. He looked so ridiculous that he would never speak to her again.

When she walked into her flat the phone was ringing. Lily was convinced it would be Ben – and not exactly phoning to apologize. Instead it was Mo, her agent.

'Hey,' Mo demanded. Clearly, she had seen the article. 'How did they manage to get the photo? Did you tip them off you were going to do it?'

Lily was horrified. 'Of course not. It was an entirely spontaneous gesture.'

'You'll have every woman over thirty on your side. You could be a feminist figurehead.'

'Look, Mo,' Lily insisted, appalled. 'I just want to forget the whole thing.' She changed the subject. 'Any more news about the play transferring? They must decide soon.'

'Not yet. Don't worry. I'm hounding them.'

Lily could believe it. Mo was like a British bulldog when it came to her clients.

'Still, you've got great reviews.'

'But I want to work, and don't quote me the statistics on actors' unemployment or I'll jump on your mobile phone.'

'I know, I know, I'll let you know the very instant I hear.'

Lily stole another look at the offending article. At least there was one consolation. It was the London-only *Evening Express*. That meant her mother wouldn't see it. She disapproved of Lily enough already.

'Troy! Troy, come here, you bad dog!' Charlotte Brandon watched in irritation as their red setter disappeared up the steep side of the valley and out of sight. It was a glorious morning. The mist hadn't yet lifted from the tops of the trees and there was an opalescent quality to the light. The sun was shining, but palely, as if through very fine muslin. Underfoot the grass was crunchy and splintered with early frost. Charlotte continued her walk along the floor of the valley. Troy, named after the notorious Sergeant Troy, because of the dog's disgraceful habit of chasing anything female and even, it had to be said, anything male if nothing more interesting provided itself, would soon come down when he failed to find any rabbits.

Charlotte drew in deep breaths of air as she walked. It was so fresh down here where only the occasional farm vehicle could penetrate. There was a tang of the sea, just out of sight at the end of their land, and gulls wheeled overhead hoping for a tractor that might be ploughing up the ground and releasing fresh worms. They were too late. All the ploughing had been done and now it was a question of waiting till spring.

Charlotte wondered how many people were lucky enough to love a place as she did this one. After a lifetime here, she knew every sign and rhythm. She could tell what month it was, what week almost, without consulting a calendar, simply from what was being done on the land.

Over the other side of the valley she caught sight of a wheeled hut, now being used to store feed for the sheep instead of its original use of providing a home for the shepherd as he moved his flock from pasture to pasture. Even at the beginning of her married life there had been a shepherd living in it, who could be tracked from valley to hillside by watching out for the curl of smoke coming from the small stove inside his hut. He'd even worn a smock which Charlotte had used as the inspiration for one of her early designs. Now one man, a farm worker not a shepherd, fed the sheep by flinging bales from his Land-Rover.

She might be a silly old romantic fool to mourn the passing of the old Dorset way of life, but other people must feel the same way, because they bought her clothes. Charlotte didn't dress anyone in cotton shepherds' smocks any more, but she did sell Victorian petticoats and nightdresses by the thousand.

She whistled for Troy. She knew the irony about nostalgia was that the past hadn't always been soft and kind at all, that for many it had been a life-and-death struggle, in which death had very often won. Nevertheless, people still had a longing for a simpler way of life and Charlotte had tapped that feeling.

But what had been the point, after all, if she had built the business up and there was no one in the family to succeed her? Again the old anxiety closed in on her, tightening her chest and making her struggle for breath. Dammit, she'd forgotten the pills she was supposed to take. She could picture the bottle sitting tauntingly on the kitchen table. It was time to go back and take one, but Troy had picked up the scent of rabbit and refused to answer any call. Cursing him Charlotte began to climb the steep bank. At the top she saw him, only feet away, wagging his tail teasingly, thinking what a good game this was. Then to her terror she couldn't move. The pain had become vicelike, crushing the breath out of her. Charlotte sat down heavily, feeling dizzy. She must have climbed too fast.

Seeing his mistress suddenly sink on to the ground, Troy whined frantically. Although Charlotte could see him with her usual clarity she couldn't even stretch out towards him. He came immediately and settled at her feet.

But it was no use. His mistress wasn't playing any longer.

Chapter 3

In the small silent room Edward Brandon reached out and touched his wife's face. Until this moment he had not fully appreciated how life might feel without Charlotte. By sixty-four you had lost enough friends and contemporaries to appreciate that life was fragile. You had even witnessed some tragic losses of your friends' children and seen those friends buckle under the guilt of feeling they should have gone first. Yet none of that prepared you for your own personal tragedies. Charlotte was quite simply the centre of his world. For nearly forty years they'd brought up a family and watched Victoriana grow from infant company to thriving business. They had spent almost every waking moment together. Sometimes they had infuriated each other, even screamed at each other, but mostly they had drawn strength, as well as fun and amusement, from each other's presence. By now a bond between them existed that nothing could seriously threaten. Nothing, that is, except death. He closed his eyes.

Gently Lily rapped on the glass door of the small room. Next to the bed in a red plastic chair pushed right up against it, her father slept with his head on the threadbare counterpane. Watching them, Lily longed to feel for someone what they seemed to feel for each other. And yet the more powerful the love the harder it would be for either to cope without the other. What would he do if Charlotte didn't recover? They were like threads woven across a lifetime into a single piece of cloth.

Anxiety shot through Lily, almost physical in its intensity. What would *she* do if her mother died? There were so many unanswered questions lying between them. She loved her mother deeply and powerfully, but she knew Charlotte had denied herself to Lily in a way that was not true of her other children. She had been so daunting that Lily had never dared to try and find out why. Instead she'd felt that there must be something wrong with her, that she must be less lovable than the others. *I became an actress, Ma, so that I could get the approval of thousands, when what I really wanted was the approval of one. Why couldn't you ever give it?*

As though he sensed her gaze on him Edward opened his eyes. 'How long have I been out for the count?'

Lily handed him the cup of tea she'd fetched from the WRVS canteen. 'Not long. Why don't I take over for a moment so you can stretch your legs. Connie's outside with the brood and Jonathan rang from the car. They're just heading into Bidchester. They'll be here soon.'

Edward accepted the tea gratefully. He stood up stiffly, looking vulnerable and old and Lily saw with a shock how crisis reversed roles. She was the parent now, her mother and father the dependent children.

Holding her mother's pale, blue-veined hand, Lily noticed that it was damp with her own tears. 'I love you, Ma,' she said softly, 'even if you don't seem to love me. Don't leave me. If you die I'll never understand.'

Charlotte did not stir. In spite of the intrusive technology she looked surprisingly still and peaceful with only a faint bluish tinge around the mouth to hint at her condition. And then, very slowly, her eyelids flickered and opened. For a

17

second they held Lily's with an almost beseeching air, like someone begging for forgiveness, but Lily was too excited to notice. 'Pa!' she shouted deliriously. 'For God's sake come. She's waking up.'

Edward was the first to run in, his face alight with sudden joy. Then Connie and Gavin followed with Tara and Jeremy on their heels.

'Charlotte,' sobbed Edward, no longer feeling he had to be strong for her sake, 'Charlotte, my darling, thank God.'

'What will you do if she dies?' Judith Brandon asked her husband Jonathan as they drove towards Bidchester Hospital in their impeccable city-clean Mercedes.

'What do you mean?'

It wasn't like Judith to initiate a conversation about his emotional life. Judith always seemed to prefer him to be strong and silent. His business had had problems lately but he'd got the distinct impression that she didn't want to hear about them.

Jonathan thought about his mother and realized that he hadn't seriously confronted the possibility of her death. Ma was a rock. She couldn't possibly die. She was too strong. She would outlive his father, he was sure. Jonathan had a habit of not confronting painful possibilities and it had stood him in good stead. He didn't intend to change it now.

'About the business, I mean,' Judith said, her extra-ordinary pale-blue eyes steady under the white-blonde fringe. 'Sell it?'

Silly him for imagining his wife might be thinking about something as trivial as his feelings.

'Why, you don't want to run it, do you? My parents'd be thrilled if you did.'

Judith thought about it. As a matter of fact Victoriana did interest her. The company had enormous potential for making more money, and if someone put real business systems in, it could be highly profitable. But Judith had other fish to fry: persuading Paula, her boss at Imagemakers, to make her a full partner, and taking the company into fresh and lucrative fields like political lobbying. Anyway the idea of burying herself in Dorset was absurd. She loathed the country. It was dull and dirty and you always ate too much there.

Jonathan glanced at his wife's perfect profile to see if there were even the slightest trace of sympathy for his mother in it. But her eyes were now hidden behind the black lenses of her fashionable sunglasses and he could only guess their expression. She turned her head to look at a mannequin in the window of Country Casuals as they passed through the small town of Bryly.

They stopped at a red light. 'You really don't give a stuff about whether my mother lives or dies do you?'

'Do *you*?'

'Yes,' Jonathan liked to think of himself as a humane person, besides which his mother was part of his security and his sense of himself, 'as a matter of fact I do.'

The lights changed back to green again. 'You'd better get a move on then,' Judith said and plugged in the earphones to her portable CD machine.

They reached the hospital half an hour later. 'Hello, Ma.' Jonathan laid a huge bouquet on the bed. 'What's all this I hear about you pretending to be ill?'

'We knew it had to be nonsense,' Judith added. 'The world couldn't turn on its axis without Charlotte Brandon.'

Lily watched her mother smile faintly and was consumed with powerful jealousy. Now that she was recovering, Charlotte seemed happier to see bloody Judith than she had her own daughters. Judith had a toughness to match Charlotte's own which she and Connie lacked.

The small room began to take on the air of a bustling airport lounge with so many comings and goings that

19

eventually the staff nurse tersely pointed to a sign reminding them that it was only two visitors at a time. With something close to a sigh of relief, Jonathan and Judith said their goodbyes and headed back for London.

A week later Charlotte was allowed home to the joy of everyone, except the small gaggle of reporters staying at The George in Bidchester who had been sent to follow her progress. They had rather hoped her stay in hospital, which coincided with their stay in a five-star hotel, would last a little longer .

Edward's delight at her return was touching. He filled every vase with her favourite white delphiniums, imported from the Channel Islands, and shopped fanatically to make sure they had all the healthy foods the doctors had insisted on. The doctors' other piece of advice was trickier. Charlotte should eat well and take plenty of exercise but avoid anything that taxed her or was stress-inducing. Like running Victoriana. The whole family knew how tough it was going to be to get Charlotte to rest. Charlotte fully occupied still radiated enough energy to run a power station, but in enforced idleness she was positively volcanic.

Despite Edward's opposition, she summoned June, her most trusted employee, to her bedside every day and sent her away with a list of things to check that would take a normal person weeks but Charlotte expected to be done by tomorrow.

Once or twice Edward went into the office but spent the whole time worrying about how Charlotte was getting on in his absence. It was on one of these days that he came home early to find her standing on a chair, resplendent in one of her own Victoriana nightdresses (the pure cotton kind that took hours to iron but which appealed to the customer's masochistic sense of being in touch with history), reaching for a pile of Victoriana catalogues on a high shelf in their study.

Edward, usually the calming influence to Charlotte's fireworks, finally lost his temper. 'What the hell do you think you're doing, Charlotte?' he demanded.

'I can't stay in bed indefinitely.'

'Blast indefinitely. You've just had a major heart attack.'

'All right, all right,' she conceded impatiently, 'I'll go back to bed. But someone's got to run Victoriana, and you're too busy fussing over me. The new catalogue needs to be sorted out. We've got to do something, Edward.'

Edward knew she was right. It had always been Charlotte's company, even though she depended on him far more than people thought to run it with her. Now that she was so ill he wanted to look after her. What was the point of running a successful business if it cost you the person you loved most? He should take Charlotte away somewhere so that she had to forget all about it; and that meant someone else was going to have to take over the reins at Victoriana.

It was time to call the family together.

Lily heard the phone ringing in the distance, as though it were in the next door flat, and realized it was because she had a pillow over her head. She and her best friend Maxie had been out to drown her sorrows last night and to dissect, glass of wine by glass of wine, her relationship with Ben Winter and whether he was an out-and-out rat or a deeply creative individual who had to have more licence to behave badly than ordinary mortals. Irritatingly Maxie had stuck to the former, adding a few alternative descriptions such as bastard, shitbag, two-timer, and insisted that he had been seen out with the twenty-year old Bambi lookalike every night since. Lily, proud of her assertive action, but missing him like hell, was inclined to backslide a little.

The evening had ended with Maxie shouting at her friend that if she and Ben Winter got back together she would never speak to her again.

The phone call, she assumed, was Maxie ringing to apologize.

'Am I speaking to Lily Brandon?' Lily didn't recognize the voice.

'Yes.'

'This is Miles Langdon. I'm the news editor of the *Sunday Special*.'

Lily shuddered at the thought of the most notorious sleaze-rag in England having her phone number.

'We wanted to make you an offer of a very considerable sum of money for an exclusive interview about your relationship with Ben Winter. It would be very good for your career,' Miles Langdon smarmed.

Lily almost felt the grease ooze out of the phone.

His voice changed from wheedling to silkily threatening. 'We can run it all anyway, you know. It's just that you could come out of it much better than him if you took the initiative. Quite the heroine even. I'm sure under that liberal façade he's just as chauvinistic as the rest of us, isn't he?'

Lily could imagine just how chauvinistic Mr Miles Langdon was. Probably told his women reporters to put on short skirts and lie down and think of England in the cause of a good story.

'Mr Langdon,' Lily wished she was standing next to him so she could stamp on his feet with her Doc Martens, 'you can forget any idea of an interview. I wouldn't dream of giving an interview to your paper. In fact I wouldn't even line my cat-tray with it.' The fact that she didn't have a cat was neither here nor there.

She slammed down the phone, hit by the terrible thought that if the *Sunday Special* were after her she had to be news, and that meant there might be others chasing her too. She sank under the covers, panicking. Where could she go? She thumbed through her vast and tatty address book for Maxie's number. Maxie lived in an enormous crumbling flat in Finsbury Park which she shared with three other actors and one poor person in regular employment who ended up paying all the bills.

Someone was answering the phone. Thank God, it was Maxie.

'Max, can I come and stay for a few days? Some horrible newspaper is after me.'

'Wanting you to spill the beans on Ben Winter's offstage performance, eh?'

'Maxie, don't you start.'

'Look, kiddo, I'm devastado about this but I'm going on tour – some of us have careers, remember – and I've rented my room to another actor. By the way, promise I won't tell the *Sunday Special*, but what *is* beautiful Ben like in bed?'

Maxie was never to find out because Lily looked out of her window at that moment and screamed. She had carried the phone into the bathroom and begun to run a bath. Up the linden tree, not three feet away, a photographer nestled, training his telephoto lens through her bathroom window.

For at least a second they both stared at each other. He was plump and balding and looked extremely uncomfortable, like a budgie trying to balance on a cocktail stick. Lily even had time to wonder if he was freezing to death before they both came to their senses and he reached for his flashgun.

'Maxie,' hissed Lily, her heart thumping, 'there's a photographer up a tree trying to take my picture. What the hell am I going to do?'

'Go and throw water over him.'

'I can't. He'll just take a picture of me doing it.'

Maxie thought about this for a moment. 'Not if you do it through the curtains with the shower attachment.'

Lily pulled the curtains and crawled along the floor, phone clutched under her chin. She turned the taps on full volume, then she switched the dial to Shower. It was absolutely freezing. Parting the curtains only an inch or two so that she was still entirely invisible, she opened the window and aimed at the intruder.

His screams were music to her ears.

She was telling herself that she'd better watch this new habit of hers of physically attacking men when her father reached her to summon her for the family meeting.

'It's not Ma?' she asked anxiously, imagining a relapse.

'No, no, she's fine. It's family business.'

It took Lily five minutes to pack. No one had yet worked out her connection with Charlotte Brandon and Victoriana. She would be safe there. It would mean five hours a day commuting for the play, but anything was better than being photographed sitting on the loo by shameless members of the tabloid press corps.

She was half way out of the door when the phone rang a final time. Lily stiffened at the thought that it could be another journalist, grateful that the answering machine would pick it up.

Ben's voice electrified her. 'Lily love,' it caressed, managing to convey both abject contrition and deep sincerity – no wonder he earned so much from voiceovers – 'I can't tell you how sorry I am about all this. Could you possibly get in touch? It's pretty urgent.'

Lily couldn't resist playing it back once, soaking herself in the beauty of his voice. But was he apologizing for how he'd treated her or because he was worried that his honourable image as the good guy of the left might be tarnished if Lily should talk to the press?

She reminded herself firmly that Maxie had sighted him bopping with Bambi not two nights ago, and firmly closed the door behind her.

The thought of Ben waiting fruitlessly for *her* call was enormously satisfying.

*

'Why do you think we're being summonsed?' Judith asked her husband snappishly, sipping the warm water with a sliver of ginger she always had first thing. Saturdays were precious and she'd thought the old bag was out of danger.

'Your guess is as good as mine.' Jonathan wondered whether it was worth slipping his hand between his wife's legs and trying to persuade her to make love before they set out. There was something about her white-blonde Nordic looks, the veins blue just under the surface of her pale skin, the bones tiny and brittle-seeming, that turned him on almost obscenely. It was almost as if you could take her delicate wrists and snap them in two. And yet, as he knew to his cost, beneath that breakable exterior Judith was purest steel. Under the covers he could feel his erection build, but Judith's expression of cool efficiency meant that her mind was already elsewhere and he didn't feel like starting the day with another humiliating rejection. He was, he knew, a bit of a disappointment to Judith. She liked winners and Jonathan didn't quite conform to her expectations.

'Right.' She threw back the covers, letting in the brutal cold air. 'There's time for half an hour on the Stairmaster before we leave.'

Jonathan grabbed her hand and, even though it went against his better judgement, pulled her down on to the bed. 'I didn't turn out to be quite the meal ticket you'd hoped for, did I, my sweet?'

'No, you didn't, darling,' she agreed with a frosty smile. 'More of a luncheon voucher really.'

She brushed off all the traces of his embrace. Jonathan was right in detecting her disappointment and she felt irritated by his remark. Had he said it as simply an honest statement of the position between them she might have admired his candour. But she knew that wasn't what lay

25

behind it. It was a request for reassurance. And handing out reassurance wasn't one of Judith's priorities.

'Have you seen my guitar music, Ma?' Jeremy put his head round the kitchen door.

Connie Brandon looked up from her favourite task of filling in her diary for the months ahead. All those school terms, half terms and dinner parties stretching reassuringly on into next year's diary made her feel life had a pattern and a rhythm to it. How Lily coped with being single Connie couldn't imagine. Connie had hated being single. The only trouble was, sometimes when she'd filled in all these events, she got the strangest feeling she'd already lived them. 'When did you last see it?'

'It was in the sitting room. Tara hid it because she thought I might impose some culture on her when she wanted to watch *Blind Date*.'

His sister stuck her tongue out at him. 'Since when was that awful crap you play culture?' Tara demanded.

'How would you know what culture was anyway, couch potato? You think *Baywatch* is intellectually stimulating.'

Connie shook her head. They were seventeen and fifteen and they'd been like this since they were two and four. Once upon a time she'd fantasized about having intelligent conversations over the dinner table with her children but Tara hardly ate and Jeremy hoovered up his food in five minutes flat, no matter how long it had taken to prepare, then rushed back to his precious guitar.

Her husband Gavin appeared, looked in the mirror next to the sink, straightened the witty tie she'd given him, and leaned down to kiss her.

'Will you be in the shop this morning? That exporter from the Philippines is supposed to be coming in with some samples.'

Connie swore into her cornflakes. It was the family meeting today and she'd have to miss him. Talking to exporters was the part of running the shop she enjoyed most, now that the recession had hit and they couldn't dash off to Morocco or the Philippines on buying trips themselves. Connie pushed her worries over the shop to one side. It had been so easy at the beginning when they'd started One World. They'd been young, idealistic and broke, backpacking round Nepal, and had come home with armfuls of glorious wooden carvings they'd bought for almost nothing. People setting up their first homes had snapped them up and Gavin and Connie found they could sell anything cheap and exotic they could lay their hands on. Now, either tastes had changed or people had less money and One World, in its new large premises, was feeling the pinch.

'Could you reorganize him? It's the family pow-wow today, remember.'

'What's it all about?'

'The future of Victoriana, I imagine.'

'Maybe they're going to ask you to take over from Charlotte. With your experience of running the shop you'd be brilliant.' She was touched at Gavin's belief in her. He was always pushing her on to try new things.

'Of course they're not,' Connie said too quickly. They would never ask her because she'd always told them she was too committed to the shop and her family. She knew the shop needed her, that Gavin couldn't afford to pay another salary, but the truth was she was yearning for change. And her family, much as she loved them, could be very trying.

She surveyed the pile of dirty crockery piled on top of the dishwasher. They could do it themselves for once. Connie wanted time to dress up like a high-powered businesswoman for this meeting.

*

Lily belted down the motorway in her Beetle with a tape blaring. It was going to be an incredible rush to get back for tonight, but family meetings were rare, and at least all this activity took her mind off Ben. Despite herself she wondered what he'd be doing. Staying in bed late probably. With Bambi. She wrenched her mind away from Ben Winter. She was getting to be like a dog chewing its own paw. This had to stop.

The sight of her parents' home did the trick. The 400-year-old farmhouse, half-hidden at the bottom of the valley, never failed to move her with its secluded beauty. Built by a farmer who had aspirations above his station, it was in mellow golden stone, sitting between two gentle hillsides as if held in an embrace. Even though it was late October, and higher up the farm track everything was ploughed and bare, down here you could almost feel it was summer.

She could see exactly why Dorset, with its unchanging agricultural rhythms, had inspired her mother to start Victoriana, so that she could live and work in one cherished place. Today, on this glorious afternoon, she felt the draw too.

Her father must have been watching for her because he was standing outside waving a welcome. In this he seemed to have a sixth sense because even when she dropped in by surprise he seemed to be there, waiting. She could picture her room with its crisp linen sheets and the fresh flowers her mother would have arranged there. All she really wanted was a hug from Charlotte, but the flowers would have to do.

'Am I the only one here?' She kissed her father. It had been such a glorious morning that Lily had dawdled and had had to race the final few miles in case she were late.

'Jonathan and Connie's cars are round the back. We're all in the dining room having coffee.'

The west-facing room glowed with the warmth from the log fire that crackled away in the vast inglenook that took

28

up the whole of the end wall. A silver coffee pot reflected the flames. Lily kissed everyone then sat down with her cup and one of her mother's celebrated ginger biscuits.

Edward raised an eyebrow at his wife then stood up.

'It seemed appropriate to hold this gathering here since it was in this room we dreamed up the very first Victoriana garment.' He reached out and smiled at Charlotte, remembering. 'A frilly nightgown your mother copied from one in the Bidchester Agricultural Museum with about a thousand flounces on it. We've come a long way since then.'

They have too, thought Lily. Victoriana was one of the most successful mail-order businesses around, its name instantly a by-word for class and quality. Lily noticed Judith exchange a bored glance with Jonathan and wanted to kick her. Both of them, it seemed to Lily, were relentlessly out of step with Victoriana's philosophy. Their own flat was minimalist and uncomfortable. Everything was stored in invisible cupboards. A knick-knack that escaped would die of loneliness. When Lily had once asked her sister-in-law if she'd do anything different next time, meaning more comfortable, Judith had said she'd get rid of the light switches.

Charlotte glanced in their direction and, noting her gaze, Judith's expression changed from boredom to one of extreme fascination. Snake, thought Lily. Of course, Charlotte and Edward were perfectly entitled to appoint whoever they wanted but she couldn't help hoping it wouldn't be Judith. Charlotte owned 41 per cent of the shares, and with Edward's 20 per cent they easily had a controlling interest. Each of the children had 10 per cent, leaving the remaining 9 per cent to Leo Orson, the friend who'd helped finance them in the beginning when they'd been desperately short of money. He had since emigrated to Australia and become rich in his own right, but so far he'd resisted all offers to sell his shares back.

'It seems to us we have three options,' her father continued. 'Sell – but Victoriana has been your mother's life's work and we also feel great loyalty to our staff, some of whom have been with us from the start; we could put in a manager, which appeals to neither of us very much; or we could ask one of you.' He glanced round at his children. 'And that's what we've decided to do.'

There was a palpable tension in the room which Lily was shocked to recognize as sibling rivalry. One of the fundamentals about having a brother or sister was that you might not want a toy yourself, but you'd drum your heels on the floor and demand it, if there was any chance of it being given to one of them instead.

Edward seemed to have anticipated this. 'You may not agree with the decision we've made, but we'd ask you to respect it. We've thought long and hard about who would be the best person. Whoever we ask will have to make some sacrifice but we feel it will benefit them as well as Victoriana.'

He smiled at Connie and her heart thudded with hope that he was going to announce her as Charlotte's successor. 'Connie, you already have the shop and your family.' His eyes travelled on. 'Lily has her stage career. Jonathan and Judith have their businesses.' Edward took a deep breath. He'd been up half the night persuading Charlotte of the wisdom of his next words. 'We feel the best successor to Charlotte at Victoriana would be you, Lily. We believe, with your determination and your sense of style, you would be just the person to take Victoriana into the next century.'

Edward waited for Lily's reaction. He'd known she would be astonished, that she might not even agree. If she did, he was convinced she would not only run Victoriana effectively, but that it could be the making of her, giving her the stability and framework, as well as the belief in herself,

30

that he believed her life lacked. It was, he knew, a calculated risk, but one he felt was worth taking.

'But I don't know anything about managing a company,' she protested, utterly taken aback.

A series of unpleasant snorting laughs conveyed that Jonathan wasn't entirely behind his father's suggestion. 'That's ridiculous Pa. Lily's never even run a soup kitchen. She's already the laughing stock of London for pouring a drink over some actor. She'd never be taken seriously.' Lily could hardly believe it when he rummaged in his jacket pocket and produced the report about Ben and the cappuccino.

'Thank you, Jonathan,' she breathed, 'you've even kept the cutting. How thorough. Did you think we wouldn't believe you?'

'For God's sake, Dad,' Jonathan ignored her, 'Lily's an *actress*.'

He made it sound like an insult.

Lily felt her temper rising, as it always did when she was up against the odds. The fact was, none of her family believed in her, apart from Edward. He'd probably talked Ma into this. Lily's eyes crept to her mother's face, consumed with the familiar longing for her mother to think well of her, to give the approval she'd always yearned for. But this would be a dangerous way of trying to get it. If things went wrong, her mother might never forgive her.

Edward seemed to read her thoughts. 'We've offered you this because we think you can do it. Will you try?'

Connie fought back her bitter disappointment. She'd been so sure they'd ask her, and equally sure she'd accept. 'Do you really think Lily's got enough experience to run a company?' she asked hesitantly.

'We didn't have any experience,' Edward reminded her, surprised that Connie at least wasn't behind Lily. 'We weren't business people.'

No, Jonathan was tempted to add furiously, and you still aren't now.

'We were art students who just believed in something passionately. Lily will have George to advise her financially, and June on the orders side, plus a team of designers. It's a lot more than we had. Well, Lily?'

'I'm in the middle of a play, Pa, I can't.' The truth was that she had never, before this moment, remotely considered running Victoriana.

'When it finishes then.'

'We're hoping it'll transfer to the West End.'

Edward looked as though he'd been kicked.

'Maybe all this has been unfair on you, too sudden. Look, why don't we go for a walk and talk about it some more? You can ask me anything you want to.' He almost added: away from the others.

She held on to Edward tightly as they made their way through the garden and out towards the fields above the farmhouse. Lily took in their mournful beauty. She wondered what it would be like to come home to this place where she'd grown up, to leave the bitchy, competitive world of the theatre and live somewhere where people probably wished her well and where they led sane and steady lives, still with some relationship with the seasons and the landscape. Her mother had understood that yearning in people and it was a great part of her success. Did she share that capacity herself? If she ran Victoriana would she be any good at it?

'I asked you to take over,' Edward read her thoughts, 'because I believe in you.' He put his hand on her shoulder and stopped her for a moment. 'You could do it, Lily, I know you could. Don't listen to Jonathan. He sees the business simply as an asset: property, machines, turnover. He'd probably call our employees "human resources", as though they weren't people at all. Victoriana matters round here. It isn't just a flibbertigibbet fashion company. Whole families depend on us who won't get jobs if we sell up. And what about the customers? We have letters from them, boxes of them, saying they've always worn our clothes. They send us photos of themselves and their children in Victoriana dresses. How can we let all that go? I know this is a big step for you. Why don't you go down to the Mill and have a look round for yourself before you make up your mind?'

Lily felt sick and shaky as she walked up the narrow road towards the Mill. The sun shone as though especially for her. A flock of sheep appeared, packed tightly into the lane. Lily recognized Mrs Field, the farmer's mother, in charge of them. Mrs Field was eighty, if she was a day. She persisted in wearing a jerkin made out of old coal sacks with the words Charringtons Fuels clearly visible on her chest, like some youth proudly sporting Nike or Puma on his expensive leisurewear, even though her son drove a brand-new Rover car. The jerkin was tied up with string over ancient waterproof trousers tucked in to what looked like her son's gum boots. Mrs Field carried a crook and as she bore down on Lily with the sun behind her, she had a magical quality of timelessness and endurance. Lily smiled at her.

Mrs Field ignored Lily and her romantic city ways. 'Get out of the bloody way!' she bellowed. Lily obliged, deciding that maybe there were more of her mother's attitudes in her than she'd realized.

It was lunchtime at the Mill, which meant Lily could wander uninterrupted. She walked quickly through the warehouse area in one of the barn conversions, then up through the design section, to the orders department. On the wall, stock supply was monitored via boards listing all the lines with different coloured stickers. Why on earth hadn't her parents installed a computer system?

She made her way towards her parents' office, over-looking the stream, on the top floor. It had a panoramic view of the countryside for miles around. The room was both spacious and cosy at the same time, the kind of feat her mother pulled off so well. There were two cork boards above the desks, one displaying the upcoming season's designs, the other with letters and photos pinned to it. Lily leaned over and read some of them. They were all from longtime customers, saying what they liked, loathed or felt could be improved about Victoriana's clothes. One photograph showed a whole family bearing a startling resemblance to the Von Trapps, with six children entirely clothed in Victoriana outfits. Another showed three generations – grandmother, mother and child – all in Victoriana. The level of feedback was genuinely touching. The customers clearly saw Victoriana as part of their lives. How many companies, Lily wondered, got customer involvement like this? She wondered why no one had thought of using this brilliant stuff in the catalogue.

In spite of herself, Lily found she was getting interested in Victoriana.

She sat down at her mother's desk and looked for something to write on. Hang on a minute, she reminded herself, you haven't even made up your mind yet.

There was no pad in sight so she opened a drawer. It contained headed writing paper and various other items of company stationery. The second had colour swatches and fabric samples. The bottom drawer was empty except for a battered decorative box with the name Charlotte Brandon inscribed on it. Lily opened it, surprised to find that it contained mementoes from all of their childhoods: faded photos of them as babies, yellowing school reports, Connie's old Brownie card promising that she would do her duty to God and the Queen; to help other people every day, especially those at home. Lily grinned. Unlike her, Connie had probably kept those rules.

At the bottom of the pile was a beautifully drawn design

of bluebells on white paper with their stalks carefully intertwined to make a lattice pattern in green. Underneath it was her mother's stylish italic writing: *By Lily, Summer 1967*.

The fact that her mother had kept, treasured even, something she'd created took her so much by surprise that she almost wept. Maybe her mother did believe in her after all.

But could she really give up her stage career just when it seemed to be taking off? Desperate suddenly for a reminder of the mad, exciting world she'd lived in for so long, she had to speak to Mo. If the play was to transfer, that would be that. As she waited for her agent to answer Lily didn't know which way she wanted the verdict to go.

'Maureen Pargiter here,' announced Mo's voice aggressively. She would by now have had her lunchtime red wine and be belligerent or full of bonhomie. You never knew with Mo.

'Lily, darling, how *are* you?' Lily could just picture her in her tiny office, piled with scripts, the walls plastered with photographs of her clients in their various roles.

'Fine.' Lily decided against elaborating about her circumstances or the importance of Mo's words. 'Any news about the play?'

Mo's pause told Lily everything. 'Sweetie, I'm so sorry. They decided against, the bastards. Not enough bums on seats. The reviews were great but the numbers just didn't make sense . . . Don't slit your wrists. There'll be other parts. Ring me next week.'

Disappointment sliced through her. She'd been so sure it would transfer. When it closed in a couple of weeks she'd have to start the humiliating round of interviews again, knowing that thirty-five was a dangerous age for an actress and that the Bambis of the world were always around to massage directors' egos – and probably other parts of their

35

anatomies. She thought of the neurosis of all her friends; how the question 'Are you working?' sent them into a tailspin of anxiety; the unfairness of a world where her fellow-actresses said she only got parts because of Ben.

Ben. If she accepted her father's offer she would be a hundred miles away. There would be no backsliding, no accidental-on-purpose meetings in the park. This way she could build herself a new, solid career, a future. Perhaps it wasn't so crazy after all.

She almost ran back down the valley towards the farmhouse, not bothering to go down the road.

Edward, standing watching for her at the sitting room window, could see from her face that she'd come to a decision. 'You're going to do it, aren't you?' he asked delightedly.

Lily answered with a smile, 'As long as you accept that I'll do it in my own way. And that might be different from the way it's been run before.'

'Of course,' conceded Edward. 'We'll be there to help, not to breathe down your neck. We'll only get involved if you ask us to, won't we Charlotte?'

'Naturally,' agreed their mother, avoiding Lily's excited eyes,'I wouldn't dream of interfering in my own business.'

Connie embraced her sister, wondering just how much her father had thought this through. If Lily failed, Charlotte might never forgive her; and if she succeeded that might be even worse. But none of this showed in her face when she held Lily tightly and wished her all the luck in the world.

Jonathan could barely contain his temper as he and Judith took their leave and drove back to London.

'It's absolutely bloody ridiculous,' he fumed, taking his anger out on an elderly woman in a Morris Minor by overtaking on the inside and scaring the wits out of her. 'So now our family business is being run by an actress whose greatest triumph was doing the voiceover for a tempera-

36

mental tampon. Pa always was soft on Lily, but I didn't realize how soft. She'll wreck it, for Christ's sake.'

'Of course she will,' soothed his wife, giving no hint to her husband that she too had felt wronged and angry at Lily's appointment. The way Victoriana was run, the almost artsy-craftsy atmosphere of the place, irritated the hell out of Judith. Part of her longed to take over the company and make it produce its maximum potential. It would be a wonderful challenge. Victoriana had never expanded into Europe or America.

All that would have to wait, however. For the moment she had other things to do. She didn't believe it would be that long before Victoriana under Lily lurched into a serious crisis and Edward and Charlotte would be looking for someone else, someone with knowledge and experience, to take over. Someone like her.

Chapter 4

It was only when her father was showing her round Victoriana after her play had closed, that Lily saw the magnitude of what she'd taken on.

She'd visited the business countless times before, both in its old smaller premises and here at the Mill. She'd watched it grow since she was a small child, eating sultanas from a matchbox while Charlotte made her calls, then watching her cut and sew nightdresses and petticoats, her mouth full of pins. She could even remember being jealous of the business as it took more and more of her mother's energies until, by the time Lily was eight or nine, whenever she wanted to see her mother she seemed to be busy.

But that was quite different from really understanding how it worked. Edward, conscious of the hierarchies and rivalries that existed within Victoriana had given this tour a lot of thought.

He decided to start in the design department because Susie McIntosh, the new chief designer, was likely to be Lily's greatest trial. Susie considered herself the creative heir to Charlotte Brandon and would probably resist any changes Lily tried to make like a tigress.

It would have been easy to mistake Susie McIntosh for

a dead leaf, thought Lily, as her father introduced them. Everything about her, from her glossy auburn hair to her chestnut lipstick and her copper-coloured tweed suit came straight from the autumn palette. If it weren't for her peacock Liberty-print scarf you might easily miss her in a wood. But Susie didn't look as though she wandered through too many woods. Country house hotels looked more her line. Five-star ones if possible.

When Susie was called to the phone Edward explained discreetly about how the collections worked. There were two a year, spring and autumn, both of which in terms of colourways, fabric choices and production space had to be planned between twelve and eighteen months ahead. Victoriana certainly wasn't high fashion – Lily felt grateful for that small mercy – but they did have to be roughly in tune with what was happening on the High Street. If mulberry and pine were that year's colours, Victoriana's customers wouldn't be happy in shocking pink.

Then there were the catalogues: the key to their business. Lily remembered them all too well. Producing the catalogues had dominated their family life, not only because the children (except her, Lily thought ironically) had to model for them, but because they always had to be shot in the wrong season, winter clothes in summer, teeshirts in freezing January. In the struggling early years her parents had even taken the photographs themselves.

'Do you remember the winter when all you kids had to put on swimsuits in January at Lulworth Cove?' Edward reminded her. 'I practically had to airbrush out the goosepimples. It's nothing like that now, we use a posh photographer and shoot in the Canary Islands.'

If Susie McIntosh's welcome was frosty, then the rest of the staff more than made up for it with the warmth of theirs.

'How's Mrs Brandon?' everyone asked with so much genuine concern that Lily couldn't fail to be touched. Charlotte seemed to inspire a manic devotion in her staff. They would lie down and die for her despite occasional outbursts and her unfailing demands for impossible standards. Charlotte liked to see her staff as one big happy family, but she brooked absolutely no doubt about who was in charge.

The next stop was a tour of the orders section, run by June Wylie, her mother's unofficial second-in-command. June couldn't have been more different from the snooty Susie McIntosh. She'd come up from the shop floor and had been with Victoriana since its dining-table days. Next to the orders department was the warehouse, sited in one of the two barn conversions. This was the province of Brian Hutchings, a Byronically handsome young man in his early thirties and the pin-up of the entire company.

By the time Edward took her up for tea and sat her down to meet George Forbes, the company accountant, Lily was staggered by how much she didn't know.

'Don't you believe it,' reassured George. 'Everyone likes to make their job sound difficult, because if it isn't, then someone else could be doing it, couldn't they?' Lily laughed at this interpretation of the endless complexities she'd had punted at her during the day. She liked George. He was only forty, Edward had told her, but he still lived with his mother and seemed much older. Lily felt the unforgivable temptation to flirt with him, but stopped herself in time. George would be easy meat. Besides, her father had told her that George's help would be crucial to her and he would be much more of an ally if he were a friend.

'What do you think?' asked her father when they finally packed up their things. 'Are you going to like it here?'

'Absolutely,' Lily was surprised at how excited she felt about the challenge. It was daunting how much she had to learn, certainly, but there were also ways she felt she could improve things. Perhaps not immediately, she needed to get the lie of the land first, but soon. 'I think I'm going to love it. But thank God I've got you and Ma around to help.'

'Well, actually . . .' Her father looked sheepish. 'I was going to tell you. I'm taking Charlotte off to Tuscany for a few weeks' relaxation. Somewhere there isn't a phone or a fax.'

Lily looked stricken. How could her father do this to her?

But Edward was wiser than Lily imagined. He'd calculated that having her mother around would be more of a curse than a blessing. Lily needed to prove herself to the staff and begin to put her own stamp on the place before her mother showed her face there. A couple of months of underemployed Charlotte dragging him round every gallery in Florence was a high price to pay, but Edward thought it was worth it.

'Don't worry. Trust George and June. You'll be safe in their hands.'

Charlotte's shadow turned out to be a lot longer than Lily had anticipated. When she moved in properly the following week she found that Charlotte's procedures seemed to be set in iron. By the end of her first full day Lily was at screaming pitch. If one more person said, 'But Mrs Brandon always does it this way,' she was going to beat them to death with a Victoriana catalogue.

The other, and unexpected, problem Lily discovered was that Victoriana was not quite as buoyant as she'd always assumed. A whole day closeted with George in her parents' office – correction, *her* office – over the millstream, learning how to read balance sheets and profit forecasts, had left her reeling. George's patience with her had finally won, though, and she began to have a glimmer of understanding.

'You've a quick brain with figures,' he was clearly surprised that this outlandish girl had such a capacity to concentrate and take in complex issues, 'just like your mother has.'

Lily glowed in the warm light of George's approval. He didn't seem like the kind of man who handed out compliments easily. 'So what do you think is the problem? Why do Victoriana's profits seem to be dipping lately?'

George looked stunned. No one had ever asked him what he thought before. Mrs Brandon had had her own decided ideas about how to run the company and consequently George had kept quiet. 'Turnover's down obviously. And it's hard to say why. Victoriana has never believed in market research, just relied on customer feedback. But what the girls in the warehouse think' – George would never have dreamed of saying this to Charlotte, but the girls in the warehouse had noticed the drop in turnover as well – 'is that young people aren't buying our clothes like they used to.'

Lily made a mental note to consult the customer correspondence. 'Look George' – now that she was beginning to understand Victoriana's finances Lily was hungry to learn more – 'are you booked up tonight or could we go and have a meal somewhere so we can go on? I really think I'm beginning to get the hang of this.'

George blushed so deeply that even his ears above the starched collar his mother probably ironed for him fresh every day burned like traffic lights. Lily realized she'd made a faux pas. She kept forgetting this wasn't London where people networked all evening in wine bars and expected life and work to spill over into each other. Here the proprieties were clearly quite different. She looked at her watch. Almost seven. His mother had probably had his supper on the table for ages. Poor George.

'Don't worry,' she said before he had a chance to get any more embarrassed, 'we'll talk about it tomorrow. You've been completely brilliant.'

George packed up his things more slowly than usual. He'd heard some odd things being whispered about Lily in the canteen, how wild and outrageous she was, but he didn't believe any of them. Charlotte Brandon was a brilliant designer and she had an amazing capacity to forecast fashion trends, but when things were going wrong she didn't want to know; and Edward Brandon had always been more of a romantic than a businessman.

Their daughter seemed more open to new ideas. In George's view – not, he supposed, that anyone was very interested in his view – she was just what Victoriana needed. And, George thought, feeling unusually brave, she was extremely attractive. He said goodnight and went out of the building whistling. If his mother got at him for being late he'd tell her to go to hell. Lily Brandon had wanted his advice.

On her way out Lily stopped in the office where they handled the correspondence from Victoriana's customers. The most recent letters were in a red box file.

They were as fulsome as ever but after a while something they had in common struck Lily. They all sounded as though they were written by people who were middle aged. George and the girls were right, Victoriana no longer appealed to the young. The girls who had danced the night away in Victoriana petticoats in the sixties were now respectable mums. They had stayed with Victoriana, but their daughters hadn't followed in their footsteps.

Lily was going to have to see what she could do about that, but first she had a call to make to Mo, who would be wondering why Lily hadn't been on the phone five times a day about her next acting job as she usually was.

Mo was stunned. 'I didn't even know you were Charlotte Brandon's daughter.' Her gravelly voice, maintained by a bottle of wine a day, was only coming from Covent Garden, yet already it felt to Lily like the other side of the world.

'I don't make a big thing of it.'

'And you're going to run Victoriana.' Mo couldn't keep

the amazement from her tone. 'Somehow I don't see you as the Victoriana type. All that virginal white cotton.'

'Maybe I'll make Victoriana a bit less virginal.'

Mo laughed. She liked Lily and was sorry to lose her. Lily could be bolshy at times, but she was talented. On the other hand, parts for thirty-five-year-olds, even if they weren't bolshy, were thin on the ground, and acting could be a thankless task. What had one of her clients said? That you had to be ready to be hit in the face with a wet cloth every day. Maybe it ought to be she who was getting out and moving to the country. 'Look, lovey, I can understand you wanting to have a crack at the old family biz, but once this gets out it'll be the end of your acting career. You have to be here, available and hungry.'

Lily bit her lip. She'd avoided facing this, telling herself she could always go back in six months, but Mo was right. By accepting the Victoriana job she'd burned her boats.

A sudden fear washed through her that she might have screwed up her life just because she wanted to prove something to her family, and especially to her mother. It reminded her of stage fright. At least she wouldn't be having that any more. If she couldn't go back to acting, she was going to have to make this damn well work.

'By the way,' Mo added, her voice curious, 'are you and Ben Winter back together? He's been getting outrageously pissed every night and telling everyone at the Blue Flame Club you're the love of his life, then falling off his stool. The management are thinking of banning him and his agent's worried sick. All for the love of yooo-oo, my dear, or so he says.'

Lily's pulse raced, despite herself. 'What happened to Bambi?'

Mo laughed her throaty London laugh. 'Who knows? Maybe he dumped her when he found she'd never heard of the Beatles. What could he have in common with her out of bed?'

Lily tossed her long hair angrily. 'If I'm the love of his life he hasn't got round to telling me so.' Then she remembered the message on the machine asking her to contact him. Had he meant to apologize after all? On the other hand if he'd really wanted to get hold of her he would have found a way. Besides, she told herself sternly, one of the reasons she'd taken on Victoriana was to get away from Ben Winter.

'Look, love,' Mo's voice had its usual gotta go urgency, 'must run. One of my clients opens tonight in *The Three Sisters* in Watford. Back of bloody beyond but you know how it is.'

Lily did indeed. Mo was brilliant like that. She had turned up at all Lily's openings, always telling her how great she'd been, no matter how dire the performance and somehow making her feel that Lily was her only client, when she had a hundred others, all needing their egos massaged too. Lily thought of the excitement that must be building up back-stage; the queues for the loo as first-night nerves grabbed the actors' stomachs; the hopes, the envy, the camaraderie. As Mo kissed a noisy departure she hoped to God she'd done the right thing in giving it all up for Victoriana. Then her mind turned to Ben, who never used to drink like that. Was this just another of his roles? The rejected lover?

Suddenly exhausted, Lily collected up her things. Thank God Connie had invited her to stay while her parents were in Tuscany and she didn't have to go back to an empty house. She grabbed the box of customers' letters to read at home. It was so late that the building was empty, apart from the caretaker, and outside in the car park the darkness was absolute, so different from the pinky glow of London she was used to. An owl hooted and Lily jumped, laughing at herself for her soft city ways. She turned on the headlights of her Beetle and headed for Connie's.

By contrast, Connie's house looked busy and enticing. Ugly from the outside, granted, it was too square and built in red brick rather than the golden stone of her parents' home. When you crossed the threshold, however, it seemed to pull you in and cosset you. Lily loved it. Inside, it was a riot of colour with glorious artefacts everywhere: graceful carved birds in the inglenook, an elephant holding a log basket, dazzling jewelled mirrors from Rajasthan. Most of them had tiny tickets attached because they'd been borrowed from the shop and would eventually be returned there.

Instead of curtains Connie had looped yards of brightly-coloured fabric and twisted them round iron sconces for tie-backs. On the floor she'd scattered dozens of Turkish rugs, often discoloured by the light or with holes in them discreetly hidden by enormous saggy sofas or baskets of wood. The house had an exotic air, underlined by the pungent smell of scented candles and joss sticks. Lily always felt she was stepping into an Arab bazaar instead of the English countryside.

She was hardly inside the door when Gavin put a glass of wine into her hand and shooed Tara and Jeremy into the sitting room. 'I've bribed them with a highly unsuitable video,' he confided, 'so you and Con can have a bit of peace. She loves it when you come to stay.' He didn't tell her that Tara especially had been outraged. She adored her Auntie Lily's stories of her racy acting friends.

Lily followed her nose towards the kitchen. Connie was so lucky. Gavin was a delight. He was wry and funny and was always trying to find ways of making Connie happy. With this house and the shop and a fabulous husband she really had cracked it.

Connie stood at the stove stirring home-made soup, looking the picture of domestic bliss in a stripy butcher's pinny. On the table was a crusty granary loaf and butter in an earthenware pot.

'Butter!' Lily exclaimed as though it were Beluga caviare. Everyone she knew used only disgusting low-fat spreads which instead of producing toast that was hot-buttered produced only toast that was damp. She sat at the table, admiring Connie's effortless cooking skills. She seemed able to knock-up a three-course meal while chatting and doing the ironing. Lily needed three days' planning, total concentration, no white noise, and had to take the phone off the hook before she could even tackle Shepherd's Pie.

'It's so great to have you here.' Connie replenished Lily's hardly-touched glass. 'I was actually feeling a bit down and you're just the tonic I need.'

Lily listened in amazement. This wasn't part of the script she ran in her head about her sister's life. 'What's the matter, Con? Everything looks pretty bloody amazing to me.'

Connie fell silent for a moment. 'Oh nothing,' she said finally, 'I shouldn't have mentioned it.'

'Stop behaving like Ma. Being stoic isn't a divine virtue. It just means you're bottling things up and they'll jump out at you later. Believe me. I know.'

Connie looked behind her swiftly to check that Gavin really had gone to watch the video. 'All right then. I feel I desperately need a change. Gavin and I live in each other's pockets twenty-three hours a day. I know it's stupid and ungrateful, but there you are.' Connie ignored the bowl of delicious soup in front of her. 'Then there's all this bloody intimacy. Gavin sits on the loo in the nude and clips his toenails and half of me thinks how wonderful, we aren't like our parents, we're so free, and the other half of me longs for a bit of mystery.'

Lily tried not to smile. Ben did the same thing. Too much intimacy was the curse of their generation. Connie poured herself another glass. She was drinking fast, and words flooded out of her. 'And then in bed we always do exactly the same thing. It's almost sex by numbers. I even know

47

what'll happen, and in what order. I can tick it off mentally. Kiss my neck, pull of my nightie, stroke my thigh, a bit of foreplay, then four minutes at it before we both go to sleep.'

Lily felt like pointing out that this described ninety per cent of people's sex after two years but decided to keep quiet. 'Couldn't you, you know, work at it?'

'I don't want to work at it. I don't want to dress up in a black negligée with a rose in my teeth and strip to the sounds of the *Bolero*. I want to have glorious, abandoned, spontaneous sex.' She looked her sister in the eye. 'Like you have.'

Lily choked. 'Like *I* have?' Lily thought of the lonely nights she'd had since she'd broken up with Ben.

But Connie hadn't finished. 'And then there's the shop. I'm so fed up with being stuck there all day with Margot I may end up killing the woman.'

'Connie . . .' A chilling thought had just occurred to Lily. 'You didn't want to take over at Victoriana yourself, did you?'

The split second of silence told her everything.

Lily felt terrible. She'd been so sure that Connie had too much in her life already with her family and the shop; she'd had no that Connie was longing for a challenge.

'Oh, Con,' Lily blurted, 'why didn't you say so at the meeting? Ma and Pa would have been delighted.'

'Pa clearly wanted you to do it. He's always loved you best.'

'And Ma's loved you and Jonathan more than me.'

Connie grinned suddenly. 'And you're taller than me,' she accused. 'And you sing in tune.'

'And you're prettier, pretty Connie. The one who got to appear in the catalogue when we were kids, remember. Ma decided I was too ugly, remember.'

Connie surveyed her sister's shining hair, creamy skin,

and the black leather jacket she kept on even indoors. Lily's style was unique. 'Yep. And you're still too ugly, aren't you? Don't listen to me. What's the betting I've forgotten about it all by tomorrow? Besides, I'm far too busy really and Gavin needs me in the shop. He couldn't afford to pay someone else.'

A thought struck Lily and she almost came out with it, then thought better of it. It might make things too hard for Gavin.

'Are you two pissed as rats yet?' Tara's head appeared round the door. 'You've been gassing through the whole of *Pulp Fiction*, you know.' She put her arms round Lily and hugged her. 'It *is* fab to have you here. Was it true about you throwing cappuccino in Ben Winter's lap?'

'Yes, and a waste of time too. He only likes double espresso.'

'He was wonderful as the defence lawyer in *Suspicious Minds*. All that passionate fighting for the underdog.'

Lily pushed the thought of Ben's glittering, almost black eyes out of her mind. 'You shouldn't believe everything you see on TV. He votes Tory.'

Tara's schoolgirl fantasies fell to the ground with a thud. 'He doesn't!'

'No, actually,' Lily conceded. 'But he is completely apolitical. He supports the Ben Winter party.'

Connie heard the pain in Lily's voice and felt guilty at going on about herself. 'Was it awful breaking up?'

Lily nodded. 'Pretty terrible. I have this horrible habit of thinking about him all the time. Suddenly the world seems to be like Noah's Ark with a big sign on it saying Couples Only. You go to a party and meet someone nice and just as you're getting hopeful a hand appears and the wife says, "Come on, darling, time we went."'

'The world may be full of couples,' Connie announced, 'but you shouldn't assume they're all happy.'

The bleakness in her tone horrified Lily. She loved them both so much and they'd always seemed the ideal couple, the one pair who'd got it right.

The next morning the atmosphere seemed to have lightened. Connie even hummed as she doled out toast and honey. Tara appeared looking extraordinarily sexy in a print pinafore with shoestring straps, a tight ribbed black jersey underneath, thick black tights, and enormous clodhopping shoes, which somehow stopped it being flowery and feminine and made it butchly witty instead.

It struck Lily that she'd seen versions of this get-up on every girl from six to sixteen and yet there was nothing remotely like it in the Victoriana catalogue. She picked up a copy of the current one and threw it at her niece. 'Have a butchers at this. Anything you want you can have free, provided you give me a report on what you do and don't like and why.'

Tara grabbed the catalogue. Two minutes later she flung it back. 'Nah, sorry,' she said in her best mock-Cock accent. 'If you want me to wear any of those you'd have to *pay* me. I wouldn't be seen dead in any of it. I'd end up looking like my mother.'

Victoriana clearly had a bit of an image problem. Lily reached into her bag for a pad and sketched all the clothes Tara was wearing. The sketches looked a bit like Olive Oyl on a bad day, but Susie could work on them. 'Why don't you and your friends come and tell me what you *would* like?'

Tara looked dubious. 'What's in it for us?'

'Tara Wade!' Connie was shocked at the mercenary nature of her youngest child. 'You're always saying we've got too much and ought to be giving it away to the homeless.'

'That's your stuff, not mine,' grinned Tara.

'How about twenty quid down and free clothes if we come up with anything together?'

'Done,' agreed Tara. 'I'll go and ring my friend Roz now.'

Jonathan Brandon left the office half an hour before the time he was due to meet Judith. She always arrived promptly and he felt like getting a couple of drinks in before she showed up. Especially today. His accountant had just delivered a stern lecture on last year's results and while Jonathan, the smart business-school graduate, had done his best to patronize a mere accountant, he knew the boring little man had a point. Things were alarmingly slow. At first he'd told himself it was just the recession and that business would pick up, but while other companies might be feeling the warmth, his financial consultancy certainly wasn't.

'What can I get you, Mr Brandon?' asked the barman at the Trading Floor, his local wine bar, handily placed minutes away from his office in Broadgate.

Jonathan, torn between being flattered by the man's recognition and nervous that Judith, if she overheard it, would deduce he spent too much time in here, ordered himself a large margarita. A jug would be nice but he could imagine her grimace of disapproval. He couldn't even say he'd got it for her because she rarely drank. Judith liked being in control. He sat alone staring into the cloudy grey-green liquid, licking the salt from the side of the glass, and thought about how to woo some new clients. The Trading Floor wasn't a bad hunting ground as a matter of fact. By this time on a Friday it began to fill up with merchant bankers, market analysts, financial hacks and brokers.

'Hello, Jonathan, drinking alone?' Jonathan turned to find Clive Green, a fellow graduate from his business course, standing behind him clutching a bottle of Dom Perignon. Jonathan didn't much like champagne, especially now that the Excessive Eighties had rendered it as déclassé as Baby-cham, but he wasn't a man to turn down a drink. Besides,

Clive Green worked for First Venture, a new firm of venture capitalists, and might prove useful for contacts.

He took the proffered glass and Clive sat down on the bar stool next to him and started laying into the snacks. Within minutes Clive had worked his way through the tortilla chips, crisps and black olives. No wonder he was as jowly as a pre-Christmas turkey. They chatted about acquaintances from the course, being careful to disparage anyone they suspected of having done better than either of them, until Jonathan spotted Judith arrive and work her way through the crowded wine bar, stopping here and there to say hello to friends or contacts. While she talked to one person, Jonathan noticed, her glance darted over their shoulder to make sure there was no one more interesting she might be missing. Once upon a time men said of women that they had bedroom eyes. Now they had networking eyes.

Finally she saw them.

'You know my wife, Judith? Judith works for Image-makers, the PR people.'

Clive Green insisted on giving Jonathan another glass of champagne and getting Judith a mineral water before looking at his watch and making his excuses. He gathered up his mac and a bulging briefcase with lap-top computer peeping out. 'By the way,' he added casually, 'aren't you Charlotte Brandon's son, of Victoriana fame?'

Jonathan's mind cleared instantly. In business it was always at the very last moment people said what they'd come to say, and the more off-handedly they raised it, the more important it often was.

'Indeed I am,' he agreed.

'As a matter of fact I have a client, North's Mail Order, who may be interested in acquiring Victoriana. That is, if your mother wanted to sell. The price could be good. North's are riding high.'

Clive Green glanced quickly from Jonathan to Judith and thought he detected a flicker of intense interest.

Jonathan had become the soul of blandness. 'Thanks for the drink, old man. And the tip. I'll put a toe in the parental water. I have to say, though, Ma's pretty wedded to her precious company. You might have to take on the whole family to get her to even nibble.'

'Interesting,' said Judith to Clive Green's retreating back. 'North's is the biggest mail order business in the UK and Barry North's a smart operator.' She had read a profile of the man in the financial pages. 'He specializes in taking over old-fashioned businesses and squeezing them till it hurts.'

'More than interesting.' Jonathan found it hard to contain his excitement. A nice cash injection from the sale of Victoriana was just what his own company needed.

'But do you think your parents would go for it? They didn't seem keen on selling.'

'They will be when Lily starts mucking up the company. We'll just have to make sure they realize their mistake sooner rather than later.'

'I'll drink to that,' said Judith. And for once she let Jonathan buy her a glass of very expensive vintage champagne.

'In fact,' Jonathan began to get even more excited, 'why don't I call up Barry North and put a few feelers out?'

'That'd be a bit unsubtle, wouldn't it? You don't want to look too keen. Get Clive Green to find out more. After all, no one loves you if you love them too much, do they?'

Jonathan watched her thoughtfully. He was sure she'd loved him once. Now her comment seemed an apt description of their own relationship.

Chapter 5

'Susie, I'd like you to look at these designs and see what you think.' Last night Tara had stayed up late and come up with some sketches which Lily had found so fresh and exciting she'd rushed straight to the design department with them.

Lily could have simply insisted Susie incorporate them, as Charlotte would have done, but she wanted to be democratic and win Susie over. Instead she could feel waves of resistance coming from the wretched woman even before she'd looked at them. 'They're just amateur drawings,' Lily explained, 'but I'm sure there's something there. With your help I think we could really use them in the catalogue.'

To her irritation Susie, soignée as usual with not a hair out of place, didn't even open the folder. Lily began to feel seriously annoyed. 'Would you mind gracing me with your opinion, Susie?'

Susie finally had the goodness to flick through them. A look of distaste appeared on her aristocratic features, at the sight of the brash and exciting clothes Lily had drawn. 'They look cheap and nasty to me. Not the kind of thing Victoriana does. We're known for our quality.'

'We should be able to keep our quality and still design for

young people. Victoriana's beginning to be seen as clothes for the over-forties.'

'The over-forties are very loyal customers. They've stayed with us since they were in their twenties.'

'Yes,' Lily tried not to let Susie's dismissive tone get to her, 'but their daughters are rejecting us altogether.' She could see she was going to have problems with Susie. There was a mulish set to her mouth. Lily suspected she would simply delay and delay, hoping Lily would eventually lose interest. Well, Lily wouldn't let her. 'I'd like your views by tomorrow, please Susie, because I want some form of these in the new season's catalogue. I'm sure you can give them a polish and adapt two or three of the best.'

Susie looked as though she was going to argue but thought better of it. Lily guessed she would go off and search for more technical ammunition to shoot the whole thing down.

As Lily politely opened her door to let the older woman out she heard a burst of smothered giggling from the other end of the Mill's open plan offices. At the sight of her, panic swiftly replaced amusement on all the faces and Lily soon saw why. Blu-tacked to one of the filing cabinets was an old newspaper article from the titillating *Sunday Splash*. It featured Lily wearing thigh boots, a skintight black rubber minidress and a riding crop. Underneath the photo some-one had invited entries to a contest for the most amusing caption. It was hopeless to try and explain that this was the outfit she had worn for a doomed lunchtime theatre production called *The Dominatrix* which had had such bad reviews it had folded in a record four days. They probably all thought this was her idea of an eyecatching outfit.

Lily willed herself to walk calmly towards it wondering if this were some kind of bizarre initiation test. She knew one thing for sure. No one would have dared do such a thing to her mother. Forcing herself to smile she approached the photograph and wrote in her bold italic hand underneath: 'Victoriana's New Boss Cracks the Whip. Only the lazy or malicious need beware.' Then she stood back while people clustered round to read it, giggling this time with relief.

She almost removed it, but decided it quite effectively got her message across and that the more dignified course would be to ignore it. One question remained unanswered. Who was it at Victoriana who so wanted to make a fool of her?

By the end of the next day there was still no response from Susie McIntosh and Lily's irritation with the woman doubled.

'Susie, I wonder if you could come into my office for a moment,' Lily asked politely at five fifteen. It was clear Susie had had no intention of doing so voluntarily. Nevertheless Lily decided to play it politely. 'Have you had a chance to work on those designs yet?'

'Yes, as a matter of fact I have. I was about to write you a memo.'

The hell you were, thought Lily, who had noted the woman's briefcase ready to be snapped shut to leave. 'Please, Susie, never write a memo when you can come in and talk. It's mad in an organization this size. Then if we need to argue it through we can do it on the spot.'

Susie looked as though that was precisely what she didn't want. 'Frankly, I feel the designs are entirely impractical for Victoriana.'

Lily waited for the predictable list of reasons Susie would produce to knock down her designs.

'The shoestring pinafore has already been in fashion this season, by next year it may be dead. There are huge risks in high fashion.'

Lily took her point but knew she was simply looking for reasons to say no. 'What would you say were my mother's greatest strengths?'

The question took Susie off her guard. 'I don't know,' she faltered.

'Would you say that one of them was the capacity for spotting a classic even in its early days?'

'Yes, I suppose so.'

'Well, I predict that Tara's pinafore will be just that. I want it in the catalogue. If you don't want to handle it perhaps I should ask one of the other designers?'

'They all work to me,' Susie pointed out sniffily.

'Then you'd better put one of them on the job or you'll lose face, won't you? And Susie ' – Susie had already stood up and was heading out of the room – 'make sure it's one of the nice young ones who understands the under-twenty-fives, will you?'

After Susie had gone Lily wondered if she was being stupid. She had only just taken over. Shouldn't she just sit back and take advice for six months before starting to make changes? Then she remembered the disturbing figures on the balance sheet and George explaining how her parents hadn't faced up to them. In six months those figures could get a lot worse. And surely she had to trust her instincts? Her instincts were telling her two things at the moment. That Susie McIntosh would put the boot into any changes she suggested, no matter how sensible, and that her designs were just what the new catalogue needed. Lily decided that the course she should follow was to be as nice as she could to Susie but to stick to her decision.

For the whole of the following week this seemed to work almost disturbingly well. Lily spent the time familiarizing herself with the warehouse and how it worked and understanding the ordering system while Susie agreed to produce proper designs from the sketches. Maybe it was going to be fine after all. She'd probably just rubbed the woman up the wrong way.

It was during the next week, when Lily was sitting on the

broad windowsill of her office wondering if she had the most magnificent view of any boss in Britain, that she decided something must be going on. Susie had just dropped in the revamped sketches. Not only was the woman smiling but actually humming.

Lily looked through the drawings. They were beautifully done, so beautifully that Lily was sure it hadn't been Susie herself who'd drawn them.

'Thanks, Susie. These are great.'

Susie smiled and made for the door, still humming. Lily watched her mystified. What did Susie know that she didn't?

When Connie got back from a gruesome day at the shop, where Margot hadn't stopped chatting all day, followed by what felt like World War Three in Safeway's, she found Lily sitting at the kitchen table with the new designs spread out in front of her.

'Look, Con, come and see what I've cribbed from your brilliant daughter and her equally brilliant friends.'

Connie dumped the supermarket bags on the floor where one of them tipped over, cannoning loose brussels sprouts and Egyptian new potatoes all over the kitchen floor. Connie kicked it with uncharacteristic viciousness.

She was deeply ashamed of her reaction when she looked at the ideas Tara had provided for the catalogue. It was good, old-fashioned jealousy. What kind of mother was it who could be jealous of her daughter instead of proud of her?

'No thank-God-it's-Friday feeling?' Lily asked, filling the kettle to make them a calming cup of tea.

'Not likely,' Connie banged the bags on to the kitchen table and began unpacking them irritably. 'I hate bloody Fridays. All day cooped up in the shop with Margot. I swear that woman never, ever, closes her mouth. And she drives the customers away with her yapping. Selling is an art and Margot does not possess it.'

'Maybe I could cook supper tonight,' offered Lily, eager to take some of the stress off her sister.

'It's okay, I'm doing goulash. It's dead easy.' Lily suspected that Connie didn't trust her cooking. She could be right. The last time Lily had cooked a proper three-course meal was probably in Domestic Science class. 'You could chop the peppers though. They're in one of those bags.'

Lily cheerfully rooted through all ten bags before admitting defeat. 'Don't tell me,' Connie clutched her head, 'I've forgotten the sodding peppers.' At this moment she caught sight of Tara watching TV in the sitting room with her feet up. 'Tara,' she bellowed in a most unConnielike voice. 'Get those bloody clodhoppers off the sofa. Now!' Tara's feet shot off the cushion in surprise. Her mother never talked like that.

Connie abandoned unpacking the shopping and took a bottle of wine out of the fridge. In the sitting room the five-thirty news blared. The fact that it was half an hour till a drink could respectably be taken made no difference. She wanted one and she was going to have it.

'Con,' Lily asked, getting her sister to sit down at the kitchen table, 'are you okay?'

Connie felt an overwhelming temptation to tell the truth. That she minded like hell about Victoriana. That the pattern of their relationship had been Connie as the successful one with the marriage and the flourishing shop and Lily the fun but feckless black sheep. Since Lily had taken over Victoriana all that was changing. How could she admit that? It was too mean-spirited to even acknowledge. Besides, it was more complicated than that. Lily taking over Victoriana had simply made her more aware of a hole in her life that she couldn't ignore any longer.

'Of course I'm okay,' Connie said bitterly. 'Good old

Connie always holds the fort, doesn't she? Don't you remember at school? I was always the one who made her bed first – and with the best hospital corners. I could have got a prize for those bloody hospital corners.' She poured herself another glass of wine. 'The trouble is, I'm fed up to the teeth with doing the right thing. Gavin needs me in the shop but I don't care if I never see it again.'

'Why don't you talk it over with him? Maybe you should get out more. Do some of the buying.'

'We can't afford to keep buying, that's half the problem, but he says buying is the lifeblood; we have to have new things. Tell you what,' though Connie hated herself for sounding so whingeing, 'having you here makes all the difference.'

Lily jumped up and hugged her sister. In recent years they hadn't seen nearly enough of each other. Being with Connie was one of the best things about her decision to take on Victoriana.

When they let each other go Connie picked up the designs from the table and studied them. Lily was right. They were talented, fresh and utterly original.

'I'm a crabby old boot who can't cope with the march of youth,' she pronounced, her usual down-to-earth nature fighting its way back, 'you're absolutely right. These are brilliant. Exactly the right thing for trendy teenagers.'

Lily had gone to bed and Connie was giving the kitchen its final once-over to check that everything was in its place when a tall figure appeared in the hall, making Connie, who thought everyone was in bed, jump. It was Jeremy.

'I thought you might like this,' he said shyly, handing her a tape and loped off before she could ask any more.

She was about to go up to bed but instead she decided to listen to it in the sitting room. It was called 'The Ballad of Lucy Jordan' and told the story of a suburban housewife filled with destructive longings. She sat back in her familiar

60

deep chintz sofa and closed her eyes. The sad, haunting song filled the room.

> At the age of thirty-seven
> She realized she'd never ride
> Through Paris in a sports car
> With the warm wind in her hair . . .

The song so exactly mirrored her own feelings. Connie too was terrified that life was passing her by while she drowned in domesticity. The tears ran down her face. She'd thought that no one understood her, but one person clearly did. The fact that it was her seventeen-year-old son, who should have been caught up with confusion and longings of his own, touched her unbearably. What kind of mother was she being?

Connie sat up in the darkness and decided that enough was enough. The woman in the song, unable to face the ordinariness of life and marriage, jumped off a building. Connie Wade was far too sensible to do that – wasn't she?

She was half hoping Gavin would be asleep by the time she got up to bed, but he was sitting up reading, his wheat-coloured hair flopping down over his eyes.

'Don't suppose you've got the energy to give me a massage?' Gavin asked hopefully. 'My back's killing me.'

Connie reached for the Radian B.

'Just there. Aaaaragh, that's bloody marvellous.' Connie kneaded and pounded Gavin's back as she'd done countless times before. 'You should have been a masseuse,' he murmured blissfully into the pillow.

'I know. I'd have made a damn sight more than in Third World imports.' She caught sight of herself in the mirror, her round neat breasts bobbing as she stroked and pummelled. 'Maybe I'll try it as a sideline at the next craft fair. One World: Exotic Artefacts and Relief Massage. It has quite a good ring to it, actually.'

Resentment nibbled away at her that it was always Gavin and not her who had the massage, but she could easily suggest he take over, starting at her shoulders and moving gently and firmly down her back to the small indents above her bum. The warm liniment made her hands tingle and she was shocked to find herself wondering what it would feel like if you rubbed it into more intimate parts.

'Gav,' she whispered, beginning to feel excited, 'how about doing me now?' But her massage had been so effective that Gavin was asleep, totally naked, a beatific smile lighting up his sleeping face. She watched him for a moment, tenderness fighting with frustration. Gently, and in as decorous a manner as possible, he farted. Connie shuddered. This, she knew, was intimacy.

She was woken next morning by Jeremy shouting from downstairs, 'Mum! Have you seen the lead for my electric guitar?'

Connie thought about this. As a matter of fact she hadn't. Maybe a neighbour had sneaked in and stolen it so that Jeremy and his friend Bazza couldn't practise in the garage any more. She eventually found it in Tara's bedroom and wondered whether she'd been trying to use it with her Styling Brush or just to spoil her brother's fun. She rather suspected the latter. The lowering thought occurred to her that her own dog-in-the-mangerish attitude to Lily fell into the same category.

By the time she went back upstairs Gavin was already dressed. He was wearing her favourite clothes, soft, unstructured suit in ocean-blue with a faded shirt. If she forgot all she knew about him, he was still pretty attractive. She tried to forget and gave him a kiss. Tara, already on the phone to her best friend Roz, pretended to puke as she always did at any signs of tenderness between her parents.

'Get off that phone,' instructed her mother. 'It's not even eight-thirty. What can you possibly have to say to Roz at eight-thirty this morning that you didn't tell her at nine-thirty last night?'

'Bags. Some of us,' announced Tara disdainfully, 'have an interior life.'

Connie poured herself a cup of coffee, feeling deflated. Maybe that was what she needed. An interior life.

Gavin glanced up from his diary where he'd been looking up the address of the sculptor in wood he'd arranged to call on this morning. He caught Connie's look of defeat. He was worried about her lately. It had all been a big adventure when they'd first started out, but Connie seemed to have lost enthusiasm. Maybe they'd settled down lately into a pattern. He did the buying and Connie minded the shop. That suited him because he loved being out and about and Connie was so good with the customers. Maybe she had started to see herself as the drudge to his more exciting role. He must encourage her to get out. Perhaps even go to the gift fair this year instead of him.

He kissed her tenderly on the neck on his way out.

'Remind me who you're going to see.' Connie sensed his concern and hated herself. He had enough worries with trying to make the shop pay without having to worry about her all the time.

'Ron. The one who carves seagulls out of driftwood.' Ron's seagulls were exquisite and they even happened to be cheap enough to sell in the shop. Once Connie would have been ecstatic about them.

We can't afford to buy anything more, Connie wanted to say. Even exquisite seagulls. It was an old argument between them.

'Why don't you come too? You'd love them.'

'I can't, love. Margot won't be in till midday. I've got to open up.'

'It won't matter if we open late for just one day.'

'Of course it will.' Connie hated her snappish tone. 'If we

aren't open, how do we expect to sell anything, for God's sake?' She started to pack up the dishwasher and finish the tasks she had to get through before going to the shop and Margot. Gavin turned away, hurt, and put on his beloved tweed coat.

Charlotte wandered restlessly round the bare, frozen garden. She hated this time of year. Donne had got it right in that poem about St Lucy's Day: winter here reminded you of 'absence, darkness, death; things which are not'. She could hardly complain, however, since she'd been the one to drag Edward back from Italy early. The weather there had been glorious but Edward had almost driven her mad, either taking her round endless gardens or treating her like a damned invalid. It was extraordinary how easily Edward had taken to retirement, simply switching his energies from the business to his new passion for creating an Italian garden in Dorset. His excitement at stealing seedlings from the flowerbeds of Tuscan castles had been extraordinary to behold. Gardening held no lure for Charlotte. She didn't have the patience and couldn't understand how it replaced sex, conversation and food in so many English people's lives. The truth was, she was itching to get back to Victoriana. She puffed out her breath into the cold air and watched the satisfying cloud of steam, then turned to go back into the house where Edward would be poring over another seed catalogue or essay by Gertrude Jekyll.

'Edward,' she chose her words carefully, 'I think I might see if I can be of any help to Lily now that I'm back. One day a week perhaps. Just to advise.'

Edward closed his copy of Vita Sackville-West. He'd been fearing something like this ever since they'd got home.

'I really don't think you should. Lily's just finding her feet. Your presence will confuse things.'

Charlotte sighed deeply in frustration. If she were honest

she knew he was right. Her problem was that she'd put everything of herself into Victoriana. While other women of her generation doted over their families, she had always put hers second to the business. Without it she felt at a complete loss. Maybe it was time she tried to be like other women. She had a home, a family, and grandchildren, after all.

Remembering that Monday was Connie's half day she decided to drop in and see her. That would give Connie a shock. Charlotte had never dropped in 'for a cup of tea and a chat' in ten years. She was just looking for her car keys when the doorbell rang, taking Edward and herself by surprise. In their new life they had few unexpected visitors.

Charlotte's face lit up when she saw that it was Susie McIntosh holding what appeared to be a folder of sketches. The woman was hardly into the front door when she had the folder open. 'Mrs Brandon,' she said with an air of great pomposity, 'I really think you should see these. Lily drew them herself and, quite frankly, they're like something out of kindergarten. She's insistent that they should go into the catalogue. I wondered what you thought?'

Bitch, thought Edward listening from his post in the sitting room. There would be no holding Charlotte back now.

Judith watched Barry North, the managing director of North's Mail Order, over the top of her vodka glass and wondered what he would be like in bed. If he conducted himself with anything like the mix of decisiveness and charm he'd shown so far, it could be an enticing prospect. He was a powerful man in both size and personality, tall and solid yet with none of the bullheaded conventionality that often seemed to go with the rugby player's build. His most arresting feature was his eyes. They were dark and magnetic and had the capacity to hold you just as much as the sheer strength of his handshake.

Tonight's meeting had been set up by Clive Green as a

supposedly social occasion but both sides knew the real agenda. Judith had been surprised he'd chosen this place to hold it. An expensively hushed restaurant or a club where he could have flashed his status at them would have been more predictable, but Barry North, she was discovering, wasn't a predictable man. All around them noisy young people were getting noisier with every round of the different-flavoured vodkas, occasionally smashing their glasses to the ground.

'Straight on their bills,' pointed out Jonathan who seemed to be working his way through as many different brands as possible.

North, she noticed, was sticking to the Stolichnaya. 'I picked up the habit in Lithuania. My father sent me there when I was eighteen to rediscover my Jewish roots. He thought my private school had made me too narrow and class-ridden.'

'I thought that's what private schools were supposed to do,' said Jonathan.

Judith listened fascinated. She hadn't realized he was Jewish. She'd never been to bed with anyone circumcised.

'I learnt a lot about buying and selling, though it was Biro pens and Castrol oil instead of three-piece suites and mail order fashion. They respect trading there.'

It was only at the very end of the evening, by which time Judith was acutely conscious of the attraction she felt for North and equally eager that neither he nor her husband should guess it, that anyone talked about business.

'So,' Barry North directed his charmingly wolfish smile at Judith and his words at her husband, 'do you think your parents would be prepared to sell if the right offer came along?'

'It's possible,' Jonathan considered the proposition, 'but only if they had no alternative. They've just had this crazy notion of putting my sister Lily in charge to keep it in the

66

family, so not yet – but she's bound to screw up. Leave it a few months and we'll see.'

'Your father didn't think of asking you, then? Even with your Master's from the London Business School?' Judith, listening intently, thought how insulting he made Edward's choice sound.

'He knows I would have turned it down,' Jonathan said with a shade of defensiveness. 'Look, don't worry. This Lily thing is just a passing fancy. There's no way she could make a go of it. She knows nothing about business. She'll be rushing back to her acting friends in five minutes and then you can buy the company. I give her six months at the outside.'

'Ah,' – there was something about Jonathan Brandon's easy assumptions that irritated the hell out of North – 'but will I still want to buy it in six months?' He gave his order to the waiter and asked Judith what she would like. She noticed with a frisson of excitement how naturally he took charge of every situation. The waiters, with their usual instinct for the most powerful person at any table turned to him immediately.

Like everyone else, Barry North had read about Lily's escapades in the papers and he was intrigued. 'Why do you think your parents have done it? It seems highly risky unless they're bent on commercial suicide, which from everything I've heard of them, I doubt.'

'Father's always been soft about Lily, even when we were kids, and he talked Ma into it. I suppose he must believe she can do it.'

'Rather an expensive luxury. So what's she like, this notorious sister of yours?'

Judith shook out her napkin irritably. She didn't like the way the conversation was going and couldn't resist putting her oar in. 'Fine, if you like sleeping in beds that have been slept in plenty of times already.'

The graphicness of Judith's sexual innuendo made

Jonathan look at her in surprise. Barry North smiled infuriatingly. 'I was referring to her professional capacities.'

Judith sipped her wine, furious with herself for showing her hand so crassly.

The nature of the sexual tension between his wife and Barry North passed over Jonathan's head. He was getting eager for his dinner. 'She's an actress. What more can I say?'

Their food arrived. Small blini smothered in cream and lumpfish roe. North demolished his in one mouthful.

'You keep talking about your father all the time,' he said, 'but Victoriana was really your mother's inspiration. What does she think of all this?'

'Now that,' Jonathan agreed, his mouth full, 'is a very interesting question.'

As they left to go, Judith caught North's eye. He gave her a look that was so frankly sexual she had to turn away in case he saw the answering glint of arousal in her own eyes.

She leaned over to take her coat from the cloakroom assistant and felt a hand stroking her behind. For a moment she closed her eyes. The overtness of his gesture sent a charge of powerful eroticism stinging right through her body – but the voice whispering in her ear wasn't North's. 'You're looking incredibly sexy tonight,' said her husband, removing his hand and looking pleased with himself at his daring.

'Oh for Christ's sake, Jonathan!' she snapped when she saw who it was. 'Have you no sense of occasion?' The kicked-dog look in his face made her feel a glancing moment of guilt, but she soon got over it when, standing waiting for a taxi, she pushed her hands into her pockets and found a business card with Barry North's name on it. His private line had been added in fountain pen. Excitement fought with irritation. Sod the man. He knew she was interested and expected her to make the next move.

It was a clever technique, Judith decided the next day at work. She was half insulted that he had assumed her compliance, half excited that he was attracted as strongly to her as she was to him. Maybe his success in sex, as in business, lay in knowing what he wanted and going for it.

When her boss, Paula, disturbed her reverie for 'a quiet word', Judith's excitement soared. Paula didn't go in for quiet words unless it was about something vital. Imagemakers was the most relentlessly open plan office Judith had ever worked in. Paula had even had some crazy idea, copied from an ad agency, that no one should be allowed their own desk. It was supposed to stop them having a 'filing cabinet mentality' and keep them open to new ideas but people had irrationally clung to wanting their own bit of space.

Judith tried not to show the powerful emotions she was feeling. For months she'd been lobbying to be made a full partner. This had to be it.

'I've got some wonderful news,' Paula announced. So far, so good. 'It's been killing me not to tell you before. I'm pregnant. Isn't it terrific?'

Terrific was not the word that sprang to Judith's lips. She listened in horrified disbelief as Paula, until now more of a workaholic than she was, stood there like the bloody Madonna after the angel Gabriel had come down upon her, insisting she was pregnant. What's more, she intended to move the whole show to Bath so she could live in the country. Judith was too furious to speak. She felt like the punter in a five-card trick. She'd been stitched up like a turkey.

Of course, Paula was saying with undisguised smugness, Judith would be *more than welcome* to come too. Bath had nothing like Imagemakers, and though it might be a little different in pace, she was sure there'd be enough business to coast along if they kept their overheads down. The rewards would probably be a lot less but think of the gain in lifestyle!

Judith cursed under her breath. If she were going to live in the country she'd rather it were running Victoriana than wining and dining dull Rotary Club members in the hope of getting their boring business. Thanks to Paula so considerately keeping her outbreak of fertility to herself, Judith had missed any opportunity of doing that – and she would have been ten times more effective than Lily Brandon, she could swear to that. The unpleasant truth hit her that if she lost her job they'd have to live on Jonathan's unsatisfactory income. Damn and blast the woman!

'And when precisely are you planning this momentous move?'

'I'd like to get the business up and running before the baby's due,' gushed Paula, so hormonally challenged that she didn't even pick up the resentment in Judith's voice, 'so in a month or two, really. I'm about to start looking for premises down there.'

Judith would dearly have loved to get up and walk out now. Unfortunately she hadn't been wise enough to accumulate what the Americans call 'Fuck You money' so she would have to stay put until she could find something else. As Paula burbled on mindlessly about maternity nurses, the relative benefits of live-in nannies versus crèches, a thought burrowed its way into Judith's consciousness. It was too early to tell yet whether Lily was screwing up, but before too long there must be *some* signs of disaster. She would just have to keep a sharp eye out for them. Phoning her mother-in-law was suddenly much more appealing than usual. She knew one thing for sure. If Charlotte had suspected that Judith was likely to be out of a job she would have fought Edward a lot harder in this crazy scheme of appointing Lily in the first place.

As she listened to Paula, pretending to sympathize with

her desire to get out of the rat race, Judith wondered how securely Lily was really entrenched.

Lily knew by the change in Susie McIntosh's manner, from surly to co-operative, that something was brewing but decided to ignore it and concentrate on tackling the ordering system. It had horrified her to discover that this was still done by hand instead of by computer. Each order either arrived via the coupon torn out of the brochure or was dictated over the phone to one of the girls on the Orders line. There was a major flaw in this system – apart from the fact that it seemed to Lily to be like riding in a sedan chair when you could be driving a Cadillac. The processing took so long it meant that customers had to allow twenty-eight days for their clothes to arrive. Yet Lily knew when she ordered something from a catalogue she wanted it *now* not in four weeks. Surely a computer system could speed that up and simplify the process of stock control at the same time?

There was only one problem. To Lily, understanding a computer system was like trying to translate the Rosetta Stone. She was even too ignorant to know what questions to ask. The Groucho Marx line about a contract being so easy a four-year-old child could understand it drifted into her head.

She might not have a four-year-old child to draft in, but she did have a perfectly good seventeen-year-old nephew. Jeremy was only too happy to help providing she supplied him with the necessary tools. These seemed to be a week's supply of veggy burgers washed down with Diet Coke. Jeremy's generation, it transpired, actually preferred the taste of sweetener.

'You're honoured,' hissed Connie. 'I haven't been allowed in his bedroom for years. Take notes.'

Remembering the former chaos of her nephew's bedroom, Lily was amazed. It was almost clinically tidy now: the bed made, CDs arranged in alphabetical order and that telltale smell of teenager – one part cigarette smoke, one part joss stick to hide the cigarette smoke, plus a smattering of old sock – no longer seemed to hang around miasmically, driving Connie to secret forays with the air freshener.

The famous poster with the tennis-playing girl lifting her skirt to reveal a naked white buttock had now gone, replaced by one for REM. She remembered how appalled Connie had been when he'd first put the tennis player up. Connie had naïvely hoped that the family tendency to wander round in the nude might have cured him of the desire for titillation. Lily had told her not to be so pompous.

After he'd been fed and watered, Jeremy switched on his computer. 'Come on, Auntie Lil,' he said, 'we'll have you surfing the Internet in no time at all,' and proceeded to explain in words of less than one syllable how the different systems worked.

'Right,' she announced after two gruelling hours, yawning and stretching at so much concentrated effort, 'I think that's about as much as my aging cyberbrain can take in today. Could I borrow the handbook though?'

'The handbook's gobbledygook, written by one nerd for another.' He reached down to pick it up, undoing the rubber band holding back his hair at the same time. The gesture was slightly feminine but at the same time almost flirtatious. She realized what a good-looking youth he was growing into and was horrified to feel herself moved. What was she? A pervie?

'Forget the handbook.' Ruthlessly he sat her back down in front of the screen. 'What you need is some hands on experience.'

She was crying for mercy by midnight. She thanked him and handed him a twenty-pound note. 'Thanks,' he said. 'I wasn't expecting actual payment.'

'Ah, but it's also for helping me hump some stuff to the flat at the top of Victoriana.' The time had come for Lily to move out and she'd decided to live above the shop. Living with Connie was great, but it made her feel like a permanent wallflower.

By the time she called in the computer sales people the following week Lily was a fan and almost knew what she was talking about, or at least had the confidence to admit what she didn't know. The sums for installing the kind of system they'd need were terrifying. There was also the small question of selling the system to June who still heartily believed in coloured stickers on charts, but she'd cross that bridge when she came to it.

After the salesmen had gone she went to look for George to find out what kind of sums Victoriana had borrowed in the past. She was staggered by his answer. In all its years of trading the company hadn't taken a penny from the bank.

'It's your mother,' George explained. 'She's always had this disapproving attitude towards debt. She used to quote endlessly from Mr Micawber on the subject.'

Lily sat lost in calculations. It amused her how completely balance sheets had replaced bed sheets in her preoccupations. The thought of bed brought Ben Winter back into vivid focus. She didn't take the protestations of undying love Mo said he'd been making too seriously. It probably meant Bambi had dumped him. Her hand strayed towards the telephone; she still knew his number off by heart. His machine picked up the call and the beeps went. Nine o'clock was obviously far too early for him to be out of bed. The machine invited her to leave a short message or fax, but Lily lost her nerve. Anything she had to say was far too complicated for an answering machine. Besides, to leave a message would be to lob the power back into his court and she was rather enjoying having it in hers.

Her thoughts were interrupted by the sound of excited murmuring from the other end of the Mill's open plan office. She could sense an unfamiliar electricity in the place and noticed that down this end most of the desks were empty. Somebody must have brought a new baby in, or maybe it was a birthday and a cake had been produced. Eager not to seem aloof she hurried along to join in the fun. In the centre of the twittering crowd, Chartotte Brandon was holding court, surrounded by as many courtiers as a Medici princess.

'Lily, darling.' There was a mild shade of guilt in her mother's tone. 'Your father and I came back early. Too much idleness. So I thought I might volunteer my services in case there's anything I can do.' She caught Lily's expression. 'Just a day a week or something.'

Lily could have killed her. She knew perfectly well that the public nature of this declaration was deliberate. Her mother was an expert at putting people in embarrassing positions. To turn down this offer of assistance would seem churlish to the staff. Surely she was big enough to cope with it? How much damage could Charlotte do in one day?

As they continued their royal progress (there was no other word for it) with Charlotte stopping to greet people as they walked past, George emerged and exchanged a brief look of sympathy with Lily. She could have kissed him. Charlotte, on the other hand, sailed past with only the slightest nod in his direction. George blushed and wondered if she'd noticed that he'd started wearing a flowery tie.

'So,' Charlotte wasted no time beating about the bush once they were inside Lily's office. 'What's all this about your doing your designs for the catalogue? You have a whole design team to do that. Don't you think you should be running the company?'

'Unfortunately, the design team designs for only the over-thirties, so no young person wants to be seen dead in Victoriana.'

'And you think you can do better?'

'Tara and her friends have been advising me. We have to do something, Ma. You must know we're heading for trouble.'

Charlotte shuddered as though Lily had committed some kind of sacrilege. 'What absolute nonsense. The company is perfectly healthy. There's absolutely nothing wrong with our turnover.'

'Except that it's falling steadily.'

'Where did you suddenly acquire all this financial expertise? From adding up the bills when you were waitressing?' Charlotte regretted how sharp her voice sounded.

Why do you never believe in me, Lily wanted to demand, but she wasn't going to give her mother the satisfaction of seeing how hurt she was. 'From your accountant, as a matter of fact.'

'Oh, George,' said Charlotte, 'George is just a glorified bookkeeper. Your father kept him on because he felt sorry for him.' The implication, not lost on Lily, was that she had got the job for much the same reason.

'If you had listened to him you'd be a lot better off.'

'What nonsense.' Charlotte was shocked by the change in her daughter who suddenly seemed to think she knew what she was doing. Clearly Lily was going to come unstuck, and Victoriana with her. She'd got back from Italy just in time. 'I'll use that desk, shall I?' She pointed with great magnanimity not to her own old desk, now occupied by Lily, but to Edward's, six feet away.

The temptation to refuse point blank to let her mother in the building flitted temptingly through Lily's mind. There was one small problem: Charlotte was still the major shareholder. The only card Lily held was resignation. She kept quiet for the moment. If her mother insisted on coming back into the business even for a day she was going to need another ally to keep her sane. She came to a decision.

When Charlotte got back home Edward was still as disapproving as ever, which irritated Charlotte intensely.

'Really, Edward, I don't know why you always take Lily's part. She's only been there five minutes and she's changing everything. No wonder Susie McIntosh is upset.'

Edward quietly continued planting out his seedlings. 'Susie McIntosh is a cow and, when you're being your usual self, you know it. Charlotte, love, I know all this has been hard for you. We built the company together, but it was your inspiration behind it. Victoriana's been like another child to you but now you've got to let go.'

'For God's sake. Edward. I'm only going in to advise. Lily will still be running the company.'

Edward smiled. Charlotte's advice was the kind you either took or she never spoke to you again. 'Is that what you were doing today? Trying not to interfere but help?' He could imagine the scene perfectly and asked himself if Charlotte, consciously or unconsciously, was trying to scupper Lily's position. 'Had it struck you, my love, that Lily might be right about doing some design herself? You might have a degree in fine arts, but that's hardly training for fashion design. It is instinct and style.' He looked at his wife slyly. 'Maybe Charlotte Brandon's creative genes have gone straight to Tara. Think of the great PR capital when the catalogue comes out. All in all I think it's rather a wonderful idea.'

'Oh, you're impossible! If Lily said black was white you'd believe her.'

'All I know is that Lily's right. Our sales figures did need shaking up and she's trying to do something about it.' He almost added, 'And she's standing up to you, Charlotte,' but knew it would only fan the flames. The truth was he found

Lily's actions rather exhilarating. She was daring to take risks and standing by them. 'Are you sure' – he wasn't convinced he should be asking this question either – 'that you aren't angry that Victoriana can exist without you? If you were, it'd be quite understandable.'

For answer, Charlotte slammed the door, took Troy's lead off its hook in the kitchen and rattled it. Nothing happened. Troy, normally eager for walks with his mistress, had clearly decided that on a freezing December day like this he would be better off in his nice cosy basket by the Rayburn. Charlotte rattled the lead again. Even the dog was being difficult. In the end she had to coax him out with a biscuit. He fixed her with his liquid reproachful eyes. Not someone else who saw her as the Dragon Queen?

Charlotte shrugged herself into her old waxed jacket which was cracked all over with tiny fine lines, and sometimes reminded Charlotte of the skin on her face. The check wool lining was chill to the touch but this didn't put her off. She loved walking in all weathers, even when the rain was so heavy her trusty jacket couldn't keep it out. She wrapped a paisley scarf of her own design round her neck and zipped up. With gum boots and thick socks to complete the outfit she looked the perfect English countrywoman. Practicality over appearance.

Eager to work off her anger with Edward, Charlotte decided not to take her usual easy path down towards the sea. Today a climb would do her good. The cold, misty weather might help cool her anger. On days like this the damp seemed to penetrate your bones, but Charlotte loved the way the light fog could suddenly clear and reveal slivers of landscape. The familiar became unknown: an adventure.

Today was one of those days. Charlotte climbed steadily up the steep hill to the left of the farmhouse. She'd been told by the doctors to try and walk every day and she and Troy had covered vast tracts of Dorset in their rambles. Both were

77

a lot fitter as a result, though sometimes, like today, Troy got lazy and skulked in his basket. As she reached the brow of the hill one of the magical transformations she normally loved so much overtook them. The mist cleared in a sudden blaze of winter sunshine revealing the gentleness of the valley beneath but today Charlotte was too wrapped up in her own thoughts to notice. What a ridiculous idea of Edward's that she was jealous of Lily. She just thought Lily was wrong, that's all. Lily was so impetuous: she had an instinct and she followed it, as though the two actions were inseparable and no other course possible. Neither she nor Edward were like that. They weighed and measured. Charlotte knew that Lily believed her mother didn't love her, but it wasn't true. She did love Lily in her way. It was just that every time she looked at her she felt smothered by guilt.

Charlotte pulled herself together. This wasn't like her. She had never believed in dwelling in the past, it was a very unhealthy place. Whistling for Troy, she started down the hill again. The brief moment of sunshine had passed now and the mist was thickening. She would be glad to be home.

Chapter 6

Half an hour later when Charlotte quietly opened the front door, feeling contrite, the second post was there waiting for her on the hall table, next to the coloured-glass lampshade which flung its jewel-like radiance around the hall. She picked the letters up and went into the kitchen to make some late-morning coffee. Perhaps she'd make some for Edward too. He'd understand, as he always did, that this was a coded apology and reach out his hand to take hers without looking up, to avoid any suggestion that he'd won. It was one of the things she loved him for.

She made the coffee and poured it into the large breakfast cups she always preferred to mugs at this time of day, flicking through her mail at the same time. There was one begging letter asking her to put her name to the masthead of a charity; another from a journalist writing about women in business who wanted to interview her – the irony struck Charlotte that now that she finally had time to see people like this she wasn't in business any more – and a reminder from the hospital about her check up. But it was the last one that caught her eye, an airmail, and she recognized the handwriting at once. It was from her sister Eve who had moved to Australia thirty-five years ago and had married and settled there. They had only kept in touch via the occasional letter and phone call. In all that time they had not once seen each other.

She ignored her coffee and unfolded the flimsy paper. The letter was typical of Eve's writing style. The first page had a no-holds-barred account of what the children of her three marriages were doing and seemed to embrace every emotional trauma known to soap opera. It was the last line that made Charlotte draw in her breath sharply.

Eve was coming back.

Panic seized Charlotte. For all this time she had buried certain truths, even to herself. With the powerful engine of her willpower she had even persuaded herself that events that had happened so long ago had simply been in her imagination. Eve was one of the two people alive who knew the reality. With Eve the other side of the world she had felt safe – now she would be safe no longer. Charlotte could feel her heart begin to race dangerously. She took deep slow breaths and reached for her medication. Why now? Why was Eve suddenly coming now?

Charlotte's immediate instinct was to put her off, perhaps to plead her illness, but Edward, she knew, wouldn't let her get away with it. On the other hand perhaps Edward needn't know . . .

It was too late. Edward had come to look for her in the kitchen. These days whenever she was out of his sight for too long he worried like an old granny. 'I saw the letter from Eve. Not bad news, I hope?' He was as familiar with Eve's erratic writing habits as she was.

Charlotte shook her head. 'She's coming over. And it seems as though she intends staying with us.'

Edward thought about this and decided it could only be a good thing. Eve had always been Charlotte's polar opposite: direct where Charlotte was devious; given to unburdening herself even to strangers while Charlotte loathed personal

intrusion; extrovert and loud where Charlotte prized subtlety and good taste. At least having her here would take
Charlotte's mind off Victoriana. Maybe with Eve around she
might even leave Lily to manage it in peace.

'You really mean it? You want me to come and work at
Victoriana too?' Connie's face told Lily more effectively than
any words that she saw the offer as a lifesaver.

'Absolutely. The most important job facing me is getting
the catalogue sorted out and I've neither the time nor the
slightest idea how to go about it. Ma used to use a freelance
but I'd much rather it were you. You've got such an incredible visual sense.' She gestured around her at Connie's
stylish interiors. 'I've wanted to ask you for ages but I didn't
know whether it'd be fair on Gavin.'

'What wouldn't be fair on me?' Gavin appeared from the
sitting room to get them all a drink. They seemed to be
getting on better lately. Maybe this would actually help.

'Asking Connie to come and join us to do the new Victoriana catalogue when you need her in the shop.'

Gavin considered his wife for a moment. She seemed to
be suddenly lit from within. Her eyes shone and her voice
fairly crackled with enthusiasm. The dramatic contrast to
her recent mood struck him forcibly. 'Better having no wife
in the shop than one who frightens the customers.'

Connie wanted to kiss him, knowing how difficult she
would be making life for him, leaving him to the undiluted
attentions of Margot. Being stuck in the shop with Margot
was rather like spending your life with the Speaking Clock,
only less exciting. 'You are a love,' Connie thanked him.
Who needed erotic titillation when you had someone who
really cared about you, as Gavin did for her?

'Would there be a salary? We'd need to get Margot to
work full-time, or Gavin won't be able to manage.'

'Of course. I'll get George to work something out.'

'When would I need to start?' Connie was practically bouncing round the room.

'As soon as you can fix up cover for the shop. The sample designs will be ready in a couple of months but there's a hell of a lot to set up first. Finding locations, photographer, models, make-up artists, hairdressers. Oh, and a theme would be nice. Why don't you come over now and get a pile of old catalogues. That'll give you an idea of how to get started.'

'I won't need to do that.' Connie gestured towards the bookcase. On the shelves, neatly stacked in date order, and going right back to the very first black-and-white line pamphlet, was every catalogue Victoriana had ever produced.

'Connie, I'd no idea you were so interested in the catalogue.'

'God, yes. I've always thought they could be much more imaginative, but you trying telling Ma that.'

'Well, with me you can have carte blanche. As long as it's classy and appeals to a few people under forty.'

Connie rubbed her hands in glee. 'This is going to be so exciting. I've even got an idea for a theme . . .'

'Have you? What's that?' Connie's eagerness was infectious.

But Connie just looked smug. 'No, I need to research it more first.' Then she remembered there'd been something she wanted to ask her sister. Something intriguing. 'By the way, have you heard the news? Ma's long-lost sister is coming to stay from Oz.'

'Auntie Eve? How amazing. I wonder what she's like.'

'I've got a photo of them somewhere.' Connie delved into the clutter on her kitchen dresser, which was so stacked with memorabilia it could have been catapulted into outer space as a time capsule, and eventually produced a faded black-and-white shot about the size of a postage stamp. Two very different women smiled out at them, dressed in the distinctive fashion of the nineteen fifties. Charlotte at nineteen was already sleek and stylish, utterly at home in her tailored suit; Eve looked like her country cousin, lumpy and drab in a dress that did nothing for her. Lily felt an immediate bonding of sympathy. Having Charlotte for a sister must have been almost as tough as having her for a mother.

'I wonder,' said Connie, putting the picture back, 'why she's coming to visit after all these years.'

'Perhaps she just misses her family,' said Gavin.

'What?' Lily demanded sceptically, 'after thirty-five years of voluntary absence she's decided she can't last one more single day without seeing us?'

It was definitely odd. Not so much that she was coming back, but that she'd stayed out of touch for so long. Lily thought of Connie and how awful it would be not to see her for all those years, but couldn't imagine it. She and Connie would have found a way of staying close no matter how many miles divided them. Maybe Charlotte and Eve had fallen out. Lily's curiosity about her stranger-aunt fizzled up enticingly.

Lily pulled a trolley from the endless snake in the Arrivals Hall at Heathrow and wheeled it towards where her parents were standing, opposite the passenger exit, waiting for Eve. She loved airports, even tatty, overcrowded old Heathrow. Airports were always such scenes of emotion: passionate goodbyes, passionate welcomings, they left soap operas standing. The airport authority had clearly declared Christmas open early and cornered the market in three-foot Santas, life-size sledges and Christmas trees. You could hardly turn round without tripping over a snowman or reindeer. The effect should have been jolly but was in fact somewhat sinister, like going to a Christmas party in Madame Tussaud's.

A flight from Naples had just cleared and an aged Italian

lady in funereal black stood looking around, laden with brown paper parcels tied up with string, before being swallowed up into a screeching swarm of relatives. How nice to have such a big family. She glanced at her mother and was surprised by the look of sharp apprehension there. Charlotte, the fearless, actually looked scared. Was she worried about not liking her sister after so many years?

The whole of the Naples flight disembarked and found its relations, followed by the Sydney flight, but there was still no sign of Eve.

The tension was getting to be too much for Charlotte. She'd taken her heart pills but they couldn't ward off the thundering headache that had suddenly come on. She'd known from the moment she'd had that letter that Eve was up to something. There was a reason behind this visit. There was a reason behind everything Eve did. Damn Eve! And how like her to make them wait. Perhaps she'd missed her flight. Perhaps she wouldn't be coming after all. Charlotte felt her spirits lift slightly.

'Where can the wretched woman have got to?' Edward asked crossly, conscious that the rugby was on television later and he wanted to get back in time for it.

'The wretched woman's right behind you.' A tall, startlingly dressed figure in a large hat and multi-coloured silks, with skin the colour of their mahogany dining table, jewel-bright eyelids – a sort of psychedelic Isadora Duncan – stood a few feet away next to a uniformed porter with a vast trolleyload of luggage. 'This nice chappie got me through before anyone else in the queue. I've just been having a cappuccino.'

'Eve.' Lily had never heard her mother sound so tentative before, what on earth was the matter with her? She should be throwing herself into her sister's arms, not treating her like some distant acquaintance. 'How lovely to see you.'

'Call me Evie,' she said as she surveyed her sister at arm's length, 'everyone else does. And these are my two nieces. You must be Connie. You look just like your mother did at your age. And you're Lily . . .' There was a beat of silence as Evie studied her niece's face.

'Come on, Eve . . . Evie . . .' Charlotte decided she didn't want any more dwelling on family resemblances. 'Edward wants to get home for the rugby.'

Embarrassed at Charlotte's lack of tact, Edward busied himself with the suitcases. 'So, how long are you planning to stay for your visit?' Even as he said it he realized it, too, might sound tactless. 'As long as possible, I hope,' he added quickly.

Evie understood the subtext of this question precisely. 'Depends how much fun I'm having. Three months? Six months?' Evie was beginning to enjoy herself. 'Six weeks? Who knows. My family think I'm an interfering old bat and were thrilled to see the back of me.'

Lily tried to suppress a giggle. Her father's face was a picture.

'What a wonderful outfit,' Connie remarked as they headed for the car park. She could have added that not everyone would think of wearing sunset-coloured chiffon on an English winter's day.

'Thanks.' Evie took the compliment as one well used to them. 'I just sold my chain of dress shops. This was one of my favourite designs. I forgot it'd be brass monkey weather in good old London.'

'Ma,' Connie chided, 'you didn't tell us Evie was a designer too.'

Charlotte looked startled. 'That's because I didn't know.'

'I only did it because I couldn't find any clothes that weren't greige, beige or café au bloody lait, so I designed my own, a little more colourful.'

I can just imagine, Charlotte thought bitchily.

'They went down a bomb as a matter of fact.'

'So why did you sell up?' asked Lily fascinated.

'The business stopped being a hobby and turned into a monster. It was taking over my life. I wanted to have time to do fun things like come and see my sister.' She threw an arm round a startled Charlotte who was relieved to see the car waiting for them. 'And of course Charlotte nearly croaking made me think about life. It's not a rehearsal you know.'

Connie and Lily exchanged glances. Things were clearly going to be lively with their aunt around.

Evie was not the kind of house guest who you only knew was there because she washed up her own cup and saucer. On her first day she insisted she would cook for them all and produced live lobsters she'd just smuggled half way across the world. Jeremy was so scandalized by this global eco-breach that she finally agreed to let him release them on to the beach at Lyme Regis. She then proceeded to bring back fish and chips for them all, announcing with relish that missing them was the real reason she'd come half way across the world.

She had gifts for everyone: Dayglo surfing shorts for Jeremy; a Ken Done watercolour of Sydney Harbour Bridge for Edward which to Charlotte's great irritation he insisted on putting up above the mantelpiece instead of the faded oil painting of a peaceful Dorset valley she loved so much; silk slips in glorious colours for Lily and Connie; and finally a bumper edition of the highly unsuitable teen drama *Heartbreak High* for Tara so she could know three months before her friends who was dumping whom, who was attempting suicide and whose mother was bonking whose father. Tara was utterly thrilled. For Charlotte herself she'd brought a palest green kimono from Hong Kong which even Charlotte couldn't take exception to.

*

It didn't take Evie long to work out what a minefield she'd walked into.

'When am I going to see round this famous company of yours?' she asked the next day. 'We've even heard of Victoriana in Oz, you know. Though I'm not sure we want to dress up in white petticoats – reminds us too much of what people wore on the transport ships. So, come on Charlotte, let's have the guided tour.'

'I'm sorry but you're asking the wrong person. Lily's running Victoriana now.'

Edward put down his paper in irritation. 'Really, Charlotte, Lily may be running it but it's still your company. You don't have to make a song and dance about showing Eve round.'

'Thank you for reminding me,' snapped Charlotte. 'But maybe it's Lily you ought to be reminding.'

Evie took in the tension crackling between Charlotte and Edward with interest. They had been married for forty years now and in Evie's experience a surprising number of friends of hers split up at this point, finally old enough to admit that they'd never liked each other much anyway. Knowing Charlotte, Edward would have had a lot to put up with over the years.

Charlotte herself clearly wanted to change the subject. 'By the way, Jonathan and Judith are coming down from town for lunch tomorrow. They're looking forward to meeting you.'

'All that way just for lunch with little me?' Evie smiled mischievously. 'I hope I'll give good value.'

Lily laughed. 'I'm sure that's one thing you always do.'

Judith and Jonathan arrived on the dot of midday in their city clothes, loaded down with Sunday papers. It was a mystery to Lily, who couldn't read a newspaper without dismembering it, how Judith could have consumed a whole pile, keeping each intact, and not getting a single smudge of newsprint on her white bouclé suit.

'She probably only reads the Style section,' pointed out Connie bitchily.

'*I* only read the Style section,' said Lily, 'but I still end up looking like Dick van Dyke in Mary Poppins.'

Charlotte excelled herself with the lunch. One thing she was using her increased leisure time for was ever more complex recipes.

'She's only interested if it has more than six stages,' whispered Lily to her aunt. 'I counted three different sauces last week, and that was with just one pudding.' While the coffee was being poured, Lily decided to take advantage of the moment.

'As the family's all here there's something worrying me I wanted to mention. It's the Christmas run-up and we're inundated with orders. The postman brought six sacks at the first post alone.'

'And that's worrying?' Jonathan demanded. 'I wish I had such worries.'

'The point is, we can't cope. We need computers to do the processing. I've looked into one that could transform our system. As it is we just won't get some orders out by Christmas. With a computer we could turn orders round in days, not weeks. People want things immediately, not in twenty-eight days.'

Charlotte tutted. 'I do so hate this society that has to have things *now* and can't wait even a week or two.'

Evie sniffed. Charlotte hadn't changed.

'That's what our competitors are offering. Victoriana's getting left behind.'

'And how much would this system of yours cost?'

Lily named the price.

Charlotte exploded. 'But that's ridiculous. It'd take us years to pay that back.'

'George and I have worked it all out: how quickly it'll pay for itself; the extra turnover it'll generate.'

Charlotte was unconvinced. 'Victoriana has *never* borrowed.'

Lily screwed up her courage. 'All businesses borrow, if it means they can expand and become more profitable.'

'Victoriana has never needed to.'

Evie could feel the sparks between Lily and her mother and wondered if Edward had ever glimpsed the potential for disaster he'd caused by giving Lily control of Victoriana. Poor Edward. He loved Lily so much he hadn't seen what a poisoned chalice he'd handed her.

'I think Lily's absolutely right,' Judith announced unexpectedly. 'Victoriana has to move with the times.' Everyone stared at her. She was somehow the last person anyone would expect to defend Lily.

After a moment's tense silence Charlotte began to pour the coffee. 'Really Lily, I think we should discuss this at a more appropriate moment. This is a family party.'

Lily dropped the subject. To those who knew Charlotte this was the beginning of accommodation.

After lunch was over and the washing up performed with all the ceremony and ritual of a religious observance, Evie retired upstairs to the bathroom. Charlotte followed her, fussing around to make sure there were clean towels. There were, each with a decorative Victoriana logo on them.

'What do you think of my daughter-in-law Judith? If she could have taken on Victoriana rather than Lily, I would sleep a lot better.'

Evie felt fury rising on Lily's behalf. Judith had struck her as cold and manipulative next to Lily's sparkling warmth. 'How could you say that, Charlotte? Lily's worth ten of that one. It's only because you can't face the truth in yourself that you treat Lily like this –'

'Why did you really come?' Charlotte broke in, unable to listen to her sister's armchair analysis of her shortcomings.

Evie put down the towel and turned to her sister. 'Because *he* wants to come and I wanted to warn you. He's been ill too, Charlotte, and he wants to sort things out.'

The face Charlotte had banned from her thoughts for so long forced its way back in. She felt him before she saw him, his energy, his passion, the enthusiasms that could win any argument. Except one.

'He wants to come here, Charlotte. I talked him out of it, but only for the moment.'

Charlotte steadied herself. 'He has no right . . .'

'That won't stop him. And what about you? It's taken its toll. Look at the heart attack. You could crack up.'

'Who could crack up?' asked a voice from the doorway. 'Not Charlotte surely. Charlotte Brandon is indestructible, aren't you, Charlotte?'

Charlotte gripped the mahogany chairback in front of the dressing table and forced herself to smile at her daughter-in-law, who was leaning on the door jamb watching the two older women. 'Of course I am, I'm as indestructible as Stonehenge.'

'Time I got some fresh air.' Evie wondered how much Judith had heard. 'All that delicious food is making me sleepy.' She closed her handbag with a snap. Watching her go, Judith sensed that something was going on here and that, whatever it was, it would be useful to find out more.

Downstairs in the hall, Lily and Edward had just got back from a walk. They stood pulling off each other's boots and laughing. Evie could feel the love flow between them, strong and powerful like a river. It should have been a touching scene, but remembering why she'd come here, Evie couldn't watch it. Lily's tragedy was that until she understood her mother's reasons for not loving her she would never be happy. And if she did understand them she might never forgive her. That was Charlotte's tragedy.

Chapter 7

Barry North sat at a discreet corner table in a restaurant he'd often used for assignations before. When Judith had finally called him he'd followed the usual pattern in these things and proposed lunch. He could have suggested a hotel but that, he knew from past experience, might be seen as moving too fast. Some women found such directness a turn-on, others needed to be courted. He didn't yet know into which group Judith Brandon fell. To cover his options he'd cancelled his afternoon meetings and the restaurant, as well as being anonymous, was well-placed for nearby hotels.

North allowed himself to feel a sliver of anticipation. Judith wasn't his usual type. She was tougher, but he found he was excited by that prospect. It lessened their obligation towards each other. He also wasn't in the habit of mixing business with pleasure – shitting on his own doorstep – but he got the distinct impression that Judith might turn out to be an asset where that was concerned.

In the back of the cab Judith checked her face in her make-up mirror. It was flawless. Hardly surprising, given the time she'd spent on it. Looking as natural as she did took a lot of effort. Unlike her host she was entirely sure how today was going to turn out. Underneath her subtle cashmere suit her bra and pants were dark blue – a colour which flattered the pale shade of her skin – and, naturally, matching. Judith had few inhibitions sexually and was prepared to do almost anything provided she could do it in toning underwear.

She waited until she was precisely five minutes late, then walked into the restaurant.

At what point, North wondered as he watched her confident progress through the restaurant, did she lose that sleek self possession and give herself up to the undignified, sometimes ridiculous contortions that no-holds-barred sex required?

When the waiter came to ask for their order neither of them had even looked at the menu. He had to come back three times before they made a selection. Excited to see North's usual assertiveness dented by her presence, Judith took the lead.

Both of them felt the tension growing as the meal progressed, but there was something Judith wanted to get out of the way. 'I went down to Dorset last week. Lily Brandon is about to computerize Victoriana.'

'Quite an outlay.' North's brain clicked temporarily back into business mode. 'How's she financing it?'

'I don't think she's got that far.'

'Why don't you get your husband to suggest she borrows from First Venture. We both know Clive Green. Keep it in the family. That way we'll be able to find out how she's doing.'

It was a brilliant stroke. Judith wondered if it were too soon for what she was going to say next. On the other hand, at this moment, she was the one who had the power and he was the one who wanted something: her. 'I might as well put my cards on the table.'

'Please do. I prefer knowing where I am in a negotiation.'

Judith enjoyed the use of the business expression. She

liked his style. 'I bet you do. It's about Victoriana. I may be out of a job soon. If you acquire it . . .'

'*When* I acquire it.'

'I might like to run it.'

'Would you now? I can't somehow see you buried in deepest Dorset with no one to play with. The country wife doesn't seem your style.'

'But I wouldn't be a country wife. I'd be running Victoriana.' She leaned towards him across the pink damask table-cloth. 'Look, I know I could do amazing things with it. It's not making money because Charlotte's run it like a holiday camp. The right person could turn it into a gold-mine.'

'I know. Why do you think I'm interested?'

'And I don't see why it has to be run from Dorset either. You'd have to keep links with the place for the sake of the rural myth but it could just as easily be run from SW1.'

'You've got it all worked out, haven't you?' The sudden roughness in his voice took her by surprise and she wondered if she'd gone too far. Some men didn't like strong women.

North leaned back and looked her over as though he were assessing his next move. 'And how do you intend to talk me into all this? I assume you've thought that out too.'

Judith took a sip of wine and watched him over the top of her glass, her eyes looking straight into his. The thought of Jonathan wormed its way briefly into her mind, but she shook it out. Their marriage was dead on its feet anyway. She had to think of the future. 'Of course I have. Shall we go? I always say actions speak louder than words.'

'It's so great to have you here, Con!' Lily enthused. She hadn't realized quite how isolated she'd been feeling at Victoriana until Connie arrived. 'Are you looking forward to it?' She could already read the answer from Connie's eager face.

Connie opened her briefcase and a pile of sketches of different locations tumbled out. Lily picked one up featuring a girl dressed in Victoriana clothes sitting in a haycart. She managed to look both modern and sexy. 'I thought we might go for a Thomas Hardy kind of look and use his different books as themes.'

It was a terrific idea, brilliantly capitalizing on their Dorset roots. Lily felt a huge sense of relief. She'd been right about Connie. Now she could concentrate on finding the money for the computer system.

She didn't have long to wait. Later that morning Jonathan rang with the name of a firm of venture capitalists to recommend. 'They're shit hot at the moment, written up in the financial press and everything. Your local bank will probably be ridiculously cautious. The advantage of First Venture is that they understand business. Obviously it's your choice but I'll send you some cuttings about them anyway.'

The cuttings arrived the next day and Lily couldn't fail to be impressed by them. First Venture even had a profile in *Finance*, the moneymakers' Bible. She had almost worked her way through the press coverage when a fax arrived from Jonathan saying he'd gone ahead and set up a meeting on their behalf with someone called Paul Allan.

'Whatever's come over Jonathan?' asked Connie. 'He's acting like an insurance salesman. You don't suppose he's getting a commission, do you?'

They giggled at the thought of their elegant brother flogging pension schemes. All the same, Lily decided she'd shop around a few other lenders as well as First Venture.

Paul Allan studied Victoriana's business plan intently for a few moments to give himself time to think. Lily Brandon hadn't been at all what he was expecting. She was sitting opposite him in a demure navy suit, the same suit that was worn by dozens of women bankers and lawyers of his acquaintance, but on Lily it looked different. Maybe it was that she'd rejected the thick, sexless, District Nurse tights that had become the modern woman's uniform. Lily's tights were sheer and crackled provocatively when she crossed her legs. With his eyes fixed on the numbers in front of him he decided what was so unsettling about her. Lily Brandon made you think of a nun who was wearing a suspender belt. Her eyes were extraordinary too, a clear tawny brown. One seemed to be a slightly different colour, more yellow than brown, giving her gaze an unevenness that was curiously attractive.

He'd read about her of course, but the public image didn't suit her either. He'd expected some kind of vamp but Lily's allure came from directness, a kind of debonair This is What I'm Like, Take Me or Leave Me air that he found far more attractive than mystery. Mystery had always struck Paul as passive – a blank canvas vain men believed they could write on. There was nothing passive about the woman in front of him, and the pitch she'd just made about why he should lend her the money was as convincing as any he'd heard. On the other hand, he had real reservations about the second generation running a business. In his experience they rarely had the talent or the hunger of the first generation. Charlotte Brandon was a known quantity, but her daughter certainly wasn't and the clothing business was notoriously unreliable.

Although he had no suspicion of it, Paul had thrown Lily into equal confusion. He didn't fit her ideas of what a merchant banker should be like at all. Lily had never had much time for them. It was no surprise to her that they were known to most people simply as rhyming slang for wankers. Among the friends she'd grown up with, only the thickest had gone into this line, and the ones with the narrowest outlook too. Paul Allan seemed neither thick nor upper class. He was boyish-looking with almost black hair and dark brown eyes, as though a rogue Italian had climbed into his mother's bed in Hayes or wherever he was from and Paul was the result. There was the faintest trace of what her mother would call *an accent*, but Lily liked him for it. The theatre had been full of people reinventing themselves and getting away from their narrow backgrounds and she suspected Paul Allan to be the same. No First XI photos or poses in cricketing whites in his hall. She found herself wondering what his flat would be like, the things he would have chosen to surround himself with.

She liked his office. It had none of the usual gadgetry of Financial Man. No powerbook computers, mobile phones, or Psion organizers. Just a beautiful blond wood desk that looked as though it belonged in the Purser's office of an elegant 1930s liner, a pad and pen, and on the walls some interesting looking abstract paintings in glorious shades of yellow and blue. Paul Allan, she suspected, was not as conventional as his profession implied.

Paul closed the report and started to wind up the meeting. He'd studied the figures at length but on the whole he didn't reckon this one as a good risk. Lily was too inexperienced and the sum she wanted to borrow was considerable. He prided himself on his instincts and they were telling him that no matter how attractive he found Lily Brandon, he should say no.

Years of trying to second-guess what directors wanted from her had given Lily pretty good intuition, and hers was screaming at her that Paul Allan was about to refuse the application. In one more minute it'd be over. Rejection had gone with the territory in acting but she was damned if she was taking it lying down in her new life.

'You don't think I've got it, do you? You're thinking Charlotte Brandon was the brains behind this operation. Why should her giddy daughter be able to hack it? Well, I'll tell you why. My mother's a brilliant woman, a woman who had a vision which she sold to millions of customers, but she became too narrow, too set in certain ways of doing things. She couldn't see that the world was changing, women's lives were changing. Don't get me wrong, I think Victoriana's core business' – she'd picked this one up from Jonathan – 'is still the same, but we have to move with the times. I've got a vision too, you know. Before you turn us down, come and see the place.'

Against his better judgement, and possibly because of the tigerish determination he'd glimpsed in Lily's golden eyes, Paul Allan found himself agreeing to look round Victoriana the following Wednesday at eleven o'clock.

Thankfully, when he did visit, only two weeks before Christmas, Victoriana performed brilliantly for Lily. The phones buzzed eternally; hopeful – and far too late – coupons still arrived by post. Everyone seemed to want to give Victoriana clothes for Christmas presents. Brian in the warehouse barked out instructions and the girls rushed around filling wire baskets with orders, the system Victoriana had used from the start. It was a perfect opportunity for Lily to point out how much business was being lost because without computers they couldn't respond quickly enough.

As they stood there, Lily could see some of the girls nudge each other and watch them, clearly taken with Paul's dark good looks. One of the boldest caught his eye. Lily half expected him to blush. Instead he smiled back. Bit of a lad, then, when he wanted to be.

Paul found Victoriana quite unlike any factory or mill he'd visited before. There was an atmosphere of quiet but happy industriousness, rather like at a well-behaved boarding school when the Headmistress was about. It reminded him suddenly of art lessons at his old grammar school where, to preserve an atmosphere of quiet concentration, their teacher had read them improving books. Any moment, Paul decided, his old teacher would start on *The Hobbit*.

Rather than subject him to a communal casserole under the watchful gaze of everyone from June to the canteen ladies, Lily spirited him off to a nearby pub. They could easily have had sandwiches in the office but she wanted Paul to fall in love with Dorset, to see what made Victoriana special.

It was so cold outside that they had to blow on their hands even in the car. On the short drive Paul looked out of the window and she willed him to feel some of the intensity she did for the place. The fields, grey and empty, had a pared-down beauty. A light mist still hung about the trees. They stopped on the top of a ridge and got out. The silence enveloped them, broken only by the sound of rooks cawing to each other to warn of intruders. 'Beautiful, isn't it?' she ventured, terrified that she'd get some trite reply.

He turned around almost full circle, taking in every aspect of the unfolding landscape. 'I used to be a keen walker. Offa's Dyke from end to end.'

'Not any more?'

'Not lately. Too much work.'

'You should take it up again.'

'Yes, I should.'

By the time they made it to the pub they were both chilled to the bone in their unsuitable indoor clothes. Inside the Harvest Home it was snug and festive. Tinsel was woven in and out of the hops hanging in garlands above the bar, and a coal fire glowed in the hearth, almost blocked out by a group of old men sitting on hard chairs, nursing halves of bitter which would be eked out for at least another hour. The landlord wasn't going to get rich on that lot.

Lily bought them both a mulled wine: 'And don't flash your fancy London ways and ask for mineral water.'

Paul took the steaming drink from her and sat in a wooden Windsor chair near the fire. 'I wouldn't dare.' He looked around him. 'Are you sure this isn't one of those snowstorm paperweights, a little bit of English heritage, packaged for export and gullible Londoners like me?'

'Nonsense,' Lily chided. 'This isn't some spot on your tourist route. At least half the people here work on the land in one way or another.' She settled back to wait for the rabbit pie they'd ordered, realizing that with the wine and the warmth she was letting her guard down – but then so, she suspected, was he.

Above them an oil painting of the four seasons painted by a local artist caught Paul's eye. Sowing in spring, harvesting, apple picking in autumn and gathering wood in a snow-covered woodland, but it had none of the sentimentality the subject might evoke. In this version life looked hard and bleak. Lily followed his gaze.

'That was what my mother understood. The kind of yearning for the past people feel, even though they can see life was tougher then. She somehow sold that along with the clothes.'

Paul felt himself falling for Charlotte Brandon's version of life just as much as any of her customers. Stuck in his city tower block, in his air-conditioned office, he had no sense of the changing seasons, no connection whatsoever with anything that seemed real. The businesses he financed were largely consultancies or services. This was the first time a company that actually *made* something had approached him and he found the old, romantic ideals flooding back that his father, a union official, had held about the manufacturing industry, the very ideals he'd spent his student years laughing at and tearing to shreds. Victoriana frocks were hardly the kind of industry his father had in mind during those heated late-night discussions about Mrs Thatcher destroying the industrial base of Britain, but they were as near as Paul was ever going to get.

Knowing none of this, Lily could still see the pull their way of life was having on him. 'It's a contradiction, isn't it? We want all the comforts of modern life but maybe we all feel more secure if we have some link with the past.' The pie they'd ordered arrived, its crust golden and flaky, decorated with pastry leaves and a piece of holly stuck festively in the top.

After the meal they sat in companionable silence, both conscious that the spell would be broken if either said the fatal words 'We should go.'

It was almost three and the pub was emptying when Lily finally asked about his train. Suddenly businesslike, he refused her offer of a lift to the station and went back with her to Victoriana to summon a cab instead. Half an hour later he was gone, after an unexpectedly stiff goodbye, leaving Lily wondering whether her plan to introduce him to the delights of Dorset had succeeded or not.

The cab was hardly out of the drive before Connie pounced. 'Well? Is he going to lend us the money?'

Lily had to admit she had no idea. She'd thought things were going well but Paul had seemed to withdraw at the end. Maybe he felt he was crossing the line between business and pleasure and was worried that she might be getting the signals wrong. She allowed herself a short droop of disappointment, which for some reason became inextricably linked with the thought of Ben Winter. The last couple of hours had been so delicious that she'd forgotten how much she'd missed being with a man who found you attractive. Maybe she ought to start making an effort: get herself on the dinner party circuit or go to wine bars. The thought depressed her even further. If only you could find a man without going through the humiliating process of searching.

'I don't think we should rely on city slickers for the loan,' Lily said. 'All they're ever interested in is quick profits. I'm seeing the local banks too. I'm sure they're far more likely to lend.'

'Pity,' Connie pointed out, watching her sister slyly. 'As city slickers go, he was pretty attractive.'

On the way back to town Paul Allan read through Victoriana's business plan three times. Despite his emotional response to the company, and perhaps even more to the person who was running it, he still felt uncertain that it was a good risk. By the time the train pulled into London he had decided against it. He would get his assistant to call Lily Brandon tomorrow and ask her to come to his office. He owed it to her at least to tell her the bad news in person.

Lily felt increasingly dismal as she trawled round the other banks in search of the loan she wanted. Even with a reasonable turnover and a big name like Victoriana's, both local banks were very discouraging. Lily began to wish they made widgets or ran a travel agency. Fashion seemed to be a universally dirty word, even anti-fashion like Victoriana's. It was too ephemeral, the bank manager in Bidchester informed her pompously, too dependent for its commercial success on the whim of a hemline.

Lily began to feel impatient. She'd heard this argument before and was convinced that Victoriana was the one fashion company this didn't apply to, but the man opposite her clearly wasn't going to lend her the money.

The message that Paul Allan had rung and invited her to a meeting cheered her no end.

'He wouldn't ask you all the way to London to give you the kiss-off, now, would he?' demanded Connie. 'He'd send you a stiff letter full of gobbledygook about margins and bottom lines. It *has* to be good news.'

On the day of her trip to London, excitement danced

around in Lily's mind like an electrical field despite her efforts to stay calm. It kept leaping out at her through each little task she performed. What should she wear? In typical Lily fashion she chose something she considered the height of demure good taste. A plum velvet crinkle-pleated skirt with a soft woollen tunic over it which clung enticingly to her shape. She decided to leave her long hair loose this time instead of scraped back, and to put on some dark red lipstick which left lip prints on everything she touched. Lily rather liked that. It reminded her of bad women in old Hollywood classics.

She surveyed herself in the mirror and decided the outfit still lacked something. She found a black velvet choker with a pretty Victorian brooch attached which always made her think about one of her favourite heroines, Eustacia Vye in *The Return of the Native*. Tempestuous Eustacia liked to wander the lonely hills with a black velvet band around her forehead and when the village girls copied her wearing coloured ribbons, Eustacia laughed at their vulgarity.

'Eustacia had disastrous taste in men too,' Lily reminded her reflection sternly, thinking of Ben Winter, and wondered if Paul Allan had any hidden mistresses, gay lovers or wives and families hidden away in Skegness.

No matter how often, or how convincingly, he had told himself this was business, Paul Allan still felt like a shit when Lily was ushered into his office. She looked startlingly exotic and totally out of place in this functional building, like an orchid stuck in an old milk bottle. Her glorious hair was loose and it hung in a polished curtain around her shoulders. There was a glow of anticipation about her which he couldn't bear to extinguish. Perhaps he had, after all, been too narrow in his thinking. The decision to lend was entirely down to him. The sum, though large, was well within the limits of his authorization, as were the stages of the payments. Victoriana, he told himself, was unique and its commitment to employing only local people would have delighted his father, no matter what he thought of the paternalistic way the company was run. Also, its owner was extremely beautiful. With Lily sitting across from him, her perfume just discernible, he could suddenly think of a lot of good reasons why he should lend to Victoriana after all.

'So,' she prompted, wondering why Paul had been silent for so long. 'What's the verdict then?' She tried to keep her voice as crisp and businesslike as possible. Here it was, the moment of truth.

Sod it, Paul decided, surprising himself, life was about more than columns of figures, the continual obsession with profit and loss. It was, he knew, an original notion for a banker. 'I've decided to lend you the money.' He didn't add that he'd only come to the decision thirty seconds ago.

In his experience even grown men sometimes got up and kissed you at such news, but Lily was watching him coolly. 'Don't worry,' she said, almost laughing at him, 'I won't lose your money. I'm really a much better risk than you think I am. You'll see.'

So she'd guessed all along how dubious he was. Paul felt a twinge of shame which he covered by buzzing his assistant for some champagne to celebrate, one of the firm's usual habits after a deal had been struck.

'I suppose that goes straight on my account?' Lily demanded teasingly. 'Another fifty quid for me to pay you back?'

As a matter of fact she was right. Another of the firm's little habits. No one else had ever noticed before Lily. 'How did you work that out?'

'I used to waitress between parts. You learn all the scams. Treating the customer to a drink then charging them for it was one of the standards. Come on, it's five-thirty. I'll take you out for one to say thank you. At least I'll know exactly how much it's costing me, won't I?'

Paul thought of the pile of reports he was supposed to be reading, acutely aware of Lily and her perfume and how she was beginning to fill up his thoughts. He didn't even pretend to fight.

Out on the street Lily suddenly couldn't think of anywhere to go. Why was it that you could have practically been born in a bar and yet not be able to name one just when you needed it?

Eventually she remembered the Blue Flame Club in Soho, where Maxie worked while resting. Although this rejoiced in the name 'club', you could get in by paying a fiver and it was certainly atmospheric.

They negotiated the doorman and climbed the narrow staircase, past wood panelling and dark green paintwork. The Blue Flame Club had alcoves everywhere, some curtained exotically rather like the Café Royal where Frank Harris, the celebrated lover, whisked ladies away for a discreet rogering while the more respectable got stuck into their dinners instead of their mistresses. Wall sconces of dangerous-looking real flames lit the alcoves, giving the lounging groups a faintly decadent air.

The waitress led them to a small niche almost filled by a huge sofa, overhung with embroidered hangings. It had the enticing feel of a harem. Paul was clearly enjoying the atmosphere. Most of his business negotiations took place in the bars and lobbies of faceless modern hotels. 'Did you work here too?'

Lily suspected that if she told him she'd picked up tips with her fanny he'd probably believe her. Actors and the jobs they did were a million miles from his world.

They ordered champagne and sat on the sofa which, though huge, was so squashy they kept sliding towards each other like a couple in a double bed with a dip in the middle. Lily was acutely aware that her knee kept touching his and so made bright conversation about impersonal things while secretly relishing the brief collisions.

She spotted the drama critic who'd once given her a rave review. He raised his glass to her, probably having no idea who she really was, causing his companion to turn round and check if there was anyone important he was missing. Lily began to see that bringing Paul to the Blue Flame was a silly mistake. This was her turf and guaranteed to put him at a disadvantage. As if in confirmation of this, a velvety, caressing voice spoke to her, making her cringe with horror.

'Hello, Lily, I didn't know you were back in town.'

He was standing there, alone, with no evidence of underage actresses in tow, looking drunk and dangerous.

'Hello, Ben. You haven't heard then – I'm running my parents' business for a while.'

'How delicious. Lily the tycoon. Aren't you going to introduce me to your friend?'

'Ben Winter, the actor, this is Paul Allan of First Venture.'

'A bank manager!' Ben's eyes glittered with drink and delight. 'Is he helping you to add up?' She realized with alarm he was even drunker than she'd thought. 'Very good at the numbers six and nine, our Lily. But I expect you've found that out already.'

Lily froze. With perfect timing their champagne arrived. Paul stood up and handed the full bottle to Ben. 'I think your need may be greater than ours.'

Ben cradled it to his chest. 'A consolation prize? How thoughtful.'

Paul helped Lily up. 'Time we went, our table's overdue.'

Lily felt Ben's eyes burn into her back as they picked their way through the tables of people pretending not to gawp. What on earth was the matter with him? In the whole six months of their relationship she'd never seen him drinking like that.

'I'm sorry,' she explained to Paul as they stood on the pavement, 'that was –'

'I know who it was.'

'He behaved appallingly. I'm so sorry.'

'Jealousy does that to people.'

'So does vodka,' Lily said unsentimentally. All the same, it had shocked her. He seemed to have gone to pieces. No wonder his agent was worried. It must be like watching a goldmine self-destruct. The awful thing was that, if she were brutally honest, Lily was a little bit flattered.

'Since we're clearly not destined to get that champagne, how about dinner? I would take you to Le Pont de la Tour, but I actually prefer the place next door.'

This turned out to be a fish and chip shop in Rotherhithe.

'Ah,' insisted Paul, clearly enjoying himself at making Lily slum it for once, 'but not any fish and chip shop. Chinese-run and it just happens to be the best in London.'

The Happy Plaice was decorated with a feast of fifties Formica. A vinegar dispenser graced each table and a juke box full of corny old tracks provided the music. They each ordered cod in crispy light batter, divinely perfect chips, thick without being soggy, and, the *pièce de resistance*, a tiny greaseproof bag filled with the crispy bits that had fallen off into the fat. Paul disappeared briefly and returned with not one but two bottles of champagne which he distributed around the tables in paper cups.

The Chinese proprietor raised his in a toast: 'To very beautiful couple. Have long and happy life together. Many beautiful children to eat fis' and chip.'

Lily collapsed with laughter. 'He thinks we're getting engaged.'

When the last of the champagne was finished they waved goodbye to the by now cheering customers, and ran off down the embankment to look at the staggering view of Tower Bridge. Unusually for London, stars scattered the sky with ridiculous theatricality. It was also achingly cold and Lily, who had left her boring old navy coat at home because it spoiled her outfit, felt herself drawing involuntarily towards the warmth of Paul's body.

They both stared at one another, each knowing all the good reasons why they should draw back. Instead Paul reached out and pulled Lily against him and kissed her hard on the lips.

Chapter 8

Inside Paul's flat Lily tried to regain her composure. It was only yards from where they'd just eaten and if you leaned out of the bathroom window, he said, there was a view of the river. The flat was tidy, without being obsessively so, and there was a smell of polish from the parquet floor, and flowers in a vase. Paul Allan clearly liked his life and organized it well.

She thought of Ben's chaotic flat. He relied on women: cleaning ladies, aunts, girlfriends to organize it for him. Paul was somehow more grown-up and responsible even though he was ten years younger.

'I'm not that respectable, you know.' Paul read her thoughts. He had just appeared with yet another bottle of champagne and one of those crinkly silver coolers. She'd seen them advertised and always wondered if they worked. 'Appearances can be deceptive.'

Lily's insides did a backwards flip at the look in his eyes and Ben vanished from her mind.

'Scientific experiment.' said Paul. 'Does this really cool it down, as it claims in the ad, in less than six minutes?'

Unfortunately to people in lust, six minutes is a very long time and, as it happened, Paul and Lily were not there to test the efficacy of the cooler's claim. Instead they were locked in each other's arms under Paul's goose down duvet.

With his body on hers, Lily was taken aback by the intensity of her passion. It was as though all the stresses of the last few months, the fears of changing her life, the loneliness of running Victoriana, were wiped out in glorious abandon. She managed to forget everything except the moment.

Afterwards they lay with only a handspan between them, smiling ridiculously, his dark eyes locked into hers as though she were in possession of the secrets of the universe. Eventually, still smiling, they fell asleep.

It must have been five in the morning, freezing and still dark outside, when Lily woke again, her head thundering and her mouth tasting of cotton wool. She sat up, not recognizing the unfamiliar surroundings. Then each embarrassing piece of the jigsaw fell into place: the loan, the Blue Flame Club, Ben, the champagne. Lily had been in situations like this countless times before, but that was in her old life. She had been to bed with Paul Allan, a man she hardly knew, someone with whom she should have been having a purely professional relationship, who was vital to the success of Victoriana. How could she have been so dumb?

She sat up and groped for her clothes. The best thing would be to quietly disappear and tomorrow write him a polite note, giving them both the chance to retrieve their professional dignity and pretend that this had never happened. Beside her Paul slept peacefully, his long eyelashes fluttering occasionally, his breathing slow and regular. A light down darkened his chest which she yearned to reach out and stroke. Instead she kissed her fingertips and dusted them across his cheek. He stirred but didn't wake.

Outside his flat, she shivered violently and looked around for her bearings. If she walked along the river she was bound to see a cab or bus. It was probably too early for a tube.

It felt as though she'd walked miles when a night bus rounded the bend, the lights inside glowing appealingly, and Lily climbed aboard. The driver, struck by the unexpectedness of someone so attractive and yet so sad suddenly getting on his bus on the last run before he knocked off, stopped at an all-night tea-stand and brought her back a styrofoam cup of coffee and lots of little bags of sugar.

'Don't worry, love,' he said kindly, stirring the hot liquid and handing it to her, 'it may never happen.'

'Thanks,' Lily took the drink gratefully, her hands still shaking, 'but it already has.'

Paul woke late and smiled even before he opened his eyes. Last night had been a fantasy come true for him. Despite his looks, Paul was relatively inexperienced with women, and had never before had the nerve to ask a woman he wanted as desperately as he wanted Lily to come back home with him. He rolled over to reach out to her and when she wasn't there assumed she must be in the bathroom.

But the bathroom was empty. So was the kitchen. Gradually it hit him with a shock of pain and panic that Lily had gone. He searched the flat one last time, noticing the undrunk champagne, flat and wasted in its cooler, then crawled back to bed. He was so bloody naïve. She must do this kind of thing all the time. He was the mug, assuming that it had meant anything, that finally he'd met someone who would really matter to him.

The first train was at six. Lily leaned miserably against a pillar on the station's tarted-up concourse which the planners, eager to discourage dossers, had designed without seats. Thankfully no one had yet turned on the festive carols. What would Paul think when he woke? She thought of the men who'd treated her like that. On the other hand, maybe he'd be relieved. He, too, might be feeling that they'd made a mistake. Later on, when she had got her courage up, she would ring him.

The moment she was back at Victoriana tiredness dragged at her. Instead of going to her office she trudged up to her flat in the rafters. And it was there that Connie found her, buried under her duvet, just before lunchtime.

'I couldn't wait to hear how you got on. What on earth have you been doing? You look terrible. Don't tell me we didn't get it.'

'Oh we got the loan all right.'

'But that's terrific. Just what you wanted.'

Lily pulled the dressing gown round her for comfort, feeling a wave of shame break over her again. 'Con, I've done the most bloody stupid thing . . .'

'What have you done? Gone back to Ben Winter?'

Lily could see that Connie wasn't taking her entirely seriously. 'I've been to bed with Paul Allan.'

She longed for her sister to sympathize and say that she'd been unwise, maybe, though not irredeemably so.

'Bloody hell, Lil, you haven't really?' Connie sounded genuinely shocked. 'But you've only known him five minutes.'

'I know.' Lily dropped her head into her hands. 'God knows what he must think of me. He probably assumes I do this all the time.'

'Don't you?'

'No I do not!' Lily was affronted.

Connie's practical mind was working on a calculation. 'Being objective for a moment, is this good or bad news for Victoriana's loan?'

'Connie,' Lily felt irritated by her sister's refusal to take her seriously, 'it's important. I really liked him. Besides if he thinks I'm this irresponsible maybe he won't give us the loan after all.'

'Since when has any man seen fancying *him* as a sign of irresponsibility? Besides, if you really like the man, you could always ring him up and explain. It might be better

111

than leaving him in the lurch. What did you do, just up and off?'

Lily nodded miserably.

Connie saw how hurt Lily was looking and put her arm round her. 'Maybe he's feeling just as bruised as you.'

By nine-thirty Paul had been in his office an hour and a half. The mornings were always the best time for work and this morning in particular he wanted to occupy himself. Even so the minutes dribbled by. Six empty plastic coffee cups testified to how he had tried to pass the time. When his phone finally buzzed and his assistant told him it was Lily, he couldn't help hoping she'd rung to apologize and insist that it had all been a mistake, that last night had meant as much to her as it had to him.

His pleasure faded instantly when he heard the distant formality of Lily's tone. If he'd known her better, he would have recognized it for hideous embarrassment, but he hardly knew her at all.

She explained that she had been going to write a letter but felt it was too cowardly. She just wanted to say that she'd been indiscreet and unprofessional and that much as she liked him, it might be better if they kept their future relationship to the professional for the time being.

After she'd rung off Paul swept the coffee cups savagely to the floor, spilling black coffee on the grey carpet. He didn't care. Men had enjoyed one-night stands for years with no sense of guilt about what the other party might be thinking. In this case the boot happened to be on the other foot. A sign of the times perhaps. It was just his bad luck that he'd hoped for more from the relationship. As he willed himself to forget the whole thing and get back to work, the bitter irony of role reversal wasn't lost on Paul Allan.

Now, because of the investment he had so rashly made in Victoriana, they would even have to go on seeing each other.

112

As Lily was doing so effectively, he'd just have to try and pretend the whole thing hadn't happened. The trouble was, he knew, he wasn't good at rejection. His mother had loved him and his older sister had adored him, and it had given him this crazy idea that people he felt something for would return his feelings, which made him tend to open up towards them much too quickly. He was just going to have to be more cautious in future.

He reached for a file, determined to forget about the whole episode, when a sudden memory of Lily's long red hair fanned out against the white of his sheets, her breasts cupped in her hands, haunted him for a moment.

'Fuck,' he said through gritted teeth, then, 'Fuck, fuck, fuck, FUCK!'

'Lily, my love, I've brought you a visitor.' Lily looked up from the pre-Christmas sales figures in surprise at the sound of Edward's voice, wildly fantasizing that it might be Paul, who'd dashed down from London. Ridiculous. There wouldn't have been time.

'You don't look very pleased to see us,' Evie teased, brushing aside the streamers from the chandelier above Lily's desk. June had arrived to declare Christmas open today and had draped everything in tinsel. 'I must say, it looks festive in here. Apart from you.' She eyed her niece beadily. 'You look as glum as a teetotaller at an office party. Charlotte hasn't been stirring it up again, has she?'

'No, no. Actually I'm not feeling too great. One of these flash flu things I expect.'

Evie decided that she certainly looked off colour but not from flu. She suspected a man in the case. There was nothing that could make a woman look worse than being made to suffer by a man. But if so, who could it be? Not Ben Winter surely? Charlotte had told her all about that episode and she was very glad the man was safely in London.

'By the way, Pa, some good news. We've got the loan from the venture capital company Jonathan recommended. So we can go ahead and computerize.'

'Good for you,' Edward congratulated her, wondering why, with the news she'd been waiting for so eagerly, she still looked glum. He hoped she wasn't pining for her old life in London. There was a social life down here, but it tended to centre on business contacts and country pursuits. Lily was hardly the huntin', shootin' and fishin' type. In fact, she was more likely to be a hunt saboteur than actually in the saddle. He wondered briefly if there were any un-attached men he and Charlotte should be encouraging, but it was hard to keep track who was single and who married these days. People seemed to get divorced and remarried at the drop of a hat and there was an unseemly scrabble for the favours of any spare man during the brief break between the two.

Evie wandered over to Connie's desk, noticing the mock-ups for the catalogue stuck on her pinboard. 'These are lovely,' she enthused, 'you're going for the sex in the hayloft look. Good idea. Sex always sells. But take some advice from my own experience back home, make sure the cus-tomer can see the design properly. The little details matter to the home shopper. They like to see what they're getting.'

'Thanks for the tip.' Lily wondered why she didn't mind Evie saying things like that, yet if it had been her mother she would have wanted to kill her. 'Did I tell you, Pa, that I've asked Connie to take over the catalogue?'

'I thought she'd be too busy with the shop for that.'

'She wanted a new challenge and Gavin said she ought to have a go.'

Edward could imagine the problems this was causing Gavin but couldn't help feeling delighted for all their sakes that she was joining them. This really was becoming the family business he'd dreamed of. If Charlotte had any complaints about amateurs he'd remind her that they'd been amateurs themselves not so long ago. 'Marvellous news. I'm off now, my basil seeds have arrived. Can't plant them yet but I can dream.'

'What I *really* came about,' Evie announced as soon as Edward had gone, 'was to get your advice about your mother's Christmas present. It's in the garden centre just outside the village and I wondered if you'd give me a second opinion. It's a statue and it is rather big.'

Lily was intrigued as to what on earth her aunt had managed to find in the local nursery, where the statuary section tended to specialise in various versions of the Wee Boy of Brussels. As it happened it was nothing of the sort. Evie had found a charming figure, about three feet high, of a male nude sitting by a stream staring into the water, a heron beside him. Beside all the naff plaster copies of the Three Graces and unidentified Greek gods in varying stages of undress, the statue shone out for the quality of its workmanship like an emerald in a tray of coloured glass.

'It's lovely, Aunt Evie!' Lily bent down to examine it.

'I thought so too. I'd take it home with me only I'd never get it on the plane and marble statuary's not really the thing in Sydney.'

'I won't offer to wrap it,' confided the gnomic man behind the till who in an attempt at seasonal bonhomie was dressed as Santa, 'but we do have some nice red bows.'

'No thanks,' Evie winked at him making the poor chap blush as red as his suit, 'I wouldn't know where to tie it.'

On the way home, with the statue safely watching over them from the rear passenger seat, Evie tried to find out what was worrying her niece. Lily brought out a strong streak of protectiveness in the older woman.

'So, spit it out, what's making you look so miserable then?'

Lily almost swerved in surprise. She thought she'd been doing a reasonable impersonation of her normal self.

'Is it a man? It usually is from my experience.'

'Oh God, Aunt Evie, *don't.*' Lily had actually managed to forget the whole lowering episode for almost half an hour. Till now.

'Ah, ha. I was right. Okay what did the bastard do to you?' Aunt Evie's overview of the male sex was not an entirely positive one.

'Nothing. He was fine. It was just that I behaved inappropriately.'

This was a new one on Evie. 'What do you mean – inappropriately? You laughed at his lack of technique?' In Evie's experience most men had all the sexual finesse of a pneumatic drill.

Lily bit her lip. 'No. I shouldn't have gone to bed with him at all. I'd only just met him . . .'

'And . . .?' prompted Evie, her mind racing with possibilities.

'And this is the man I was supposed to be impressing with my leadership qualities and mature decisiveness. So what did I do? Only went and jumped into the sack with him.'

'Good heavens.' Evie chortled. 'Not on the boardroom table?'

Lily shook her head.

'Under his desk?' she asked hopefully.

'Under a duvet. In his flat.'

'Sounds boringly respectable to me.'

'But Aunt Evie, he was the banker giving me the loan. God knows what he thinks of me after this.'

'Probably that you were the most wonderful surprise a man could wish for. I bet he's busy rubbing his lamp at this very moment hoping you'll reappear. Lily, love, I can see you regret it and maybe it would have been more sensible to choose someone you aren't professionally involved with. But hell, life would be boring if we always did the right thing. Stop flagellating yourself. You've got the loan, so now forget about all this regret. Que será será and all that. Presumably you're going to have to see this chap from time to time anyway. Leave him to do the running if he wants to. I'd be very surprised indeed if he feels like you do about this. He wasn't married, was he?'

'Not unless he'd hidden her in a broom cupboard and destroyed all her possessions. It was a very male flat.'

'Then let's hear no more of it. Come on, I'll take you for a quick drink in the pub and we'll throw our glasses to the ground.'

'You're on,' said Lily, but she couldn't bear to go to the Harvest Home where she and Paul had spent that happy lunch-hour such a short time ago; the memories were too raw. If he chose to contact her, so be it. Otherwise she would be the very model of the top executive when they next met and give no sign of what had happened between them.

'You look more cheerful,' said Connie when she arrived back in the office an hour later.

'Aunt Evie's a wonderful tonic. She's been giving me her thoughts on men and morality and how none of it matters much in the end.'

'Then maybe now, Miz Scarlett, you better dry dem eyes,' advised Connie, 'and get on with some work runnin' dis here company. Like have you got any idea on photographers? I don't want the usual catalogue type. They make everything look cheap and awful.'

Lily got out her address book but most of the photographers she knew took mugshots for *Spotlight* that were one step up from a photo booth. There was a thought tickling the back of her mind, though, trying to fight its way through all the brain cells slain by thirty-five years of hard living and too much alcohol. Finally she retrieved it. 'Maxie had some staggering publicity pictures done by a young photographer a while back. With a ton of gel and the right light he actually made her look young and innocent.'

Connie was impressed. Anyone who could achieve that with Lily's best friend was clearly an artist in his craft. 'Do you know his name?'

'No, but Maxie will. She fell in love with him and promised when she was rich and famous he could be her personal photographer.'

Maxie was busy painting her toenails in Pulp Fiction Purple, with a cotton wool lozenge between each toe, when the phone rang and she had to waddle around looking for the telephone, wondering who could be insensitive enough to phone her at such a crucial moment. The nail polish was made by Chanel and if she smudged it it would probably cost a whole evening's wages. Still, an actress always answers the phone. This could be the big one, after all. 'Hi, Artistic Director of the Royal Court, would I be free to take over the starring role in *Plenty*, now let me see . . .?'

When she discovered it was Lily she was even gracious enough not to be disappointed. 'Lily! How's life in Chocolate-box Britain? Are you coming up for any Christmas bashes?'

Lily shuddered at the thought of the usual parties she and Maxie got invited to. Three hundred aspiring actors fighting over the Moldavian Chardonnay and chunks of cheddar while pinning to the wall any hapless casting director who'd been mad enough to show up. Lily was glad she'd be missing them. 'Actually, I was wondering if you had a phone number for that photographer who made you look like Maria in *The Sound of Music*.'

'And a bloody miracle that was. His name's Euan Brady.' Maxie dictated his number. 'You better not mention my name, though. I don't think I've paid him yet.'

'Maxie, that's awful! He did it incredibly cheaply anyway.'

'I know,' Maxie recalled guiltily. 'I did offer him settlement in kind though.'

Lily could just imagine it now. 'And what did he say?'

'That he'd rather wait until I had the cash. If you really are thinking of employing him, maybe I'd better warn you about something.'

'Don't tell me. He's unreliable?'

'Nope.'

'Dishonest?'

'Nope.'

'Can't be trusted in taxis, lifts or any isolated places?'

'No.'

'What then?' Lily had run out of options.

'Euan Brady is the most attractive guy I've ever met.'

'Come on, Max, what about the leading man in that Beckett play?'

'Apart from him maybe.'

'Or your driving instructor when you took all those extra lessons and pretended you couldn't do three-point turns?'

'Okay, apart from him.'

'And that one who came to repair your washing machine and stayed for a week? And your shrink, the one you were convinced was in love with you, and that accountant who did your books free?

'Okay, okay. But Euan Brady is still pretty bloody amazingly attractive.'

This might once have been of interest to Lily, but at the moment she didn't care if she never saw another man under eighty. She was giving them up for Lent. Early.

She handed the number over to Connie and decided it was time she had a session with June about the impending computerization of the order system. June considered computers to be like video recorders, devised with the sole purpose of making her life more complicated. Lily had already explained that they would have the opposite effect but June was about as receptive as an Eskimo with a Psion organizer.

The orders department had even more Christmas decorations than Lily's office, some of the same ones that had come out every year since Lily was a child. June must have kept them from the earliest days at Victoriana.

'The girls are very worried about all this computer stuff,' June said. Lily knew the truth was that it was June who was most worried. She was in her fifties and had grown up in the days when stocktaking in shops meant closing the whole place and going up a ladder to count every item, not just pushing a button on a till. Most of the girls were much younger than June and some of them almost teenagers who'd probably have used computers at school. Lily was sure they would cope. 'Come on June, be positive. The computer company's giving us a week's training. By the end of that you'll be making Bill Gates look like a beginner.'

'Who's he when he's at home?'

'The man who started Microsoft.'

'Well, he's got a lot to answer for.'

Hoping that Bill Gates never got to hear of June's poor opinion of him, Lily went back to her office. On her desk was an exquisite blue and white china bowl containing six delft-blue hyacinths. Their heady scent filled the room. Lily held her breath. Maybe Evie was right. He did want to see her again.

She tore open the card. Her stomach somersaulted and then, just as suddenly, plummeted. 'Try and forgive the unforgivable. I behaved appallingly. Love makes one mad. Ben.'

The irony of how excited this would have made her only a few months ago slammed into her. But not as hard as the disappointment that the flowers weren't from Paul. Evie might be her own personal wise woman, but even the oracle had off days.

Bloody, bloody Ben.

Judith Brandon often woke earlier than her husband and had a session on her Stairmaster. The exercise not only kept her lithe but also she found it a useful space for thought. Today there was one problem in particular occupying her mind: what she was going to do when Paula moved Image-makers to Bath?

She'd had a few offers but none of them attracted her. They were mainly short-term consultancies and, though they were well paid, hardly amounted to the kind of job she had now. What she would really relish was some kind of role at Victoriana, so that she could see from the inside how things were going and lay her plans for later on, but it was hard to see how she could pull that one off unless she convinced Lily that her PR skills were just what Victoriana needed.

She stepped up her speed until light drops of moisture dampened her face and hair. Why bother going through Lily at all when her mother-in-law thought so well of her? It was time to play the family card, and what better moment than Christmas, the season of good cheer. Feeling optimistic, Judith dressed, kissed Jonathan goodbye, and then fought her way through Harrods' pre-Christmas crowds to look for a suitably extravagant present for Charlotte.

After two exhausting hours she found a Celtic brooch that would look good on one of the woollen wraps Charlotte favoured. She'd chosen it with particular care and spent much more than someone who was about to be out of work ought to be spending. When she got home she wrapped the present so dramatically it looked like a work of art in itself. Wrapping was one Judith's strengths. She often gave presents so dazzling to look at that the lucky recipient didn't notice that the actual present rarely lived up to the promise of its exterior.

It was Christmas next week and Imagemakers would be closing its London office permanently. Paula had thought about having a party but had decided to put the money towards a couple of extra weeks maternity leave. It occurred to Judith that she could go down to Dorset and make herself useful to her mother-in-law. On the way she could stop at New Covent Garden Market and buy a bunch of lilies so large and impressive that no one could miss them.

Charlotte herself was feeling more cheerful than she had for months. Christmas gave her a focus. She was exceptionally good at swagging mantelpieces with tartan fabric and making her home look like something straight out of one of her own catalogues.

Throughout the entire house no surface was undecorated, no mantel unadorned, she had even laid a trail of glass jam jars, each with a nightlight in it, up the front path to the house to signal a festive welcome for guests.

The rooms were already allocated, the beds made. With remorseless efficiency she had ordered the turkey, made the stuffings, two Christmas puddings, plus a chocolate version because the children preferred it. Her star attraction this year, with so much time on her hands, was a large iced cake which she had decorated with frosted green and black grapes, ivy leaves winding exotically round its base. It was, she had to admit it herself, a work of art. Consequently it was likely no one would dare eat any of it, but then they never did anyway. The conundrum of Christmas cake was that unless you started eating it way before Christmas when it seemed sacrilegious then it never got eaten at all.

Eventually Evie had had to take her in hand and say 'For God's sake, Charlotte, stop it. Anyone would think you

122

were auditioning for the part of Martha Stewart. We're all convinced.' By the time Judith arrived to put herself at her mother-in-law's disposal there was very little left to do.

'Judith, dear, what a lovely surprise, but why aren't you at work?'

Judith handed over the vast bunch of lilies. 'I thought they'd look nice in the hall on that stand under the portrait. All they need is the Charlotte Brandon touch in arranging them.'

Creep, thought Evie, who was sitting on the sofa behind a biography of Anaïs Nin. Anaïs, without putting up too much of a struggle, was about to go to bed with both Henry Miller and his wife and Evie was keen to know who was going to put what where, but she also felt honour bound to listen in to Judith and Charlotte's conversation. She hadn't liked Judith Brandon from their first meeting.

'But didn't Jonathan tell you?' Judith smiled bravely. 'The company I work for is relocating to Bath. As from the day before yesterday I've joined the ranks of the unemployed.'

It was on the tip of Evie's tongue to ask her if she'd be checking out the job centres but Charlotte was already clucking with outrage at the unfairness of it all. 'But you're so talented! Surely you'll get snapped up in five minutes?'

Charlotte began arranging the lilies and carried them to the stand in the hall under the portrait where they did indeed, Evie had to admit, look sickeningly effective. It would be an awful pity if they happened to run out of water though.

'Maybe it's the time of year,' Judith produced a perfect imitation of a talented woman whose gifts were going to waste. 'All I've had is a couple of paltry offers for consultancy work.'

Evie began to see the way the conversation was heading. Anaïs would clearly have to wait to get into Henry Miller's trousers for a while longer. 'I'm sure something will turn up,' she said. 'You'll obviously have to ring a few people up and tell them you're on the market. I had a friend who lost her job and she made ten calls a day till she got another one.'

Charlotte looked appalled. 'She shouldn't have to. I'll tell you what . . .' Evie had a horrible feeling she knew what was coming next and tried to signal to her sister to think again, 'why don't you come and help out with Victoriana's publicity? I'm sure Lily would be delighted to have someone as capable as you on board.'

'Charlotte,' Evie counselled, 'don't you think perhaps you should ask her first?'

'Oh, for heaven's sake, Eve, I must be allowed to make *some* decisions in my own company. Lily's brought Connie in, which is lovely. She can't possibly object to Judith helping out. She's family too. We're very lucky to get her.'

'Are you sure Lily can afford Judith? She told me she was trying to cut costs,' Evie argued desperately.

'Oh, money's not a problem,' Judith lied. She'd have to view this as an investment. 'I'd love to put something back into the family. You've all been so kind to me.'

'That's decided then. I'm sure everyone will be thrilled.'

Evie went back to Anaïs and Henry in disgust. She wasn't at all sure that was the word Lily would use when she heard.

'What do you think, Ma, am I going to be the belle of the ball?'

Connie surveyed her daughter and was struck by the inadequacy of such a quaint expression in capturing Tara's appearance. Tara had aped her aunt Lily at her most outrageous and dressed entirely in black: black velvet miniskirt; a black bandeau top offering acres of bare midriff to the freezing December air; black tights with so many holes in them they looked as if they'd been colonized by moths, except that Connie knew Tara had spent all afternoon making them with a penknife; and a cloche hat with flowers on it which had belonged to her mother in the seventies and had spent the intervening time in the dressing-up box. The effect was startling to say the least.

It was the Christmas party season and Tara had more invitations on the mantelpiece than the rest of the family put together. Jeremy had pretended not to mind but Connie had caught him looking through them the other day with a resentful expression. Where Jeremy had two friends, Tara had ten. Connie had once tried to explain to him that Tara was at the gang stage when even going to the loo had to be achieved in a group of no less than six; but she knew it was also that Jeremy, handsome though he was, found talking to new people difficult. Tara, on the other hand, shone at parties.

Connie didn't have time to worry further because the doorbell rang and she heard girls squealing in the hall and saw Jeremy run for cover as they poured in, giggling. She waved goodbye, discovering exactly what the arrangements were for Tara's return. Watching her daughter get into the car, she realized what was faintly disturbing about Tara these days. It was her emerging sexuality. It seemed to Connie that just as her own chance of passion was dwindling, Tara's sparked into existence. That pattern might be biologically sound but Connie didn't feel ready for joining the bingo and bridge brigade yet.

In the welcoming yellow-painted kitchen Gavin had just poured them both a glass of wine. An overwhelming sense of familiarity overtook her. He would complain about suppliers and deadlines, then ask her about her day before announcing that he was off to bed. She knew she should talk about her feelings but didn't. Guiltily she kissed the top of her husband's head, hoping that he wouldn't want to make love to her tonight. Later on, as they were undressing she noticed him watching her and, feeling mean, she made an excuse to finish in the bathroom.

The next day her old energy was back. She went in to work early, eager to get the catalogue shoot set up before the Christmas break. Since they were ruled by the peculiarities of shooting the summer catalogue in the middle of winter they usually decamped to the Canary Islands or Jersey, but Connie's idea of using a Thomas Hardy theme meant staying in Dorset and shivering.

She'd already had some success in finding models. There was a wonderful milky innocent she'd found for her Tess, and a sulkily beautiful Bathsheba. Who ever was to take the photos might have thoughts of his own of course, but she doubted if they'd find anyone better. She had three well-known photographers bringing in their portfolios to show her tomorrow. One had shot catalogues before, another had taken photographs she'd liked in a fashion magazine, and the third was Euan Brady.

As she listened to the first two explaining their techniques Connie saw how hard it was going to be to get this particular relationship right. What she wanted was someone who would take her ideas and interpret them through the filter of his own imaginative style, but what she was being offered were either fixed ideas about how things should be done, or no ideas whatsoever. By mid-afternoon Connie was depressed. She'd hoped to find the photographer, choose the models and meet them all by the middle of next week. Perhaps that had been impossibly ambitious.

When the message got through to her from Euan Brady that he wasn't going to be able to get there after all, she felt unreasoningly furious with the man. He'd been sent on a last-minute assignment to Paris, said the message.

Well, screw him. In Connie's view it was entirely unprofessional. If he let them down over the interview he might do the same with the shoot. She'd have to start looking for someone else.

'How's it going?' asked Lily the next morning. 'Have you found your Richard Avedon yet?'

'Don't. The two I met yesterday were about as inspiring as *Exchange and Mart*. And Maxie's friend just didn't show up.'

By the end of the day she'd booked appointments for two more possibles and felt she was entitled to pack up and go home. All the preparations for Christmas still waited for her. She'd done most of the present buying, apart from Jeremy and Tara who were always impossible and never knew what they wanted except that it wasn't what you got them, but the wrapping remained to be done and she'd been conned into making six chocolate roulades for the school bazaar. She was just wondering how she could possibly have let herself agree to this when she walked into reception and bumped into Euan Brady. He was a tall, rangy young man in his late twenties with shoulder-length hair, wearing the unusual combination of blue jeans, sports jacket and an earring. He was surrounded by photographic gear and he reminded her faintly of Jeremy.

'Hi!' He got to his feet as though it were the most natural thing in the world for him to be sitting there at close of business on a Friday evening.

Connie's reaction was simply annoyance. All right for him to appear out of the blue, he hardly seemed weighed down by commitments – clearly he jetted off at five minutes' notice – but other people were.

'You'd better come upstairs to the office,' she said curtly.

'Great place you've got here.' She could hear the trace of a Canadian accent. 'Look, I'm really sorry about missing that meeting yesterday. I've been waiting five years to photograph Joseph Krantz and he finally agreed if I came straight over. You know artists.' His tone implied that

127

Connie probably came across the artistic temperament in world-famous painters every day.

Connie couldn't fail to be just a little impressed. 'I thought you were a fashion photographer.'

Euan Brady grinned. 'That pays for the rest.'

Connie wasn't sure she liked the sound of this. It was impressive, of course, but Brady could just as easily turn out to be a prima donna who thought something like shooting a catalogue well below his station.

He held the door to the old-fashioned lift open for her. 'And, no, I am not some poncy type who thinks he should be doing the cover of Vogue. I don't take on anything I won't enjoy.' He leaned back lazily against the wooden wall of the lift. 'So, go on, convince me why I'll enjoy this.'

'Look,' she snapped, having to stop herself adding 'young man,' 'me client, you photographer! You convince *me* why I should want you to do it.'

She might find his cool unnerving and his relaxed manner wildly irritating, but she couldn't argue with his portfolio. This ranged from big fashion spreads through advertising campaigns selling beer to hard journalistic shots of wars and riots, and one clear thread ran through it all. Extraordinary originality.

She held out the beer advertisement and a newspaper still of a child in Bosnia. 'They seem to sit so oddly,' she said.

'Nonsense. Technically they had similar problems. I only had one shot at photographing the child or she'd have been in more danger than she already was; and with the beer shot, how long do you think that foam stayed like that? And, yes, the lager did pay for the Bosnia trip.'

Money had been the next thing on her agenda. Victoriana had always budgeted for a top photographer but not one who could command vast fees from ad agencies. 'Victoriana seems rather small potatoes after some of the work you've done before.' As she said it she was aware she seemed to be constructing barriers for him to jump instead of finding ways of making the job attractive but then he had inconvenienced her considerably. He had a lot of convincing to do. She was also unnerved by his extraordinary self-confidence.

'You said you wanted to use the places Hardy put in his books. He's my favourite writer.' He closed his eyes and intoned the opening paragraph of *The Return of the Native* and then topped it by quoting, word for word, the entire Monty Python sketch parodying Hardy's prose style. By the end of it Connie was almost crying with laughter.

She wiped her eyes finally. 'Before we make a final decision you really ought to meet my sister, Lily Brandon, who's really running the company.'

'The one who dumped cappuccino over Ben Winter?'

'The very one.'

'I photographed him once.'

'What was he like?' Lily tended to be a little one-sided on this subject.

'Nice guy until I took the lens cap off, then he got all Byronic on me. Had to be photographed from the left side only. Incredibly talented, but I hear when he flies he has to book an extra seat for his ego.'

Connie giggled. 'Anyway, don't remind my sister of it. I think she's got over him.'

'My lips are sealed.'

She helped Euan load some of his gear back into his car and offered to put him up in a hotel for the night at Victoriana's expense but he preferred the idea of going home. 'Save it for the budget. I'm sure I'll need it.'

'Euan, this is my sister, Lily Brandon.'

Lily had to admit that for once her friend Maxie had been telling the truth about how attractive Euan Brady was. Normally she was about as reliable as a fake Cartier watch, but Euan actually lived up to his billing. He was tanned and relaxed as though his assignments were all in Caribbean hideaways, yet Connie had told her about the Bosnia stuff.

'As a matter of fact I think you know my friend Maxie.' How had he reacted, Lily wondered, when Max had offered him her body instead of cash for taking her picture. 'She told me her unusual suggestions for payment,' Lily couldn't help adding.

'Ah,' he nodded, 'but did she say she'd offered me weekly instalments?'

Lily could imagine all too well. 'I think you'll find us more conventional in our methods of payment.'

There was a beat of silence when she thought he was going to say how disappointing but instead they all discussed models and locations and settled a date to do the shoot. Still hurting after her disaster with Paul, Lily couldn't help finding Euan's laid-back charm appealing.

Connie and Euan walked ahead to the design studio and Connie showed him the samples of a sarong-style skirt with toning jacket from the catalogue.

'Try it on, I can't possibly see it on the hanger. It's all in the draping.'

Connie looked round for a young girl to model it but they'd all gone home. It was silly to fuss so she wrapped the softly alluring garment round her waist.

'That's no good,' he pointed out and nodded towards the pretty screen they kept in a corner of the studio so that the clothes could be tried on when necessary. 'The folds are all wrong with your trousers underneath it. Try it on properly.'

Minutes later she emerged from behind the screen and walked up the room as though it were a catwalk, twirling at the end.

Lily watched her in amazement. They'd both forgotten about her presence altogether. It was as though Connie and Euan Brady were in an entirely separate room. And then she was amazed she hadn't seen it before. While she'd been fantasizing in a mindless teenage manner about Euan's attractiveness, it wasn't Lily he was drawn to at all.

It was her very married sister, Connie.

Chapter 9

Whoever dreamed up family Christmases had a lot to answer for, Lily decided. Three whole days of enforced idleness after three weeks of stress and tension preparing for it was a surefire recipe for the Christmas from hell. On top of that, Charlotte didn't approve of television. Lily had to admit it was a relief not to scan the credits after every performance to see who was getting the leading roles, but it did leave a lot of time to get through from Christmas Eve to Boxing Day. They'd played charades, which everyone except Jonathan and Judith had enjoyed, but then no one expected those two to enjoy a game that involved making yourself look ridiculous. If anything they looked rather more tight-lipped and sullen than usual. Lily thought wickedly, it must be hard to assess whether your marriage was going well when you were both self-serving yuppies who seemed to see acts of generosity as manifestations of weakness.

Judith was, however, making herself extraordinarily helpful to her mother-in-law, praising every arrangement, decoration and item of food and drink so profusely that even Charlotte's pleasure in her rightful due was turning to embarrassment.

Despite the shock of no TV, Jeremy and Tara were having a good time and Tara had even shown an unsuspected talent for acting which might well cause her mother grief if she decided to take it seriously.

Edward always enjoyed playing the genial host, especially now that he had his garden plans to tell everyone about. Gavin was the only one who worried Lily. He looked tired and anxious. He seemed not to be able to concentrate but wandered about, picking up magazines and putting them down again, and drumming his fingers on the tartan upholstery of his chair.

'Everything okay, Gav?' Lily asked him gently when they were both collecting up the glasses after supper. Gavin smiled back at her briefly. 'Just a bit wiped out. We stayed open late every night hoping for the Christmas rush.'

'And did it come? You were packed the night I drove past.'

'That was because we gave free mince pies and mulled wine.'

'And made lots of dosh, I hope.'

'We got through a lot of mulled wine.' There was something in Gavin's tone that upset Lily a lot. Maybe things were worse with the business than she'd thought and taking Connie away had done real damage. The trouble was, joining Victoriana had transformed Connie who at this moment was giggling with Tara like a seventeen-year-old.

After nearly thirty-five years of Christmases on the beach, Evie was finding a Real British Christmas quite a novelty. Edward had instantly assumed she'd be thrilled by lashings of turkey and stuffing and Christmas pudding, but the truth was she was pining just a little for her usual seafood and champagne. She was also wondering whether she ought to mention the fact that Charlotte had invited Judith to join Victoriana to Lily. In the end she decided against it. Family Christmases needed all the help they could get.

It was only when she and Lily were carrying out another quaint British ritual, the washing up, on Boxing Day that Evie felt it was time to bring the subject up. 'By the way,' she said, swirling a dishcloth ineffectually over the Wedgwood dinner service, 'did Charlotte mention that she's asked your dear sister-in-law to come on board?'

Lily almost dropped the precious plate she was drying.

'Poor Judith is apparently poised to join the ranks of the unemployed and your mother took pity on her. She's going to be helping out with your publicity.'

Lily's chest tightened with anger. Judith was fine at corporate PR but, since that largely consisted of taking hordes of grey-suited businessmen to Ascot, Wimbledon and the Henley Regatta to get pissed as rats, it didn't seem to Lily to have much to do with securing press coverage. She was convinced she could do it better herself.

'I'm sure you're brilliant at getting publicity,' her mother soothed when she marched into the sitting room to protest, 'after all you've attracted enough of it in your time, but it needs to be the right kind of publicity. Besides Judith is going to be at a loose end and it's such a waste of her talent. Really, Lily, you could be more generous. We've given *you* a chance after all.' Lily found herself rendered speechless at the idea of taking pity on poor, unemployed Judith.

'Charlotte,' Edward asked tetchily from one end of the red brocade sofa, 'have you been shoving your oar in again?'

Charlotte ignored him.

'Of course she has,' Evie insisted. 'My family think I'm bad but I'm a rank amateur beside you, Charlotte. You make Stalin look like someone who minded his own business.'

Charlotte went on pouring the tea, unperturbed. 'Look, Lily may be running the company but Judith is family. I obviously wouldn't have made an offer to some stranger.'

'Oh wouldn't you, Ma?' Lily was furious now. 'Do you realize that you haven't once asked me how things are going, not seriously. It's your precious company, as you keep reminding us, but you've offered me no real advice. George the "glorified bookkeeper" has been six times more helpful than you. All you've ever done is make decisions over my head. If you weren't my mother,' Lily's eyes flashed at Charlotte, 'anyone would think you wanted me to fail.' Lily kept her eyes angrily fixed on her mother, desperate for some response at least. Charlotte sat supremely calm, refusing to recognize the bitterness in her daughter's words. It made Lily want to shake her out of her killing complacency.

At that moment Judith and Jonathan came downstairs from an afternoon nap which had happily coincided with the washing up. 'Hello all.' Judith looked round at the angry faces. 'Everyone having a happy Christmas?'

Lily had no time to dwell on her annoyance with her mother. January, with its vital post-Christmas sale, was one of Victoriana's busiest months. As George pointed out, if you were left with 15 per cent of unsold stock you could survive, but 20 per cent was a disaster, wiping out most of your profit and vital investment for the next year. She just hoped to God the new computer system would make a difference. It had to. In March they were due to make their first quarterly repayment to First Venture.

She decided to go and see for herself how things were going. The first thing that struck her as she walked through the sunlit barn that housed the orders section was the air of calm and efficiency. The old system had involved a great deal of shouting and running about; now the only sound was of keys being stroked as the girls took orders through their headsets.

Everyone seemed to have taken to the new system with the exception of June, who was clearly struggling. 'Drat the thing!' she cursed her computer. 'It's gone and lost my order again!'

Lily was wondering how to tackle the problem tactfully when one of the youngest girls, Shauna, strolled up to June and sat down casually. 'I hated it at first, until I realized it's just like a video game.' She leaned over and pressed a couple of keys. 'You just have to think like the computer instead of like you, then you can beat it. See here . . .'

Lily watched fascinated as the eighteen-year-old quietly demonstrated exactly how the system worked. Lily held her breath. How would June react to being shown how to do it in front of her entire department?

She needn't have worried. June was simply grateful. 'Thanks Shauna,' she said, 'it makes sense for the first time.' Shauna grinned. 'Sign of a misspent youth, they say, understanding video games. Besides I'm the one who should be thanking you. You gave me the job, even though I'd got rotten qualifications.'

From her post in the corner of the room Lily felt a lump rise in her throat. Shauna might only be eighteen but she had an extraordinary feel for the dignity of the older woman.

Without making her presence felt, Lily went back to her office. She'd check up how sales had been going at the end of the day. Connie was already installed at her desk, one phone under her chin and the other in her hand, samples littered over her chair, models' cards piled up on her desk. She was clearly loving every moment. It struck Lily that there was a change even in the way her sister looked. Connie's clothes had become more individual and stylish.

'How's it going?' Lily asked.

'Great. The models are booked. I'll know about the stylist, hair and make-up today. Most of the samples are ready for the shoot. Oh . . .' she paused marginally, 'I hope you don't mind, I've gone ahead and booked Euan Brady. We're off to look at locations tomorrow.'

The news by six that evening was enough to take Lily's

mind off any niggling little problems. They'd had a bumper day and the computer system had outdone itself.

The next morning Lily decided to have a brisk walk before going to her office. It was a gloriously sunny day, still below freezing but with the clear biting cold that expanded your spirits as it numbed your feet. She thought of the photographs she'd seen of New York businesswomen walking to work through the urban caverns of Manhattan in their trainers. Here she was in her wellies, tramping across the English countryside. A sudden sense of happiness spiced with relief warmed her as though the hot summer sun were beating down on her back. The computer system was working brilliantly and she loved Connie's plans for the catalogue. She was making a success of it. All around her the early morning mist was lifting to reveal the gentle beauty of the valley in front of her. Her father had been right, running Victoriana *was* something she could do well.

Euan Brady certainly took his work seriously. Immediately after their meeting, even before they'd offered him the job, he'd been straight to the bookshop in Bidchester and bought every Thomas Hardy novel he could find and re-read the lot. Connie could see that her own role would be to curb his colourful imagination from anything too excessive.

'What I want to do,' he was enthusing, 'is take some of the key scenes from the books: Bathsheba's Harvest Supper, Tess in the dairy at Talbothays, Eustacia on top of Rainbarrow, and build the catalogue round those.' He caught a slight look of doubt in Connie's eyes at the scale of the thing. 'Don't worry, I know all this is really about flogging frocks. I'll make your frocks look better than they've ever looked before. And we'll be offering a free fantasy with each one. Irresistible! And, yes, before you ask me, I am accustomed to staying within my budget.'

They had almost reached the farmhouse Euan wanted her

to see. Like her parents' home it was in one of the hidden valleys that were such a feature of this part of Dorset. Most were developed but now and then you came upon one like this where time literally had stood still. The house was mellow stone with two wings that stretched round like arms almost into a courtyard. It would be perfect for re-enacting Bathsheba's Harvest Supper.

'I've spoken to the farmer already. He was tickled to death by the idea of being in a catalogue. He's always felt the house was a gem. He'll let us shoot interiors as well, so we can knock off a couple of other pages here too. And he doesn't even want a facility fee, just a namecheck for the house.'

'Euan Brady,' Connie asked, 'is there no end to your talents?'

He leaned against the stone wall. 'That's a question I hope you'll be able to answer for yourself one of these days.'

Connie felt herself flushing. No doubt this was how photographers went on all the time. The whole of the fashion industry was probably fuelled by flirtation. She just wasn't used to it, that was all.

Even when Susie McIntosh put her head round the door and asked if she could have a word, it didn't dampen Lily's pleasure in how things were going, but she could tell from the smugness of the woman's tone that a problem had come up.

'The samples for the dresses your niece suggested have come in. I thought you ought to look at them.' Why don't you just break into song, you old crow, Lily felt like saying.

Lily's best design, a short flowery dress in a silky material with shoestring straps was being modelled by one of the girls in the office. Susie had teamed the dress with pale tights, soft feminine shoes and a pastel straw hat that would have been more suitable at a wedding. It looked awful, dowdy and old-fashioned. Lily tried to fight off her sense of bitter disappointment. She'd set such store by this design. It was going to be one of the cornerstones of the catalogue, convincing young girls that Victoriana wasn't just for their mothers. This tired rag would have them skipping back to Top Shop in five seconds flat. Lily looked at her watch. It was gone three. Maybe she'd go and see if Tara had come out of school yet and ask her what she thought.

A few hundred yards from Tara's school pupils were streaming along the pavements with cokes and packets of crisps in their hands, their brown and white uniforms suddenly overrunning the streets like brown ants. She'd never find Tara in this lot.

Lily was about to give up when she saw her leaning against a bus shelter, immediately recognizable by the flair with which her uniform stood out from the others'. Her skirt was shorter, not much, but enough to greatly improve its drab appearance. Her cardigan, on the other hand, was four inches longer than all her friends'. They all had backpacks in gaudy colours but Tara had a battered satchel which she was using as a shoulderbag. Their hair was long and bushy, hers short and gamine. There was only one word for it. Style.

'Auntie Lily, what on earth are you doing here?' Tara had been standing freezing in her self-shortened skirt and though she was prepared to suffer for style, especially as the boys from the Secondary Mod would be appearing any minute, the sight of her aunt in a nice warm car seemed the answer to a prayer. 'Is this your good deed for the day?'

'Actually,' Lily said, 'I wanted your advice. The designs we sketched have arrived but they don't look quite right on the model.'

'What's she wearing with it?'

Tara raised her eyes heavenwards in inimitable teenage

horror at such rank ignorance when Lily told her. 'Can we go via home and I'll pick up some gear?'

Half an hour later, Tara, still in her school uniform, disappeared behind the screen with the model and the girl emerged wearing a skimpy black ribbed teeshirt under the dress, thick woollen tights with a rip in the knee, Connie's old cloche hat, black-lensed granny sunglasses and Tara's trademark clodhopping boots.

The outfit had been transformed from Good Girl to Grunge Girl and Lily hugged her niece. 'She looks fabulous. You are brilliant, Tara.'

Susie McIntosh, however, was tight-lipped. 'I'm sure Mrs Brandon wouldn't like it.' Lily could have hit the woman. 'It may have escaped your notice, Susie, but I'm running the company now.' Tara, who had already picked up a precocious understanding of subtext, knew exactly what was not being said. 'Hey, I've got a great idea. Why don't we rename the company Mrs Brandon Wouldn't Like It?'

Emboldened by her successes, Lily devised a strategy to deal with Judith when she arrived. She would set up some small sponsorship project, similar to those Judith was used to dealing with in London, but on a microscopic scale. Then, perhaps, Judith would have her pants bored off and rush back to something more exciting in town.

It was February before she could believe it and Lily opened her copy of the local paper to find that even down here whole pages of subscribers paid good money to print Valentine messages like 'To Bunnykins from Your Bad Rabbit' and 'For Wee Willie Winkie: I'll Scratch Yours If You Scratch Mine'.

Bloody love. How was it she could get the rest of her life right and still be alone? She closed her eyes and pictured Paul Allan's smooth, tautly muscled body. The familiar rush of shame and regret ruined the picture like spilt black ink.

She'd heard nothing from him except for a polite and efficient letter setting out the terms of their agreement and including the appropriate documents for her signature. Maybe it was all for the best. It was one of her failings to get intensely involved before the other person had even had time mentally to unpack his suitcase. She was sure that, apart from a natural sense of embarrassment, he hadn't given her a second thought.

Here she was wrong. Paul Allan had thought about Lily Brandon almost every day since they'd last met. If it were not for a keen sense of rejection, made keener by his suspicion that for all his achievements Lily didn't think he was good enough, he would certainly have called her.

Lily pulled herself together and went back to work, consoling herself with the thought that her first repayment of First Venture's loan was due soon and that she would be able to meet it with absolutely no problems. Apart from the pleasure of achievement it would mean meeting Paul on equal terms.

Chapter 10

Later in February Judith joined them. As it turned out the experience wasn't as bad as Lily had been expecting. Familiar with Judith only in a social context, where she managed to be in equal parts ingratiating and bossy, Lily was impressed by how effective she could be professionally. Her ideas were good and her contacts with journalists seemed to be limitless, though most of them were on the consumer and motoring pages rather than the more useful fashion and features. It was still a great relief, however, when Judith suggested she spent half the week working in London.

It would be Judith's major job to get publicity for the catalogue launch and to try and make sure that the press wrote stories when it would be useful to Victoriana rather than because the paper had a gap to fill or wanted to get in before their rivals. It was, Lily learned, an extraordinary game of bluff and double bluff just to get the simplest story in when *you* wanted it in, rather than when it simply suited the paper's deadlines. The logic seemed to be that both of you had something the other wanted but neither of you was supposed to admit to the commercial nature of the transaction.

After Judith had departed back to town, Connie put her

head round the door cautiously. 'Has she gone then, She Who Must Be Avoided?'

Lily answered with a giggle. 'You can't always avoid her. She's going to be doing the PR for the catalogue. She'll have to liaise with you.'

'You didn't tell me I'd be working with the sister-in-law from hell when you offered me the job.'

'I didn't know, did I? God it must be great to be chairman of ICI and make your own decisions. I bet his mother doesn't interfere.'

'But then she probably didn't found the company. Anyway, hark at you, wanting to run ICI now.'

Lily grinned and stretched. Things were going well despite Judith's appearance, and she was feeling tentatively pleased with herself. She'd taken risks and they'd paid off. She felt particularly proud of the computers. That had been entirely her idea. Now the catalogue was underway and Judith's arrival was less cataclysmic than she'd feared. Her next task would be to try and predict how much stock to have made up of each garment, the trickiest of all tasks facing a fashion business: too little in the warehouse and customers had to kick their heels in irritation, sometimes cancelling the order altogether; too much left and it decimated their profits. It was a problem most businesses had to face but in fashion it was a nightmare. She picked up the analysis she'd asked George to prepare of last year's sales figures. Then, pleased with herself for having had so much foresight, she worked her way through the things in her urgent tray and was amazed when she finally consulted her watch that it was eight p.m.

She was about to leave when a thought occurred to her. She'd been angry with her mother about not taking enough interest in how the company was doing since she'd taken over. If she wrote a brief report to coincide with the first repayment to First Venture then Charlotte would be forced to acknowledge it.

When she finally switched off her computer she was tired but glowing with the sense of a job well done. She tidied her desk and noticed an order that needed her initials to confirm it. She must have missed it earlier. Exhausted but happy she glanced at it briefly and signed it. Now she could go up to her flat for a well-earned rest. Tomorrow she'd have the report printed up beautifully for presentation to her mother. Charlotte would then have plenty of time to read it before the first repayment in two weeks' time.

Connie was almost home when she remembered that they were out of decaffeinated coffee and she'd promised Tara faithfully this morning that she'd buy some. Tara claimed she shook like a leaf at the merest hint of caffeine. Since Connie had started at Victoriana the larder had been less plentifully stocked and she'd noticed the Whinge Chill Factor at home had soared astronomically. She thought about stopping at the petrol station but they sold a disgusting instant version which Tara could spot in any taste test even if she were blindfold and had just been eating a vindaloo curry. The trouble with the children of the baby boom generation, Connie was forced to admit, was that they were spoiled rotten. Maternal guilt struggled with a healthy Puritan sense that to drive five miles to buy decaffeinated coffee for her daughter was pathetic over-indulgence. Pathetic over-indulgence won.

When she finally got home she could hear laughter coming from the kitchen which cheered her no end, but the scene awaiting her wasn't quite the one she'd pictured.

Tara was sitting with her booted feet on the table. Her friend Roz, who had come to share homework duty, clearly now abandoned, was sitting next to her and both were giggling furiously. Leaning against the Rayburn, Jeremy brooded out disapproval of Heathcliffian intensity. There was no sign of Gavin. Sitting at the head of the table, in her own place, a glass of Gavin's precious malt whisky no doubt provided by Tara in his hand, Euan Brady held court.

'I apologize for dropping in like this,' he said unapologetically, 'but I've found the most perfect location and it really needs to be seen at dawn.'

Connie unpacked her shopping stoically. She supposed if you hired people for their artistic ideas they were prone to crazy schemes like this. 'You don't mean dawn tomorrow by any chance?'

'Absolutely. I'll have to get back to London afterwards. It's the most staggering place, a folly in a lake and it sort of rears up out of the mist at you.'

'Can I come, Mum?' beseeched Tara, 'I'll get my homework done tonight if you say yes.'

'You'll get your homework done tonight anyway and, no, you can't come. You can't go to school with your shoes soaked from wading about in the foggy, foggy dew, can you now?'

'I could wear wellies,' pleaded Tara.

'No,' Connie said firmly, 'and go and finish your essay before supper. Where's Dad anyway?'

'He rang earlier. He's driving back from Devon with a new shelf-system on the roof rack. Slowly, he said, or it'll fall off and into the path of the car behind and cause a pile-up with multiple fatalities.' Connie recognized Gavin's thought patterns in this. She remembered now that he'd told her about the shelf system. It had been going dirt cheap, and would mean they could revamp the shop a bit. He wouldn't be back till late.

'Would you like to stay to supper?' she finally asked, wondering what the hell she could offer. Probably Baked Beans à la façon de Dorset. At least there was the decaffeinated coffee for afterwards.

'You know,' Euan was watching Tara's retreating back,

'you really ought to put your daughter in the catalogue. She's as stunning as any model. They're all about that age now. She might even be a bit old. The magazines like them at thirteen or fourteen. That slanty, angular look of hers is all the rage. The agents even go off to Eastern Europe to look for them.'

'Sssh!' commanded Connie, not entirely sure of the purity of her motives, 'I can tell you're not a parent. I'd much rather she got her A levels than anorexia. Besides we were all shoved in the catalogue when we were kids and hated it.'

'I must go and look you up in the back numbers. You must have been a beautiful baby . . .'

'Euan,' Connie demanded, 'are you flirting with me?'

'Oh no, absolutely not. Flirting is a process where both parties derive pleasure from stirring each other up verbally with no intention of taking things any further. Personally I can't see the point of that, can you?'

Connie busied herself unpacking the shopping, wondering if hiring Euan Brady had been such a good idea after all.

The date set for the first repayment of Victoriana's loan was March 15th. The week before, Lily took immense pleasure in dictating the covering letter to Paul Allan. The appropriate tone, she'd decided, was formal but friendly, not simply giving the bare details but also an idea of how well the company was doing and could therefore meet its repayment early.

She then rang her parents to check that both were in so that she could discuss the report she had given them a few days ago. Edward was in the garden, ecstatically excited that he could finally start planting soon, and she had to submit to a tour of his newest planting scheme before they went inside. They all sat around a pot of tea while Lily went over the details of her report for them.

When she'd finished Edward embraced her. 'Congratulations, darling, you've done spectacularly well, hasn't she, Charlotte?'

Both of them waited for Charlotte's reaction.

Charlotte had listened with conflicting emotions. Lily clearly had more of a flair for business than her mother suspected, and she'd worked hard too. Charlotte looked into those odd yellow-brown eyes of Lily's which waited, too proud actually to ask, for some love and affection. Part of Charlotte longed to give it, to see them light up with pleasure and relief, but then the panic started, the familiar cocktail of regret and disbelief at her own conduct all those years ago. The only way she could effectively deny this turmoil in herself was to batten down her emotions and hide beneath her usual distant calm.

'You've done well, Lily darling, I'm impressed.'

Edward glared at her. Surely she could rouse herself to something more positive?

The words of praise, lukewarm though they might be, were almost too much for Lily. She bit her lip and looked away. It wasn't what she'd hoped for, but it was something. She leaned over and kissed her mother's cheek and took herself back to Victoriana.

It was late afternoon by the time she got back and lights blazed in all the windows. A lorry was unloading into the bay at the side and there was a hum of purposeful activity about the place. Lily allowed herself a moment's pride that her family, and now herself, were providing jobs for so many people from the village nearby. People who, without Victoriana, might be on the dole, or doing night shifts in a service station, or having to move to one of the big regional cities in search of work.

From the epicentre of the bustle George came towards her. She could see instantly from his face that something was wrong.

'Lily, I think there's been a bit of a mix-up. The suppliers must have sent the wrong order. We ordered two thousand camisole tops and they've sent twenty thousand.'

Lily snapped out of her self-congratulatory dreaming to attend to the crisis. Huge boxes were being unloaded from the van and were stacked until a wall of cardboard towered over them. The beginnings of panic swept through her. There was bound to be some honest mistake. She ran through reception and, ignoring the lift, took the stairs to her office. A fax was waiting for her on her desk: 'Herewith your order. Business must be booming. Congratulations.' It was signed by the MD of their firm of silk suppliers.

Lily scrabbled among her paperwork, then remembered that in a fit of efficiency she'd filed it all away. Their copy of the order was exactly where it should be. Lily felt the taste of fear in her mouth. It was indeed an order for twenty thousand camisoles, countersigned by herself that night when she'd been working late. She'd obviously been too tired to check it.

For minute after minute she simply sat at her desk without moving. Then she willed herself to get out her calculator – not that she really needed it. She had just cost the company twenty-four thousand pounds. It was exactly the amount they were due to repay to First Venture.

Had her secretary sent off that letter to Paul Allan which she'd so enjoyed writing? No, thank God it was there. She tore it up and threw it in the bin. Unless the supplier could take some of those camisoles back, they wouldn't be able to meet it after all.

Chapter 11

'Oh God, George,' Lily appealed, perched amid the papers and box files piled upon the desk in his tiny office. The walls were papered with bird posters, bird calendars and rare bird identification charts. In his spare time George was a fanatical birdwatcher. 'What on earth am I going to do?'

At that moment, seeing the anguished look in her spectacular eyes, George would have walked across the Gobi desert for Lily, or even – and this was asking something – defend her to his mother who thought Lily a fast trollop, but neither action seemed immediately useful. She'd worked so hard and just as it looked as though it might pay off this had happened. If he'd been braver he would have put his arm round her but because George had never so much as patted a woman in his life, he didn't. Then he thought of something concrete he could suggest. He could always borrow against his pension scheme. 'As it happens, I've got a fair bit stowed away,' he offered. 'I could lend it to you for a few months till everything's back on course.'

Lily was unbearably touched. 'I don't deserve you, George.' He blushed furiously. 'But save your money. You know the rules. Never use your own cash. First Venture can afford it better than you.'

'In that case you're going to have to ask them to defer the first payment.'

Lily's spirits drooped even further. Her small moment of triumph would become an apology. 'I suppose you're right. How do you think they'll take it?'

'They won't be over the moon, but I imagine they'll wear it as long as you meet the payment next time.'

The thought of explaining all this to Paul Allan filled Lily with horror. To think she'd actually been looking forward to meeting him again.

'George,' she knew what she was about to say was ignoble but what the hell, 'what are the chances of keeping this cock-up quiet?'

'So Mrs Brandon doesn't hear of it you mean?'

'This is only a temporary blip and you know how people's confidence can be hit.'

'I'll put it about the camisoles are for a special order, shall I?'

'That's a brilliant idea. Say it's something I negotiated personally, then store them till we can work out what to do with the buggers.'

There was still one slender hope left. She tried the supplier to see if he could take any back. A tough but friendly factory manager from the Midlands, he said he'd love to have helped her out but he had problems of his own. The camisoles had been made to Victoriana's specifications and he doubted he could find another customer. The most he could do was offload a few hundred on market stalls at cost price.

Lily thanked him. 'Funny,' he sympathized, 'we were going to check with you about the numbers, but we thought it sounded a bit cheeky, as though you didn't know what you were doing, so we didn't bother.'

There was a tiny beat of silence while both of them

contemplated the implications of this. 'Never mind,' she said brightly, wanting to kill herself, 'I'm sure we'll manage to sell them.'

As interviews went, Lily's with Paul Allan was somewhere on the scale between intense embarrassment and sheer bloody hell. They had each adopted a tone of slightly chilly formality to get them through what both clearly saw as a fiercely uncomfortable situation. Paul, Lily noticed, had unconsciously taken on the mannerisms of a much older man, his notion perhaps of how a banker *should* behave, since his natural instincts had led him into so much trouble. Any minute she expected him to hook his thumbs in his waistcoat, if he'd been wearing one, or start striding up and down.

Instead he sat uncomfortably behind his desk, avoiding her eyes, trying to act as though this were a conventional business meeting when both were acutely conscious that the last time they had seen each other was in bed.

'I think you'd better take me through it,' Paul said stiffly. 'What exactly went wrong?'

Lily thought briefly about lying and saying they had miscalculated their cash flow, but that wouldn't help Victoriana.

'It was my fault entirely. I sanctioned an order for twenty thousand garments instead of two thousand. It wiped out the profit we'd made in other areas. I've learned my lesson, believe me. Every order now has to be signed by three people and, if possible, the Pope. I won't make a mistake like that again.'

'How did it happen?'

'I was pretty exhausted. There was a lot to learn at first.'

Paul could see the dent it had made in her self-confidence and longed to reassure her, but this was serious and he'd be doing her no favours if he didn't make her see that. He had to keep his eyes on the file in front of him to stop remembering the fullness of her breasts against him, the nipples an unexpected dark pinky-brown, 'You do realize that businesses are all about cash flow?'

Lily, already sitting as straight as a ballet dancer, stiffened with embarrassment at the memory of her body touching his. 'Yes, I know, long-term profitability is no use if you don't have immediate liquidity. Lesson one.'

Sensing the tension in her, Paul wanted to hold her. Lily Brandon confused him as no woman he'd ever met. He'd started the meeting angry at her treatment of him and now he was feeling protective, for God's sake. He half wished he'd never made her the loan. It had come between them and would do so even more if she couldn't handle the repayments. What if they were ever faced with a real crisis?

'Look, Lily . . .' The concern in his voice melted her insides, but his words sobered her. 'First Venture is a pretty hard-headed company. If you need any advice I'll try and be impartial. Whatever you do, you *must* meet the next payment. Are you absolutely sure you can do that? If there's any worry, you must start taking action now or – I can't stress this strongly enough – you could lose Victoriana.'

Lily sat rigid, all thoughts of their last encounter shrivelling at the chilling nature of his words.

'We'll meet the next payment, I assure you.'

'If there's any more advice I can give you . . .'

They both stood up at precisely the same moment, like something from a comedy routine. Both of them laughed, embarrassed but relieved that the tension had been broken. It was Paul who spoke first. He hated the idea of the meeting finishing with no acknowledgement of what had passed between them. 'Lily, I just wanted to say . . .' His eyes held hers, dark and intense, the black brows almost meeting in the middle.

Lily stopped him, 'Don't Paul. I think we both know. When this is all sorted out, perhaps . . .'

He nodded and held open the door for her, wondering if this constituted encouragement or brush off.

On the train going back Lily stared out at the disgraceful beauty of the day and felt even more miserable. She'd hoped she'd be able to treat Paul Allan with dignified formality like a dowager duchess, but she'd found it impossible to achieve any neutrality at all. If only she hadn't behaved like a chimpanzee on heat that first night there might have been some future in their relationship, but now things would always be too complicated. It was typical of her that the first time she met a straightforward, single man she went and screwed it up. Maybe there was something wrong with her, a streak of masochism, that meant she would always fail in her relationships. The prospect of a manless, childless future reared up at her out of the glorious spring day and she thought of Connie, who was blessed with so much.

To be gloomy for too long wasn't in Lily's nature however. Allowing herself one gusty sigh she decided she was like Hardy's Eustacia Vye, doomed always to love the wrong man. Somehow the thought made her feel better, and she tossed her long hair, Eustacia-like, and headed for the bar. If she was doomed to the single life she might as well have a glass of wine in her hand.

Connie hummed with pleasure like a greedy bee as she dressed for work. It was one of those days that mid-March sometimes provides to tantalize you with the thought that spring really wouldn't be far behind. There was a bright blue sky and a sharp invigorating wind that blew all thoughts of winter from the brain. Today they were going to look at the final location on the top of Rainbarrow, where Eustacia Vye had often stood in *The Return of the Native*.

Outside a horn beeped and she waved from the bedroom window down at Euan who had somehow acquired an open-topped Land-Rover painted in camouflage colours for the recce.

'Where on earth did you get this?' she asked when she came down, throwing her bag in the back and climbing in.

'From a mate in the Territorial Army. They do manoeuvres round here.'

'I'm amazed you have any mates in the Territorial Army,' Connie marvelled, thinking of the unlikely allegiance between trendy earringed Euan and the rugger buggers she knew who joined the weekend soldiers.

'He helps me when I shoot things undercover. I'm not just a fashion snapper, darling.' He pulled a poncy face like the most camp of catwalk followers and Connie held on as he executed a life-threatening three-point turn, causing their gravel to jump three feet in the air. Life with Euan certainly wasn't dull.

Upstairs in his bedroom. Jeremy abandoned his computer to see what all the commotion was about. He was just in time to catch his mother holding on to her hat, laughing like a teenager as she drove off with that bloody photographer bloke, and watched them as they raced along the bumpy drive to the main road beyond.

It was a particularly successful day for Connie and Euan. Rainbarrow was a perfect location and Euan had tracked down a working granary belonging to English Inheritance, who were happy to let them shoot there. There was even a classic English duck pond and green next door to it. Connie could just picture the dancing scene in *Tess of the D'Urbervilles* unfolding as she sat and watched. Euan had even found a friendly pub nearby with rooms above it where they could all stay cheaply.

'You must be kidding,' Connie said when Euan told her how cheap it was, 'the stylist won't settle for less than five star.'

'Oh yes he will,' Euan pulled her in the direction of the

welcoming little pub, 'you haven't tasted the landlady's cooking yet.'

Connie settled herself into a cosy corner in a small bow window and sighed with satisfaction. They'd sorted out two whole days of the shoot and it was only lunchtime. Euan Brady would have been good value if he'd demanded twice the fee. Scanning the menu hungrily Connie chose Stargazy Pie. She'd always wondered what it would be like and this seemed a day for adventure. Euan ordered something called a Dorset Priddy which turned out to be a kind of light pasty filled with spiced meat. It was delicious. So was Connie's pie once she'd recovered from seeing all the mackerel heads sticking out from the pie crust.

'That's them gazing at the stars, duck,' explained the landlady.

Afterwards, warmed by the pie and a glass of cider, in the warm fug of the tiny bar, listening happily to snatches of uneventful conversation, Connie had the desire never to move again.

'Go on, have the other half,' tempted Euan.

Connie knew she should force herself back to reality, to the work remaining to be done at the office, to her family commitments, but for once she felt like being selfish.

Euan put her drink down on the table and sat next to her, his thigh brushing against hers. Although it was the merest touch it felt to Connie like volts of electricity crashing through her and she jerked her knee away, almost knocking the cider over. To hide her confusion she fished about under the table for her handbag, then clutched it to her like a chastity belt. Five minutes later she suggested they left.

Back in the office Connie's usual energy had deserted her. She sat with the beginnings of a Things To Do list which, astonishingly, given the number of things to do she had in reality, had stopped at one. Finally she noticed a scribbled piece of paper which said 'Gavin rang' on it.

Banning from her mind all thoughts of Euan she willed herself to think of Gavin and the children. She'd been ignoring them lately. She packed up early and stopped in Bidchester at the fishmongers where she bought highly extravagant sea bass, and then some outrageously expensive strawberries flown in from the Canary Islands. They couldn't afford either but there were moments when you had to be extravagant.

By seven the table was laid with an unheard-of proper white cloth, the fish sautéed with ginger and spring onions, and delicately spiced with wifely guilt. She'd spent hours in penitence garnishing it with hand-cut beans, radishes in the shape of stars and new potatoes so tiny it seemed immoral to be eating them. How could she have sat in a pub with Euan only four hours ago, longing for him to suggest they go upstairs? She must have been mad.

Connie was just lighting the candles when she heard the front door open and waited for the expression on Gavin's face. Jeremy, starving and tired after two hours of electric guitar and headbanging in the garage followed his nose to the kitchen and looked at the feast in amazement.

'I thought you were Dad,' Connie explained.

'It's not your anniversary is it?' Jeremy asked.

Connie shook her head. 'I just thought I'd spoil him a bit. He's been working so hard since I started at Victoriana.'

Jeremy scanned his mother's face suspiciously. More odd behaviour. First dashing off like a bride on her honeymoon with that photographer, then coming back and cooking gourmet meals instead of the instant pasta they'd all got used to.

'You chose a funny night then. He rang to say he's staying over in Oldworth with that sculptor chap. The one who does the wooden fairground horses.'

Connie struggled with the uncharacteristic desire to burst into tears. Instead she put her arm round her son. It was hard to achieve as he had overtaken her in height years ago. 'I don't suppose your principles would allow you to eat sea bass?'

When she woke up the next day, slightly hung over after self-pityingly drinking the whole bottle of wine she'd intended for them both, Connie rolled over to snuggle up to Gavin.

His absence, even though she immediately remembered its explanation, still struck her as ominous. *This is what it'd be like all the time if you left, a big hole, bigger than the one you think you're in already.* She looked round the familiar bedroom, drawing comfort from its much-loved objects: the faded chintz of the curtains round the four-poster bed which she'd been so thrilled at finding because they were so right, so unsmart and yet so pretty; the matching blanket chest at the foot of the bed; the oak Windsor chair; the cheval glass Gavin had given her because she complained she could never see more than six inches of herself in any of the others.

Maybe she was just feeling middle-aged, that life had passed her by like in the song. She pulled her dressing gown more tightly round herself and sat at the dressing table. Her hair had kept its colour, but here and there she saw grey hairs dulling the gold. She searched for her tweezers and began to pull them out, one by one, the satisfaction of feeling she was somehow outwitting time immediately cheering her.

'I'm seriously worried about you, Ma,' announced Tara's voice from the bedroom door, 'do you think this behaviour is normal? Maybe it's a sign of The Change. Are you having hot sweats? Irregular periods?'

'Look, Dr Ruth. I'm not expecting the change for another ten years, thank you very much. I'm just removing my grey hairs.'

'You'll be here forever then.'

157

'As a matter of fact I only have a few.'

'You'll be wanting a toy boy next, then we'll *really* know you're menopausal.' Tara leaned over her mother's shoulder in the mirror. 'Look, you've missed one,' she pointed out kindly.

Connie stared at her reflection when Tara had gone. She supposed it was natural to view your mother in the same age bracket as the Queen Mum or Mother Teresa. It must be loathsome to have a mother so young and glamorous you saw her as competition. Connie had always distrusted women who dressed the same as their daughters and claimed to be their best friends. At school a pal of hers had had a mother like that and Connie had been deeply relieved that Charlotte never turned up in miniskirts or blue jeans, and tried to compete.

Anyway she wasn't *that* bad. Apart from the sprinkling of pepper her honey-blonde hair still shone. Her body was fine as long as she didn't compare it with Tara's or any of the models she was hiring for the catalogue; but then they were all so young they thought cellulite was something to do with baby's blankets. She wasn't forty yet and recently there'd been times when she actually felt like a girl again. She brushed her hair vigorously, refusing to admit that those times all had one thing in common.

Downstairs the usual morning nightmare was waiting for her.

'My guitar music's gone again. Have you seen it?' Jeremy's tone was full of reproach, as though it were written in stone during pre-conception that mothers should always know the exact whereabouts of their children's possessions.

'When did you last see it?' Connie asked.

'On the dresser last night. I need it. My test for the Royal College is next month. I have to practise every day.' It had somehow become her fault, she noted, that he was prevented from pursuing this noble path.

She refused to nibble the bait. 'You'd better find it then, or you'll never grow up to be Eric Clapton, will you?'

'Ma.' Jeremy looked at her reproachfully. Normally she would have found it for him. 'You've been very peculiar lately, are you okay?'

'It's the menopause,' confided Tara, 'we worked it all out upstairs, didn't we Ma. She'll start shoplifting soon, to attract attention.'

Connie grabbed Jeremy's backpack and riffled through it, pulling out a crumpled sheet of music from its murky sock-ridden depths. 'Is this what you're looking for?' she asked through gritted teeth. 'And by the way, *I am not going through the menopause, all right*?'

'Don't worry, Ma, it always makes you moody,' Tara said. 'I read that in a magazine. Just don't go into Safeway's alone when you're feeling depressed, okay?'

Driven to distraction Connie took a swipe at her daughter but Tara ran off, leaving Connie to wonder how many years you got for killing your teenager. However long, it might just be worth it.

'Have you seen Lily this morning?' Judith asked Susie McIntosh. 'Only there's something I need to run through with her urgently.'

Susie hugged the knowledge of Lily's whereabouts to her and wondered whether to share it with Judith. The temptation to find an ally in her low opinion of Lily was too much to resist. 'She's in London. We were due to repay some of the loan for the computers this week, but there was a mix-up over an order and it's cost us a fortune.' Susie saw with pleasure that she had every particle of Judith's attention. 'So we can't make the payment.'

'How do you know?'

'One of the secretaries told me. She was scared for her job.'

Judith's mind raced. This was just what she'd hoped for but she didn't want it broadcast round the building quite yet. Timing was important. 'Thanks for telling me, Susie. You were absolutely right to pass it on in case anyone got wind of it from the press. We don't want that, do we? Otherwise your friend could be right. We'll all be out of a job.'

Judith tidied her already immaculately neat desk. She didn't want Susie McIntosh blabbing all round the company. There was one person who certainly ought to be informed, however, and Judith had a feeling Lily hadn't yet done so.

Charlotte Brandon.

'I really think you should talk to Lily before panicking, Charlotte,' Evie was furious with Judith for having 'let slip' – though Evie would lay a hundred to one it hadn't been accidental – that Lily had had to defer the first of her repayments. 'She's probably got a perfectly good explanation.'

Evie had been suspicious from the moment that Judith had arrived earlier that morning, without her usual telephone call in advance, announcing that the weather was so glorious she couldn't stay in London another minute. If Evie's assessment of her character was correct, and it usually was, spontaneity came as naturally to Judith as modesty did to Margaret Thatcher.

The conversation had progressed to how much Judith Brandon was doing for Victoriana's image, with Judith managing to convey that until her arrival this had become a sadly neglected area, and then moving in for what Evie deduced to be the real reason for her visit.

'By the way,' Judith had enquired, 'is Lily back from London yet?'

'I don't know.' Charlotte sounded surprised. 'I assume she went to tell the bankers how well things are going. She came over the other day to show me the figures for the last quarter.'

'How extraordinary.' They were walking in the garden and Judith bent down to pick a bluebell, then held it to her nose. Will you come into my parlour, Evie thought to herself, watching her sister fall trustingly into the trap.

'Why?' asked Charlotte anxiously.

'Because she couldn't make the payment. I wanted to ask her what had gone wrong in case the press got wind of it. You know what they're like. Nothing they like better than sniffing out a bit of bad news, especially about someone successful. It'd be everywhere.'

Charlotte looked devastated. 'I can't understand it. She said things were going so well. I was just beginning to feel she might pull it off after all.'

Poor Lily, thought Evie, wondering if that was why Judith was making trouble, because inexperienced, outrageous Lily *was* finally doing rather well, apart from this one problem, and Judith, successful and highflying, wasn't.

'So, Judith,' Evie asked her crisply, 'are the job offers flooding in? Surely there must be a black hole in the world of PR without you? I should have thought the great and the good would be beating their way to your door by now.'

'Actually' – Judith was clearly nettled – 'I've been working pretty hard on Victoriana's account. Someone has to.'

'It's nice to know there's still some self-sacrifice in the world.' Evie skewered Judith with her piercing gaze until the younger woman finally looked away, 'Otherwise one might get the impression that some people were entirely out for themselves. By the way, Judith, how did you come to hear about this? I would have thought it was pretty confidential.'

Judith looked guarded. 'Oh, just some gossip around the office, you know.'

'Gossip certainly travels fast, then. I understand the payment was only due yesterday.'

Judith flushed under her perfect make-up. The bloody old cow. She thinks I'm up to something. 'Well, you know,' she offered lamely, 'news travels fast in the City.'

'Then I'm sure you'll make it your business to deny any rumours and assure everyone that Victoriana is in perfectly good shape.'

'If I were you,' Evie counselled when Judith finally disappeared leaving behind a cloud of gloom and Arpège, 'I'd watch that one. Why don't you ask Lily what the problem is instead of listening to Judith stir?'

'That's exactly what I intend to do.'

Evie slipped upstairs. She wanted to give Lily some warning of what had been going on. As she did so, she felt a faint pang of apprehension, and hoped Lily knew what she was doing. Stop it, she told herself, believe in the girl for God's sake. You're sounding like your bloody sister.

Charlotte had to admit, when she casually dropped into Victoriana's offices later that day, that it hardly seemed like a company in trouble. The telephone orders section had grown since her last visit and even now the switchboard seemed to flash continually with waiting calls.

'Would you like me to show you how the computer system works, Mrs Brandon?' offered June, by now so enamoured of new technology that she wished only to spread the gospel to others, 'it's really easy when you get the hang of it. I couldn't even set the video before.'

'No thank you, June, I'm glad to say I don't possess a video.'

June was about to argue when she remembered that Mrs Brandon coped with arguments she might lose, as she was doing now, by simply walking away. Well, it would be her loss. June had booked herself on to a course next month in advanced word processing. Mrs Brandon might just wake up one day and find herself part of a world she didn't recognize. That wasn't going to happen to June.

The warehouse, too, was buzzing with activity. So much so that Charlotte noticed, with a flash of annoyance, that her visit was passing without the usual pomp and ceremony.

Susie McIntosh cheered up visibly at her arrival in the design department, but even this didn't compensate for the next incident. Charlotte had just slipped into the Ladies, shared by both shopfloor and management, by Charlotte's own decree, when she encountered a young girl looking so guilty Charlotte suspected she had gone in there to smoke. Worse still, she didn't appear to know who Charlotte was.

Charlotte was too shocked to speak. Never before had Victoriana had an employee she didn't know. When the girl left, Charlotte hurried off in search of Lily, bursting with moral outrage. She finally found her trying samples on two models in her office. 'Lily, I've just seen a young girl in the lavatories who I've never met before and I'm sure she's gone in there to smoke.'

Lily tried not to smile at the seriousness with which her mother took this crime, though she had an inkling that the real sin the girl had committed was not recognizing Charlotte. She could see what a blow that might be to her mother's pride. 'What did she look like?' There couldn't be many employees Charlotte didn't know, and even fewer who didn't know Charlotte.

'Bushy red hair and that pasty white skin that looks as though it never sees the light of day. She looked like one of that shifty Robinson clan.'

Lily nodded. It must be Shauna, who'd helped June so much with the computer. Lily had a good idea that it wasn't to have a smoke that Shauna was lurking in the loos, looking pale, though what her mother would make of that when she discovered, God alone knew. 'Sounds like Shauna Robinson. She's a really helpful girl. Just eighteen and quick as anything. I have high hopes for her. I'll take you to meet her in a moment if you like.'

Charlotte studied her daughter carefully. Once she would have stopped what she was doing and listened to Charlotte's complaint. Instead, she seemed to be side-stepping it. Lily clearly felt in control.

Charlotte was honest enough to recognize that instead of the joy she ought to be feeling at this subtle shift in her daughter, what she actually felt was resentment. Had Edward been right then? Did she want Lily to fail?

Anyway, she had no desire to be trailed round as the old lady who should be humoured, 'Don't worry about that. There's something more important I need to talk to you about.'

Lily told the two girls she'd finish later.

'This business about missing your repayment. I want to know how serious it is.'

Lily kicked herself for not telling her mother about it before someone else did. She'd been cowardly and short-sighted, but that brief spell of Charlotte's approval had been so wonderful that she'd wanted to hang on to it, to hold it to her like a hot-water bottle. 'I'm sorry. I should have told you. It's true that everything is going well. It still is; and the projections George and I have been doing are even better. It was just a stupid mistake on my part.'

'And you tried to cover it up?'

'If I'd thought there was any risk to the company, I'd have told you at once. As it is, the way the orders are going we can easily meet it at the next quarter.'

'You sound very confident.'

'Yes,' Lily was surprised to realize that she actually meant it, 'I am.'

'So what was the stupid mistake you made?'

This was the moment Lily had been dreading. 'I counter-signed an order for twenty thousand garments instead of two thousand, at a loss of twenty-four thousand pounds.'

'What was the garment?'

'An ivory silk camisole.' Lily waited for the withering reply. To her surprise none came.

'Let's hope the bodice-ripping look's in this year then,' said Charlotte. 'Perhaps you should give away a copy of *Tom Jones* free with every one.'

Lily was so surprised at her mother making a joke that she forgot to ask her how she'd found out in the first place.

After Charlotte had gone she sat thinking about Shauna Robinson. She'd been in the Ladies herself the other day and had heard someone in one of the cubicles throwing up. It had been Shauna. When she'd emerged Lily had asked if she were all right. Fine, Shauna had insisted, just a bit of a bug.

Lily had wondered at the time, since Shauna was nor-mally the most robust of employees, always laughing and joking, a joy to have about the place. At eighteen Shauna was the youngest of the Robinsons, the most numerous clan in the village. If anyone was seen underneath a motorbike, covered in grease, at the roadside, it would be a Robinson. If the glass in the bus shelter were broken again, it would be attributed unanimously to a Robinson; if anyone sat outside the pub drinking lager past the witching hour of two-thirty, that would be a Robinson too. Shauna, she knew, was brighter than the rest and might just have a chance of breaking the mould. She'd come to them for work experi-ence and had been kept on by June. She was a nice kid.

Lily picked up her phone and asked June if Shauna could be spared for five minutes.

'Not a problem, I hope?' June asked anxiously. Lily could tell from the tone of her voice that June, too, was fond of Shauna.

'No, no. I wanted her advice on my computer, that's all,' lied Lily.

'She'll sort you out in no time then. I'll send her up.'

Shauna was looking so healthy and rosy when she bounced in, wearing a pair of denim dungaree shorts with thick black tights underneath just like Tara wore, that Lily lost her nerve.

'June said you had problems with your WP,' Shauna announced breezily, 'let us at it then.'

'I think I may have sorted it out.'

'Oh, well then,' Shauna started to go out again.

'Look, Shauna, there's something I wanted to ask you.'

'Oh?' A wary look replaced the bounce.

'The other day you were in the Ladies . . .'

'Throwing up? Yeah, I said, I had a bug.'

'Are you completely better? Only I gather you were in there again a little while ago, and you seemed quite ill I'm told.'

Shauna looked at Lily levelly, her eyes narrowing with suspicion. 'You think I'm up the spout, don't you?'

This bald statement of exactly what she had been thinking made Lily falter momentarily. She'd never been in a situation like this before and began to see how much tact it took. 'Well, if you *were* pregnant we'd try and be as helpful as we could.'

'But I'm not, am I?' Shauna challenged her.

'Fine. Look I'm sorry I mentioned it.'

'I mean,' the young girl toyed with the buckle on her dungarees, 'I've heard about Mrs Brandon from June. I never met her, but when my cousin Kathleen had a baby without being married June said it was a good thing she didn't work here, because Mrs Brandon didn't hold with that kind of thing.'

It was true that Charlotte had always disapproved of illegitimacy, seeing it as another sign of the breakdown of

166

the values she held dear. 'But then I'm not my mother, am I?' Lily said. 'And I wanted to ask you something. If you *did* ever have a baby, would your mum look after it for you?'

Shauna laughed. 'Not my mum. She's likes her fun. She's always saying thank God that part's over, shitty nappies and that. She says she's washed enough nappies to last a lifetime.'

'They are disposable now,' pointed out Lily.

'Not disposable enough for my mum. She'd only look after the baby if it were disposable too.'

'How about your gran?'

'She moved away years ago. Thought we might start sponging.' Knowing the Robinsons' reputation this seemed a fair bet, but Shauna was different. Come to think of it, the poor kid was probably having to hand most of her own wages over to fund the Robinson appetite for afternoon lager sessions.

'Oh well. I expect I was being presumptuous. I just wanted you to know I'd do all I could to keep your job for you if you were having a baby.'

'You mean you wouldn't chuck me out? Even though I've only been here a few months?'

'Of course not. As long as you were serious about coming back and sorted out your childcare.'

Shauna suddenly made up her mind. 'All right then, I am pregnant, miss. I'm sorry I lied, only I like it here so much. I thought I might get the sack if I were pregnant and I couldn't bear that.'

Lily was appalled at the girl's perception of what Victoriana required of its employees. While she was here she intended to set up proper maternity leave and stop June going on about the shame of unmarried mothers.

The parallels struck her between Shauna and Hardy's Tess, the classic victim of Victorian morality – but this was the 1990s! Here they were featuring Tess in the catalogue while perpetuating the kind of hypocrisy that had destroyed Tess's life.

'Of course you won't have to give up the job. Does your family know?' Shauna shook her head. 'Well, tell them first. And tell them your job's safe. I promise.'

Shauna leapt up from her chair and pumped Lily's hand. 'You won't regret it, I promise!' And Lily, watching Shauna's intelligent face, alight with gratitude, knew instinctively that this was the truth.

'Great, great, great, great . . . GRRREAT!'

Connie had always wondered why photographers sounded half way between a bossy gym mistress and a soft pornographer, and now she understood. It was to offer the model encouragement to keep up that relentless smile during the vital ten minutes that followed the incredibly tedious two hours the shot had taken to set up.

Connie had to admit it was worth it. In the middle distance a cart lumbered out of the haze towards them, with a model dressed as Bathsheba Everdene, but in Victoriana clothes, sitting perched on top, the light glinting off the small mirror in which she inspected her ravishing beauty. Forgive us Hardy, muttered Connie to the great writer, telling herself that plagiarizing a scene out of *Far From the Madding Crowd* to flog clothes was a tribute of sorts. Anyway, it was a truly glorious shot.

It was strange, thought Connie, how powerfully nostalgia worked in selling us things from Hovis bread to Victoriana clothes – and yet, nostalgia for what? What was it that we wanted to buy along with the flowery prints and the bread with Nowt Left Out? A notion of our past that felt safe, perhaps; a time when jobs were for life and everyone knew their place, and children played safe on the streets. She felt the draw of nostalgia herself, she knew it, with her unfitted kitchen, her vast Welsh dresser loaded with mementoes.

She'd once even bought a bread board, hand carved with sheaves of wheat, for thirty pounds, probably more than the carver would have earned in a year. She'd wanted it because she felt loaves had been sliced on it for generations and, stupid though it was, she wanted to feel part of that history.

Would some young girl, seeing their Bathsheba, want to buy the frock so she could imagine herself as an independent young woman a hundred and fifty years ago? The irony was, of course, that now the humblest shop assistant had more freedom and independence than Bathsheba did, for all her money.

Lost in thought Connie hadn't noticed that the shot was finished until she felt a hand in the small of her back and knew instantly whose it was.

'Come on, Connie, we're stopping for lunch. Or are you going to spend the day contemplating the splendours of nature?' Euan helped her down off the stile from which she'd been watching the proceedings. 'Connie. Is that short for Constance? How wonderfully Victorian. Of course Lily and Constance, your mother would choose those. Would the third have been Ruby?'

'Too much like a barmaid for my mother's tastes. No she would have been Florence. Instead she turned out to be Jonathan.'

'I shall call you Constance, it has a ring to it that reminds me of you. The fair maiden, once awakened into the full blossoming of her sensual passion, who remains constant to her awakener for time immemorial.'

'I'm not sure Gavin sees himself quite in that light.'

'Maybe I wasn't talking about Gavin.'

Connie looked away, knowing she'd somehow been wanting him to say that and feeling foolish once he did. 'So,' she briskly changed the subject, 'how did it go this morning?'

'The light was marvellous and that model is terrific. There's a touch of the classy baggage about her that's perfect for Bathsheba. Of course, half your customers won't know who the hell Bathsheba was anyway but it'll make a pretty picture.'

'Nonsense. Our customers are intelligent, sophisticated women.'

'Like you, you mean.'

This is just a game, Connie told herself, and I'm out of the habit. 'Yes,' she said, 'just like me.' And Constance Brandon, who was at that moment feeling remarkably inconstant, abandoned herself to the heady delight of what she told herself was harmless flirtation.

Later on, at home, reality hit her with unusual ferocity. The kitchen was a mess, the result of Tara at her petulant and unhelpful worst; a pile of Jeremy's filthy rugby kit leered at her from the kitchen table, where, in an effort to be helpful, he had placed it among the debris of breakfast which she had abandoned in a rush to get to the shoot, shouting a request that between them they should deal with it, which they clearly hadn't listened to.

She ignored the lot and sat down to read the paper, feeling furious with them all. They just assumed she would be there to sort out their lives, their crises and their washing, yet no one gave a stuff about *her* needs. She sat at the uncleared table and allowed herself a moment of self-pity before a few home truths wormed themselves into her consciousness. Gavin wasn't some mean shit who took without giving; he had made a considerable sacrifice so she could join Victoriana and had been generous enough to hide from her quite how difficult her departure had made things. Tara and Jeremy were behaving no different from usual; they were simply being teenagers.

She was the one with the problem.

A few minutes later, Gavin's key turned in the door and

she felt a little sink of the spirits which she made herself ignore. Instead she stood up to greet him.

'How did it go?' he asked and then, noticing the mess, 'my God, those children are savages. They promised to clear this lot up.' He began to pick up plates and carry them to the dishwasher.

Connie stopped him, lashed by guilt. 'Let them do it. Why don't you and I go upstairs for a bit?'

Gavin hesitated for a moment.

'Why not?' He put his arms round her gratefully. 'What a nice surprise.'

But the sex, engaged in for the wrong reasons, didn't bring Connie the closeness she'd hoped for. Afterwards, she asked herself how it could have. She'd done it in the spirit of wifely prudence rather as she might try and remember to put the washing on before she went to work, or make two batches of something, to save time later. She watched Gavin's eyelids flicker into sleep, and saw the awful truth. They would probably both have got more satisfaction from clearing up the kitchen together and putting on the dishwasher.

Euan dumped the first batch of prints for the catalogue on Connie's desk two days later with a flourish.

'How are they?' Connie asked, not daring to open the envelope.

Euan's face clouded over. 'Pretty disappointing I'm afraid. I seem to have overexposed the Bathsheba shots and the light up on Rainbarrow was worse than we thought. You can hardly see the model who's supposed to be Eustacia.'

Connie's face was a pantomime of shock and horror.

'Go on, open the box,' Euan urged.

The photographs were staggeringly beautiful. He had captured the haunting quality of the misty early morning perfectly, and Bathsheba's coquetry, patting her hair in the tiny mirror, gave a touch of humour. It was the kind of photograph people would tear out and stick on their walls.

By the time Lily arrived Connie was bounding around like a spring lamb, waving them at anyone who'd stop and look. Lily laughed. 'I think you're supposed to keep the catalogue a secret till the great unveiling. Like with cars.'

'I just couldn't resist showing them off. Look at these, Lil, they're *wonderful*!'

Lily had to concede that they were indeed wonderful. Euan Brady was clearly a talent. There was one particular shot that caught Lily's eye more than all the others. It was the dancing scene from *Tess of the D'Urbervilles* with each girl wearing a different Victoriana nightdress. What made it stand out from the others was its almost orgiastic abandon.

'It's all there, it's in the book.' Euan said, before she had a chance to comment. 'Hardy says it's like a pagan ritual. I just recreated it.'

Lily studied it again. The girl in the foreground had a look of imminent climax in her eyes as she tried to hold up the thin strap of her nightgown. It was certainly eyecatching and it would generate huge publicity, of that Lily was entirely certain.

And Charlotte would absolutely loathe it.

The main question was, as Euan had put it so aptly, would it flog frocks? Lily decided that undoubtedly it would. Their customers could all imagine themselves as a nymph in a Victoriana nightgown, waiting wide-eyed for the arrival of that wicked satyr who would carry them off into the woods, instead of their boring husbands from Surbiton.

'It's wonderful, a classic. You're both incredibly clever.'

Lily saw them exchange a smile of acceptance. The electricity between them was so powerful that it closed them off into a secret world of their own, but what startled and scared Lily was the frank sensuality of it. From the look in her eyes, Connie could be imagining herself as one of those dryads with nothing but a metre or two of flimsy cotton lawn coming between her and the man standing next to her.

Chapter 12

Connie could hardly remember feeling this happy in years. Outside spring was unfurling in the most shamelessly glorious way. Black lambs butted their mothers, skylarks swooped and trilled, daffodils nodded, and even the gruffest old sods in the village smiled in the face of all this rampant beauty and renewal. There was nothing more exciting – especially if you had been exposed to five years of seeing mainly Margot – than going to work to a job you really enjoyed, especially in weather like this. The element she left out of this particular equation, for reasons she would have been reluctant to admit, was at this moment sitting in Victoriana's canteen, studying some colour prints and charming the socks off the canteen ladies.

Connie, meanwhile, got herself ready to go. Tara, with her usual self-absorption, noticed neither spring nor her mother's unusually happy mood. She was examining her chin, aware of a sensitive patch that would soon erupt into a spot of volcanic size so that she wouldn't be able to face Roz's jokes, nor the disco at the art college in Bidchester on Saturday night.

Gavin didn't notice either, but that was because he was trying to protect his family from an increasing sense of anxiety about his business and the strain of doing so took all his energy. A few months ago, before she started working for Victoriana, Connie would have noticed without him needing to say anything. She would have taken in the slowing down of activity in the shop, almost to a standstill. She would have remarked on how few customers even came, and how little they spent when they did, contenting themselves with buying a card where once they might have splashed out on a gift. One World was only existing from hand to mouth and she would have sat down with him and talked about it. Together they would have come up with a plan which would have made him feel more optimistic. There would have been painful changes, even letting Margot go perhaps, but they would have done it together. They would have had each other, two of them standing against harsh reality, and that would have been extraordinarily comforting to Gavin.

Instead, Connie had noticed only how well the catalogue shoot was going, how much turnover it would generate for Victoriana, and what enormous fun it had been to find locations for it.

Watching her put her coat on, her face alive with eagerness, Gavin suddenly resented her. She seemed so much in a different world, obsessed with things that seemed trivial to him, even though he knew they were probably important to how well she did the job. For days she had been endlessly disappearing at dawn and coming back late, thrilled at having discovered some new place to photograph when it seemed to him they could as well have done it at the bottom of the garden or in a ploughed field. Yet Connie had always had a feel for these things. Maybe it was the loss of her touch in the shop that had hit business so badly. She had always made it look so appealing. Just the way she arranged the window display and the things on the shelves seemed to bring people in, and neither he nor Margot had the knack of leaving people to themselves until the precise moment of decision, then easing them into a sale so that they thought they'd decided entirely on their own. Gavin cheered up marginally. He'd ask Connie to come and wave her wand over the shop one night this week.

What's the matter with them both? Jeremy had been watching his parents for weeks and knew what neither were admitting, that something was wrong. His father wasn't cracking his usual terrible jokes and seemed withdrawn; his mother was unnaturally cheerful. She was like one of those wind-up rabbits, brimming over with energy, but driven by some mysterious hidden power source. Jeremy even had a good idea what it was, but if he was right why wasn't his father doing anything about it? To just ignore the whole thing was madness, surely? It occurred to Jeremy, as yet entirely innocent of the complexities and compromises of love, that perhaps his father did know and didn't want to face the consequences. Surely, he thought with a shock of pain, the father he loved wasn't simply a wimp? Jeremy, more used to the dilemmas thrown up by Dungeons and Dragons than real life, decided that if it ever came to it, he might have to be the one to take some kind of action. What action, he had no idea.

On his guard, the parfit gentil knight in a Cure teeshirt, he resolved to watch his mother carefully and, if necessary, save her from herself.

'So, what do you reckon? Pretty bloody amazing, aren't they?' Lily had spread the roughs of the almost-completed catalogue out on her desk to show Judith so they could discuss how to present the finished article to the press.

Judith was taken aback. The roughs were, quite simply, stunning. Every page had an extraordinary mood and sensuality. What Euan had managed to suggest was the explosive sexuality hidden behind the modesty of the Victorian era.

176

The press would go mad, not least because it was such a departure from Victoriana's previous maidenly image. This catalogue was going to be a landmark of its kind.

It was also, Judith suspected, going to come as an enormous shock to Victoriana's founder. Modesty and practicality had been Charlotte's watchwords. There had always been a hint of the buttoned-up governess in Charlotte's concept of the Victoriana ideal and this catalogue was going to blow that sky-high.

Lily waited for Judith's reaction.

'It'll certainly make an impact,' Judith conceded. 'We should get early copies out as soon as possible. Why don't I make a list of who we should offer it to first?'

Judith surveyed her sister-in-law with an unaccustomed prick of envy. She'd come shooting down here, expecting Victoriana to be wrapped in deep gloom. Instead, it seemed to be buzzing with excitement and Lily seemed to have a new confidence which even permeated down to her appearance. Leaning over the desk in a dark green wrap skirt and velvet body, her dark red hair rippling down over her shoulders, she looked unnervingly in charge of herself and of her surroundings.

It struck Judith, with all the pleasure of an unexpected tax bill, that Lily Brandon was beginning to do rather well at running Victoriana. This was one eventuality that she hadn't examined. The likelihood of Lily actually making a success of the business had seemed about as likely as Madonna Ciccone being canonized.

At that moment they were interrupted by the arrival of Connie and the photographer, whom Lily had asked to join them. Away in London pursuing her consultancy work, Judith hadn't seen Connie for a couple of weeks and was startled by the change in her. She positively sparkled. From her shining newly-styled blonde head to the well-cut lavender silk suit she wore, which for once certainly

177

wasn't from Marks and Spencer, Connie seemed like a parched flower after a rainshower. At her side, laughing down into her eyes, holding on to her arm protectively and totally unnecessarily, was, if Judith wasn't much mistaken, the reason for this. Euan Brady had clearly been caught in the same downpour.

Judith wondered if Connie had thought about the consequences: the risk of exposure, of losing her husband. Had she weighed up these things and decided to go ahead anyway? Judith always thought people who risked all for love were mad. Barry North's face flashed through her mind. Did she love him? She felt a vulnerability, certainly, that she'd never felt with her husband. Jonathan would never give trouble, he quite liked the feel of the boot on his neck. Barry was different, though: dangerous, unpredictable, strong. She suspected he also had a tender side and that given the right woman he was capable of loyalty. Could she be that woman? Judith realized with a shock almost of dismay how much she wanted to be. She suspected he still saw her as a diversion, though possibly a useful one. She also saw a way of proving her loyalty to him and maybe getting him for keeps.

'Connie,' she exclaimed, 'the catalogue's sensational.' She turned to Euan: 'Or is it you I should be congratulating? You'll set a whole new trend with this.'

'It was all Connie's idea.' The affection in Euan's voice would have warmed the coldest day. 'She knew exactly what she wanted from the start. I just translated it.'

'Like Van Gogh just translated the sunflowers,' chided Connie. 'You had no creative input whatsoever, did you?'

'When do you think we should have the press launch?' Lily asked Judith.

'As soon as you can get the catalogue finished and print some early copies. I'll start setting up interviews with the magazines now.'

Instinctively Connie waited until Judith had left before she asked the question that neither of them had yet faced up to. 'When do you think we ought to show it to Ma?'

Lily summoned all her strength of will. 'Not until it's set in stone and too late to change.'

Lily watched Connie and Euan depart to get on with the catalogue. Was the relationship between them simply a flirtation? Whatever it was, it was becoming noticeable even to Judith. She wondered if she ought to tackle her sister but in the event she didn't have time to do so, because another more immediate crisis presented itself. June had discovered Shauna's pregnancy and wanted to know what she should do.

'What do *you* think, June?' Lily asked.

'I like her tremendously. She's got nerve and she's bright as anything – amazing in a Robinson. But, Lily, she's only eighteen. Do you think she'll manage?' June stuffed her hands anxiously into the pockets of her long cardigan, one of Victoriana's designs from ten years ago. She liked Shauna and didn't want to lose her, but it was a huge thing to be taking on, a job and a baby.

'If we don't keep her on what will happen?'

'She'll stay at home, I suppose.'

'And live on what?'

'Benefit, I should think. Don't the council give you a house or something? The papers are always fussing about unmarried mothers jumping the housing queue.'

'Exactly. We'd be pushing her right back where she came from. Back on benefit like the rest of her family. Shauna's trying to get away from that.'

'Mrs Brandon will be horrified if she hears.'

'Look, June.' Lily tried to keep the irritation she was feeling from her voice. Mrs Brandon. Still. And from June too. 'I'll deal with my mother if she makes a fuss. You can tell Shauna her job will be safe and that I'll be writing to confirm it.'

She sat down as soon as June had left and wrote the promised letter. Of course Charlotte would disapprove, but there was an issue here about the way her mother had run the company. The atmosphere at Victoriana was almost feudal. Charlotte's tentacles had spread too far into people's personal lives. Her employees were frightened of losing their jobs if they didn't live by Charlotte's own moral code. That might have been acceptable in the days of the mill owners, but this was a hundred years later. In her own way, Shauna was striking a blow for independence on behalf of all the other employees too. Providing she did her job Lily would support her to the hilt.

Charlotte, when she did discover, Lily suspected through the good offices of the interfering Susie McIntosh, was incandescent with fury. She swept into Lily's office wearing a black velvet cloak lined with lilac silk, Boadicea-like, and insisted she speak to her.

'Lily, you can't be serious about keeping on this pregnant teenager. It's outrageous to even consider it.'

'Why? Because she'll set a bad example? Ma, this is the 1990s not the 1890s. What kind of example will she set if I don't keep her on? Another unmarried mother on benefit, probably accused of getting pregnant to jump the housing queue. I don't suppose you're too keen on the dependency culture are you, Ma?'

'Really, Lily, that's beside the point.'

'No, it's not. Shauna comes from a long line of scroungers and, miraculous though it might seem, she isn't one. She's bright and ambitious and loves working here.'

'Not so bright she didn't get pregnant.'

'No. She's made a mistake, but she shouldn't have to pay for it for the rest of her life.'

'The workforce will think you're weak, that anything goes.'

'No, they won't. They'll see that a good worker is valued

and that, unlike under Charlotte Brandon, their private lives are their own concern. Has it never occurred to you, Ma, that your employees were terrified out of their wits by you?'

Charlotte couldn't believe Lily's tone. Lily was actually challenging the way she'd run Victoriana. 'What nonsense. They respected me. We were a family.'

'A family maybe, but one where the mother ruled with a rod of iron.' She almost added, just like ours.

Lily noticed that the pages of the catalogue were on her desk and instinctively she made a move to cover them. Furious with herself, she halted the gesture. Who was running the company, her or Charlotte? She'd meant to work up to this moment, choosing it carefully as her father would have done, strewing the path with compliments, but she'd had enough of trying to keep Charlotte happy. She would run Victoriana her way and if they hated it, they could fire her. 'By the way, the new catalogue is almost ready. It went off to the printers this morning.' This was an exaggeration, since it hadn't actually been sent yet, but she didn't want Charlotte to know that. She handed the mock-ups over and waited, conscious of the sudden trickle of sweat in her palms.

But these are brilliant, said a voice in her head, congratulations, darling, I think they're marvellous.

Charlotte studied them carefully. They were atmospheric certainly, and beautifully photographed. They even managed to show the clothes off in considerable detail, essential for a catalogue, but their sensuality shocked Charlotte rigid. This wasn't the Victoriana she'd spent thirty years of her life building up.

'They're lovely photographs, I grant you, but they're quite unsuitable for Victoriana. Our customers would be appalled. You can't possibly use them. You'll just have to stop them at the printers. I'm sure they can wait a week or two while you re-shoot. You're well ahead of schedule.'

Lily felt like a small child, put in its place for expressing a stupid opinion in adult company. The sensation was so powerful that unconsciously she began to question herself. Was her mother right? Was she wrong and out of step with the mood of the times?

Lily willed herself to keep her nerve. This hadn't just been her work. It had been Connie's and Euan's. Even Judith had appreciated what a stir they'd cause. 'I'm sorry, Ma, but I'm not changing a thing. I was asked to run this company and that's what I'm doing, to the best of my talents and abilities. I think this catalogue is going to cause a sensation.'

Charlotte suddenly felt old, as though she were a rubber tyre with the air hissing out of it. Once she would have fought back, now she just wanted to get home. 'I'm sure you're right,' she said, but she couldn't resist adding, 'but maybe not the kind of sensation you want.'

Lily opened the door for her, feeling uneasy. She'd been prepared for her mother to stamp and shout, not simply cave in. For once she'd been ready for a confrontation, but Charlotte had managed to move the goalposts, as only Charlotte could.

She glanced down at the mock-up, hoping to God her judgement was right. Pull yourself together for God's sake, she told herself angrily, if you don't believe in yourself it's sure as hell no one else will.

Evie was sitting out on the lawn when Charlotte got back, her face directed towards the sun but wrapped in millions of layers, like a sunbathing walrus. Edward pottered somewhere in the background.

Charlotte sat down in the Lloyd Loom chair opposite her sister's. If only she could just settle down to retirement like Evie and Edward. They seemed to positively thrive on it, but Charlotte missed the cut and thrust of running the company. Did she also miss seeing her employees jump?

She'd been hurt by the picture Lily painted of her. People liked to know where they stood and be sure of what was expected. She had simply shown them.

'The new catalogue's almost finished,' she said carefully.

'Oh? What's it like?' Evie knew just how important a moment this must be for Lily and Connie: the symbol of their independence from Charlotte.

'I hated it.' Charlotte shuddered. 'It's dramatic enough but quite wrong for our image. The press will have a field day. "Victoriana Loses Its Virginity", I can picture it now.'

Evie picked up the hurt in her sister's voice. She reached out her hand and squeezed Charlotte's. 'Poor Charly, they really are getting on all right without you, aren't they? That must be tough.'

Charlotte sniffed. The unexpected use of her baby name had taken her unawares, and she hated being offered sympathy. Only the weak needed reassurance. 'I think I'll go and find Edward. That flowerbed he's just weeded still looks like black hair with dandruff. He never was any good at it.'

Evie watched her sister's straight figure walk across the lawn. She was such a strong woman that it was easy to forget the toll the last months had taken: almost dying, having to give up her beloved company, and then there was the troubled relationship with Lily. If Charlotte would only admit to the past, and the mistakes she'd made in it, terrible though they were, then she might be able to open up and enjoy the present, take pride in Lily's achievements; but that moment hadn't come yet. For all their sakes Evie hoped it would. Wrapped in her cocoon of rugs, she wondered if it would ever come. If it didn't, then her trip half way across the world would be wasted. As the dusk fell she asked herself if there was anything she could do to hasten it. There was only one way, she thought, and if it backfired it could cost Charlotte everything.

*

183

Connie never knew whether it was really by design that Judith rang and asked her and Euan to go to London to do an interview.

'Don't they want Lily too?' Connie asked in surprise.

'Not for this one. It's a design mag and they asked for the people behind the look. There'll be plenty of other interviews for Lily. Why? Would you rather hand her all the credit when the idea was yours? The interview's at six, the woman can't do it before then for some reason, so I've booked you a hotel. She'll do it there. Do you need me to come too?' Judith made it sound as though only a complete incompetent would need her there, so Connie declined. The family were surprisingly supportive when she told them, except for Jeremy who shot her a hostile look when he found Euan was going too. Connie made herself ignore it.

To her surprise she rather enjoyed the interview. Her ideas for doing the catalogue had been born simply of instinct and having to think them through for the benefit of someone else – especially with Euan there to flesh them out – was enlightening for them both. The hotel was one she'd never heard of, near the back of Harrods, small and unpretentious, but with a distinct personality of its own.

She unpacked her overnight bag and hung the dress she was wearing for dinner with Euan that night in the closet. Then she poured all the little bottles of bath foam extravagantly into the bath and raided the minibar. There were tiny packets of Planter's peanuts and wildly expensive bars of chocolate with Buckingham Palace on them. She put one on the side of the bath. She might as well satisfy all her sensual demands at once. Then she climbed in and let the waters lap round the island of her body, trying to unwind. Relaxing was almost impossible with the terrifying but wonderful knowledge that she was in

London, alone, with a large empty bed, no responsibilities, and Euan.

What was she going to do later, if he asked her to come back with him or wanted to come up here? Connie closed her eyes. Fantasy and flirtation were one thing, but this was different. She let herself think about Euan: the way he looked at her and how it made her feel hot and wet; the excitement laced with desire each time she heard his name or knew she might see him; the way he seemed to understand her and listen to her. How many times a day did she think about him? She didn't want to count. Going to work had become not just satisfying but an adventure, with the chance of his presence lighting up her day.

But what about Gavin, generous, loving Gavin who trusted her? Didn't only unhappy people have affairs? Couples whose marriages had dimmed and dulled until nothing could revive them had affairs, the deliberate first stage on the road to separation. Later they would say it was a symptom not a cause and that the whole process of disintegration of their marriage had been inevitable.

What nonsense that was. There were choices at every stage. She hadn't done anything to commit herself yet. She loved Gavin. She was restless, but that was different – and it was no doubt just as much her fault as Gavin's. Probably they should take up bridge or some such God-awful thing. There was probably some worthy organization she could contact through Relate. Bridge Evenings for Couples in Crisis or Golf for the Maritally Stressed. Besides, Euan's job on the catalogue was over now and he would be staying in London.

She only had tonight to get through.

Feeling shriven of her ignoble feelings she got out of the bath and enveloped herself in the towelling dressing gown thoughtfully provided by the management, then draped herself over the bed sipping the last of her white wine.

When the knock on the door came she told herself it was only the chambermaid coming to turn down the bed.

But she knew it wasn't.

Chapter 13

'Connie, it's me. I need to talk to you urgently.'

When she heard Euan's voice Connie had the absurd temptation to pretend she was out, but that would be ridiculous. His voice was cheerful and reassuring. Maybe there had been some problem with the interview. She opened the door.

Euan closed it roughly behind him and stood in front of her. He seemed agitated. There was a deep furrow between his pale blue eyes and his hair hung untidily over his face. He brushed it back with an angry gesture. Connie couldn't think what had gone wrong. The lab couldn't have messed up his prints, surely.

'What's the matter?' she asked, wanting to reach out and smooth away the preoccupied look as though he were Jeremy.

'You,' he accused, 'you're the matter.'

Connie, knowing exactly what he meant, pretended not to. 'What have I done to offend you so much? I thought we were friends.' Wicked that last line, designed to stir things up.

For answer he pushed her on to the bed and buried his face in her neck. 'God. I want you so much. I can't go on with this.'

Connie, who had decided not five minutes ago that she would resist any advances, felt his body pressing into hers, and wanted him more than she'd wanted any man, even Gavin. She could feel his breath on her neck. He was waiting for her to make the next move.

She could still change her mind.

Of course she couldn't. This was what she wanted, had wanted for weeks. Her body was singing, burning, aching with wanting him. In that moment nothing else mattered.

She slipped astride him and began to undo his buttons.

His eyes opened wide and wild with desire as he pushed her robe down over her shoulders and tugged at the belt until she was exposed to him. Feverishly Connie undid his jeans and zip and delved inside until she held his erect prick in her hand. It was beautiful. He began to try and remove his shirt but she stopped him, pushing him gently back. He was at her command. Leaning forward to kiss him she eased herself on to him and moved up and down as his hands caressed her breasts. Moments later he cried out, pumping into her all the frustrated longing of the last weeks.

'But you didn't come,' his pleasure clouded over at the realization.

Connie turned with him still inside her until he was looking down into her eyes. 'That was only the first time.'

An hour later they forgot about their restaurant booking, just as they forgot about everything that existed outside the four walls of their hotel bedroom. Room service had finished by the time they fell apart, exhausted and starving, so they were forced to picnic on the contents of the minibar, champagne and chocolate and Planters peanuts, which to neither Connie nor Euan had ever tasted so good before. Finally, Connie, who always insisted on a two foot comfort zone in the marital bed, fell into a deep sleep wrapped in

Euan's arms, firmly pushing from her mind all thoughts of tomorrow.

Gavin decided to take advantage of Connie's absence by going into the shop early. Jeremy and Tara needed booting out of bed, but he left them to their own devices after that, both wildly complaining that they got a better service from their mother.

'That's because she's too soft on you,' he whipped the duvet off Tara, 'unlike your cruel father. You can get your own breakfast. The milk's on the table.'

'Thanks a lot, Dad,' muttered Tara. 'Aren't you going to offer us a lift? What if there are perverts hanging round the bus shelter?'

'They'd have found you ages ago,' he pointed out unsympathetically, 'the way *you* dress.'

Once inside the shop, Gavin could drop the veneer of cheerfulness he'd kept up for home. He'd wanted half an hour alone to study the books, before Margot came in. She would overreact if she suspected the level of his worry and start volunteering her notice. Obviously she must know there was a problem; even Margot would have taken in the fact the shop was like a morgue and that stock was moving as slowly as if it were nailed down. He had hidden his worst fears in a flurry of activity, moving things around, arranging exhibitions down one end of the shop to try and bring people in. He hadn't dared invest in new stock because so much of the old remained unsold. Painted horses from Indonesia stood in lonely splendour where once the shelves were packed with sun-face candlesticks, papier-mâché picture frames from India, Moroccan incense burners, and statues of fat ladies from Mexico. So far he'd put off facing the worst, but it was becoming harder. If the rent review, due next month, meant another hike, they might have to give up the shop.

The thought depressed him beyond measure. It had been their livelihood for twenty years, ever since they'd left university full of hope and optimism and had come back with armloads of Nepalese carvings. He thought of the buying trips they'd made together since then: to Java and Bali, Goa and Singapore. It had been such a wonderful feeling to spend thousands of pounds on beautiful things without feeling guilty.

He didn't hear Margot arrive and she stopped in the doorway, surprised and concerned to find him here so early. She was worried about Gavin. She knew a lot more than he suspected about the state of affairs at One World. She knew, for instance, that they couldn't afford the big trips round the world, but they'd even stopped going to their supplier in Amsterdam. Gavin hadn't even been to the annual gift fair he always attended and she had a good idea why.

She also knew that losing Connie to Victoriana might well have been the death-blow, since it meant Gavin had to spend more time in the shop and also pay Margot for the extra hours to cover for Connie. She wondered if he'd told his wife any of this. Knowing him, he wouldn't have. He was one of the most generous men she'd ever met.

Maybe, Margot wondered, she should drop a hint to Connie about it. Margot was a doer, the type who kept charity shops staffed, and road schemes at bay, and woolly mittens knitted for Bosnian orphans. She liked to feel she was contributing her bit to keeping the world a decent place. Having come to a decision about Connie, she realized quite how much she'd been worrying lately.

She greeted Gavin, hung her coat on the lifesize statue of a eunuch that no one had ever wanted to buy and put the kettle on. He'd feel better after he had a nice cup of tea.

'One lump or two?' Connie woke up to find Euan wearing

the towelling wrap she'd discarded with such enthusiasm last night. He was holding out a cup of tea.

'Just milk.' Connie propped herself up, thinking how strange it was to be in bed with someone who didn't know whether she took sugar or not. Gavin knew her tastes so thoroughly he could order a meal for her and choose exactly what she would have selected herself. She sipped the tea, watching him in amazement as he put four lumps of sugar in his own cup.

'Blood sugar replacement,' he explained, 'you've been wearing my stocks down to danger levels.'

'Have I now?' She popped another sugar lump into his cup. 'Then we'd better build up some resources for the next round.'

'No time like the present, I always say. I wouldn't want to get out of practice.'

They shut out the world for another hour, making love more gently this time, without the desperate passion of last night. Then they ordered breakfast in bed. Connie made sure she was in the bathroom when the waiter knocked, knowing she couldn't meet his eyes.

Having missed dinner last night they fell on the pastries like siege victims, tearing either end of the same croissant and stuffing it into their mouths. Then they devoured the brioche and the French bread. Euan spilt strawberry jam on his chest and Connie licked it off, pretending to be a faithful hound. So Euan pounced on her and made love to her from behind, doggy fashion, until their laughter turned into groans of pleasure. Finally they fell back exhausted again and Euan was so starving he phoned for another breakfast.

It was the same waiter.

'Great idea,' hissed Connie as he left with a large tip. 'Lesson one in how to be anonymous. He's probably ringing up the Guinness Book of Records to tell them about us. Biggest breakfast consumption in recorded memory.'

'I don't want to be anonymous.' Euan took her face in his hands. 'I want to shout how wonderful you are from the rooftops.'

'Just make sure it isn't the rooftops in Dorset then.'

And then the phone rang. Both of them looked at it as though it were a tip-off that the Gestapo were on their way to put a jackboot through the door. Connie couldn't bring herself to answer it and Euan reached for it instead. Connie remembered herself just in time and grabbed it. What if it were Gavin? Her face flushed and she felt her heart race at the thought of pretending everything was completely normal. She'd never be any good at lying.

'Hello. Connie Brandon speaking.'

It was only Judith, giving her the details of another interview to be slipped in before she went home.

Connie dressed and packed her bag, knowing that the awful moment approached when they had to say goodbye.

'I thought I might come with you,' Euan insisted, kissing her neck again. 'I've still got plenty of tidying up to do on the catalogue.'

'No, Euan, please.'

The panic in her voice was infectious. Euan had visions of Connie pretending last night had never happened or that it was some meaningless one-night stand. 'When will I see you then?'

'I don't know, Euan. I need to sort things out. To find out why this happened.'

Euan was suddenly angry. 'It happened because we wanted each other and because your marriage is dead, Connie. Face it, all you have in common is your children.'

Connie knew that this wasn't true. Euan wanted it to be true, and it *ought* to have been true, given the way she'd just behaved. Life would be easier if it were true, but the hardest thing she had to face was that it wasn't.

She felt a breath of fear dampening her happiness. If she'd

192

just wanted to have an affair she'd chosen the wrong person in Euan. He wasn't the type to fit neatly into a slot once a fortnight for some abandoned sex because that was what happened to be missing from the rest of her well-ordered life. She saw now that she'd made things a hundred times more complicated for herself because of last night.

'I'll ring you soon,' she promised.

His look softened his next words from a threat into a tease. 'You'd better. Or I might be tempted to ring you.' He headed for the door, then came back one last time to kiss her. 'Look, Connie, I love you. But I'm not prepared to hang round for crumbs from the rich man's table. You're going to have to make up your mind.'

On the train back Connie veered from wild excitement at the thought of Euan's touch to horror at what she'd let herself in for. Was it possible to love more than one man?

It was almost lunchtime when she reached Bidchester and Connie, conscious of not having rung Gavin from the hotel as she should have, decided to call in at the shop.

The window of One World had a forlorn air. Connie had always made a point of changing it every week or two, using different brightly coloured cloths as a backdrop for any spectacular pieces they might have in. When she'd left she'd put in a magnificent Noah's Ark in carved wood from Sri Lanka. Now its brightly painted colours were dusty and fading and a spider's web trailed from one corner of the ark up to the top of the window. Connie studied the rest of the shop, her irritation boiling over. It reminded her of a badly stocked charity shop just after Christmas when the best stuff had all gone.

'Connie, what a surprise!' Margot appeared from the back office carrying a bone china cup of tea with two shortbread biscuits balanced precariously on the side. While the shop had become dowdier, Margot's personal appearance had achieved the opposite. In the dressing stakes Margot had let rip, teaming her usual olive cashmere jumper and pearls with long exotic earrings and an ankle-length Indian skirt. The look was somewhere between upper-class county and rural earth mother. It was not a happy marriage.

Still annoyed. Connie opened her mouth to comment on the window, but Margot got in first.

'I'm really glad you came in because there was something I wanted to raise with you.' Margot's tea slopped over the side and drenched her biscuits. She didn't seem to notice. 'In fact I was going to ring you today, isn't that funny?'

Connie sighed inwardly. This would probably be a half-hour drone about the efficiency of their cleaner, or the vagaries of the computerized till. 'As a matter of fact, Margot. I'm in a bit of a hurry. I just popped in to see Gavin. Do you know where he is?'

'Actually it's about Gavin I wanted to talk to you. I'm really worried about him.'

What on earth could Margot be on about, Connie wondered, but she sat down anyway. 'Go on. What's the problem with Gavin?' She knew her tone was discouraging but it was the best she could do.

Margot hesitated. She was a bumbly old thing, she knew, and she didn't like intruding on personal matters. She was still smarting at the obvious glee with which Connie had abandoned the shop and Margot's own companionship. Maybe she should leave her employers to sort out their own problems and let the business go down the drain. But, no, she was too fond of Gavin and she knew how much he cared about keeping it going.

'He's very worried about the shop, Connie. I found him in here going through the books at eight o'clock this morning. I think he'd seen your accountants and the news wasn't good. He's not himself. No jokes. And he looks like a wet Wednesday. I'm surprised you haven't noticed.' It was as near as Margot ever came to a tart remark.

Exasperation at Margot for blaming her, when part of the responsibility for how awful the shop looked was clearly Gavin and Margot's own, struggled with guilt at how far things seemed to have gone. Maybe Margot was overreacting. 'He hasn't said anything about this to me.'

'No, well . . .' Margot made it sound as though the reason for that was screamingly obvious: Connie's selfish behaviour in going off to work for Victoriana.

'Where is he now?'

'Gone to deliver a set of vine-leaf candlesticks.'

'He shouldn't be doing that. Why couldn't they pick them up?

'I think he was nervous they'd change their mind if he didn't. He feels we can't afford to lose any sales.'

Connie clucked in exasperation. Getting the car out and delivering a sale of a few pounds could hardly be cost effective. Things must have gone downhill lately.

'Sorry, Connie,' Margot cut in on her thoughts. 'I didn't want to speak out of turn. It's just that he's a wonderful man and I hate seeing him like this.'

After she left the shop Connie didn't feel like going to Victoriana any longer. She'd go home and wait for Gavin. She wanted to simply dismiss Margot's revelations but Margot, though irritating, was good-hearted.

Home, when she got there, now seemed to her to share the same sad air as the shop. Busy with the catalogue and her preoccupation with Euan, she hadn't been waving her house-wifely wand with the usual dedication lately – but why should it always be the woman who created the homely atmosphere?

Tara was the first back. 'Good time in London? Did you wow them with your witty quotes?'

'Absolutely. Sit down and have a cup of tea. Tell me what you've been up to lately.' Shaken by Margot's suggestions, Connie wondered if there were things she didn't know about her children too.

Tara smiled at her suspiciously. 'You're very caring suddenly. Is this the Working Mother's Burden striking?'

Connie banged down her Gary Larsen mug. 'That's not fair. I'm always interested in what you're doing. Usually you just won't tell me.'

'Not so interested lately, though, now you're the catalogue queen. Don't slit your wrists, Ma, I think it's brilliant you're enjoying it so much. You do realize, though, you haven't shown this masterpiece of yours to me or Dad?'

It was a shock to admit that Tara was right. She'd so effectively separated her home and working life since she'd left the shop that she'd never even thought of it.

'Have I made you feel terrible?' Tara decided she could get away with putting her feet on the table. 'All manner of goodies follow when the woman of the house feels guilty. I've noticed that with Roz's mum.' Tara blew her a kiss. 'Go on. Don't let us get away with it. Why shouldn't you have your moment of glory. You've worked hard enough for it.'

Tara's generosity was almost too much for Connie to cope with. If she'd behaved like a brat, grasping and rude, just as if Gavin had been grudging or threatened, at least she could have told herself she had a reason for behaving the way she was with Euan. As it was, she couldn't think of a single excuse except that she wanted him wildly, dangerously, selfishly.

'Hello, love,' Gavin said as soon as he got home. 'What was it like being fêted by the glitterati? Still speaking to us humblebums?' He leaned down and kissed her cheek. His was cold and he hadn't shaved that morning.

'I don't think half a page in *Design Weekly* will change my life too much.' She stroked his chin. 'No time to shave this morning?'

'It's the Bob Geldof look.' He was, as Margot had said, looking exhausted. She was amazed that she could have missed it. His wheaty hair hadn't been washed lately either.

'Come on,' she pushed him into the chair next to hers. 'How about a whisky? I'm just about to start supper.'

He held up a tumbler and she poured in three fingers.

'Whoa, steady on, are you trying to get me drunk?' he asked hopefully, the anxiety beginning to clear from his eyes. 'You seem in a good mood. Are we celebrating something?'

To this, Connie had no answer.

In bed the next morning she watched the dawn creeping in and tried to decide what to do. She should give up Euan, that was obvious, but she couldn't. She might resolve to, but she knew as soon as she heard his voice she'd weaken. On the other hand she had to do something, so Connie took the course of action most natural to her. She launched herself, like Joan of Arc with a Brillo pad, at the practical problems surrounding her, starting off with sorting out the shop.

The quickest and most effective change she could make, Connie decided, was to the main display wall. She dashed into the ironmonger's and bought jade and yellow paints and a couple of sponges.

'This looks more like Blue Peter,' commented Gavin. She ignored him. First she painted the wall jade, then sponged it to lighten the effect. The new display shelves were soon yellow with a jade wave design running along the front edge.

They had always tried to tread a fine line between emporium and art gallery but lately One World had been teetering too far towards thrift shop. Connie remembered Lily's description of the Blue Flame Club and she pulled up their old sofa and covered it with a throw, in the glorious red natural dye of Rajasthan. Next, she took Noah out of the window, replaced the faded cloth with another throw, bright blue this time – it was an extravagance but this was an emergency – and put a jewelled horse in the window instead. Then she rearranged what stock they had on the yellow shelving to look elegantly spaced rather than sparse. Even now the shop looked too bare.

'You'll have to go and get some more stuff at the next fair. We've got nothing to sell.'

Gavin looked stricken. 'I'm not sure we can afford it.'

'Surely we can afford some.' Business must be worse than she'd suspected. 'Even if you only spend a few hundred. We've got nothing to sell at the moment, no wonder no one's coming in.' She picked up an ancient broom handle kept for the purpose and directed a spotlight on to the horse where he shone magnificently.

Gavin stood back and looked round him. 'Connie, you're extraordinary.' He stared at her handiwork. 'You've transformed it!' He'd put on the small, goldrimmed glasses he'd just acquired for reading and they gave him the air of an earnest PhD student. Sudden tenderness for her husband overcame her – but would tenderness be enough to protect her from the raw longings Euan had released? She knew he would be waiting to hear from her, probably angrily suspecting her of capitulation to the ordinary and the domestic.

'Why don't I come and revamp it every couple of weeks. Do you think that'd help?'

Gavin took off his glasses and rubbed the bridge of his nose. Connie was appalled to see that he was fighting back emotion. Was this just business worries or did he suspect her affair? She rubbed the red mark on his nose tenderly. How could she behave so badly? No matter how painful it was, she was going to have to break it off with Euan. She put her arms round him: 'Cutting right back on stock isn't the answer you know. Why not go to the trade fair in Bromsbury next week and order some more? We'll pay for it somehow. And take Terri with you.'

Terri was a divorcee friend who ran a similar shop in the Bidchester Galleria. Her weakness for Gavin was a joke between them, mainly because Terri had a pretty face but the body, in Connie's view, of a sumo wrestler. 'Just don't come home with her lipstick on your collar.'

'No,' the old Gavin grinned back, 'I'll make sure it's only on my underpants.'

Both Tara and Jeremy felt relief that the atmosphere in the house seemed to have lightened, though only Tara showed it. 'Dad says you've tarted up the shop brilliantly,' she said. Then, noticing her mother's preoccupation, added, 'You two are all right, aren't you?' There was an edge of anxiety under the cool mock-tough accent. 'You never snog any more, you know.'

Connie burst out laughing at this quaint expression. 'You'd be the first to go Yeucch if we did,' she pointed out. 'And I have been just a tiny bit busy with the catalogue, but I will try and remember to snog. Publicly, just for you.'

'Don't make it too public, I wouldn't want any of my friends to see.'

In the end it was Euan who contacted her. She knew it was him because there was a long accusing silence on the other end of the phone. It either had to be him or a heavy breather.

'Euan, is that you?' she whispered. Fortunately he had at least rung her at the office.

'I can't live like this, Connie,' he said at last. 'I have to see you. I'm coming down.'

Connie reminded herself of all the reasons she shouldn't see him. There were too many to begin to list, but the sound of his voice stole away all her resolve. 'No, I'll come to you. Not this week though, I can't. On Monday. In the afternoon.'

I'm having an affair. Connie hugged the knowledge to her, half-shameful, half-excited, wishing she could share it with someone, knowing that wasn't possible. Lily would disapprove. Since Paul Allan she seemed to have abjured men altogether and with the zeal of the reformed would probably extol the virtues of celibacy. Besides which she adored Gavin. She would think Connie was mad.

In the four days that followed, Connie decided that Lily would be right. She was mad. Why was she putting herself through all this guilt and anguish and risking the happiness of the people she loved most?

On the fifth day she knew the answer.

Euan's flat was in North Kensington. As she searched for it Connie glanced round guiltily, as though she might bump into one of her Dorset neighbours out walking their dog down the seedy end of Ladbroke Grove. Finally she found the right address and plucked up courage to ring the bell.

Euan answered immediately. He was barefoot, in blue jeans. His fair hair was tousled as though he'd just been working and had his mind on other things, she thought jealously. She'd been unable to think of anything but him since they'd made the arrangement. Why are women doomed to make men their whole world, she wondered angrily, while women will only ever be one part of men's?

Without a word he pulled her into the flat and kissed her hungrily, pushing her up against the front door, not even giving her the chance to put down the carrier bag of shopping that had provided her cover for the visit. Before she'd had a chance to say I can't do this, his mouth was on her neck, one arm round her, holding her against the door, the other pulling up her skirt. Connie, respectable and wifely, flung down her carrier bag and began to slide off her coat, arching her back at the pleasure of his touch. They never made it to the bedroom. It was only afterwards as they lay in the hall, their clothes scattered around them, that Connie wondered if their lovemaking had been visible to half the street. Worse than that, she didn't care if it had.

Several days later, she lay in the bath at home contemplating marriage and its limitations. She should, she knew, be eaten up by guilt, but all she could think about was Euan and the feel of his hands roaming over her body. Every time she closed her eyes it was Euan who filled her mind. She knew she was going round grinning like a village idiot and tried as hard as she could to concentrate on the usual props of her life: gym kits and shopping lists, car insurance and dry cleaning. She repeated like a mantra: I have a husband and family I love, I have a husband and family I love.

It was no good. The demands of domesticity had no chance against the powerful magic of Euan's exploring fingers. Even the criticism, valid she knew, that she was a middle-aged woman lost in lust, couldn't penetrate the extraordinary joy of her hours with Euan.

Was it love? God alone knew. To risk so much, it ought to be. In her more rational moments she tried to think through what would happen, but the prospect was too ghastly. There was too much pain and loss, all of it caused by her, pitting the road. She would think about it another time. Today she was going to be happy because she would be seeing him.

She stepped out of the bath and soused herself in body lotion, then dressed with extra care. He was coming to the office so it wouldn't be a meeting of bodies, but just the thought of seeing him made her smile and touch herself. She liked her body better because he liked it so much. He had reclaimed it from motherhood and endowed it with a sensuality she'd never known she had.

When he arrived a few hours later at Victoriana's offices she let none of this show – or so she thought. She treated him with simple friendliness until it was time to go, and then she couldn't let him. She offered to come down to the car park with him, and when he suggested a walk through the beauty of the spring afternoon, she flushed because her mind was jumping ahead to secluded spots where they might make love.

In the end it was just a walk because Connie lost her

nerve. Acting out Tom Jones in the middle of the gentle Dorset valleys was a step too far, so they ran and teased and talked until Connie remembered her promise to Gavin that morning to do the shopping.

'Saved by Safeway,' she laughed. 'It'll always have a new meaning to me.' But he didn't see the joke.

Instead he insisted on dropping her home. Connie, nervous at being seen, was reluctant.

'I'll let you off miles from home. Please.'

She agreed, wanting another few moments of him, just as he wanted them of her, but she felt increasingly nervous the nearer they got. When they were within quarter of a mile Connie began to panic and demanded to be let out.

Jeremy, cycling home, bumped into her just as she was turning into their driveway. 'Hiya, Ma, what are you doing creeping around?'

'I am *not* creeping around,' Connie insisted huffily. 'I got a lift home, that's all.'

Jeremy glanced behind him for the car that had dropped her off, puzzled that it was nowhere in sight, but said nothing.

Connie avoided his glance and pushed open the garden door into the kitchen. Tara sat on the worktop swinging her legs and eating Shreddies from the packet. 'Tut, tut, Ma,' she chided, 'you're in the doghouse. You promised to go shopping and there's nothing for tea. Dad's gone instead. Where on earth were you – meeting a lover?' She laughed uproariously at the absurdity of her little joke, but Connie felt Jeremy's eyes bore accusingly into her back as she opened the fridge and realized how bare it was.

Jeremy couldn't know. She was just imagining it. But the fragile spider's web of her happiness snagged a little on the sharp edges of reality.

Chapter 14

The weeks building up to the launch of the catalogue passed in a blur of activity for Lily. She'd never been busier in her life. Everyone seemed to need her attention and she could suddenly see the attraction of being the mother of a large family. You might be worn out by all the different demands, but it was a deeply satisfying kind of exhaustion.

It also served to distract her from the inescapable fact that this was the moment of truth. All the work she or anyone else had put in depended virtually one hundred per cent on these few glossy pages. If they'd got the look right and the press went for it, the sales could rocket. If they didn't, then Victoriana was seriously in trouble.

Judith was neither happy nor exhausted. She was wound up and angry. Even trying to relax on her Stairmaster didn't work. After so many years spent wooing them, she knew exactly what caught the press's attention, and they were going to gobble up the new Victoriana catalogue. As a story it had everything. A family business that's been a big success story but still kept its personality suddenly loses its guiding force. Everyone predicts disaster when the giddy daughter who knows more about being in the gossip columns than running a business takes over. And then, sod her, she only goes and does it. Changes the image and gives Victoriana a whole new look. They'd lap it up all right. And she had the task of selling ringside seats.

A thought occurred to Judith that made her switch off her machine. If she was in charge of the press launch, then she was in a perfect position to screw it up. Accidentally, of course. She pulled on her sweat shirt and headed for the desk. She stopped for a moment, her pen poised. Could she really sabotage the event that mattered so crucially to Victoriana's future? She didn't owe anything to Lily, Lily had the job *she* deserved, but Charlotte had always been generous to her. On the other hand you could argue that by hastening Lily's departure she would really be doing Charlotte a favour. The draft of the press release only needed the most minor alteration and it could go to be typed and despatched.

Afterwards, she went into the kitchen and squeezed herself some lemons which, spiced with a slice of fresh ginger, were all she ever had for breakfast.

'You look happy,' her husband commented sourly. 'I suppose that means some poor bastard's for it.'

'How on earth did you get so cynical?'

Jonathan went back to the minuscule portion of breakfast he was allowing himself, to try and get fit for summer. 'Through living with you I expect,' he muttered into his muesli, wishing he could get up the nerve to leave her.

Judith tapped him on the head with her newspaper with surprising affection. 'Just be grateful it isn't you.'

By the morning of the launch Lily had never felt so nervous in her life. Not even first nights came close to this. She'd caught herself throwing a coin in the fountain in the shopping mall in Bidchester to make a wish that all would go well. The Bidchester Galleria, she'd had to remind herself severely, was hardly the Fontana di Trevi. It was just that there was so much riding on today.

'Don't worry,' Judith reassured her, 'they'll flock here in their dozens. You see.'

As she helped Judith arrange the chairs in the meeting room looking out over the millstream Lily wondered how many journalists would really come all this way without the powerful lure of Charlotte Brandon's charisma. The press adored Charlotte and Charlotte understood just how to handle them. She knew that they loved the myth she embodied. Her ascent from kitchen to boardroom was to them as important in its way as log cabin to Presidency. It meant anyone could achieve what Charlotte had achieved. Of course, this ignored all the things that made Charlotte different from most people, her determination and superhuman energy, her unique instinct for what her customers wanted, but it made for good copy.

Charlotte, of course, fed the myth brilliantly, telling the journalists tales of how she had struggled, straight out of college, with a baby on her hip, sustained by her dream. Lily's favourite story – which even happened to be true – was about the matchbox full of raisins. In the early struggling years Charlotte had kept this by the phone to bribe whichever baby was crawling around when an important call came through. It had given her five minutes, she said, while the infant in question found out how to open the thing and to eat its way through the booty within. From this Charlotte had evolved the now-famous Five Minute Rule. No phone call to her from anyone at Victoriana was supposed to last more than the legendary five minutes.

Charlotte understood, with far greater mastery than a PR person, that it was little gems like these that the press hungered for, because it made her business, and the odds she had worked against, come alive to the ordinary reader. But Charlotte had refused to say whether she was coming, and even though Lily still desperately wanted her mother's approval, a sliver of Charlotte's own steel had entered into her daughter's soul.

All the changes at Victoriana were down to her, Lily, not her mother. And she wanted to take the credit for them. On the other hand the press might absolutely loathe the collection. They might feel, as Charlotte herself did, that Victoriana should stick to the tried and true, the maidenly image in all its purity. In that case, Lily thought, rather enjoying herself, they would be in for a shock.

They put a catalogue on each seat and checked that there was enough wine. Soon the canapés would arrive – tiny pizzas, mouthwatering little quiches, mini brioches with cheese. Early in her acting career Lily had learned that when you dealt with the press you should never underestimate the importance of the catering. She glanced at her watch. Only five minutes to go. She stationed herself by the huge picture window where she could see any cars arriving and took a deep breath. Where on earth was Connie? Surely she wasn't going to miss the moment they'd all been working towards for so long?

At the back of the room she could see her father and Evie arriving and knew instantly this meant her mother wouldn't be coming.

'Good luck, my love. Your mother sends her good wishes but thought her presence might be limiting for you. This is your day.'

Lily wondered if her father had just made that up to protect her, but it didn't matter. She wasn't going to let Charlotte spoil today.

Evie, a veteran of many a press launch, looked in surprise at all the rows of empty seats. 'Where is everyone? Not like the hounds of the press to miss a piss-up.'

'They'll be here any minute. Judith has been doing the organizing. She's been super efficient.' Lily stifled the small

206

panicky voice that was beginning to start up in her head. Judith smiled brightly.

Finally, Connie arrived with Euan in tow. Lily was slightly surprised to see him, photographers didn't usually show up at events like this, but Euan wasn't a usual photographer. Then she took in the way Euan's hand was holding Connie's elbow. He was guiding her as though he were her husband.

'What about a glass for everyone?' suggested Judith and busied herself with opening a bottle. Lily wandered over to the window again, puzzled. Normally a few press turned up early to get the best seats or an early quote, or simply to gossip with their rivals. In spite of her attempts to keep calm she felt dampness spread across the palms of her hands and wiped them on a napkin.

Come on, she willed them.

'This is ridiculous,' pointed out Evie as the minutes ticked by. 'Are you sure it said eleven on the press release?'

'Absolutely,' Judith insisted. 'Maybe there's some rival event in London. You can never tell what other people are planning. It's one of the risks of a press conference.'

'I would have thought,' Evie drawled, 'it was the PR's job to find out.'

In the end Lily couldn't stand it any longer. She strode over to the phone and called the fashion editor who'd always supported them best. 'Hello there, this is Lily Brandon of Victoriana speaking. We seem to have a bit of confusion over the details of our press launch. Could you look in your diary and tell me what time it's down for?'

There was a long pause as she heard pages being turned. At last the voice came back, 'Hello, Lily. It says here 11 a.m. on the 27th. Okay? I'm looking forward to it.'

After a word or two of thanks, Lily put the phone down. She felt her head pounding horribly. The 27th was in two weeks' time and the catalogues had already been despatched. It was the way of the world that the press were only interested in you when your story was brand new. In a fortnight they would be old news. It was a complete disaster.

'Judith,' Lily rounded on her sister-in-law furiously. She knew how much was at stake today. 'How the hell could this have happened?'

Chapter 15

'I can't understand it. I know it had the right date on it when I gave it to the secretary. The stupid girl must have cocked it up.'

Lily watched her sister-in-law closely. She was either genuinely dismayed or had acting skills which could have got her into RADA. Either way, Lily loathed people who shifted the blame on to others beneath them, especially when the people being blamed weren't there to defend themselves.

'It was your responsibility to check the invitation before it went out. I want a full report on how this could possibly have happened.' Reluctantly Judith stood up. 'And, Judith. I'll be talking to the girl who did the typing myself.'

They glared at each other, Judith's cool blue eyes locked into Lily's tawny brown. 'Are you implying I'd try and cover up my own inefficiency?' demanded Judith.

'As long as it *is* only inefficiency.'

Judith's eyes narrowed. She swished angrily out of the room, her ivory Chanel slingbacks tapping on the empty parquet floor which should have been covered with a milling crowd of journalists.

'She did it deliberately,' hissed Evie, popping a tiny

quiche into her mouth, 'you'd better watch that one. She's more of a Venus fly-trap than an English bloody rose if you ask me.'

'But why should she want to sabotage our press launch?'

'I'm amazed after all your years in the theatre that you haven't learned by now. Some people want you to fail.' She gestured round with her wine-glass to the sad sight of empty rows of seats and uneaten canapés. 'What are you going to do now?'

Lily found everyone looking at her. They all expected her to have an answer. This was the moment for decisiveness.

'I'm going to call another press conference in three days' time.'

'But will people come at such short notice?'

'They'll have to. In two weeks they'll have lost interest. We'll just have to find a way of luring them down here, though God knows how.'

'I know,' Connie chipped in, 'we could have a fashion show with all the clothes in the catalogue.'

'In three days' time?' Lily sounded unconvinced. 'Won't they expect something incredibly professional? These are fashion writers, used to covering Paris and Rome. This is deepest Dorset.'

But her brain had already begun to race ahead. 'We could make a virtue of that, though. I know, why don't we bill it as a family affair? Use Tara and her friends as models – clothes look best on skinny fifteen-year-olds anyway – and get Jeremy to do the music. I'm sure Ma would promise to come just to give it an extra appeal, wouldn't she, Pa?'

'Of course she will,' Evie insisted, not waiting for Edward to answer. 'It'll be fun.' Evie clearly loved a crisis. 'We did loads of shows from the shop in Sydney. No probs.'

'I'll muck in,' offered Euan. 'I've photographed enough of the bloody things. I ought to know what's involved by now.'

While Evie and Euan set about collecting garments and anyone attractive enough and thin enough who worked for Victoriana to model them, Lily rounded up half a dozen girls from the orders section to help them make phone calls and fax a new press release to all the fashion and features editors. She would have to concoct some intriguing explanation that would catch the editors' imagination.

'I know,' suggested Evie, her earrings clanking against her glass in excitement, 'tell them spies have been trying to steal the new collection because it's so hot, so you've decided to launch it sooner than planned!'

'Done!'

Even as she sent the new release off, Lily sensed a delicious feeling of excitement which, if it communicated itself to the press, would have them falling over each other to get here. At least she hoped so.

Then she went to look for the secretary who had typed out Judith's original release. It was interesting in itself that Judith hadn't asked the girl who usually did her typing, but an inexperienced new recruit who was fresh out of college and flattered to be asked. Today she was almost in tears because of the dressing down she'd just had from Judith.

'I'm *sure* I wouldn't have put the wrong date. We were told at college to check everything we've typed and I did.'

Lily could believe it. The girl had only graduated a couple of months ago and Lily could remember from her acting training that at that stage you still did every single thing your teachers had told you, right down to going to the loo and making sure your hair was tidy.

'Was it on dictaphone?'

'That's why I remember it. Most of our work is on cassette but this was handwritten.'

'I don't suppose you kept it?'

The girl shook her head miserably.

'Oh well, never mind. We're not blaming you.'

'Mrs Brandon Junior is. She said the whole launch was wrecked because of me. That I might lose my job.'

What a bitch Judith was. 'Of course you're not about to lose your job. I gather you're doing very well.' The youngster looked as though she might lie down at Lily's feet like a faithful Labrador reprieved from its last journey to the vet.

There was no way Lily could prove that Judith had deliberately sabotaged the press conference and she could hardly come out and accuse her brother's wife unless she had powerful evidence against her. But that didn't mean she had to trust her in future with anything more important than giving the press a laundry list. She'd make any important announcements herself.

Back in her office, everything was mayhem. Euan seemed to have commandeered her desk and phone and was haranguing a well-known marquee supplier. When the man wouldn't come down to Euan's price he decided to do it himself via duckboards and a firm that did tents for agricultural auctions at a third of the price.

'But how on earth are we going to make it look presentable?' demanded Connie, panicking.

'And this is from the woman who could make an outside toilet into a work of art if she put her mind to it. What happened to all those stooks of corn you collected for the Bathsheba shoot?'

Connie clapped her hands. He was right, they'd be perfect. She could just tie big bows on the front and hang agricultural implements everywhere. There was even a trendy London florist who specialized in decor like that and charged people an arm and a leg.

'You're a genius,' she congratulated him.

'I only thought of it. You've got to do it.'

'Easy.' She turned to Lily. 'What about Ma, have you asked her yet? We're telling everyone she's coming.'

'I'd better go and see her then,' said Lily, dreading it.

When Lily found her, Charlotte was writing letters in the summer house which, like George Bernard Shaw's, could be moved around to follow the path of the sun. It was bright and cold, but Charlotte loved this view down over the valley towards the sea so intensely that she sat here in all weathers, wrapped in coats and blankets.

'My dear Lily,' she insisted when Lily explained what they needed her to do, 'I've handed the company over to you and you've produced a catalogue that's very different from my own taste.' *You mean you hate it*, Lily wanted to blurt, *go on, say it*. 'So what possible advantage would there be in my presence?'

'Look, Ma, this is an emergency. If we don't do something dramatic we'll never get anyone to come.' Lily suddenly heard the echoes of herself as a little girl, always feeling that there was something she'd done to offend her mother but never even knowing what. Lily cast around for some argument that would convince her. 'The press adore you, Ma. Victoriana will always be you in their eyes.'

'No, Lily. This version of Victoriana is *your* idea. I hope it all goes very well.'

In desperation Lily blurted out, 'Please, Ma. Judith's nearly sabotaged the whole thing. We can't let her get away with it. You have to help. *You* gave her the job.'

'Lily, what are you talking about?'

'She was in charge of the invitations for yesterday. They all had the wrong date on them.'

'I'm sure it was an honest mistake.' Lily almost laughed out loud. Under Charlotte's regime anyone making such an 'honest mistake' would have been out in five minutes. Lily was the one who was the old softie, who couldn't bring herself to fire her own sister-in-law. Her mother, however,

213

could be infinitely stubborn if she chose and there didn't seem to be much point pushing her any further now. Maybe if she were left alone she'd come round.

Evie, however, was less patient. After an exhausting day trying garments on the would-be models, pinning them and giving them lessons in how to sell the clothes not themselves, Evie wasn't in the best of moods. In fact her family back home would have identified it as her 'taking no sodding stick from you lot' mode, a reasonably common occurrence where Evie was concerned.

'You do realize, sister dear,' her voice grated with annoyance, 'how much is riding on this for Lily?'

'Of course I do.' Charlotte was equally impatient. What did Evie know about it anyway? 'I just don't think my presence would help. What am I supposed to say when nosy journalists ask me if I like the collection. Lie?'

'It wouldn't be the first time, Charlotte, would it?' Evie came up very close to her sister and gripped her arm hard. 'You've lied to Lily about some pretty fundamental issues. It wouldn't kill you to tell a mere few lies now, for her benefit.'

Charlotte wrenched her arm free, staring at the red mark which was already subsiding into the yellow and blue of a bruise on her delicate skin.

'We're pretty uncivilized in Oz. We have some pretty outlandish beliefs. Like blood being thicker than bile. She needs you, Charlotte.'

Chapter 16

Half an hour before the show's appointed time they were all still running round crazily and Lily was beginning to lose her nerve. What if no one came after all?

But people did come. They came in their dozens, lured by the sense of excitement laced with skulduggery that the sudden new invitations had contained, until there was no little gold seat left unoccupied. Being townies to a woman, they adored the decor with its theme of agricultural work through the seasons. It's amazing what you can do with a few rakes when you put your mind to it, Connie confessed later. She had left a tiny basket filled with early strawberries on each seat and the sophisticated fashion journalists, more used to free samples of designer perfume and wildly expensive cosmetics, were enchanted.

And they loved the show. Under Evie's skilled direction it tiptoed its precarious way between a real family party and a properly organized catwalk event, never once descending into amateurishness or farce. Lily, watching from the wings, had almost cried with pride as Tara stomped on, wearing their own designs. Shauna Robinson came behind her, her long pre-Raphaelite hair trailing and floating to the wild haunting music which Jeremy had put together from

215

English folk tunes, played by himself and his friend Bazza on their electric guitars. When they'd finished the crowd clapped for ten minutes.

Euan pushed Lily and Connie on to the duckboard stage for another round of applause. Lily had to bite back tears of relief and gratitude that they'd headed off the looming disaster. Then she saw her mother slip in at the back and her heart leapt. She wanted to summon Charlotte up to the platform to share her joy, but a small voice warned her to leave things to lie. It was enough that her mother was here at all.

A buzz of excitement spread through the tent as the fashion writers checked out each other's reactions and angles. Lily looked round for something to use to tap her glass and get the attention of the assembled crowd. Evie appeared beside her proffering a fork: 'Always carry one in my handbag,' she said. 'Nothing like it to shut the buggers up.'

Lily tapped her glass. 'Ladies and gentlemen, thank you for coming. The most important thanks are to my sister, Constance. She has been a powerhouse of talent. The inspiration behind the shooting of the catalogue is really hers. And my niece, Tara, is only fifteen but modelled today with such style and panache that I'd watch out if I were you, Naomi Campbell. We're all incredibly proud of her. My aunt, Eve Brandon, produced the show and my nephew Jeremy, did the music. And, of course, none of this would be possible without the genius of my mother, Charlotte Brandon. A truly family affair! Now, help yourselves to a drink and if there's anything we can do to help, we'd be delighted.'

All of them were in demand afterwards as each journalist tried to find a different angle from the others. Even Evie was being pinned down in the corner by an Australian writer who had fallen upon her with delight.

So far so good, thought Lily, as the first of them began to head back to London. The new look seemed to have gone down well, but they wouldn't know till they saw next week's papers.

'Congratulations, darling, that was brilliantly handled,' said Edward. 'Ma says so too. She's slipped off quietly.' Lily nodded, understanding that her mother hadn't wanted to meet too many of the press. Her appearance here at all was what mattered.

Since almost all the guests had departed, Lily flung herself into her father's arms. 'Do you think she liked it?' She knew the question was unanswerable, but couldn't help asking. Finally, she allowed herself a glass of champagne and was just about to drink it.

'Tell me, Lily dear,' a voice behind her asked, and Lily turned to find one of the sharpest women's features editors, standing behind her, 'why didn't your mother join you on stage? We all longed to see Charlotte basking in her daughter's reflected glory.' Next to Lily her father stiffened like a cat and she had to hold on to his hand to stop him reacting. 'If it were my daughter I'd be dying with pride. Not a rift, I hope, between mother and daughter over these gorgeous sexy clothes?'

There was no holding Edward, despite Lily's warning pressure on his hand. 'My wife, if you remember, had a heart attack not long ago. Naturally she wanted to be here, but she slipped away before all the fuss. She can't cope with crowds these days.'

'How sad,' purred the frightful woman. 'And she used to love crowds so much. Especially when they'd come to see *her*.'

Lily spent the next few days biting her nails. Would they get the coverage they desperately needed, or be pushed off the page by some new designer telling people to wear their underwear on the outside?

In the event she needn't have worried. Almost every fashion editor immediately saw that a sexy look for

Victoriana was a great story. Victoriana clothes were featured in double page spreads everywhere; the Bathsheba look was suddenly how everyone wanted to dress and the clothes were given the highest accolade of being immediately copied by the High Street chainstores. But no one got the look quite right except Victoriana.

'Come here, Tara,' Lily gasped as they pored over the papers, 'there's our frock and see who's modelling it!'

The paper in question had cleverly dressed Stark, the female pop idol of the moment, in Tara's outfit. She had worn it just as Tara had done with a skinny-rib teeshirt underneath and ivory-coloured lace up boots, so heavy they wouldn't have disgraced a navvy. She stood gazing out at the camera with one finger in her mouth, jailbait personified.

'Wow!' Tara's eyes widened in astonishment, 'Stark wearing my outfit! And it looks great! Wait till I show them all at school!'

'Yes!' Lily shuddered slightly at the blatant sexuality of the way the girl was modelling it. 'I don't think we'll show that article to Charlotte, do you?'

'No fear,' Tara agreed, 'she'd start recalling all the frocks, saying they were a safety hazard.'

'If you wear them like that they probably are,' chipped in Connie. 'That one's three sizes too small.'

'That's how you're supposed to wear it, Ma. They're not supposed to flap around like a marquee. I think she looks wicked.'

On that at least they all agreed.

If Lily had ever doubted the power of the press, she now saw its effects dramatically demonstrated. Everyone seemed to want a Victoriana outfit and they wanted it *now*.

The spin-off on morale among everyone working for them was equally dramatic. Where the staff had been prepared to shoulder adversity with Lily and Connie, they now felt they were sharing the triumph. Every day the atmosphere at

Victoriana was partylike, with people bringing in cakes and streamers.

Paul Allan wasn't much of a reader of the fashion pages, but he couldn't fail to notice the barrage of publicity for Victoriana's new catalogue. He stopped at the kiosk by Tower Bridge and bought a selection of tabloids, upmarket papers and magazines. He spread them over his desk, amazed that every single one featured Victoriana, and settled down to read a half page interview with Lily.

Afterwards he studied the photographs of her, taking in the fall of her long hair, the red wrap dress in shot silk which accentuated her body, and the high heels in mulberry suede. He'd never seen her in high heels before. They changed the shape of her leg, pushing her calves into a pronounced curve which he found wildly alluring. In one picture she was sitting on the edge of her chair with her skirt split above the knee, hinting at hidden delights. Telling himself that it was purely for business purposes, he carefully cut out the photograph and slipped it into the pocket of his briefcase.

He tried to devote himself to the mountain of work that beckoned to him but it was no use. Lily's silk-wrapped body came into his mind each time he tried to ban it. Finally, although he knew that he was probably inviting rejection again, he couldn't resist ringing her.

'It's nice of you to call,' Lily said when he got through. She almost added: after all this time, but made herself resist. She'd been through all that and she was over it. For weeks after their last meeting she'd longed for this call even though she'd been the one to do the rejecting. By now she'd had time to rebuild her defences.

'I've been reading about you everywhere. I just wanted to offer my congratulations. You've obviously done a brilliant job.'

'Thanks largely to my sister and a very talented photographer.' Despite herself she felt a leap of excitement at his voice. Lily was feeling wildly happy with the world and why shouldn't he be a beneficiary? Besides, he sounded genuinely pleased for her. 'The coverage has been rather extraordinary hasn't it? No earthquakes in Brazil this week, I suppose.'

'You shouldn't be so modest.'

'I don't feel modest. I feel absolutely bloody brilliant!' It was the truth, she realized. 'I just don't like show-offs, it's different. Anyway,' she couldn't resist adding, 'you must be pleased to see your investment isn't going down the drain after all.'

Paul was nettled. 'I never thought it would be, but as a matter of fact this isn't a business call.' He took a deep breath, rushing his words slightly and hating himself for it. 'Actually I wondered if I could take you out to dinner to celebrate. We needn't mention Victoriana.'

Lily laughed at the impracticality of this plan but said Yes all the same. She felt like celebrating. She felt like being taken out to a cityfied, prettified meal in a ludicrously expensive restaurant. 'That would be lovely.'

'Really?'

'Would you rather I refused?' Lily suddenly felt powerful, desired.

'Just try. Shall I come down to you?'

'Certainly not. All the restaurants round here are far too cheap.'

'I'd better think of somewhere special then.'

'Absolutely. I'm not being fobbed off with fish and chips again.'

This time he took her to a tiny restaurant in Primrose Hill and it was everything Lily could have wished for. Romantic, delicious and wildly expensive. Knowing what might be for dessert, Lily was surprised she hadn't lost her appetite but the food was far too tempting and Paul clearly enjoyed watching her eat.

'Go on, have another petit four,' he teased since she'd demolished both her share and his. 'There's one you seem to have missed.'

After the meal they walked in the park, both aware of the possibilities ahead, but putting off the moment because the anticipation was so incredibly delicious. Suddenly they couldn't wait any longer. Paul grabbed her hand and they ran like children the quarter mile back to Regent's Park to find a taxi. Half an hour later they were in his flat.

'How's the wine cooler? Did it work?' Lily asked, knowing she was filling the shy silence that had fallen between them.

'I've no idea.' Paul's eyes burned into hers. 'I had my mind on other things.' He leaned forward and slipped down the strap of her black cocktail dress from each shoulder in turn. Lily did her bit by reaching behind her and pulling down the zip so that the dress fell enticingly around her hips.

'God, you're gorgeous,' he murmured before his mouth was too busy doing other things to speak any more.

The next day Lily woke up feeling unbearably smug. She'd done it. She'd found a man who made her laugh, turned her on and who was, unless he had the lying capacities of Bluebeard, single. It was utterly wonderful. There was still the small complication of their business relationship but maybe she'd got that out of proportion.

At nine, after breakfast in a nearby café, he announced it was time for work.

'You're not going off to the office after a night of matchless passion surely? Aren't you going to luxuriate a little?'

'I have. Normally I go in at seven.'

'Revolting yuppie. So when will I see you?' Confidence, warming and unfamiliar, oozed through her.

'This weekend?'

'Absolutely. There's a little pub I know.'

Paul laughed. 'There's always a little pub you know.'

'Too true.' Lily agreed sadly. 'You might as well know the truth. You've fallen for an old soak. You can withdraw now.'

'I love old soaks. As long as they're buying.'

'Anyway, it might be more tactful now that I live above the shop.'

He ran his fingers through her long red hair, knowing there was something he ought to tell her. He'd decided, for both their sakes, to hand the day-to-day decisions for Victoriana over to Clive Green. He could still keep a fatherly eye on the arrangements, but it would at least give them both a little distance in which he hoped their relationship might flourish. He couldn't risk losing her again because of their business entanglement.

He wasn't absolutely sure how she would take it, though. She was so sensitive when it came to Victoriana, and he didn't want to spoil this glorious, magical moment.

Chapter 17

'How are things going, June?' Lily hardly needed to ask. The rows of computer terminals on the ground floor of the Mill were flashing like demented Belisha beacons. Fingers raced across keyboards, hardly able to keep up with the sudden surge in demand and there was a delicious hubbub of female voices asking for names, addresses and credit card numbers. It was the most glorious sound Lily had heard in her life.

'Amazing!' June grinned with delight. 'Thank God we've got the computers or we'd never be able to cope.'

Lily's lips twitched at the memory, only a few short months ago, of June's technophobia. 'What's moving fastest?'

'Tara's little frock, I'd say. What do you think, girls?' Those that could nodded or raised their thumbs.

'It must be something to do with the way it was modelled,' June teased, 'either by Shauna here or that popstar. Anyway they're walking out of the place.'

'What about the dreaded camisoles? Is anyone buying my white silk elephants?'

'A few.' June said tactfully and tapped the keyboard with the air of a lifelong computer whiz. 'Six actually.'

'Sod the things,' Lily swore cheerfully, refusing to be cast down. 'Everything else is going brilliantly.' She felt a low glow of satisfaction and hoped that Susie stuck-up McIntosh had noted the success of the little dress. I must make a point of telling Tara when I go back, she thought.

Down in the warehouse Brian, the manager, was beaming. Here they had stuck to the old method of filling wire baskets with each order, taken from vast racks of hanging clothes or from shelves if they were small items. The process was still done by hand as each order needed to be checked before it went down to the packing department.

After so much tension it was hard to contain her excitement. She wanted to go and tell Charlotte, to boast immoderately, to say: There now, I could do it after all, couldn't I?

Instead she went back upstairs and dragged Connie off to lunch at Bidchester's only Greek restaurant, where the food was awful but the atmosphere unfailingly joyous and holidaylike. Connie deserved a celebration too. In fact, the way Lily was feeling this morning, she felt like giving everyone the day off. Maybe if things went well, she might even get a real holiday before too long. She closed her eyes and imagined Crete in May, before the tourists arrived, the sky a disgraceful blue, goats leaping, wild flowers running riot, the taste of ouzo on your tongue and the warmth on your back. For some reason Paul Allan, lying on a beachtowel for two, also featured in this fantasy.

'We've done it, Con.' Lily clinked her glass against her sister's. 'We've actually bloody well gone and done it!' She didn't let on, though, that with all the superstition of fifteen years in the acting profession, she was crossing her fingers under the table as she said it. 'Here's to making Victoriana a real success again!'

'You seem in an amazingly good mood. Your fairy godmother didn't happen to leave you a hunk in the gooseberry bushes, did she?'

'Connie,' Lily announced pompously, not wanting to admit to having let Paul back into her life, 'it is possible to be happy without it being anything to do with a man.'

'Oh yes? Just remind me how.'

Now that the catalogue was safely launched, Connie's role would soon officially be over and she could pick up the strands of her old life. Connie suddenly saw how scared she was of that.

After the celebration lunch she drove home through the glory of the late spring afternoon. The apple blossom was still out, palest pink and fragrant, mingling with the faintest scent of honeysuckle. The hedgerows, or at least those remaining, were garlanded with it. The hot weather of the last few days had brought out the first roses and the villages she drove through struck her as almost comic in their perfection. This was how England was supposed to look but rarely did.

Her family needed her. Gavin needed her, the shop needed her. Connie detected in herself a desire not to go home, a feeling so unfamiliar that she didn't at first admit to it.

Tara pounced on her even before she'd had time to put down her bag. 'There's no sliced bread. Ma. What am I going to do for sandwiches tomorrow?'

'You could eat pitta.' Connie might have laughed at the Marie Antoinette overtones if she hadn't felt so overwhelmingly angry. 'Or you could take yourself off to the shop.'

'What about homework?'

'That's not usually much of a priority unless you want to get out of something. Really, Tara, I'm not your servant.'

Tara's eyes glinted with teenage resentment. 'I suppose you're too high-powered to bother with cooking for us now.'

Connie felt the temptation to strike out. This was nothing to do with being high-powered, or busy, or getting above herself. It was just that she'd begun to feel fiercely resentful at all this dependency. Yet, how could Tara know that, when only a few months ago Connie had treasured it? Being the hub of her family had seemed to give life meaning. Now it was grating against her desire for freedom. It wasn't Tara who had changed. It was her; and the thing that had changed her was meeting Euan.

How could men carry it off, she asked herself angrily? How could thousands of husbands start an affair, determined that it wouldn't affect their marriage, and it wouldn't. They might be a bit bad tempered with their kids, annoyed at their wives' obsession with trivia, but they could compartmentalize their two lives perfectly adequately. Yet she couldn't. Her obsession with Euan was seeping into everything, soiling the clean white linen of her old life. When she tried to force it back to normal through the old familiar tasks she'd once enjoyed, all she could feel was the memory of his mouth on her breast or his hand slipping between her legs and she had to give up the unequal fight.

A thudding sound brought her back to reality. Jeremy had just wheeled his mountain bike into the hall and toppled the neat row of wellingtons there. 'Jeremy,' she heard herself scream, 'be more careful, can't you, you stupid boy? You're forever crashing into things.'

Jeremy leaned his bike against the wall and began sorting out the boots with great precision, refusing to look at Connie. She watched him, a wave of guilt washing over her. She shouldn't be taking things out on him. He was at an awkward age, no longer a boy, not quite a man, towering above her physically but still unsure of himself. She remembered how Charlotte had called Lily clumsy at his age and how Lily had hated it.

As Jeremy pushed past her to get to his bedroom she caught the look of accusation in his eyes, and an expression almost of disgust, far beyond anything the immediate circumstances could warrant.

She reached out to touch him, remembering how he had always made a point of bumping into her, still wanting physical contact though he was too old for cuddles. He shrugged her off roughly and ran upstairs, three at a time, desperate suddenly to get away from her. She wondered if he was just discovering sex himself. Most boys of his age already had, but Jeremy was different, dreamier, less confident. Could it be that he was searching for his sexuality just when she was so gloriously indulging hers? She pushed from her mind the effect this might have on him, but it crept insistently back.

'Damn and blast it!' She kicked the pile of wellingtons Jeremy had so neatly aligned so that they scattered satisfyingly along the hall.

'Morning, Miss Brandon.' Mr Seacroft, whose family had run the greengrocer's in Darcombe for three generations, spun his boater, a party trick of his Lily remembered from childhood. 'Congratulations. I gather things are fairly humming over at the Mill.'

'Pretty busy,' Lily agreed, smiling and choosing herself some early strawberries for Paul's visit. They were never as sweet in early summer as they would be in July or August but she'd take a chance.

'Your family's always done us proud, keeping jobs round here.' He selected a shiny red apple and presented it to her as if she were Snow White. 'Them ones are lovely. French,' he almost spat the word, 'but lovely all the same.' Mr Seacroft sounded desolated to have to admit that anything French could be superior, but he was an honest man.

'I'll have it with my lunch. It looks like it came from the garden of Eden.'

'I do hope not, Miss Brandon. We haven't finished paying for the last one yet.'

Lily continued down the village street, nodding at passers-by. Was she imagining it, or was everyone being extra friendly? It was almost like one of those black-and-white pre-war comedies where everyone was cheerful and knew their place.

Lily was glad she'd left the car and walked into the village. It was too beautiful a day to be cooped up in a car. She felt incredibly lucky. How many company directors could stroll to their jobs with the sun burning into their backs, the goodwill of the local citizenry propelling them along, knowing that their office, when they reached it, was a gem of an old mill, set in the rolling acres of Dorset?

Hi ho, hi ho, it's off to work I go, she hummed, thinking of her Snow White apple.

Outside the Sunne in Splendour, a smart, shiny four-wheel drive disgorged a family of trendy Londoners. Lily bit her lip with pleasure. The mother and daughter were both wearing Victoriana dresses. She felt so thrilled she almost dashed up and told them. The pair stood for a moment, leaning against the car, getting their bearings. The mother, in her early sixties, wound her arm through her daughter's as they consulted a map. The easy affection of the gesture grabbed at Lily's heart. If only *her* mother felt towards her like that! The old longing she hoped she'd conquered bit into her. I almost hate you, Ma, she thought, but she knew that hate would have been easier than what she really felt: a painful, dry, bitter thirst for love.

June winked at her as she walked through the orders section on the way up to her sunny office. The explanation was waiting for her on her desk. It was the biggest bouquet of flowers she'd ever seen: deep blue delphiniums, pink and white larkspur, Canterbury bells, lilies, all tied up in a fat blue bow; country flowers, all of them, with no showy hothouse blooms to jar the senses. She breathed in the scent of the lilies and tore open the card.

This time they were indeed from Paul. It was almost as though at that precise moment he'd known she needed cheering up.

Don't be ridiculous, dumbo, she told herself, but she felt better all the same.

She was just fantasizing about a rather adventurous way of thanking him when June burst into the room. 'Lily, you've got to come downstairs.' Lily had never seen June look so agitated. 'It's the computers. The system seems to have seized up or something. We're all going mad, tearing our hair out. Orders are flooding in and all we can get are blank screens.'

Lily refused to let herself panic. There had to be some simple explanation for this. 'Have you called in the people who installed them? I'm sure they'll sort this out in no time.'

The scene downstairs, Lily had to admit, was awful. Of the rows of terminals only four were processing orders. The other girls sat in front of blank screens, powerless to deal with the orders that were pouring in. With the unprecedented demand the system had overloaded and crashed.

'Can't they take the orders manually?' Lily demanded anxiously as they waited for the engineer to arrive.

June shook her head. 'We've looked into that. The real problem is that we've been phoning orders through all day and only some of them have got through to the warehouse. We don't know which orders are being processed and which aren't.'

'So when will we know?'

'Only when people ring up to complain that they haven't received their goods.'

'God, what a week.' Lily's stomach churned as the implications of this hit her. They'd spent a fortune on this system and being able to meet their next payment to First Venture depended on an increased turnover of orders. It *had* to work. They *had* to be able to put more orders through and work out which ones it had already processed.

''Fraid not, love,' the engineer informed her with patronizing cheerfulness when he arrived. 'This system could never have dealt with a load like this. Whoever told you it could?'

'Your sales people,' Lily blazed, not admitting that even she hadn't anticipated quite this level of demand.

The man clammed up then and Lily could have kicked herself. The more she could prise out of the engineer, proving that the system could never have coped, the more ammunition she had to force the company to sort it out.

'What's the maximum number of orders it can deal with then?'

'Five hundred a day? Eight at a pinch, with some more software.'

'But that's crazy,' shouted Lily. 'We need it to handle three times that. That's why we got it in the first place. Surely we can just get some more terminals or something?'

He looked at her as though she were a rather backward toddler. 'It's nothing to do with the number of terminals. It's the operating system. It just can't process that number of orders. You need a bigger system.'

'How much would that cost?'

He drew in his breath sharply. 'Hundreds of thousands.'

'But surely there must be some gizmo we can bump it up with so it can cope.'

'I'll try,' he conceded, 'but I can't promise anything. You should have told us you anticipated this level of demand.'

'I had no idea. None of us did.'

'Nice problem to have, too many orders. A lot of companies would swap places with you.'

Lily could have cheerfully hit him with his little black diagnostic box. She imagined the customers at home, sending in their cheques and looking forward to receiving their new clothes while they were still young enough to wear them – and not getting them. 'Not if your bloody computer can't put through the bloody orders, it isn't.' The engineer shook his head. He liked a lady to behave like one.

By the end of the day, Lily was in despair. The horrible patronizing service engineer had been right. Their new system hadn't a hope in hell of servicing the number of orders the press coverage had brought in its wake. Willing herself not to think about all the orders piling uselessly up, Lily slipped away to her office feeling sick and shaky. This was her fault again. She should have checked that the system could deal with this level of demand. It was typical of her, always rushing headlong into things she didn't really understand, thrilled with her capacity to be bold and imaginative.

Brian Hutchings, the Byronic warehouse manager, caught her just as she was phoning frantically round for a second opinion. 'Miss Brandon, we've run out of that pinafore dress, the one that's been so popular.'

'We can't have.' Lily couldn't cope with any new problems. 'We had five thousand of them.'

'We're down to the last couple of dozen, I thought you'd like to know.' Lily willed herself to see this as good news. At least some orders were getting through. But her optimism didn't last long. She dialled the manufacturers to order some more, but they were desolated, they had no more of that cloth. They'd have to reorder from Brussels and it might take weeks. Lily dropped her head in her hands. She'd heard of things like this happening, but never quite believed it. They were the victim of their own success.

When there was a knock on the door, she actually jumped in her skin. It was an ominously smiling Susie McIntosh. 'I don't want to be a party pooper,' – she clearly did – 'but I thought you'd want to see this week's post.' She handed a large batch of letters to Lily with barely concealed delight. They dripped with middle-class vitriol. In changing Victoriana's image, Lily had put herself on a par with moving the Shipping Forecast or modernising *The Archers*. From the howls of anger, you'd have thought the collection had gone from creations in cotton lawn to surgical rubber. She half expected to see letters about it in *The Times*.

For comfort she turned to the bouquet of flowers, but she had forgotten to put them in water and they were already drooping. It was one stupidity too much for Lily. A sense of failure reverberated through her. She covered her face with her hands, blocking out the sight of her office, the flowers, everything. As she did so, she caught sight of her forearm, bare under a loose sleeve. It was her mother's arm, exactly reproduced in every detail, from the bony wrist to the light sprinkling of freckles that came with the first summer sun. Even the way the skin folded when she twisted it was so exactly like Charlotte's it was uncanny. If she was her mother's daughter in this way, why didn't she share her mother's steely determination, that intensity of purpose and capacity for believing in herself that had propelled Victoriana from a tiny company into a highly successful one that everyone had heard of? Now, just as everyone was no doubt expecting, Lily was wrecking it. She knew it was cowardly to wish her father hadn't put her in charge, but she found herself wishing it all the same.

It was Shauna Robinson who turned out to be Lily's unlikely rescuer. She knocked on Lily's door, carrying a cup of coffee, announcing that she'd come to offer any help on behalf of the girls downstairs. 'We thought maybe we could put some orders through by hand, like the old days. June's thrown away the forms but I've made a few up we could try for now.'

A lump came to Lily's throat. If an eighteen-year-old girl could think of positive action what the hell was she doing wilting like an overblown tulip. 'Thank you, Shauna, and to all of you. It's definitely worth a try.' She didn't add that according to the engineer two and a half thousand orders were coming in a day and the system was processing only five hundred, that their best-selling line had just run out of cloth, and that letters were flooding in from their staunch fans saying how much they hated Victoriana's new look. 'Thank you, Shauna,' Lily hoped she sounded as encouraging as a boss could, 'that's a brilliant suggestion.'

Shamed into action by Shauna's initiative, Lily summoned George and his calculator. It would be better to know the worst. Their next payment was due soon and she'd better start trying to do something about it.

'George, hi,' Lily tried to jolly them both into better spirits, 'come and pull up a deckchair on the *Titanic*.'

But he didn't laugh.

'How serious is it?' she asked quietly.

George, his starched shirt collar cutting into his neck, reddened at having to be the one who brought her such bad news. He would have given anything to fudge the truth, but giving her false hope would hardly help her. 'Disastrous would be a better word. We were relying on the increased sales to pay back the loan. Until we can get our hands on those orders we're in real trouble.'

He shuffled the printout of their cash flow he'd brought in with him and avoided her eye. He didn't want to show her the depression he was feeling. She could do without that on top of everything else she had to cope with. 'I'm afraid if we don't get it sorted out, we aren't going to be able to pay the next instalment to First Venture. It's double this time, remember.'

Remember! How could she forget for a single second?

'And if we don't meet the payment?'

George couldn't even bring himself to spell it out, but they both knew the implications.

Chapter 18

Bankruptcy. The Dickensian word, with its shadows of the workhouse and debtors' prison, kicked at Lily in the pit of her stomach. She'd always seen it as somehow sleazy, something that happened to crooks who intended to lose their bad debts and start again tomorrow under another name, or incompetents with a no-hoper of an idea, or megalomaniacs who over-reached themselves in property – but never Victoriana. Victoriana that had been her mother's favoured child for thirty-five years – and in less than a year, Lily had brought it to the brink of disaster. Thank God Paul was coming tonight. She would just have to tell him the truth and see what he recommended.

By the time she picked him up at the station she was feeling calmer but he knew at once that something was wrong.

'I'm frightened, Paul.' Lily hated admitting the truth, to him of all people, but had an instinct that he wouldn't hold it against her professionally. 'I seem to have nothing but problems.'

Ignobly, Paul looked at her huge troubled eyes and longed to get her to bed as quickly as was decently possible, but he reminded himself sternly that putting his hand down her dress wasn't what she needed at the moment. She needed a strategy for survival. 'How likely is it you can meet the next payment?'

'What are the odds on winning the lottery?'

'That bad? Okay, you're going to have to raise cash quickly. Have you got anything you could sell straight away? A piece of machinery, a lorry? Some stock you could sell off fast?'

Lily thought of the silk camisoles, another of her stupid mistakes, but how could she sell those unless she set up a market stall of her own. Lily's Lingerie. At least it had a ring to it. She shook her head. 'George and I have been through it all.'

'That leaves property which would take too long, and people. You're going to have to lay staff off.'

'Paul, I can't. The reason my parents never wanted to sell was to save jobs.'

'You may have to. First Venture won't let you off the hook this time. You could lose everything. What would your mother think about that?'

With Paul's help they came up with a package of measures which would keep Victoriana afloat – for the moment. 'I'm really grateful to you for coming. I think I'd have gone mad if you hadn't.'

'No you wouldn't,' Paul stroked her hair. 'You've done amazingly, you know, for someone with no experience.' His praise was so unexpected that she had to choke back a sob. 'I know it looks bad at the moment, but the mistakes are easy ones to make.' He felt angry with her parents on her behalf. What had they been up to in handing her the responsibility of running the company without the back-up to follow it through? 'You've had good ideas, essential ones even. Don't blame yourself. All you've done is uncover Victoriana's weaknesses. Once they're sorted out, they'll thank you.'

The remote chance of her mother thanking her flitted into Lily's mind and she smiled.

'Let's have some more of that.' Paul leaned over and kissed her, to the immense delight of the girls in the orders section who were watching them through the plate-glass window, and to the disapproval of Susie McIntosh, who saw it as a clear case of screwing while Rome burned.

Half an hour later they were tucked into a corner of the Sunne in Splendour, under the close scrutiny of the small group of drinkers who propped up the bar on a dull Friday night when there was nothing on the television.

It was barely nine when, blind to the degree of interest they were exciting among the other customers, Lily and Paul finished their drinks and said goodnight.

'Aye aye, Doris,' commented one of the regulars to the landlady, who was making a great play of discretion and pretending not to notice Charlotte Brandon's daughter disappearing upstairs with an unknown young man, 'reckon in the morning you'll have to prise those two apart with a crowbar.'

To the general joy and entertainment of all the Sunne's clientele, Paul and Lily rarely surfaced during the whole weekend, and when they did, had to run the gauntlet of a Greek chorus of neighbourly advice.

'Give 'em some mead, Doris, they'll need their strength building up,' offered one.

'Guinness'd do it,' suggested another.

The landlady's mother, ensconced under a rug in the snug, a TV set blaring only inches away, contributed the wisdom of years: 'You'd best stay off the drink altogether, my ducks, if my Bert is anything to go by.' Beside her, Bert snored rumbustiously, ninety if he was a day.

By Sunday evening Paul knew he'd never met anyone like Lily Brandon – but he still hadn't told her that, for both their

sakes, he'd asked Clive Green to take over Victoriana's affairs. He'd put off breaking the news for too long.

'Lily, before I go back, there's something I ought to tell
you. I've handed over the running of your account to Clive
Green. I'm getting too emotionally involved and I can't
make business judgements any more where you're
concerned.'

Lily couldn't believe what she was hearing. 'For God's
sake, Paul, why didn't you tell me?' His words soiled the
beauty of their time together. Anger splintered into her
mind with the force of an axe through a door. He was
treating her like a child. 'You're scared!' she accused. 'You
want someone else to make the decision if it comes to the
crunch, don't you? That way it won't be your fault.' Her
eyes blazed at him, yellow as a big cat's.

Paul was silent. Was there a grain of truth in her
suggestion?

Lily didn't wait to find out. She sprang out of her chair
and ran from the pub, red hair flying, before a delighted
audience who declared it more exciting than *Home and
Away*. Her eyes blurred as she thought of Paul's betrayal,
doubly wounding after the closeness of the last two days.
He had simply handed Victoriana over to a stranger
without even discussing the matter with her. How could
he?

The list of redundancies she was trying to draw up
smudged with her tears. She'd known laying people off
would be awful, but it was ten times worse.

The only person Lily could happily do without was the
troublemaking Susie McIntosh, but she was the one person
she couldn't fire, precisely because she *was* a troublemaker.
Not now anyway. Maybe when things were going well
again and they could afford a decent payoff and wouldn't
mind if she ran crying to the press.

Equally typically, it was the one person she wanted to hang on to who offered to go – Shauna Robinson.

'Go on,' Shauna insisted. 'I'll be having the baby in a few months anyway and I'd have to have time off. I'll just start earlier. Don't worry about me. A diet of daytime TV and junk food is just what I need. You can take me back when everything looks up.' She held out her hand. 'It will, you know. You've really bucked this place up. Everyone says so.'

Lily was so moved she hugged the girl, kicking herself that it had to be Shauna of all people who went. 'It won't be for long, I promise.' She looked up, to find Judith had arrived for their weekly briefing.

'What was all that?' Judith asked after Shauna had departed, sniffing back a sudden attack of tears.

'I've just had to lay Shauna and ten others off to save money. You've heard about this computer business I suppose.'

Judith nodded. She had in fact been briefed in great detail and with even greater glee by Susie McIntosh, right down to Lily's performance in the pub, running away from Paul Allan, which was already an item of village gossip.

'Do you want to make any kind of press statement?'

Lily shook her head. 'I don't care if I never see another journalist in my life. I just want you to keep Victoriana *out* of the papers.' That shouldn't be too tough for you, Lily almost added, given your record with the press conference. Instead she waited for Judith to offer to cut back her own services in the cause of economy. But Judith didn't. If Lily failed to make enough economies and Victoriana was about to go under, she wanted to be there to witness it. Instead, she tried to look suitably serious and concerned as she took herself off to call Barry North.

North was in the middle of dictating a letter into his miniature tape recorder when Judith got through. He felt a flicker of irritation. She was a more demanding mistress than he liked and the sex, though still exhilarating, was less adventurous than it had been at the start of their affair. At the beginning Judith had been prepared to do anything, indeed had suggested various practices even he hadn't attempted before, all of them deliciously disgusting. Now she seemed only to be interested in activities that gave her pleasure, and that meant a far more limited repertoire.

'Hello Judith.' His tone was brusque, designed to remind her that she was interrupting an important man, and it had better be for a good reason.

'Barry, I've got some interesting news.' Judith felt like a dog bringing its master a juicy bone to win back his affection after some misdemeanour and resented him for it. 'It's about Victoriana. Lily's finally fucked up. The computer system's lost all their orders and they can't meet their next payment. They're starting to lay people off.'

Barry North considered this information. 'Try and disguise your delight, Judith dear. Has it never occurred to you that if Victoriana goes bust, your husband's inheritance will be considerably reduced?'

'By then I'll be running the company under your ownership though, won't I, Barry darling. Look, I think you should ring Clive at First Venture and see if there's anything he can do to help.'

She had a point, of course. It was time First Venture put the screws on, but Barry North was the kind of a man who didn't enjoy being given advice. Especially by a woman. And especially when she was right.

All the same he had the good sense to take it. 'Clive, old boy,' North used the expression advisedly since he knew that neither he nor Green were the public school type. 'I hear Victoriana isn't going to be able to pay back your loan. How much say do you have in their affairs?'

Clive Green's jowls wobbled in delight at the beauty of North's timing. 'Rather a lot, actually, *old boy*.' His intonation of the words was equally ironic. 'As a matter of fact, I've just taken the account over, and my professional analysis is that they're in deep shit.'

'Anything you can do to dig them in deeper would be most welcome. I don't suppose you could call in the debt, for instance?'

'Not yet, unless they miss this payment. Then Bob's your Mother's brother. No problem.'

'How are those two boys of yours getting on at Winchester?' North asked suddenly. 'Fees must be a bit steep. Did you do a plan?'

The fact that Green and his wife hadn't been circumspect enough to do a wretched school fees plan was one of their constant regrets now they were saddled with the crippling costs of private education each term, but how the hell had North worked it out? He knew that dramatic shift in the conversation meant North was offering him assistance.

'I'll fix you an appointment with my broker. He'll sort you out. I'd hate to think of you having to worry about money.'

'Thanks a lot. On the other matter, I can't do anything directly, but why don't you get one of their suppliers to put the screws on. If one of them makes things dodgy, then I can step in. They must owe their suppliers – maybe one of them should decide they need paying a bit sooner than usual. The rest'll follow like lemmings and bye-bye Victoriana. It happens all the time.'

North tapped his desk decisively. It was an excellent idea.

For the moment Connie's role at Victoriana was over. She told herself that she was grateful, that she needed a beat of time in her life, a moment's peace to stand back and ground herself, to remember the old familiar props, the things that had been so central to her and had faded into insignificance since meeting Euan.

Unfortunately for Connie, Tara's school had chosen this

same time to give her study leave and she sat, looking out-rageously sexy, with her clodhopping feet on the kitchen table, reading an article about groupies in *Rave* magazine which rejoiced under the headline of COCK AU VAN.

'Glad to see you're taking an interest in domestic science,' Connie remarked pointedly, 'but shouldn't you be im-mersing yourself in sociology or English Lit?'

'It *is* sociology. One of my topics is the impact of the six-ties on youth culture.'

'Well, at least take your shoes off the table.'

Tara looked at her mother as though her request was un-reasonable beyond belief and went on reading until Connie swiped her, leg, hard, with the *Guardian*.

'We don't hit in this family, Ma, remember?'

Connie glared, thinking that what sociology papers should really cover is the crisis in parental authority since nice middle-class people had stopped walloping their offspring. Tara had been unusually stroppy lately. Maybe she was picking up Connie's dissatisfaction and throwing it back at her.

'Are you okay Tara? I mean nothing's worrying you?'

Connie knew that what she really wanted was for her daughter to say she was fine, apart from her usual daily preoccupations with which member of REM she fancied most.

Tara paused, reluctant to let such an opportunity for whingeing pass, then simply admitted to being a tad wor-ried about her GCSEs. Three months ago Connie, as thrusting a mother as any other in the face of her daughter's educational opportunities, would never have imagined her-self uttering the words, 'Is that all?' But she did.

Half an hour later, with her daughter safely shuttled into her bedroom and showing every appearance of commitment to her revision, the phone rang and Connie pounced on it before Tara could, which was just as well since it was Euan.

When she explained that she'd taken a couple of days off he was thrilled. 'Wonderful. You can come to see me tomorrow then.'

Connie hesitated at the insuperable challenge of explaining that it was to get away from him that she had stayed home. She had wanted to try and lay herself back down into her old life, like a fork in a drawer of cutlery. 'I can't, Euan.'

'Of course you can. I *need* you, Connie. I have to see you or life has no meaning.'

Connie noticed a brown ring staining the white of the worktop, where someone had put a teapot, and wanted to scrub it until it was pristine and sparkling. She was beginning to feel the same way about her marriage.

'No, Euan, I can't. We're hurting too many people.'

'And hurting me doesn't count?' She heard the anger in his voice and an edge of petulance that reminded her of her children. Overwhelmed with sudden exhaustion she sat down at the table and twisted the phone lead round her fingers. Surely even in an affair she didn't have to be the mother? 'If you don't come,' Euan's voice was teasing but with the hint of a threat, 'I might just have to come and see you.'

For the first time in the relationship Connie was tempted to slam down the phone but, just in time, he apologized and the old tenderness sprang back into life.

'All right. I'll come to you. Around lunchtime.'

The rush-hour was over by the time she parked at the station and she travelled in off-peak comfort, hoping there would still be a refreshment trolley coming round. British Rail had long since abandoned one of the great attractions of travelling, the bacon sandwich, but did better coffee than of old. Connie settled back to sneak a look at the other people in the carriage. Mostly businessmen but also women off for a day's shopping, no doubt to the mecca of John Lewis to buy things that no other shop seemed to sell: decorative ribbons, stiff net for fairy costumes, navy uniform knickers; things for their families, in all probability, not for themselves. A small smile curled itself round her features. The women were all similarly dressed in attractive, sensible clothes, just as she was. Maybe they too were off to meet their lovers?

'Mrs Wade, how nice to see you. Off on a shopping spree like me?' A booming voice interrupted her fantasy and the awful Mrs Wallington, the queen of Bidchester's cocktail party circuit, sat down opposite. What would the ghastly woman do if Connie told her the truth? I'm going to sleazy Ladbroke Grove for two hours of sleazy but exciting sex, in fact the sleazier the better, then I'll get the 3.12 back to Dorset in time for the kids coming home.

Despite the warm weather, Mrs Wallington wore what used to be called 'a costume' in thick puce tweed ambitiously teamed with a coral angora beret worn at a rakish angle. She reminded Connie of an enormous tropical parrot let loose in the treetops of suburban London.

Connie had to endure Mrs Wallington's gossip, which ranged far and wide from village to county, until they reached London, where the older woman watched eagerly to see if anyone was there to meet Connie. For a brief second Connie imagined Euan rushing up the platform unexpectedly and sweeping her off her feet. Fortunately only the ticket collector awaited her and she waved goodbye and made for the underground and Ladbroke Grove, incurring a raised eyebrow from Mrs W that she didn't want to share a cab to Oxford Street and the safety of the John Lewis haberdashery department.

For Connie wilder shores beckoned.

She shivered involuntarily as Euan bent his head and licked the pool of sweat that had gathered at the base of her neck. Today they had hardly spoken, just driven into each other with an intensity that thrilled Connie, but also frightened her. There had been no laughter today, no exchange of news, none of their usual teasing and petting.

Euan lay back and watched her. 'How was it for you, as they say? Did I perform satisfactorily or would you have preferred more manual stimulation? Speak up, Constance, if you're in this just for the sex you might as well get your money's worth.'

His bitterness made her sit up and instinctively reach for the sheet to cover herself. 'Of course I'm not just in it for the sex.'

'Leave him then.' He jumped astride her, and grabbed her arms so roughly they hurt. 'Come and live with me. You love me, you know you do.'

'I can't leave.' Connie held his eyes with hers, skewered by the pain of knowing that every option was agonizing.

'You're going to have to choose, Connie. We can't go on like this. I can't do anything else. My work's fucked. My concentration lasts about ten seconds. I need to be with you all the time, you're my harbour. I can't live without you.'

Connie felt herself shrivelling up with fear. Love was so dangerous. It could be used to justify everything, even breaking up families and starting again. She closed her eyes, then slowly reached for her clothes. 'I can't, Euan. I can't do it to them.'

Euan jumped out of bed. 'You'd better go then,' he yelled, 'and get back to your cosy little family.'

On the way home, feeling bruised and empty, Connie turned her face against the electric blue velvet of the train's upholstery to disguise her red eyes and the black streaks of mascara that ran down her face.

'Mind if I join you?' Connie couldn't believe her bad luck as the dreadful Mrs Wallington eased her bulk into the seat next to hers and patted Connie on her hand. Connie, expecting an uninterrupted hour of snivelling, wiped the streaks from her face as best she could. Why wasn't the wretched woman still in John Lewis, selecting microwave cookware?

'All's not really fair in love and war,' Mrs Wallington announced, 'is it, my dear? I expect it was one of those male myths put about to justify their bad behaviour.'

Connie jumped and prepared to say she had no idea what the other woman was on about.

'I expect you've done the right thing. Women are more aware of the complexities than men. They can just wade through the debris to get what they want, and expect someone else to clear it up. We're not like that.'

Connie listened in amazement. The sheer nerve of the woman. For all the interfering old bat knew, Connie could have just been told she had terminal cancer or had been at the bedside of a dying parent. Mrs Wallington clearly read her thoughts. 'I work for Relate as a counsellor. You get to recognize the signs. They're written all over you.'

Connie felt furious and invaded, as though Mrs Wallington represented a Neighbourhood Watch of the soul.

'It happened to me once, you know. Hard to imagine, isn't it? I met him at the Chelsea Flower Show, next door to the alpines and rock plants as a matter of fact. We started with gardening tips and ended up in the potting shed.'

Connie thought of Mr Wallington, the incredibly pompous Chairman of the Rotary Club.

'My husband was never keen on gardening. No patience.' She winked at Connie. 'In that or anything else.'

'What did you do in the end?' Connie realized her own denial should have come already, if it were going to come at all.

'I gave him up. It would never have worked. He was too much of a horny-handed son of the soil. Nothing in common bar the begonias and the bonking.' Mrs Wallington stared wistfully out of the window, as though in retrospect that sounded quite a lot. 'So I stayed with Hugh and threw myself into good causes and became a pillar of the community, campaigning against all the things I used to enjoy. You should try it. It's surprisingly satisfying. And you don't need a man.'

It was a frightening prospect yet Connie felt cheered nevertheless. Mrs Wallington was gently reminding her that life went on.

'Our stop, I think,' pointed out the older woman.

Connie gathered up her things, feeling unaccountably confident that her secret was safe with Mrs Wallington.

In the kitchen Tara was raiding the fridge, glowing with smugness that she had completed the tasks the school had set for her. 'You're late. Where've you been? I thought you had today off.'

'Shopping,' lied Connie, then, remembering she had no bags, 'I couldn't find anything I liked. Where's Jeremy?'

'Upstairs. Behaving very oddly actually. He swept in ten minutes ago and dashed up to his room.'

Connie put down her coat and wondered whether to go and investigate. Jeremy had been so difficult lately, jumpy and sensitive.

He was lying on his bed. Connie sat down next to him and tried to stroke his long hair. He pushed her hand away with startling force. 'You forgot, didn't you?' he demanded.

'Forgot what?' Her mind raked the possibilities. Had she promised to buy him something?

'Forgot what day it is.' He pulled himself up from the bed and kicked his treasured guitar. It was almost more shocking than seeing him attack a living being.

'Oh my God, your test for the Royal College. It wasn't today? Why didn't you remind me?'

'Because I wanted you to remember yourself, like any

246

decent mother would,' he kicked the guitar again, 'if she hadn't got her mind on other things.'

Guilt bit into her. How could she have forgotten the day that would decide the next three years of her son's whole future? And yet his failure to remind her had clearly been quite deliberate. A spark of rebellion fizzled damply in Connie. Why was she always the one who had to carry the burdens?

'It was your responsibility too,' she said gently. 'You made a choice in not telling me and I'm not sure that was fair.' She waited for the look of pure loathing that would be her due, but Jeremy kept his eyes firmly on the wall.

'Supper's in half an hour,' she reminded, 'see you downstairs.'

'Mum . . .' She was at the door before he spoke. 'Maybe I wanted to hurt you.'

She longed to fold him into her arms like she had when he was a small child, but wasn't sure that was what he wanted. 'I love you, darling,' was all she could think of to say, 'and don't worry, I'm hurting quite enough already.'

In bed that night Gavin rolled towards her, sensing the depth of her anguish without understanding its cause. She'd been unfamiliar lately, excited, private. But Connie couldn't bear his touch, even in comfort, and withdrew. Gavin, feeling powerless and excluded, could only listen as she sobbed silently into the pillow. An hour later, as he finally drifted off to sleep, his thoughts turned guiltily not to Connie but to the warm and welcoming Terri. Terri had taken to dropping into the shop lately, after Margot had gone, and he'd very much welcomed her sympathy, but last night things had gone a step further. She had offered to massage his neck and it was so delicious Gavin had wanted it never to stop.

'Morning, Mrs Brandon, not often we see you these days.'

Mr Seacroft put the two bundles of asparagus into Charlotte Brandon's basket and pointed out the virtues of his delicious, English-grown strawberries. 'None of your Canaries rubbish, these beauties are local. And none of that pick-your-own nonsense either, a real con that, getting your customers to do the work for you. Try one?'

The other customers in the shop were treated to the rare sight of old Mr Seacroft feeding an enormous strawberry to the regal silver-haired figure of Charlotte Brandon, who happened to be two inches taller than he.

These proceedings were watched with disapproval by young Mr Seacroft who disliked too much intimacy with the customers and had long battled to transform Darcombe's small greengrocer's shop into a self-service emporium, staffed by a school leaver, so that he could remove himself to a sun-bed in his back garden.

Charlotte conceded to the sales pitch even though it was about as subtle as a Sherman tank, and bought two large punnets. Old Mr Seacroft wrapped these in brown paper bags, twirling the corners with a triumphant glance at young Mr Seacroft, as if to say: try pulling that off with self-service and a surly sixteen-year-old.

Young Mr Seacroft resisted the temptation to point out that well-heeled customers with their old-fashioned baskets and old-fashioned full purses like Mrs Brandon were few and far between, especially as there was a Safeway's in Bidchester. Instead he raced his father to hold the door open for her.

'Sorry to hear about your bad news, Mrs B.' Young Mr Seacroft shot an equally triumphant look at his Dad, a staunch Tory who would never concede that his beloved party had ruined the economy. 'I gather you're having to lay folk off.' Young Mr Seacroft didn't notice Charlotte's horrified reaction and bore on: 'I blame the government. They're putting the boot into business instead of helping it,

248

if you ask me, but it wouldn't be the same round here without Victoriana. You must be worried sick.'

Charlotte clutched her shopping bag as if it were her only hold on reality and took herself out into the village street. In all the thirty-five years of Victoriana's existence it had been expansion all the way. In fact they'd had to run to keep up with themselves. The shock was making her feel faint.

Across the road, on the edge of the village green, the Sunne in Splendour already had a few people sitting outside at white tables and chairs. Charlotte decided to break the habit of a lifetime and get herself a glass of mineral water which she could sit in the shade and drink till she felt better. Maybe she'd better take one of her pills too. Her heart was racing worryingly.

She put her basket down on one of the tables to forage for her purse, noting that the group at the next one was from the notorious Robinson family. They must have forsaken daytime television for outdoor activity for once. Charlotte was about to tell herself not to be such a snob when one of them addressed her belligerently.

'I hope you're proud of your daughter, Mrs Brandon. The way she's carrying on, I certainly wouldn't be.'

Charlotte picked up her basket, thinking better of the mineral water idea. She could hardly drink it peacefully with this lot around anyway. Noting that Charlotte was about to escape, Janet Robinson moved in for the kill. 'She's laying folk off, our Shauna included, pregnant and everything. I thought that was against the law these days. Disgraceful I call it. Shauna's having to sign on the Social.'

'I'm sure my daughter is doing her best in a difficult situation.' Charlotte felt her blood pressure rising at the idea of everyone in the village knowing her business except her. What was going on at Victoriana, and why hadn't Lily told her?

'One law for the rich,' mumbled Janet's husband audibly to Charlotte's departing back, 'I bet they're not selling their great big house to save the company. They'd rather put everyone out of work. You should tell the local rag. They'd be interested in what's happening to our Shauna.'

Charlotte was so shaken up she could hardly drive. It had taken her a lifetime to create Victoriana. She'd put her soul into that company and every part of it had borne her imprint.

Edward was in the garden, as always, when she finally got home. He seemed to opt out of everything for that wretched garden of his, it was like a retreat from life. Sometimes she felt tempted to go berserk with the hedge trimmer and destroy everything he'd created, so she could drag him back to reality.

He stepped out from behind an avalanche of climbing roses with Judith by his side, telling her about his new greenhouse. Charlotte felt a warm glow of gratitude at the sight of her daughter-in-law. Here was someone who would understand her concern.

'Are you all right, Charlotte?' Judith's voice rang with solicitude. 'You look as though you've seen a ghost.'

'I have. The ghost of Victoriana. Its death is already being predicted by everyone in the village. For heaven's sake, Judith, what *is* going on?'

Judith arranged her features into deep concern. This was perfect. 'I didn't want to worry you with it. Lily's frightened the debt will be called in by First Venture if she can't make the next payment, so she's making staff cuts. She's convinced that things will be all right then.' Judith managed to subtly convey that she did not herself endorse this rash optimism.

'And if not . . . ?'

'I'm sure it won't come to that, Charlotte.' Judith's eyes were modestly downcast to hide her delight at this new development. 'Victoriana's been such a success story. It can't possibly go under.'

As soon as she got back into her car, Judith Brandon called Barry North. 'Now's the time to put on the pressure,' she said tersely, 'the old witch is definitely rattled – and make sure whoever it is, they talk directly to Charlotte. Edward Brandon won't want to admit his mistake in letting Lily run it.'

Barry North had given considerable thought to choosing which of Victoriana's suppliers to lean on. Eventually he had found the perfect candidate, perfect because S. J. Wilson's also supplied his own firm and wouldn't be able to survive without North's custom; perfect also because they had problems of their own. S. J. Wilson supplied cotton dresses, made to Victoriana's design, and since Victoriana sold an awful lot of cotton dresses, the sums involved were large. If, instead of allowing Victoriana to pay them at their usual leisurely pace, they demanded immediate payment, Victoriana would be in a lot of trouble.

Barry North picked up his phone and asked to speak to Mr Samuel Wilson in person, telling the secretary that what he had to say was important and also highly confidential.

Lily had never imagined she would live with a calculator as her constant companion. She even took the thing to bed. In the old days, if she'd taken anything to bed that needed batteries it certainly wouldn't have been a calculator.

Tonight, as she sat at her desk with her columns of figures, Lily felt utterly alone. Everyone had left hours ago. She'd tried to call Connie for some moral support, but Connie always seemed to be out. For a moment her thoughts crept back to Paul. She'd heard nothing from him since their fight. There'd been moments when she'd longed for his precious support but she'd sloughed them off. She would show him she could do it alone. Maybe she should never have given up acting, and said no to her father's plea. Lily loathed people who gave in to self-pity, but tonight she found herself succumbing to a large dose of it. In London she could have rung Maxie and gone out on the town, but here all that waited for her was an empty flat and an empty bed.

She was giving herself a lecture on not being a pathetic wimp when the caretaker called up to say that there was someone to see her in Reception. In a brief moment of weakness she hoped it would be Paul, knowing she was being silly. It might be Evie though. Evie was just the tonic she needed. She grabbed her coat and ran downstairs.

Ben Winter, looking neat, well-dressed and astonishingly attractive, stood chatting pleasantly to the caretaker as though he were really interested in the man. Lily watched in amazement. Ben didn't usually waste his precious time on nobodies.

Even without an audience he had enormous presence, but there was something different about Ben Winter tonight that she couldn't put her finger on.

'Lily, my love,' he swooped down on her and kissed her on both cheeks. 'I've been filming in Bidchester and couldn't miss the chance of seeing you. Come and have dinner.'

His dark hair was neatly cut, giving him an air that was romantic rather than his usual saturnine, and his eyes held none of their usual glitter of sarcasm. He held out his hands, laughing. 'You're wondering what my secret is. Have I done a lifeswap with Dorian Gray? It's simple. I've given up the booze.'

The caretaker pretended not to listen but Lily could tell he was riveted all the same. It couldn't be often that a star unburdened himself in the reception area.

'Losing you was the last straw. I'd told myself I was in control till then. After you it all went wrong.'

Lily remembered the last time she'd seen him. He'd been drunk then but she'd had no idea it had become a habit. She'd noticed that bottles of wine arrived miraculously at their table in restaurants, just as they were about to leave, yet she hadn't seen Ben ordering them. She'd thought they were gifts from wellwishers until she inspected the bill and realized that they were actually paying for them.

'I was very clever; drunks are,' he said, reading her thoughts. 'Bottles of vodka hidden in every nook and cranny. Now I've put Satan firmly behind me. The lips that touch liquor shall never touch mine. Though I'd be prepared to make an exception for those that have touched Australian Chardonnay.'

Lily smiled in spite of herself at this reference to her favourite wine.

'Come and have dinner. Please.' He produced a smile that would have melted the resolve of a nun. 'My agent said I shouldn't admit I had a problem, but I had to tell you. You deserve an explanation for how badly I behaved.'

The caretaker looked bereft when Lily finally agreed and they both headed for Ben's car. This was more of a cliff-hanger than the telly. He couldn't help hoping she gave in. He was a charmer, that one, and Miss Brandon didn't seem to have any personal life, despite her racy reputation. His Biddy wouldn't approve, of course. She'd say the man was a rascal, but women liked rascals, didn't they?

As soon as they were sitting in the car, Ben took her hand. 'Can you ever forgive me?'

Lily eyed him warily. Was this another of his acts? He was certainly different, and there had to be some explanation. But she was far from convinced. He'd hurt her too badly.

'Drink might explain your unpleasant behaviour in the Blue Flame, but I've never heard of it as an excuse for dumping someone in public to run off with a nymphet.'

'God, Lily, that was so dumb. I knew the next morning

what a mistake it was, and I kept her on for months out of guilt. That's when I really hit the booze. Please will you come to dinner?' Ben's personality was capable of filling the National Theatre; in a small estate car it brooked no refusal. Besides, Lily was so lonely she would have had dinner with King Kong, so she ignored the alarm bells that were ringing faintly in her head and agreed.

In the bar of the Crown Hotel, everyone turned to watch as Ben Winter dutifully drank Perrier and Lily sipped her wine. Ben, on the other hand, saw no one but her. The dinner was surprisingly good and Ben was wonderful company, just as he'd been when they first met. Afterwards they sat in the private lounge until finally, at midnight, Lily insisted she had to go.

Just as she was about to get into her taxi he pulled her to him, firmly but not roughly. 'I meant it, Lily, losing you was the stupidest thing I've ever done. Can you ever forgive me?' And he kissed her with more passion than she could remember in the whole six months of their relationship.

Breathlessly she broke away, her emotions in complete confusion. There were so many things she was unsure of, but one thing she knew instinctively. This wasn't another of Ben's poses.

'Give me another chance, Lily.'

'No more nymphets?'

He shook his head.

'No more booze?'

He held her eyes with his powerful dark gaze. 'I can't promise to be Little Lord Fauntleroy. I may even fall off the wagon. But with the love of a good woman . . .'

Lily kissed him gently. 'No one's ever called me a good woman before. Flatterer.'

'You'll think about it, then?'

'I'll think about it.'

'Don't take too long. We're only here a few more days.'

His smile held a teasing hint of lasciviousness. 'It would be a pity to waste my four-poster bed.'

Connie Brandon was well acquainted with all those nice expressions like Snap Out Of It, and Pull Yourself Together, and had often used them herself in the face of other people's irritating inability to do so. For some reason, in your own case, it was different. Nothing seemed to make her slot back into her normal life, not family responsibilities, affection for Gavin, guilt about Jeremy, nor even worry about what was happening to Victoriana or the shop could wrench her back. Her mind kept being drawn irresistibly to Euan, his beauty, the way he made things come alive, the way he made *her* come alive; but was she really ready to give it all up, the very foundations of her life, for this feeling? Panic swept through her as she sat on the stairs of her familiar beloved house. What if it was, after all, just an illusion based on not being able to have him?

The trouble was, Connie couldn't imagine herself, sound and sensible Constance, as a fixture in Euan's gypsy life. Until he'd met her, he'd told her once, he'd never stayed anywhere more than a few months before he was off, moth-like, to fly into the flame of the latest exciting assignment. The idea of him and Jeremy even tolerating each other was hard to picture. Jeremy would be outraged by a man in her life who was only ten years older than he was, and Euan wouldn't have the patience to understand that. Tara might eventually come round, but neither of them would forgive her. Then there was the difference in her and Euan's ages, which seemed not to matter now, but would in ten years' time when everything began to droop. She had never given two thoughts to ageing before she'd met him, indeed had pitied women whose obsessions with youth had led them to the scalpel and the step class, never letting go and enjoying life for fear of getting fat or flabby, but now she began to understand them.

'Are you planning to sit there all day?' She heard the exasperation in Gavin's voice and tried to rouse herself.

Gavin saw that he, too, had a choice. He could try and force his wife to tell him what was going on, with all the risks that such knowledge held for their life together, or he could wait and see what happened. Today, at Connie's suggestion, he was going to a gift fair in Bromsbury. Terri was going too and they had agreed to drive there together.

'I'm off to Bromsbury then,' he reminded Connie. 'I'll be staying the night. Will you be all right?' Gavin, angry and hurt as he was at Connie's rejection, had told himself he would put Terri off if his wife showed the slightest concern about him, but Connie simply nodded as though she hadn't really been listening. Gavin shouldered his bag and went out to the car.

It was only after he'd left that Connie managed to take her own advice and shook herself up enough to wonder if she should have shown more interest in what Gavin had said. There had been something odd about the way he'd told her he was staying overnight, almost as though he wanted her to discourage him.

Connie told herself she was imagining it and headed into the kitchen to tidy it for what seemed like the millionth time.

When Sam Wilson took the call from Barry North he hadn't been at all happy. He liked to think he was a decent man and he knew how hard it was to survive in business, especially these days. His relationship with Victoriana had been long and mutually productive. Right from the beginning he'd supplied Victoriana with cloth. At first Charlotte Brandon had put together the dresses herself with just a handful of workers to cut and stitch for her. For the last few years S. J. Wilson had taken on that role and made them up for her to Victoriana's designs. He liked Mrs Brandon and respected her toughness. You didn't build a company like Victoriana up from nothing without nerve and imagination. News travelled faster than hemlines in the clothing business and he'd heard the rumours that they had their difficulties, yet he'd also seen the amazing press they'd got. If they really were going bust, as Barry North had insisted, he would be a fool not to get his money out quick, or he'd be dragged down with them, but there was a bad smell about all this.

Weighing it all up, he'd decided to resist the pressure from North's and see what happened. Then he'd opened the *Bidchester Herald* this morning and found this. A double page spread on how Victoriana was laying off staff, and some row about sacking a young girl because she was pregnant. If he didn't move now, all the other creditors would get in first *and* North would put the boot into him too. S. J. Wilson's would be forced to close down after three generations of trading.

He might dislike the times he lived in more than ever, but Sam Wilson came to the conclusion he had no choice: he would have to demand payment at once.

Charlotte was sitting in her favourite wing chair with Troy at her feet and a cup of tea at her elbow, incandescent with fury.

'Where do they get this tosh?' she flung the offending paper at the Rayburn, frightening Troy so much he yelped and ran off to the scullery. 'This is perfect. It says Victoriana is so starved of cash it's firing people right left and centre and may not be able to meet its payroll. This is libellous.'

'You know what the press are like. This Robinson girl must have been stirring things up. I think we'd better talk to Lily about all this as soon as possible.'

'I knew she was trouble when I met her. I told Lily . . .' Their conversation was cut short by Sam Wilson's call. Edward answered the phone but the caller asked expressly to speak to Mrs Brandon. Charlotte listened silently as Sam Wilson attempted to explain his reasoning for requiring payment from Victoriana instantly, ending with an apology that sounded remarkably genuine.

Charlotte had to hold on to the arms of her chair. She knew exactly what this meant for Victoriana. 'Forget any sessions with Lily, Edward,' she announced wrathfully. 'If Wilson's wants paying then they'll all start. Victoriana will be bankrupt in no time. I don't care what you say, I'm going to take over again myself.'

Chapter 19

'Have you seen this, Lily?' Lily was lost in a daydream, endlessly re-running her extraordinary evening with Ben. If she hadn't been so angry with Paul, perhaps Ben's sudden return wouldn't have made such an impression. She would have simply reminded herself of the past and sent him packing. Instead, all she could think of was that, even after all the months, Ben was still obsessed with her. The thought, mad or at least unwise, was as exciting as finding an unopened Christmas present in the middle of July.

This morning she'd woken up with the same feeling, a forbidden thrill whose source she couldn't for a moment trace. Then she'd remembered.

Lily took the copy of the local paper from June. The headline jolted her back to reality. SHOCK LAYOFFS: END OF THE ROMANCE FOR VICTORIANA? The report went on to list in detail all the employees they'd made redundant, noting that one, Shauna Robinson, was pregnant.

'It says we're in trouble and the company might not survive,' June pointed out anxiously. 'That's not true, is it Lily? This is just a glitch, isn't it?'

'Of course it is,' Lily said, forgetting Ben in her anger at the unfairness of the article. She'd spent days at her desk with her calculator and knew every detail of Victoriana's cash flow, right down to how many toilet rolls they used (too many for the number of bottoms) and the unit cost of the paper cup sitting filled with coffee on her desk. She had made a list of economies which ranged from sending things by second class mail to banning expensive Post-It stickers. In her calculations, thanks to the staff cuts, they could just scrape by and make their payment to First Venture, but this story in the papers wouldn't help.

She had almost succeeded in reassuring June that things would be all right when a tearful Shauna appeared in her office, clutching the paper. 'I just wanted you to know,' Shauna half-sobbed, 'that this horrible stuff didn't come from me. I didn't tell them any of that and I certainly didn't give a quote saying how bitter I felt. You and June have been brilliant to me. That's what I told the reporter but she didn't even bother to write it down, the cow. Oh, Lily, I'm so sorry.'

'Look, don't worry,' Lily tried to calm her. 'We were sure you wouldn't have said those things, weren't we, June?'

June nodded vigorously. 'We knew you couldn't spell victimization anyway,' June teased.

Shauna slumped down in the chair opposite Lily's desk, looking more visibly pregnant by the moment. She followed Lily's gaze down to her burgeoning belly. 'It just sort of bulged the moment I stopped work, as though it knew we could both be couch potatoes,' she attempted a grin. 'God, I'm missing you lot. All my Mum talks about is who's screwing who in the soaps, the cost of living now I'm at home and how young people Don't Know How Good They've Got It Today. She was thrilled that I was in the paper.' Shauna looked sheepish. 'In fact I suspect it might have been her who told them in the first place.'

Lily was about to offer her a cup of coffee when reception rang to say that Charlotte was on her way up. Shauna and

June got up immediately. It was like being told, Shauna thought, that the Head Teacher was on the warpath, without knowing quite what it was you'd done. She suspected the visit might be something to do with her and wished fervently that her bloody mother had kept her mouth shut. 'I'd better go. Mothers, eh? Dontcha love 'em?'

June and Shauna scuttled away giving Lily a look of commiseration. She steeled herself for Charlotte's anger and arranged all the figures she'd been working so hard on.

Charlotte swept in with all the subtlety of a nuclear warhead. Judith, her beautifully-made up face studiously neutral as though it would be incapable of an expression that said I told you so, was in her wake.

'I'm sorry about this, Lily, but I'm afraid I've got bad news. The managing director of S. J. Wilson's rang me yesterday. If they aren't paid in full by the end of the month they're going to start bankruptcy proceedings against us. I feel I have no alternative but to take over.'

Lily sat down, aghast. She'd talked to Sam Wilson only last week and he had been as friendly as ever. What had changed? Something dramatic for Sam to behave like this. She'd been half killing herself worrying about their paperclip consumption while Sam was bulldozing down the whole building. A sliver of panic slid between her bones. Maybe he'd seen the article. Maybe he wasn't the only one and all their suppliers would start doing this.

'I really am sorry, Lily' – and indeed the sight of her stricken daughter did hurt Charlotte more than she'd expected – 'but business is business. I can't stand by and watch Victoriana collapse. We have a duty to our staff and to our other suppliers. Now this is out, they'll all be wanting to be paid. I'm going to take over running things myself for a while and Judith here is going to help me. She can fend off the press interest we're bound to get after this.' She indicated the article about Shauna. 'Of course you're welcome to stay on board. I'm sure there'll be plenty to do. For now, would you mind asking George to come in? I'd like to run through the financial situation with him before we do anything else.'

Judith. Lily couldn't believe it. Her sister-in-law had tried to sabotage the catalogue launch and now her mother was installing Judith in Lily's desk. Anger jabbed at her and she almost walked straight out, but that would mean turning her back on a year of her life, on the people she'd come to know and respect, like Shauna and June and George. She couldn't do it. She was going to have to fight, even if it meant fighting her own mother. She longed to say that she had everything under control, that once they got over this bad patch Victoriana's long-term future was good, all of which happened to be true, but Charlotte wasn't in the mood for listening. Instead she dismissed as piffling all the economies Lily had sweated blood to make. Lily's mind wandered insistently back to Sam Wilson. This gesture was so entirely out of character with the gentlemanly managing director she'd learned to know and trust over the last months, especially the fact that he'd rung Charlotte and not her. The thought that she should find out more sustained her through the awful session that followed.

At the end of the gruelling session with George, Charlotte insisted she needed time to think. It was clear to Lily that she intended to do it at Lily's desk. The office that Lily and Connie had spent such happy months in was Charlotte Brandon's once more.

Now that she was no longer in charge the strain of the last weeks caught up with Lily and she felt an almost irresistible temptation to break down, get drunk or go to bed for a week. Determined that Charlotte and especially Judith should not see this outbreak of weakness she disappeared to the safety of the Ladies. Thank God it was empty. For the first time since she'd taken over at Victoriana Lily allowed

262

herself to give in. She'd put so much of herself into the business and she'd been so sure it would pay off in the end.

'It's all your own fault, you know.' Susie McIntosh seemed to appear out of thin air. The bloody woman must have heard her crying. 'You've wrecked this company. You should never have tried to run it in the first place.'

Lily stared into the mirror above the washbasins, fighting back the tears. Was Susie right? Did everyone else at Victoriana share her view? She thought of her father who'd trusted her and had wanted her so much to succeed. She'd failed him too. For a moment she was tempted to run away, to go back to London and acting, but that would be the coward's way out. She still believed in Victoriana, and she was going to have to find a way to fight back.

She heard Judith's voice calling her and quickly wiped her face. She was damned if she was going to let Judith see her like this.

'Ben Winter's on the phone for you. He said it was urgent.' Judith watched her curiously. 'I didn't know you two were seeing each other again. Has he invested in asbestos underpants in case you throw another coffee over him?'

'I'm not seeing him,' Lily snapped. 'Not like that, anyway.'

Things were always urgent with Ben, but this time he had a point. It was the last day of shooting and he wanted to see her before he left. Lily, miserable and angry and fighting against a powerful sense of failure knew she wanted to see him too.

It was Evie who came up with the lifesaving idea in the end. She was so angry with Charlotte for sweeping in and taking control that she decided she and Lily must find a way of saving the company themselves.

'We'll show her,' Evie promised over her third glass of retsina in the Greek restaurant where they'd gone to drown their sorrows and plan their fightback. She flung the end of her cyclamen silk wrap gaily over her shoulder in emphasis, almost knocking over the glass of Metaxas brandy she'd just ordered from the waiter's tray. The man only smiled. He'd spent a fortune having his restaurant redecorated with a mural of the Acropolis plus a few Bacchanalian scenes from the Daphynis wine festival and Evie had been the only person in over a year to make a point of praising it.

Normally they only got sober businessmen in on Wednesday lunchtimes who stuck religiously to the set lunch, drank mineral water and rarely tipped. This lady had started with calamari, then moved on to pricey red snapper which the locals avoided because of British prejudice and too many bones, and rounded it off with *two* kataifi, only one of which defeated most of their clients half way through. Now she was calling for Turkish delight. The manager opened a special box for her, spurning the usual one they gave out, which was made in Cleethorpes, and offered her the genuine Istanbul variety.

'Are you absolutely sure there's no way of raising some money fast to pay this man off?'

'I went through all that with Paul Allan.' Lily winced at using his name.

'There must be something.'

'Only the camisoles.' The thought of the camisoles, her first stupid mistake, depressed her so much she joined Evie in a brandy. 'We've sold a few through the catalogue, but there's twenty thousand of them sitting in the warehouse.'

Evie's elbow wobbled dangerously as she tried to lean on the table, but through the haze of retsina one pure light shone direct and dazzling. She stood up like Moses after being handed the Ten Commandments.

'I've got it! We could do a Special Offer in one of the colour supplements. That's what we did in Sydney. We had loads of black lace basques which no sensible woman would be seen dead in. We advertised them in a Sunday paper and – wooomf –' Evie's expansive gesture deposited brandy over the couple at the next table while Lily smiled apologetically, 'the buggers all went!'

'Evie,' Lily made herself sound more positive than she felt, 'you're completely, utterly brilliant!'

'And Connie can get that young man to take the photographs,' Evie went on. 'It's going to have to be pretty damn amazing. He'll never have taken a photo with more riding on it.'

'But how will we handle the orders?' Lily suddenly worried. 'The system's already overloaded. I'm spending a small fortune on gizmos and software already to try and sort it out.'

Evie looked like Boadicea stopped in mid battle-cry by a common soldier complaining about the state of his footwear. 'We'll do it like a Telethon. Get in loads of lines for a week. It's incredibly straightforward. Just one product, not your usual 300. I'll find you some volunteers, don't worry. It'll be a party. Like hop-picking.'

'Tell you what,' Lily suggested, her mouth full of another square of Turkish delight which the waiter had just given her, reluctant to see his star guests leave just when Christos from the kitchen was about to join them for a rousing chorus of Zorba's dance. 'Don't let's tell Ma about this.'

'Wouldn't dream of it. Here's to our new venture.' Evie shook her hand tight, then, unable to resist the lures of a man half her age with dark flashing eyes and a bouzouki, followed Christos to the postage stamp of a dance-floor, and joined arms with the delighted waiter.

It was only when she was back at Victoriana that Lily realized she hadn't mentioned Ben Winter to Evie, probably because she could imagine her aunt's robust reaction.

*

Connie wandered round the kitchen restlessly, trying to get on with the business of life. She had tried all her usual stand-bys to confront the blues. Yesterday she'd tidied the larder, putting down clean newspaper on its sticky shelves, washing all the jars of Worcestershire Sauce, barbecue relish and organic honey, then grouping them by category and arranging them in descending order of height. If the WI found out, they'd probably hand her the Cleanest Larder in Dorset award. Usually, imposing order on the domestic world soothed Connie's inner one, but not today. The squalls still persisted, rocking and jagging the smooth waters of Connie's once peaceful and uneventful life.

Euan was like an addiction, Connie saw, as she ruthlessly turned out the bedroom cupboard, restacking each drawer with military precision. Gavin, if only he knew it, could have read the barometer of his wife's emotions from how neatly his shirts were folded.

Addiction was dangerous, Connie reminded herself. It didn't matter what to: food, alcohol, chocolate, drugs, it was all the same. There were, Connie had read, people with addictive personalities and the only way to break the pattern was to cut the object out of your life completely. There could be no half measures. It started off, so the famous twelve-step programme decreed, with admitting that you were addicted.

'My name is Constance,' Connie said aloud, 'and I am erotically dependent.' She had just made another final decision to cut Euan out of her life when Lily and Evie arrived.

It struck Lily, still full of optimism and Greek brandy, that when she and Evie descended on her sister, Connie's kitchen didn't exude its usual enviable mood of comfort and joy. The appearance was the same, sun streaming on to polished boards, summer flowers in a bright jug on the blue-checked plastic table-cloth. Rayburn on for the still-chilly

266

evenings, Tara's boots possessively hogging the space in front of it, school paraphernalia everywhere and the washing machine humming reassuringly. It was Connie who seemed removed and distant, as though this weren't *her* kitchen at all. Even her beloved Radio Four was off and there was silence. Lily saw how crucial her sister was to the whole enterprise of the Wade household. If Connie switched herself off, just as she had Radio Four, the whole atmosphere changed.

Connie listened to their proposal and smiled faintly at their enthusiasm, until they came up with the suggestion of Euan.

After three agonizing days of cold turkey, trying not to think about his touch for every moment of every hour, their timing seemed especially bitter.

'I can't ring him, Lily, I just can't.'

Evie looked nonplussed at Connie's emotional outburst, but Lily, more attuned to her sister's way of thinking, saw at once what was going on. 'Of course you shouldn't,' she soothed. 'We'll easily find another photographer, won't we Evie?'

Evie, her usually sharp mind dimmed by disappointment and a second Metaxas, protested, 'But we'll never find anyone to touch Euan. He's got a rare talent, that boy. We've only got one crack at this, girls. Think of Victoriana.' An afterthought came to her which she decided might clinch it: 'Think of showing Charlotte how wrong she is.'

'There are plenty of other photographers with talent around,' Lily insisted, suddenly brisk. 'I think we should approach a few more.'

After they'd left, Connie walked purposefully to her supermarket-neat larder and helped herself to three of Tara's Jaffa cakes. Then, very calmly, she swept a row of jars off the shelf on to the slate floor where they would attract all manner of insect life and went to look for her train timetable. If she left now she could be with him by four and still get back tonight. Willing herself not to think about children or broken promises, she scribbled a note and took a pizza from the freezer. In the distance she could hear Jeremy playing a snatch of his test piece, the Aranjuez concerto, its mournful notes suggesting unbelievable sadness and pain.

Bromsbury wasn't the most romantic of locations. The gift fair was shoehorned into a hall normally used for double-glazing exhibitions, but it still managed to have the vague air of a middle Eastern bazaar. Traders from all over the world came here to sell everything from Christmas trinkets to carved African sculptures. Gavin was feeling buoyant, having just negotiated with an exporter from Bombay for jewelled silver picture frames of quite extraordinary beauty and surprisingly reasonable price.

'How did it go?' asked Terri who seemed to have an unerring instinct for where Gavin was at any one time.

'Pretty good, actually. I got a good deal, I think.'

'You are clever,' Terri said, her voice overflowing with warmth and sincerity.

Gavin glowed. He knew it was pathetic, but he couldn't remember when someone had last bothered to flatter him, or even been interested in him for that matter.

Terri was, he knew, eccentric. She disguised her size by wearing extraordinary old velvet clothes, often with beads and appliqués on them, which looked as though they'd come out of a steamer trunk in the 1920s. Somehow they suited her. She reminded him, though she might not have been entirely delighted at the comparison, of a well-worn but comfortable velvet sofa: not as smart as a Biedermeier chaise longue but an awful lot easier to live with.

'Do you fancy a drink? Everyone's starting to go. There's a bunch going over to the Frog and Ferret.'

It reminded Gavin of his student days, drinking pints of

bitter in noisy and hot surroundings, pregnant with possibilities. Even the muzak featured Marrakesh Express.

At ten a group of revellers peeled off to go for a curry, the one thing Bromsbury was famous for.

'Do you want to join them?' Terri asked. Then she added softly, 'Or we could go back to the hotel, it's only round the corner.' They'd discovered earlier that they were both staying in the same hotel. Gavin heard the invitation implicit in her question and had to drag his mind back to Connie. Infidelity is not the answer, he told himself, I should be getting things sorted out with Connie not screwing someone else.

Summoning every ounce of willpower, he tore himself away to look for a phone. Connie didn't have to make any declarations of undying ardour; just hearing her voice would be enough to remind him of what was at stake. It was Jeremy, however, who answered the phone and told him, with angry bluntness, that Connie had dashed off to London leaving them a note, frozen pizza, and an awful mess in the larder.

Back in the rapidly emptying pub, Terri was waiting for him. She reached out a silver-ringed hand, her smile melting the last of his dwindling resolve.

Charlotte was finding her return to Victoriana less triumphant than she'd expected. She had assumed there would be a communal sigh of relief and that everyone they employed would be humbly grateful. Instead, there was a surprising amount of rumbling resistance.

On her first day she had felt, certainly, a sense of tremendous pleasure as she sat at *her* desk, drinking in *her* view across the soft green valley towards the sea, but the irritation had soon arrived.

During her time in charge, Lily had altered almost every system in the company and Charlotte had the unfamiliar response of being told, often quite firmly, that 'Lily changed that. It works much better now.' In fact, Charlotte concluded waspishly, the whole atmosphere had changed. There was even pop music in the warehouse, with jokes and raucous remarks being lobbed to and fro. Didn't they realize there was a crisis?

By the end of her first day back she had to admit that her daughter must have possessed skills that Charlotte hadn't suspected, both with systems and with people. Still, Charlotte reminded herself, not quite able to take off the blinkers that had stood her through thirty-five years of successful business, she can't be that good or the company wouldn't be in this mess.

It took the session with George Forbes to really get to her.

Charlotte had always seen him as a boring little man, with those spots on his neck and his tendency to blush, and still living with his pushy mother at his age! She'd bracketed him, without too much thought, as an anorak-wearing train-spotter. The fact that his passion was for birds and that George was in fact a minor expert of some distinction, often asked for articles for birding journals, would have surprised her, but she might well have pointed out that train-spotters and bird-watchers weren't so very different after all.

What did surprise Charlotte was the way he dared talk to her, and in front of Judith too, which made it harder to ignore. Whether it was her age or the fact that she'd lost her nerve as a result of her heart attack, Charlotte didn't know, but she did know that she'd lost her taste for confrontation. Tearing a strip off people like George when they made mistakes had once been a pleasure. It braced the mind and kept the blood pumping, as well as keeping employees on their toes. Now, for the first time, she suspected it simply made people scared of you. Was that such an honourable or effective aim?

'George, I'd like you in my office in five minutes, please,' she had announced earlier today. Ordered might have been a more exact description, but then it was her company.

He had arrived and proceeded to outline to her, almost breezily, how things might look bad for Victoriana in the short term, but that the future of the company, thanks to Lily's miraculous improvements, was actually safer than it had been under her own management.

'There were lots of problems when she arrived. I did try and tell you that things were likely to go wrong, Mrs Brandon, that we had no real idea of our costs. Your daughter's dealt with all that extremely effectively.' He looked up from his printouts, a knight in shining polyester, jutting his chin combatively in Lily's defence. 'You should be proud of her.'

'Then why,' Judith butted in, during Charlotte's astonished hesitation, 'if Lily is so miraculously talented, is Victoriana on the verge of bankruptcy?'

'Because you, for one, didn't help her, did you, Mrs Brandon, at the beginning when she really needed you?' Charlotte was unprepared for the vehemence of George's reply. It was like finding that your faithful dog, whom you had treated badly and largely ignored but whom you had expected to offer his loyalty anyway, had suddenly turned and savaged you. It hurt both in the injury and in the surprise. 'Any normal mother would have helped all she could when her daughter had so little business experience, but you just left her to it. No wonder it was hard for her. Anyone would think you *wanted* her to fail.'

'Look, Mr Forbes, I think it's time you apologized to Mrs Brandon instead of making ridiculous accusations,' said Judith icily.

George ignored her, and took his glasses off to polish them, a glint of water in the corner of his eye. 'In all the years I've worked here, you never once asked my opinion. You just thought I was too unimportant to have anything worth listening to.' It shocked Charlotte to have her thoughts articulated and she was glad that with his glasses off the man probably couldn't see her expression. 'But Lily asked me, and she listened.'

And look where it got her, Judith was about to point out when she caught Charlotte's quelling eye. Charlotte shook her head slightly.

George, feeling himself to be standing up not just against Charlotte but against his own suffocating and autocratic mother, had the heady experience of taking life by the horns. Then, just as suddenly, it eluded him. 'I apologize. I've said too much. I think it'd be better if I went now. It won't take me long to clear my desk.'

To Judith's astonishment, Charlotte put a hand on the boring little man's arm. 'That won't be necessary, George. By all means go home now, but come back tomorrow and we'll go over the figures then.' The sympathy in Charlotte's voice was clearly genuine. 'My daughter was lucky to have you. As I am.'

George shuffled his papers together. He would take up Charlotte's invitation and go home – and if his mother objected, she could get lost. In fact he might drop by the estate agent and pick up some details of flats. It was time he moved out. He should have done it years ago.

'Why on earth did you do that, Charlotte?' Judith demanded. 'The man was appallingly rude and he'll clearly put a spanner in any plan you come up with. You should have fired him.'

'I'm sure I should,' Charlotte smiled affably, 'but I happen to rather like loyalty. It's so unusual these days.' She gestured to the insulated cafetière that sat on her desk. 'Cup of coffee?'

Judith shook her head. Charlotte might be harder to handle than she'd thought.

Euan loved the idea of photographing the camisole. Lingerie

ads either looked so romantic and vaseline-lensed that they had no sex appeal or so tacky, with boobs popping out all over, that they'd put off anyone with a sliver of subtlety. It would be a challenge to try and come up with something that was romantic *and* sexy.

'When's the deadline?' Connie could already feel the excitement of working with Euan refresh and renew her. He was so good at firing you up. Was the difference between him and Gavin that to one the glass was always half full and to the other half empty? Connie decided the thought wasn't fair. It was only lately that Gavin's natural optimism had been dented.

The paper needed the photographs in a week's time and they would be hard pushed to sort everything out by then. It would also be expensive. Were they completely mad to spend money when things looked so bad?

'Euan, what if no one wants to buy it?'

'Don't even think about failure,' he commanded. 'Our photograph will be so gorgeous that they'll be clipping the coupons the length and breadth of the land. Any ideas where we're going to shoot this masterpiece?'

'I've made a list of hotels with romantic four-poster bedrooms.'

At the thought of checking four-poster beds, Euan brushed up against her so that she could feel how hard he was through the faded denim of his jeans. Connie groaned with pleasure, forgetting all the resolutions she'd been trying to make to forget him.

'How did you get on at the fair?' she asked Gavin when he got back the next day. This time it was his turn to look shifty. 'Not bad actually. I found some beautiful mirrors and a ceramic horse from China that will look fantastic in the window. I can't wait for the stuff to arrive.'

Connie hugged him, delighted that he sounded cheerful

and energetic for once, and Gavin relaxed. He must stop feeling so jumpy or he'd go and confess to going to bed with Terri. Gavin was, he knew, the guilty-conscience type. At school when the Head had demanded who the culprit was for a particular crime, Gavin found himself tempted to volunteer, even though he'd been miles away from the scene, just so that the school wouldn't be kept in detention. He also slowed down every time he saw a policeman. This morning, he'd half expected to walk into the kitchen and find Connie, arm outstretched, pointing at him accusingly and saying 'Adulterer!'

In fact, Connie seemed rather better tempered than she had for days and almost insultingly devoid of suspicion.

'Would you like me to come and sort out the window of the shop this morning?' she offered.

'I thought you had this fashion shoot thing to organize.'

'I have, but I can fit the window in as well, if you like.'

'That'd be great.' He just hoped Terri wouldn't do anything silly, like ringing him at the shop. He'd better phone this morning and forestall her.

Jeremy watched his parents between the cereal boxes. They were being unnaturally polite to each other. There were none of the old jokes and insults that provided the usual breakfast-table atmosphere. He wanted to say: For God's sake pull yourselves together, why can't you, we're the kids round here. Maybe pretending nothing was happening, as his parents were already doing, was a safer strategy.

Lily read through the letter from S. J. Wilson's for the second time. It was a written confirmation of their request for payment in full within thirty days or they would be forced to start bankruptcy proceedings. Strictly, the letter should have gone to Charlotte but, touchingly, one of the secretaries clearly felt Lily should have the chance to read it first.

The letter sounded nothing like Sam. It was stilted and

official, with none of the warmth and sympathy of the man himself, almost as though it had been dictated by someone else. There was something strange about it, she knew it intuitively, although it could be that the tone was simple lawyerese, born of embarrassment.

She put the letter back on her desk and marked it for Charlotte's attention, then picked up her shoulder bag. She was going to drop in on S. J. Wilson's this morning to find out why Sam had done it.

Chapter 20

'We used to be in a converted church, a bit like you up at the Mill,' Sam Wilson told Lily as he showed her round his purpose-built factory, sited in a featureless industrial estate on the outskirts of Bindon, 'but it makes financial sense to be here.'

Charlotte's financial advisers had often suggested she move to a modern factory near the motorways, just as Sam had done. Perhaps if her mother had taken their advice they would be in less of a mess, but they would have lost their soul in the process.

'Don't you miss the old place?' she asked.

Sam Wilson grinned. 'God yes. There's nowhere for five miles to even go and get a decent pint. The old place was in the middle of town.' He was sixtyish with sandy hair and pale skin which looked as though it never saw the light of day. 'Still, turnover's up. No distractions I suppose. Lily . . .' he began. 'I'm glad you're here because . . .'

Lily knew he was about to apologize for the situation. 'Actually, Sam, I just wondered – was there any particular reason you suddenly asked for the money?' He looked shifty. He'd been expecting this since the moment she'd arrived. 'I mean you normally allow us ninety days. Why the hurry all of a sudden? Was it just the article in the paper?'

Looking at her lovely, sad face, the eyes glowing with concern, and remembering what a breath of fresh air she'd been after the sternness of her mother, Sam wished he could tell her the truth: Barry North had put him up to it and he couldn't afford to cross North's Mail Order. If he told her, however, he would lose North's business and go under in Victoriana's wake.

'It's true we've laid off a dozen people,' Lily went on, 'but we're coming round now, Sam. It's been a difficult few months, but I know Victoriana's going to survive. Please let us have a while longer to pay. If you give us a vote of confidence, it'll encourage other suppliers to do the same.'

There was an embarrassingly long silence which Lily resisted jumping into. She'd once read an interview with an investigative journalist who said he often left five whole minutes before interrupting a subject who had something to hide, even though those five minutes stretched out agonizingly as if he were on the rack.

'Look, Lily . . .' he began, then stopped abruptly.

'Yes, Sam,' she encouraged. There was something. She'd known there was something. People didn't change their business practices of thirty years for no reason.

They were walking through the bustling factory now. On all sides young girls were cutting out fabric on intricate machines, managing somehow to jiggle to Radio One at the same time. 'Nothing,' he said. Whatever it was, Sam Wilson had clearly thought better of coming out with it. 'I'm just sorry about all the problems it must be causing you, that's all.'

This was no time to let him off the hook, Lily decided. 'Yes. It's a tragic situation. If Victoriana did have to close down, a hundred and fifty people would lose their jobs.' She almost added 'All because of you', but decided it was too unfair. The implication was there whether she spelled it out or not, but he didn't take the bait. Lily had to bite back her disappointment. She was so sure there was something he was keeping from her.

'I'll see you to your car,' he said.

The cars were parked tightly and Lily had to concentrate on getting out without taking the wing off the one next door. She had just safely manoeuvred herself into the street when Sam Wilson leaned down to the passenger window.

Lily sensed the pressure he was under too. 'Look, no hard feelings, Sam. You're an honest man. I know you wouldn't have done this unless you had to. It's a tough world out there.' She smiled at him encouragingly, shaming him with the genuineness of her sympathy.

Sam looked at her silently. He'd heard she'd been an actress and had given it up to run Victoriana. He could see her on the stage. She had a kind of polish that didn't come into his world very often, but she didn't look happy. There were black fingerprints round her eyes and her skin seemed to have lost that creamy quality he'd noticed in her before. She was a brave girl to risk standing in her mother's shadow.

'Goodbye, Sam.'

'Goodbye.' He hesitated, then seemed to come to a reluctant decision. 'Look, Lily, do you know a character called Barry North? He runs North's Mail Order.'

'I've heard of him, certainly.'

'Well, watch out for him.'

Sam turned abruptly away, leaving Lily's mind racing. Barry North occasionally appeared in the gossip columns, and had something of a reputation as a Casanova, but she didn't think it was her moral welfare Sam Wilson was warning her about.

Her first thought was to tell Paul, then she thought again. She was so angry with him for handing over their business. She'd sort this out on her own.

*

278

'How are things with Victoriana?' Paul Allan asked Clive Green. Paul was worried about Lily. Although she would never believe him, he had great faith in her abilities, but he could see that her problems were building up into tidal wave proportions. Even if she'd been a highly experienced businesswoman, it would have been tough, but she wasn't. She was a novice, a fast thinker who'd made some mistakes and learned from them.

Clive Green jumped at the question even though technically he had nothing to feel guilty about, unless Paul had found out about his link with North's. But that was almost impossible.

'Dodgy. One supplier's demanded payment and there could be a rush.'

'But none of the others have yet?'

'I thought you were off the case?' Clive pointed out resentfully, his jowls wobbling in irritation.

'In a day-to-day sense, yes, but I told you I wanted to keep a fatherly eye on it all the same.'

Clive raised a sarcastic eyebrow. Paul clearly couldn't decide whether he wanted to get shot of the whole embarrassing thing, or be a Sir Galahad, charging to Victoriana's rescue. Paul Allan was First Venture's golden boy and nothing he'd touched yet had ever gone remotely wrong. Maybe he was scared if it did, the shit would stick.

'Do they look like they can make their next payment?'

'Not unless someone's got a hotline to the Almighty. The old lady's taken over the reins again, so they must be panicking. Pity. I was hoping for a few long sessions with the daughter, poring over the cash flow. She could warm my cockles any time.'

Paul banged out of the room, seething. He was within a millimetre of slugging that creep Green. Christ, poor Lily, how much she must have hated that, having to let her mother take the business back, saying I told you so. Things must be pretty desperate for Lily to let her.

He knew from a career point of view he should stay on the sidelines, but he couldn't. He dialled Lily's direct line.

Judith, the new occupant of Lily's desk, answered it. She held the receiver against her chest for a moment, thinking fast. She'd always suspected there was something between Lily and Paul. He clearly wanted to be Lily's knight in shining armour and since North's was also a client of First Venture, he'd be well placed to make trouble if he started digging.

'She's out, I'm afraid. We're not seeing much of her at the moment. I think she may be going back to acting.' Divine inspiration struck Judith. 'She might be with Ben Winter, of course. He's filming round here and they've been out together a lot. I don't suppose she'll want to stay in Dorset much longer. Ben will want her in London.'

Paul's throat closed up so much he found it hard to speak, 'I didn't know. Thanks a lot.'

Paul held on to the phone for so long a mechanical voice had to remind him to replace the handset. She was back with Ben Winter. He'd thought when all this mess with Victoriana was over there might be a chance for them. How bloody naïve he'd been.

While Charlotte was still out of the room Judith made a swift call. 'Your idea of getting Wilson's to threaten bankruptcy was a master stroke,' she congratulated Barry. 'There isn't a hope in hell that Victoriana can meet the payment. If you make an offer now, I think Charlotte will go for it. She loathes the idea of bankruptcy. She sees it as a public disgrace. Say you'll try and save the jobs. That'll probably clinch it.'

'I'll have my lawyers draw up the offer today.'

Judith wished she were there in person to see his face.

'Things will happen fast, then. It might be useful if I started looking for a new HQ,' she said.

She knew she was pushing her luck because Barry had never actually come out and conceded her partnership with him, nor that Victoriana should be run from London.

'Remind me when the payment's due,' he said quickly.

'Less than a month.'

'Why not?' he said finally. 'Not long now.' He loved this moment when complicated plans finally paid off.

'No.' Judith smiled to herself. 'Not long at all now.'

The door behind opened and Charlotte, looking strained, came back into the room. Taking in her mother-in-law's drawn expression, Judith experienced a rare moment of guilt, which she swiftly suppressed. Charlotte and Edward deserved to lose their beloved company. They should never have asked Lily to run it in the first place. If she had children she wouldn't dream of letting them run her company just because of their genes. Sentimentality had no place in business and Charlotte Brandon would never have been in this mess if she'd had the sense to see that.

Lily lay in the bath, trying to decide what the hell to do. She wanted to make up her mind now, not in the heat of the moment, about whether or not she was going to jump into bed with Ben. The rational part of her mind was shocked at how attracted she still was to him, how much she'd thought about him since his reappearance in her life. But what about Paul? There had been complete silence from him since their fight. He'd certainly managed to get over her quickly. Unlike beautiful, bad Ben Winter.

In the Crown Hotel Ben was also thinking about Lily. He hadn't had to bother much with seductions. Women had always queued up for his attentions, though often it was the character he played that really attracted them. Half the women in London had wanted to screw the anguished defence lawyer in *Suspicious Minds* and Ben had been happy to oblige, though he'd found it boring when they wanted to talk about the legal issues as well.

The thought of seducing someone you'd already been out with for six months was both daunting and intriguing. What would stir Lily up? It was quite a blow to his ego to admit how little he knew about her preferences. The therapy must be helping, he supposed, if he was actually thinking about someone else for a change. The only thing he knew for sure was that she liked Australian chardonnay so he made sure he had enough to lower the defences of a Mother Superior.

He tidied his suite, a very unfamiliar feeling, wondering whether to leave out the video of himself in *Suspicious Minds*, but Lily wouldn't be fooled by that. Dressing gowns and Noël Coward wouldn't work either. He had to make her laugh.

Every diner in the restaurant watched with envy as Ben regaled Lily with gossip, stories and jokes until her jaw ached so much she had to beg him to stop. Finally, Lily looked at her watch. Embarrassed, she tried to cover the gesture but Ben caught her wrist in a grip that was both gentle and firm. 'Lovely Lily,' he said softly with a smile that would have melted the hearts of the toughest audience, 'will you come to bed with me?' And then he added the word she'd rarely ever heard from him, 'Please.'

Chapter 21

The door had barely closed behind them before Ben's arms were around her, half-carrying her to the huge curtained four-poster.

On the bed she felt his weight pinning her downwards as she sank into the soft enveloping mattress. His hands reached insistently for her breasts. 'Slow down,' she murmured, 'there's plenty of time.' But Ben seemed driven by a kind of desperation she'd never seen before. His eyes were closed and she could feel his hot breath on her neck.

'I've got to have you, Lily, you're my survival.'

She felt his hand rip her tights and froze in horror. 'For Christ's sake, Ben, stop this . . .'

'Lily, Lily,' he muttered, groping for his fly, 'I need you. I need you so much . . .'

Lily felt herself close up. She couldn't believe this was the charming companion of a few moments ago. Had he gone mad? She began to try and push him off, but Ben hardly saw her now. He was grinding himself into her, his insistent fingers ripping her tights still further.

It was over in seconds. Her thighs ached from the violence, but that was nothing to the pain of being used as though she were simply an object for his gratification.

His eyes lost their glazed look. 'I'm sorry. I just needed you so desperately. I've been thinking about nothing but tonight for days. My whole future depends on you, Lily.'

Lily gasped. Even now he didn't seem to see the enormity of what he'd just done. He tried to stroke her face but she pushed his hand away furiously. Ben looked at her searchingly, seeming to take in her torn tights for the first time. 'I've blown it, haven't I?' He even had the nerve to look miserable, but she wasn't falling for it this time.

'You certainly bloody well have.' She pulled down her skirt and shrugged his attempt at tenderness violently off.

'Forgive me, Lily, please.' His dark, luminous eyes glistened with tears, but she knew at once they were tears for himself, not her.

She felt sick. 'I'm going Ben, and I don't want to hear from you ever again. If you write to me or send me flowers, I'll agree to that interview the *Sunday Special* were so keen to get.'

He didn't try to stop her, but watched soulfully from the bed, as though *she* were the one who was acting strangely. In his disturbed world-view he already seemed to be constructing a story in which he was both hero and victim.

To her immense relief there was a taxi waiting outside the hotel with a driver who took her home without wanting to make cheerful conversation.

Lily handed him a ten pound note and dashed in, without waiting for any change, straight up to her flat and tore off her clothes. Under the hottest shower she could bear her mind was still numb with pain and betrayal. How could she have been so wrong about him? She should never have gone up with him. No, her mind cried out in rebellion, don't take the responsibility, that's how men always get away with it. It wasn't your fault.

She stumbled out of the shower into a huge warm bath

towel and without even bothering to find a nightdress buried herself under the duvet and cried herself to sleep.

The shock and pain of last night hit her even before she was fully awake. By a supreme act of will she blanked it out of her mind. She wasn't going to let this ruin her life. She had enough to worry about as it was. The only real relief was that Ben was going today and she knew he would take her at her word. She wouldn't be seeing him again. She'd seen it in his eyes that he'd believed her threat.

Lily hid her face in the pillow, not yet able to face the reality of everyday life and all she had to do to save Victoriana. A loud banging on the front door finally penetrated her consciousness and she recognized Evie's voice shouting for her.

Eventually Lily dragged herself out of bed and opened the door. Evie stood leaning on the frame as incongruous in her vibrant clothes as a budgie in a tree of sparrows.

'Come on, girl, what kind of time do you call this? I tried to get you at the office, but they said they hadn't seen you. Get yourself up, for God's sake. I'm taking you to lunch. You look terrible,' Evie pointed out cheerfully.

Lily half ran into the bathroom and scrubbed her face till it shone like a novice dedicating her morning wash to Jesus. The clothes she'd worn last night were a tangled heap. She bundled them into the dirty clothes basket, desperately wishing the memory was so easily dispensed with, and dragged on a white teeshirt and jeans.

Realizing her lack of tact, Evie hugged her niece tightly. 'Fancy telling me about it?'

For a moment Lily was tempted, but she didn't want to admit how stupid she'd been in letting Ben Winter back into her life.

'Come on,' comforted Evie, 'spit it out.'

'I'm scared, Evie.' She might at least talk about one of the things that was getting to her. 'What if we really can't meet the payment?'

'Forget lunch.' Evie could see that what her niece needed wasn't food but confidence-building. 'Let's go for a walk instead and talk about it.'

Lily felt herself calm down. Finding Evie on your doorstep was like being handed a cool cloth to soothe your brow when you had a raging headache.

They walked out into the blinding summer's day. From either side of them the branches almost met and there was a sense of lulling, protective shade in the narrow lane by the Mill. The silence was so deep that it was almost audible.

'Now then,' Evie prompted gently, 'what are you worried about?'

'I feel so alone, more than I've ever felt. Connie's caught up in a fantasy of her own . . .'

'That young man, you mean?' interrupted Evie.

Lily nodded. 'So many people are going to be hurt and there's nothing I can do but watch. And the business is in real trouble because of me. Ma never thought I could do it and she was right. They should have asked Judith. She's the kind of daughter Ma wanted. Why doesn't she believe in *me*?' Evie bit her lip at the depth of pain in Lily's voice. 'I've tried to ask her, but she always dismisses me. I'm not imagining it, am I? She's never loved me, even when I was a child.'

Evie felt as though the whole world had ground to a stop, waiting for her answer. If only Lily had been her child. She would have given Lily so much love it would have overflowed. She would have made her believe in herself, see her own beauty, her courage, her intelligence.

Evie knew she had to defend her sister, tempting though it was to appropriate Lily's love. 'Charlotte is an amazing woman, Lily. Look how she built up Victoriana from nothing; how much she cares for all the people who work for her.'

'She loves them all right. And Connie and Jonathan. I'm the one who's the problem.' Evie wished passionately there was something she could do to take away the pain. 'If only *you* were my mother. You're everything she isn't.'

She longed to be able to tell Lily the truth: that there were reasons why her mother had found it so hard to love her; that it wasn't as Lily believed, had always believed, that there was nothing in herself to love. We have children so recklessly, thought Evie, without seeing how much we hold their future, their whole beings, in the palm of our hand.

Bloody Charlotte. Bloody love.

But she couldn't tell her. It wouldn't be fair to Charlotte. She couldn't deliberately be the one to push over the edifice her sister had so carefully constructed over so many years – but on the other hand, perhaps she didn't have to strive officiously to keep this tower of illusions alive . . .

'Come on.' She hugged her niece tight. 'Where's the Brandon fighting spirit? We've got the special offer coming up. You mustn't give up yet. We're all relying on you.'

Some of Evie's strength miraculously began to flow into Lily. She was right. They couldn't give up now, and throwing herself into the fight might even make her forget about Ben.

For the next two weeks she threw herself into work to heal her wounds. She might not be running the company, but there was plenty to do: answering the angry letters they'd had, criticizing the new catalogue; leaning on the manufacturer to get more of Tara's dress back in stock – the fabric still hadn't appeared from Brussels – and trying to solve the computer problem. Three sets of experts had been now, each with a different, wildly expensive solution. To make things worse complaints were starting to come about the orders that had been lost in the system. Then there was Sam Wilson's tip-off. How could she find out more about Barry North? Her first impulse was to ring Paul, but that simply brought the memory of her encounter with Ben back. Fortunately, Ben must be safely back in London by now and at least he'd taken her at her word and left her alone. She wouldn't be hearing from Ben Winter again.

Charlotte knew she looked as if she were in control, but that was her natural bearing. The truth was that, for the first time in her life, Charlotte was frightened. Death hadn't scared her when she'd had the heart attack. She didn't believe in either God or the afterlife: they were, in Charlotte's view, props to take one's eye away from reality; but the public humiliation of bankruptcy was one thing she couldn't face. Her concern for all the people who worked for her was genuine and heartfelt but there was something that scared her more – the thought that if Victoriana went under, the press coverage would be enormous, there would be retrospectives on her life and her climb to the top, no more privacy ever. And if they really started digging, God knows what they would find. It all seemed to Charlotte too much · to bear.

She leaned on the edge of the window watching everyone go home, a dull pain thudding in her head. What was the right thing to do?

It was beginning to get dark outside and the columns of figures were swimming in her head. In the middle of her desk was a letter that had arrived today from their company lawyers which so far she had mentioned to no one, not even Edward. It came from North's Mail Order, and it contained an offer to buy Victoriana from them as soon as possible.

Chapter 22

The sum they were offering was much less than Charlotte believed the company to be worth, but it would be a swift and decisive answer to their problems. If she sold Victoriana, there would be no bankruptcy, no public humiliation – and no dangerous digging into Charlotte's past by journalists as there would have been if the company collapsed publicly.

It was, she had decided, the only answer; but she would need one other family member to back her up.

She draped her jacket round her shoulders. She'd walk home, the heat had subsided and it would give her time to think. The office was already empty. She paused at the notice board with all the letters and photographs sent in by their customers. With a leap of pride it seemed to her that Victoriana must be unique. What other business had customers who wrote to them, chatty letters giving their opinions on the product? Would a Victoriana owned by a conglomerate like North's be able to sustain that relationship?

She went back to her desk and wrote a memo out by hand, summoning the family to a board meeting to discuss an issue vital to Victoriana's future. Instead of holding it at home, as they usually were, it would be here in

Victoriana's offices. Charlotte couldn't bear to discuss selling the company while sitting in the home where, with fumbling inexperienced fingers, she'd cut out Victoriana's very first garments, all those years ago. She'd had no idea then that she'd be so wildly successful. Just as she'd had no idea, less than a year ago, that it would all end as sadly as this.

Edward was waiting for her outside on the steps, concerned at the lateness of her return. She handed him the letter from their lawyers.

'Have you decided what you want to do?' The beauty of the evening had already faded for him. He already knew the answer. He read the letter again. The sum offered was ludicrous, much less than they could have got a year ago. He tried not to remember Jonathan and Judith's predictions that this was exactly what would happen, but no doubt they would remind Lily at the earliest opportunity. Poor Lily. Maybe in his desperation that she should prove herself he'd left her too much alone.

'I'm calling a board meeting to vote on it. Will you support me?' Charlotte suspected Edward was going to oppose her, but that was a risk she had to take.

'But why sell now, for such a ridiculous sum?'

'Because any minute we'll be bankrupt and I can't bear that to happen. Besides, North has offered to save at least some jobs. If we go under, he'll just pick off the parts he wants and everyone will be out of work.'

'Have you talked to Lily about it? You might at least find out what she thinks.'

'Lily's hiding her head in the sand and still thinks everything's going to be hunky dory.'

'What about Connie and Jonathan?'

Charlotte shook her head. She'd tried to contact Connie, but been told she was in London. Jonathan would support her because at least he got something this way – and anyway, he would do what Judith told him. Connie was harder. Lily, of course, would oppose. That left Edward.

And Leo. She could have kicked herself at the irony of Leo Orson, the friend they'd turned to when they were desperate for money to fund the company, still owning any of her shares. At the time, Leo had been the only person they knew with enough cash to lend them the last few thousand they'd needed to start the company. Despite all her attempts, he'd never agreed to sell them back to her. It had been his way of keeping a link. Yet in all these years, he hadn't voted on anything. Did he know that Lily had been running the company? If so, that might complicate matters, but she'd had no sign that he did.

Charlotte allowed herself the rare indulgence of thinking about Leo. She hadn't seen him in more than thirty-five years and yet she could picture every line of his face. Would that wonderful red-gold hair be grey by now? And the height that had always dominated any group be stooped by age or twinges of arthritis? She couldn't imagine the years catching up with Leo Orson. His attraction had always come from within, from the power of his personality. A room always seemed smaller with Leo in it, and when he left, it was as though someone had turned out the light. That was how she had felt after she had seen him that last time, as though someone had hit a switch in her very soul, leaving only half of her alive, like a stroke victim who has to relearn the simplest things. Charlotte had had to learn to live again – but she'd done it, like she did everything else, with determination, and only allowed herself the faintest shadow of regret. The only way she had performed this miracle was by shutting down her emotions. It had taken resources of willpower that few people possess, but willpower was a quality Charlotte had in abundance. She wasn't going to start asking herself now if that choice she'd made so many years ago had been the right one.

'Are you going to support me?'

Edward met her eyes steadily. 'I haven't heard both sides of the case yet, have I Charlotte?'

'No,' she said slowly, 'and you've always been a fair man, haven't you, Edward?' He scanned her face for a glint of sarcasm, but there was none.

'You're determined to sell to North, then?'

'What other option is there? You know I can't watch Victoriana go under.'

Edward glanced around him at the room where they'd started Victoriana all those years ago, when they were young and eager and it had all been such an adventure. The house had been full of friends from art school then – drawing, designing, talking, drinking – with Leo Orson sitting at the end of the table, dominating everything with his fiery charm, explaining his theories that life and work should be one seamless activity, lighting them all up with the taper of his enthusiasm.

'We could start again,' Edward insisted, his voice suddenly charged with eagerness, 'on a small scale. Maybe we just got too big. It could be just like the old days. At the very beginning.' His mind raced back to the excitement they'd felt then, staying up all night, discussing their theories of design, living almost in a communal way in this beautiful farmhouse, romantics all, surrounded by friends. They had believed utterly in what they did. What an incredible time it had been.

'It's too late, Edward.' Charlotte's voice sounded tired and defeated. 'We can't recapture the old days.' That time was gone. And Leo with it.

'Don't do it, Charlotte.' Edward's voice vibrated with emotion.

'I care about Victoriana as much as you do, but has it never struck you that selling it might be the only way to save it?'

Edward shook his head. 'I can see you've already made up your mind.' His eyes held hers, locked in sadness. 'I can't support you, Charlotte.'

Charlotte pulled her jacket round her, as if it were cold. 'Then I'll have to see who will.'

They both contemplated the fact that Charlotte was the major shareholder. She only needed one other person to support her to carry the deal through.

Evie had intended to say goodnight, but when she heard their raised voices she decided not to. It was so unusual to hear Charlotte and Edward quarrel that it had to be about something important – and she had a good idea what.

Connie's mind was so full of Euan and misery that she hardly took in the significance of being summonsed to a board meeting by her mother, but Lily, sharp-eyed and suspicious after Sam Wilson's hint, guessed what was going on at once.

A rap on the open kitchen door made them both jump, until Evie's face appeared. For once their aunt's expression was grim.

'She's had an offer for Victoriana, hasn't she?' Lily guessed.

Evie nodded. 'I heard them quarrelling about it last night. It was pretty heated.'

'I can even tell you the buyer.' Now that it had happened, Lily felt surprisingly calm. 'It's Barry North of North's Mail Order.'

'How on earth did you know that?' Evie was amazed. 'They didn't mention a buyer.'

'From something Sam Wilson hinted at when I went to see him a couple of weeks ago. I wonder how much he's offering.'

'Not much I gather. Edward said it was ludicrous.'

'Evie,' Connie teased, trying to break through the impenetrable gloom that had taken over the room, 'you must have had a glass to the door.'

Evie laughed. 'I have exceptionally good hearing.'

'Especially when your ear is adjacent to the keyhole.'

'Look, whose side are you on?' demanded Evie.

'Sorry,' said Connie. 'But she can't sell unless one of us agrees, and if Pa's opposed that leaves only us three and that man in Australia. Lily and I aren't going to sell, are we Lily?'

'Jonathan might,' reminded Lily, voicing what they were all thinking.

'You mean Judith might,' Connie corrected. 'Even Sooty's got more independence than Jonathan.'

'But why would she want to sell, if North isn't offering much money? She won't get many Gucci handbags with Jonathan's share, supposing our dear bro hasn't converted most of it into margaritas by the time they get it anyway.'

Lily's mind fizzled with sudden insight. 'She sabotaged the press launch, remember. Maybe it wasn't just out of spite. You don't think she could be getting some kind of kickback from North's, do you?' She thought of her manipulative sister-in-law with distaste. She wouldn't put anything past Judith. It had been amazing to watch how Judith had wormed herself into Charlotte's respect and affection. All that flattery, not to mention the odd expensive gift. Charlotte had come to rely on Judith more than her own daughters. A perfect position to be in to influence someone.

'Okay, then,' Connie demanded, 'if you're right, how *are* we going to save the business in exactly two weeks?'

'With the profits of the special offer, of course. I've done the sums. It's going to be a huge hit and with the money from that we'll stave off First Venture and give Wilson's something on account. I'll talk Sam Wilson into accepting it.'

'I don't want to put a damper on things, but how can we process the orders when the computers can't cope already?' Connie asked.

Lily smiled, a hint of the old reckless Lily who poured cappuccino into lovers' laps peeping through the seriousness of their predicament. She tapped her nose. 'Evie's already thought of that. Old technology.'

Connie smelled a rat. 'Meaning what exactly?'

'Meaning you, me, Evie, June – and I'm sure Shauna would come back and help us – plus some temps we're hiring in, working twenty-four hours a day between us, with order forms and Biros.'

'There won't be time, surely?'

'Yes, there will. The ad goes in on Sunday and Evie says most of the response is instant. People whip out their credit cards and get on the phone. The beauty of it is, it's cash up front. They pay before you deliver so, if it works, which of course it's absolutely one hundred per cent bound to, we'll have all the lovely money before the board meeting and we can make a real case.'

Connie's spirits drooped. There were so many ifs involved.

'But what if . . .' Connie didn't know where to start. Lily's salvage plan had more holes in it than a teabag. She could imagine Lily in her acting days, geeing up the cast for some potentially disastrous first night, willing them to ignore the critics waiting to savage them, or an audience of one, or discovering that the 'profit share' deal they'd all agreed would founder because there weren't any profits. 'How many first nights have you had, Lil?'

'Zillions.'

'And how many second nights?'

'That would be telling. Now come on, O ye of little faith. When's the shoot for the camisole ad?'

'Tomorrow.'

'I don't want to worry you, Connie love,' Evie chipped in, her flaming hennaed hair lit from behind like a harpy at sunset, 'but we're all depending on you over this. Just make sure it's completely, utterly bloody brilliant, will you?'

'Thanks a lot,' Connie flashed back acidly, wondering how the hell they could pull off what sounded to her like a miracle. 'It's nice to know we're all sharing the responsibility.'

As she waited for the others to turn up for the photo session the next morning, Connie was glad she had something practical to do, rather than simply sitting about worrying.

Euan was already there and in his usual way had charmed the management into giving him extra facilities: free champagne and flowers that some middle-aged Lothario had ordered for his nubile young mistress three doors down. Connie had to admit, the hotel had done them proud. Unprepossessing and featureless from the outside, the interior had been turned into a paradise of camp Edwardiana. Dark polished wood gleamed down at them, lit by enormous chandeliers and art nouveau glass. The four poster, lined with red damask and piled with cushions, would have lured John Knox from the straight and narrow. It was perfect.

Connie itched to straighten the cushions but her palms were damp and sticky with tension. Instead she watched the make-up man unpacking his box of tricks, which reminded Connie of a mechanic's toolbox, on to the lavish dressing table. Inside were stashed row after row of eyeshadows, lipsticks and face powders.

The stylist busily arranged froths of lace he'd brought with him on the bed, plumped up the pillows and fiddled with the drapes until he was satisfied. He then stretched out in the pose they'd selected for the model. 'How do I look, pets?' he demanded. 'Even I'd go to bed with a rich businessman in this gaff, I tell you.'

'Surprise, surprise,' commented the make-up artist drily. The stylist was his current lover and they took jobs together. 'You'd go to bed with a double-glazing salesman in a Happy Eater, you would.'

Euan surveyed the stylist's work and removed the roses that the man had just strewn artistically over the bed. 'This isn't an ad for Interflora, you know. She'll probably sit on one and end up with Band Aid on her bum. By the way, where is our model anyway?'

Connie jumped. She'd been so nervous, with so much riding on today, that she hadn't noticed the absence of the most important person. The girl should have been here half an hour ago. She scrabbled around for the call sheet. It was there perfectly clearly. She dialled reception but they were none the wiser. Finally Connie got on to the model agency.

'I can't understand it.' The booker sounded as angry as she was. 'She should have been with you hours ago. I'll chase her up.'

Connie had just ordered them all a cup of coffee when the agency woman was back, grovelling. 'I can't tell you how sorry I am, she's overslept.'

Connie couldn't believe it. They only had the room for the morning, otherwise the cost would have been prohibitive. 'How long will she be?'

'No more than an hour or so,' lied the booker.

'Where does she live?' Connie demanded suspiciously.

'Sevenoaks.'

'She must be WonderWoman, then,' pointed out the stylist, 'if she can get here in an hour.'

'Right,' Euan commanded as soon as Connie put the phone down. 'Get your clothes off.'

'*What*?' squawked Connie. 'You've got to be kidding. I'm a 38-year-old mother of two.'

'Think of all those readers' wives in the naughty magazines,' encouraged the stylist helpfully.

'They're all bought by porn-mad men who'd fancy their mother-in-law if she took her clothes off,' Connie protested, hanging on to her jumper with all the zeal of a virgin martyr. 'I can't, Euan, we'll have to re-shoot.'

'It's the only way we're going to get this done. There isn't time to find anyone else.' Euan was wearing his charm-the-old-birds-from-the-trees expression. 'I'll make you look more beautiful than any eighteen-year-old. Trust me, Connie.'

'I've never trusted men who say Trust Me.' Connie backed away as the stylist and make-up artist moved threateningly in on her.

'Constance,' Euan clinched it, 'it's for Victoriana. You're our last hope. Remember?'

'Poor Victoriana.' Connie began undoing her buttons, sighing deeply. 'Some last hope.'

Lily told herself that ten days was not an absurdly small amount of time to save Victoriana. A lot could happen in ten days if you wanted it to. She'd approached one of the young, keen designers to produce the art work for the Special Offer and it looked beautiful. She'd checked the details six times – the one thing they couldn't afford was a mistake – and now she was wondering whether to show it to her mother or not.

Eventually she decided against it. She would simply leave a copy of the offer in her mother's In-tray and Charlotte would come across it next week, by which time the newspaper carrying it would have safely gone to bed.

Neither Charlotte nor Judith, who shadowed her everywhere these days, doing little errands for her and appearing to consult her on the smallest thing, were in the office. Lily put the artwork under a pile of samples and turned to the window. It was glorious weather and Lily couldn't resist leaning out. A warm wind lifted her hair and caressed the back of her neck, tempting her to abandon the struggle and head out into the inviting green arms of the country-side. The shady lane at the end of Victoriana's drive looked dark and cool, with sunlight playing patterns on the stony white of its surface. Little knots of staff sat on the grass by the millstream chatting. It was idyllic. But for how long?

Turning miserably away, her pleasure lost at the constant nagging thought that if the company folded it would be her fault, she began to close the window. A sudden breeze blew some papers, neatly piled on Judith's desk, to the Turkish-carpeted floor.

Lily bent to pick them up, leafing through them at the same time to see if there was anything even vaguely incrimi-nating. There was absolutely nothing linking Judith to North's Mail Order. Most were everyday correspondence with suppliers, some requests for Charlotte to speak or give interviews – something she hated doing unless the whole thing had been her idea, whereupon she loved it – and memos from George about financial questions. Only one thing looked remotely interesting: a letter from a famous London firm of estate agents, laying out the details of some offices the agent had clearly just shown Judith round. The letter, which must be a summary of a previous conversation, confirmed that the space would be available at short notice, should any sudden eventuality arise. Lily couldn't see any possible link with Victoriana. Maybe Judith was considering starting up on her own again.

Then the size of the space hit her. This couldn't be offices for a one-woman PR company. The square footage was huge. A suspicion, crazy but persistent, planted itself in the back of her mind. Looking round to check that no one was around, Lily wrote down the agent's name.

In the peace of her own office she dialled his number. The man was out; would she like to leave a message?

Suddenly decisive, she gave her number. 'Tell him Miss Lily Brandon called, *not* Mrs Judith Brandon, and ask him to phone me back, please.'

Once she'd made the call, Lily felt faintly ridiculous, convinced that there had to be some sensible explanation. A wave of sudden exhaustion hit her. This wasn't like her. She had the constitution of herds of oxen. Wasn't she the one who could stay up forever after first nights, drink till dawn, then start all over again?

She searched in her drawer for a couple of paracetamol then went off to get a glass of water from the machine that dispensed it, iced, into silly triangular cups you couldn't put down anywhere. The water was refreshing but the dragging tiredness came back instantly. Back at her desk she laid her face on her arms for a moment and was instantly asleep.

The phone woke her and for a second she had no idea where she was.

'Miss Lily Brandon?' enquired the male voice.

'Speaking.'

'This is Mr Nutley of King, Flitch & Montague.'

Lily pulled herself back into the living world. 'Hello, Mr Nutley. Thanks for ringing me so promptly.'

Encouraged by her friendly tones, Mr Nutley unbent. 'Tell me, Miss Brandon, though it's rather cheeky of me to ask' – he had a friendly camp air that reminded her of her acting friends – 'are you Miss Lily Brandon of Victoriana?'

'I am indeed.'

'I thought so.' The man sounded pleased, as though she'd just confirmed a bet. 'And Mrs Judith Brandon is also involved?'

'She operates on behalf of other people too. She's a consultant.'

Mr Nutley sounded confused, 'So it's not Victoriana that's

moving its HQ to London then? Pity. I've found the perfect place: Duke's Reach, a riverside development in Richmond.'

'Then I'm sorry to disappoint you. Victoriana isn't planning to move anywhere.'

'Ah. My mistake.' Mr Nutley didn't sound to Lily as though he thought he were making a mistake at all.

Her thoughts were interrupted by the arrival of Connie, looking flustered and sheepish, clutching the transparencies from the photo shoot.

'How did it go?' Lily demanded, grappling with the envelope.

Connie snatched it back. 'Fine,' she insisted, mysteriously brief.

'How was the hotel? How was Euan? How was the model? Did it look brilliant?'

Connie blushed. 'Not too bad considering.'

'Considering what?'

'Considering that the model didn't turn up and I had to stand in for her.'

Lily laughed unflatteringly. 'You didn't really.'

'Actually I did. Look.'

Connie took out one of the transparencies and held it up to the light. 'With the aid of soft focus, clever lighting, and the best make-up artist in London . . .!'

'God, Con, you look staggering!'

And she did. Her hair shone in the warm glow of the flattering lighting, and her pale skin gleamed enticingly. She reminded Lily of one of the early Hitchcock heroines, classy and sophisticated but somehow vulnerable at the same time. But the thing that shocked Lily was the expression in her eyes: there wasn't even the merest suggestion of the house-wifely in Connie's expression. 'I had no idea you were so sexy!'

'I only got them by jabbing my elbows into my ribcage.' Connie peered down the front of her blouse. 'Look, they've gone now. By the way, thanks for not saying My God Who'll Buy Anything From that Raddled Old Tart?' Connie noticed for the first time how pale and washed out Lily was looking. 'Speaking of raddled old tarts, you look terrible.'

'Thanks. Actually I feel terrible,' Lily conceded. 'I have done for a couple of weeks now. Ever since . . .' She caught herself just in time. She'd almost said ever since that night with Ben. 'I keep falling asleep in the middle of the afternoon.'

Connie sat down on the desk and stared at her sister, an ominous thought occurring to her. 'I don't suppose there's any chance,' – she hardly dared mention it – 'that you could be pregnant?'

Lily stared at her, appalled. Of course there wasn't.

She'd never been one to keep a tab on her cycles, in fact she hardly ever thought about it. The mini-pill might not be the best form of contraception for someone of Lily's headlong disposition, but it was the only thing that suited her. Diaphragms jumped out of your hand like slippery white frogs, pessaries reminded you of oven cleaner, and PC or not PC, she couldn't cope with condoms. And then the full horror of the thought struck her. If she were pregnant, could it be from that night with Ben? Lily made herself be sensible. The chance of her being pregnant was so remote as to be ludicrous.

'Your boobs aren't sore are they?'

Lily's hand went automatically to her left breast. The nipple was tender but she'd assumed that was because of rough treatment. She couldn't be.

As soon as Connie had gone, Lily dashed into Bidchester and surveyed the chemists. Superdrug seemed the most anonymous. She could hardly go into Smithson's where her mother used to drag her for prescriptions for everything from whooping cough to outbreaks of teenage acne.

She chose a one-step test, even though they were the most

expensive, because it promised an answer only a day after your period was due.

She couldn't even wait till she got home, but peed into a paper cup in the Ladies in Bidchester Galleria. Then she sat in the car, with the testing device standing upright in front of her on the dashboard, for the longest three minutes of her life, waiting to see how many small blue lines would appear beneath its tiny window.

Chapter 23

It was time. Lily had a strong temptation to fling the whole contraption into the nearest litter bin and ignore the whole thing. Instead she closed her eyes for a second, then stared at the white plastic device. Two blue lines had appeared. Lily fumbled with the packet to double check, knowing exactly what they would confirm. It was positive.

She sat in the car park, hardly able to face the horror of her situation. This had to be the result of that awful night with Ben, two weeks ago. She shuddered at the thought and pushed it from her mind. She hadn't heard from him since, thank God. And now this. She couldn't do it. The baby might be entirely innocent, but how could she have a child that would daily remind her of Ben and that horrible night?

Slowly Lily's head sank on to the steering wheel and stayed there until there was a rap on the window. Lily jumped.

It was a large jolly woman with a string of noisy children. 'You okay, love?'

'Fine, thanks,' lied Lily and willed herself to reverse out of the featureless car park and drive home.

She was numbed by the horror of what she had to face up to. She was going to have to see a doctor. Dimly she recalled conversations with actresses who'd been overtaken by fertility at disastrous moments, but she'd hardly listened. Maxie would know. Maxie had been pregnant herself once.

Lily thumbed through her address book, appalled that she could no longer remember Maxie's number without looking it up.

Maxie was thrilled by the sound of her friend's voice. 'Lily, fab to hear from you. It's been *months*. How's life in darkest Daaar-zettt?' Maxie's attempt at a Dorset accent was about as convincing as Michael Caine playing an English aristocrat. 'Have you met a lantern-jawed vet who wants to put roses round your door and a bun in your oven?'

Lily almost laughed hysterically at the unknowing accuracy of her friend's question. 'Look, Maxie, there's something very personal I need to ask you.'

'Oh, goody.' Lily could imagine Maxie snuggling into her chair for a choice titbit of gossip. 'Fire away.'

Lily tried to be delicate. 'Max, you know that termination you had a few years ago?'

'What termination?' Maxie sounded confused. 'You mean when that lunchtime theatre thing closed down early because nobody came?'

'No, love.' Delicacy had always been wasted on Maxie, 'Termination of pregnancy.'

'Oh, you mean *abortion*.' Lily flinched. For once Maxie was lost for words. 'But I've never been pregnant,' she insisted.

'Max, are you going mad?' Lily wondered whether booze and hard living had finally scrambled Maxie's brains. 'I remember seeing your signature in *The Times* with lots of other actresses, saying you'd had an abortion in your youth and that they mustn't tighten up the law.'

'Oh that.' Maxie sounded sheepish for once. 'That was a bit of a white lie, actually. My agent said it'd be good for my career when she heard who else was signing.'

Lily was speechless for a moment and felt deeply grateful that there were so many miles between her and the politically correct madness of London.

'So you've never had one at all.'

'As a matter of fact, I've never even been pregnant,' Maxie confessed, 'though come to think of it I've taken more risks than the Dangerous Sports Club. I wonder if I've been doing it right? You do take that long waggly thing and dance round it three times singing "What a Thing is Jesus"?'

Despite her horror at the situation she found herself in, Lily giggled.

'Look, there is a man in Harley Street quite a lot of people go to. He's stage struck. Why don't you go and see him? He probably gives a reduction for Equity members.'

The sole appointment the trendy gynaecologist could offer was for next week. It was two days before the board meeting but it was the only one available for months. As she accepted it, Lily found that one of her hands had strayed down to the flat of her stomach and was cradling it, in the age-old protective gesture of the pregnant woman. She imagined the embryo tucked optimistically into her womb. She wouldn't think like that. She mustn't think like that or she wouldn't be able to make a rational decision.

At least she wasn't going to have time to sit and think about it. This coming weekend, their Special Offer would be appearing and there were endless things to double check. The new phones, the temps, the relays of their own staff during that time. She'd put so much of her hopes on to this, and she hoped to God she was right.

On Sunday morning Lily had the brilliant idea that if they were all going to work all day taking orders for the Special Offer they had better have a treat to keep them going and she stopped to buy huge bags of croissants, still warm from the bakery in Bidchester.

They were all tucking in, the new phone lines tested,

when Evie arrived, flourishing the Sunday paper. All the Victoriana staff flocked around her to look at their advert. Connie herself cringed. Posing had been so unexpected that she hadn't had time to think of what other people might make of it.

'Good heavens, Mrs Wade,' June said primly, 'I didn't realize you were so, er, well developed.'

'She's not,' teased Lily. 'Go on, Con, show us how you get instant knockers.'

Connie pushed her elbows into her sides and squeezed until her breasts rose and stuck out provocatively. Shauna, hugely pregnant, tried to copy her but couldn't find anywhere to put her elbows and they all fell about laughing. Suddenly, the phones jumped into flashing life and they dived for the switchboard and the pile of order books specially drafted in for the exercise. This, they all knew, was the moment of truth for Victoriana and quite possibly for their own jobs as well.

By the end of the day they were exhausted and stunned. The phones hadn't let up at all. A mound of sandwiches and drinks lay untouched in the corner of the room, because no one had had time to stop and help themselves, and the order forms were piled high in front of each girl, ready to go to the warehouse tomorrow for packaging and delivery.

Holding her breath, Lily counted them. There were fifteen girls and each had taken a hundred or so orders. Even allowing for returns that was incredible and this was only the first day when credit card orders came in by phone. By Tuesday the coupons enclosing cheques would arrive.

Lily cracked a bottle of champagne and poured it into paper cups. Then she stood up on a table and made the announcement. 'Thank you all very much for coming in today and spoiling your Sunday, or rather your husbands' Sunday, because they've actually had to lift a finger at home for once.' There was a roar of approval at this gentle dig at

307

men. 'It's been a terrific success so I'd like to propose a toast . . .'

'To Connie's tits,' suggested Evie.

Everyone sniggered and Connie stuck them out obligingly, as though they were nothing to do with her, and pouted. '*Mrs Wade* to you lot,' she demanded.

'I *am* sorry not to have offered the proper respect,' Evie apologized, jumping on to the table next to Lily. 'To Mrs Wade's tits!'

Connie was still laughing when she got home, until she saw the expression on her son's face. He was standing by the kitchen door, watching for her, the colour supplement in his hand.

'Bazza brought this round,' he said accusingly. 'His Dad went out and bought six copies.' Bazza's father was a policeman. 'He's going to stick one up in the station, he says, instead of Kim Basinger.'

'I'm flattered,' Connie said gently, then regretted it when she saw how upset he seemed. 'I'm sorry, darling, I should have warned you all, but it only happened by accident when the model didn't turn up.'

'Yes, you bloody well should. This'll be all over our class tomorrow. Everyone'll be laughing at me. How *could* you Ma? It's disgusting.'

Connie wanted to explain how it happened, how she half agreed with him, but that her intentions had been good. Tentatively she reached out a hand to stroke his long hair.

Jeremy wrenched his whole body out of her reach, as if her touch would defile him. '*He* took it, didn't he? That photographer? Dad may not have noticed what's been going on, but I have. Look at you,' he waved the magazine at her. 'You look like you're begging for it.' He threw it on to the floor and ground it with his heel. Then, before she even

308

took in the meaning of his gesture, he grabbed a wine bottle from the recycling box by the back door.

I must move that stupid box, Connie thought irrelevantly, people keep tripping over it. The thought died as Jeremy smashed the bottle on the fridge and slashed it across his wrist. Then he stood, smiling at his mother's screams, while blood pumped out on to the floor, soaking Connie's photograph in an incriminating red flood.

Chapter 24

'For God's sake, Connie, how did it happen?'

Connie simply stared at her husband like a victim of shock, clinging to the side of Jeremy's hospital trolley as though she might be swept to sea if she let go. This was a punishment. She could see that clearly now. People like her didn't have abandoned, passionate affairs and get off un-scarred. The emotive word triggered off a devastating picture in her mind of Jeremy – the child she'd protected from scalds, warned against dog bites, and sat up with through endless illnesses – marked for life, each stitch a constant reminder of her own act of madness.

In the end, Gavin had to shake an explanation out of her. When he'd heard there'd been an accident, he'd somehow known, without being told, who had been hurt, that it was somehow connected to Connie and himself, and the wound they'd allowed to grow between them.

'He cut himself with a broken bottle,' Connie's eyes didn't move from her beautiful son, lying flat like a corpse on the narrow hospital bed.

'But why? Was it something to do with his music test? He's been under a lot of pressure, I suppose. Maybe we didn't take it seriously enough.' She could hear the guilt seeping into his voice and wanted to stop him, tell him that it wasn't his fault but hers. 'What did the doctor say?'

'He's had twelve stitches, but he's going to be all right. He lost quite a lot of blood.' The memory of the newspaper, drenched in red, filled her memory. 'They've sedated him and they want to keep him in for the night.'

Gavin leaned over the bed and held his face against Jeremy's. Connie heard the sounds of a muffled sob. He kissed his son's forehead and stroked his long hair with the tenderness almost of a lover. From this angle he seemed smaller than his son, something she'd never noticed before, but perhaps emotion was colouring her perception.

'I just can't believe it. What on earth made him do it? Are you sure it wasn't an accident?'

Connie's eyes fixed on Gavin's anguished face. She could explain about the photograph, ascribe her son's motive to some kind of Oedipal jealousy, a mother-son thing. Gavin might even accept it and she had the feeling that Jeremy wouldn't tell him. Would that be fairer? The urge to tell him the truth was overwhelming, but that was probably for her own sake. The temptation to be purged, the hope of forgiveness were irresistibly seductive, but truth was hard to escape. Whatever she did, Gavin would be hurt.

'Come and get a cup of tea,' Gavin urged, slipping his arm round her protectively, 'you look as though you're going to faint. He'll be fine. He's a big strong lad.' He glanced at his son and smiled faintly. 'Bigger than me, I'd hardly taken that in.'

It was the kindness and concern that undid her. She knew she didn't deserve it. 'Gavin, don't. It's all my fault. There's something I need to tell you.'

She could see from the closed look that crossed his face that he didn't want to know and she almost changed her mind. But Jeremy groaned in his sleep and his good arm

311

slipped off the bed, the white skin vulnerable and exposed and Connie couldn't hold back the tears.

'What is all this, Con?' Gavin prompted, his voice wary.

The words tumbled out, hardly making sense, into the chilled silence between them: a catalogue of her infidelity. Connie offered the bare facts, pared and unemotional, and presented them without excuse or explanation because either would have been an attempt at exoneration.

Then the doctor arrived, greeting them both extra cheerily, seeing the horror on Gavin's face and assuming its cause was their son, lying on the bed. An overreaction, but understandable – he was a father himself. 'He's going to be fine. No arteries affected, thank God. The damage is superficial though it looks dramatic. He'll sleep now till the morning when you can come and get him. He'll be right as rain in a week or two. Why don't you go home and have a nice, cosy cuppa?'

Connie wanted to laugh, long, loud and hysterically. Instead they were ushered silently out, like two good children, towards the exit and their car.

The drive was silent and hostile. Already it was as though neither wished to speak, in case it was used against them. They thought their separate thoughts, no longer a couple.

The kitchen was a mess, just as she'd left it two hours ago. Connie found a bucket and brush, then dropped to her knees and scrubbed the stained floor, wondering crazily how a murderer could ever get away with it. There seemed to be so much blood. Behind her she heard Gavin run upstairs and the sounds of packing.

'I'll let you know where I am in a few days,' he said, suitcase in hand. 'And of course I'll come and see Jeremy.'

'What shall I tell them?' Connie knew she was using the children as a tool to gain his sympathy but couldn't stop herself.

312

Gavin shrugged, his face blank with pain. She noticed that his fair hair was finally becoming flecked with grey and it suited him. 'Whatever you think best,' he said finally. 'I'll go along with what hurts them least.' His generosity cut through her like a knife through liver, smooth and bloody. She thought briefly of Euan and couldn't imagine him reacting anything like this, with such dignity and largeness of spirit.

'Gavin . . .?'

'Yes?'

Time hung suspended for a moment as their eyes locked. 'I'm so terribly sorry . . .' She wanted to add that she could see now it had been a mistake, a madness, necessary perhaps but too destructive, that the fire of her passion had been built with the kindling of other people's feelings. In order to feel alive she had killed things in the people she loved. Trust. Security. The expectation that someone stood with you against the world. She reached out a hand to him and for an instant it looked as though he might grasp it.

'Hi, all,' shouted Tara, bundling in through the front door, scattering possessions around her, oblivious to the drama that had happened a few hours ago or the one that was being played out now. 'Can someone give me a lift to Roz's? I should have been there hours ago.'

'I will,' Gavin wrenched his gaze from Connie's and turned away.

'What's this?' Tara demanded gaily, prodding his case with her boot, 'not more junketings at gift fairs? You're on the road more than a rock band these days.'

Gavin took her arm and steered her out, leaving Connie staring after them, her mouth dry and painful at the effort not to cry. 'Come on,' he said firmly, 'I'll tell you about it in the car.'

After they'd gone, Connie methodically tidied up the kitchen until there was no sign of disaster. It looked, she thought, as it always used to, peaceful and alluring. The sun lit up the late summer roses in the jug on the kitchen table, playing patterns on the dull sheen of the wood; the yellow walls reflected a warm, contented glow; the huge dresser with its shrine-like range of mementoes gave evidence of a full and busy life.

Connie sat down at the table, feeling utterly alone and dialled her sister's number. My one phone call from the cells, she thought crazily, would be to Lily. I'll go mad if she's not there.

But she was there, and she told Connie, in tones that were gentle and firm, to stay where she was, that she would be there in half an hour. As she waited, Connie turned over in her mind how extraordinary life was that Lily should have longed for love all her life, from their mother, from men, and didn't seem to have found it. And she, Constance, had always found love easy to gather to her, had feathered her nest with it, and had thrown it away.

The phone rang, shrill and startling, making her jump in the uneasy silence, and she knew, with absolute certainty, that it would be Euan, ringing to be congratulated about turning her into a sex symbol. Euan, above all others, was the one person she didn't want to speak to. She let it ring.

Lily, when she arrived, said nothing. Just held her.

When Connie stopped crying, Lily sat her down at the kitchen table. 'Is Jeremy all right?'

'I think so. No thanks to me. And poor Tara. What a bloody awful way to find out about me and Gavin.'

'He'll have told her gently, Gavin isn't the kind of person to blame you.' Lily thought of how her brother-in-law had always been kind and humorous when she'd got into a mess in her own love life. Instead of disapproving of her like everyone else, he'd teased her with amused patience, making her feel that without his bad sister-in-law life would be a duller experience. 'Oh, Con, you poor old thing, what are you going to do?'

Connie's shoulders slumped, knowing that this was a mess of her own creation. 'Wait and see, I suppose. Funny isn't it, you're usually the one who gets into trouble, not me.'

'Oh I'm not doing so badly myself, believe me.'

'Lily, I'd forgotten. Any more news? You weren't really pregnant? It was a false alarm?'

'The little blue lines say otherwise, but don't worry about me. I'll sort it out. It's you and Gav we've got to think about. Maybe all this will blow over and you'll come out stronger, as they say.' A small sob shook Connie. Lily reached over and put her arm around her, filled with protectiveness, wishing she could think of the right thing to say to ease her pain. 'He's a kind man, Con, he won't do anything malicious.'

'Oh God, why can't we just love kind men, instead of wanting something more?'

Lily felt a trickle of irritation for her sister. Surely she wasn't still underestimating Gavin? 'He's not just kind,' she said sharply. 'He's fun. And more subversive than you think.'

The tears started to flow down Connie's face. 'I know.'

'Why don't you tell him you want him back then? It has to be up to you.'

'I've no idea where he's gone.'

'The shop?' Lily handed her the phone.

Connie dialled, messing up the numbers at first in her nervousness. 'One World. Can I help you?' Margot's voice boomed down the line so that even Lily could hear it.

Connie quickly put the phone back in its cradle. 'I can't talk to Margot. Oh, God, what a mess.' She suddenly felt selfish, so utterly caught up with her own pain that she'd forgotten about her sister's problems. 'Lily, what about you? Have you decided what to do?'

'I'd like to stick my head in the sand but as the rest of me will just get larger that's not going to work, is it?'

A weak smile crept across Connie's face. 'What a pair we are, eh? Thank God we've got each other.' For a moment they just held each other in silence.

Gavin sat for a long time outside Tara's friend's house after he'd dropped her off. He had expected his daughter to shout and protest, but she took in what he said sullenly and silently, jumping out of the car half way through his insistence that they both loved her, as though she'd heard all this before.

He thought of Terri and how much she wanted him to go and live with her. Now there was nothing to stop him. Her difference from Connie made her all the more attractive. Pushing away the thought of Connie, entwined in lust with a taut young body and a spirit too young to have come up against life's compromises, he came to a decision.

He would move in with Terri.

London was in the middle of a sweltering burst of late summer heat on the day of Lily's appointment with the trendy gynaecologist. She took the tube to Oxford Circus, a short walk from Harley Street. All London's outlandish street characters seemed to be about today, from dossers and grungies to keen and efficient tourists with their maps and sensible shoes. There was a distant chant of some grubby but ever-optimistic Hare Krishnas. All these had been part of her daily life, but now seemed amazing to her after the peace and order of Dorset. Outside the underground a cheerful youth was singing perkily, selling magazines to help the homeless:

Buy the Big Issue, seventy pee,
If you don't, I'll get no tea.

Lily delved into her bag, giving him a pound for effort, and headed off for Harley Street.

The waiting room was stuffy and pretentiously mock-Georgian, with only copies of *Vogue* and *Country Life* to pass the anxious moments. Lily sat miserably turning the pages. To her horror, Ben's face smiled up at her, looking devastatingly attractive, at a first-night party for his new play. She dropped the magazine as though it had last been read by Lucrezia Borgia, incurring a disapproving look from the doctor's assistant who had arrived to fetch her, precisely one minute before her appointment. At least in the private sector the abortions ran on time.

The consultant stood behind a vast mahogany desk, looking so disgustingly prosperous that Lily assumed any attempt to tighten the abortion law must have been a failure.

'Hop on the couch, will, you please Miss, er . . .'

Lily briefly fantasized about using a false name but she'd only forget it and her notes would get lost. 'Brandon.'

'. . . Miss Brandon. Do you know the date of your last period?'

'I'm afraid not.'

'I see.' His tone was censorious, as though any woman with the slightest sense of decorum would know precisely where she was in her menstrual cycle.

'But I have done a positive pregnancy test.'

'Pants and tights on the chair please. Now let's examine you, shall we?' He stuffed two gloved fingers up Lily and poked around painfully. 'Tell me, Miss Brandon, how did you hear of me?'

Lily stiffened – surely this wasn't the moment for social chit chat? 'I used to be an actress . . .' she began.

The odious man's face wreathed itself in smiles. 'And Nature's such a Philistine, isn't she? A little accidental meeting of sperm and egg and bingo, another promising career down the drain. I can assure you, many's the Miranda who would have had to get her wardrobe in Mothercare if it weren't for us.' Lily loathed him more by the moment.

He withdrew his fingers triumphantly.

'Right, you can put your things back on now. You are indeed pregnant. Have you considered what you want to do about it?'

Oh, no. Only during every sleepless night since she'd discovered. She thought of Ben's face above her, eyes closed, not seeing her, as he forced himself into her.

'I'm pretty sure I don't want to have the baby.' As she said the words she wondered desperately if she could really go ahead and have an abortion.

'Wise decision. Life can be tough for single mothers. Not the same stigma as it used to be, of course' – his tone sounded wistful as though he yearned for the good old days of Victorian disapproval – 'but lonely and demanding. Most of my patients want to choose when they have a baby rather than be blackmailed by Nature.'

'How long have I got to decide?'

'The legal limit is, of course twenty-four weeks, and you're only twelve weeks. Still, the earlier the better for all concerned . . .'

Lily stood on one leg, her tights only half pulled up, and hopped from behind the screen. 'Did you say I was *twelve weeks* pregnant?' she demanded. How could she not have noticed the missed periods, even with her temperamental cycle? But then she had had a few other things to think about – like saving Victoriana.

The great man looked at her as though she'd gone mad. 'I did indeed, but you'd have to have a scan to be exact.'

Lily sat down heavily, floored by the implication of whose baby it therefore had to be. Now what was she going to do?

'When would you like to come in for the termination?'

Lily grabbed her coat and bag and practically ran to the door with one shoe still off. 'Actually, I've had second thoughts. I'll mull it over for a day or two.'

The doctor watched her mournfully: another silly girl

who'd make herself a burden on the state. The only people who were having children these days were the unmarried. He'd read about it in the paper. The married ones couldn't afford the expense. Something was going very wrong with society when an honest doctor couldn't make a living out of terminating pregnancies in unmarried women.

Lily almost ran round Cavendish Square, feeling absurdly happy. The basis of her happiness, that she wasn't pregnant by a man she loathed but by a man she only professed to dislike intensely, was one she didn't care to examine too closely. The back entrance of John Lewis beckoned enticingly and she decided to stop for a cup of coffee, forgetting that to get to the coffee shop you had to go through the nursery section.

Mothers to be, proudly pushing their stomachs before them, chatted with their own mothers about the virtues of layettes and Moses baskets. She imagined herself and Charlotte, wandering arm in arm, bursting with pre-maternal pride, through the baby department, talking of nothing more important than prams versus pushchairs. She felt a pang of pain that was nothing to do with the cramps of pregnancy. It was unlikely that she would ever achieve that kind of loving, easy intimacy with her mother. Instead she pictured coming back with Evie, loud and bossy, but fun, who would insist she went right over the top and bought every frilly furbelow that the shop had to offer.

Except, of course, that she hadn't finally decided to go ahead, had she? A wave of sudden exhaustion overtook her and she decided to phone Connie and see if she could come and meet her train. As she began dialling the number, she remembered how little time they had until the board meeting. It would be cowardly to rush straight back home. She was sure that Judith was somehow involved with Barry North. She had to find some way of proving it – and the only real lead she had was the estate agent here in London.

When she rang King, Flitch & Montague, the secretary informed her that Mr Nutley was out at a meeting in Richmond. Lily was about to ring off when she remembered that the offices Judith had been interested in were in Richmond. 'At Duke's Reach?' Lily dredged the name of the development miraculously from her brain. 'Is that with Mrs Judith Brandon? Only my boss was wondering if he ought to be there too. Would you be a love and see if Mr Nutley's expecting anyone else?'

The girl disappeared just as the man in the phone queue behind Lily started tapping restlessly with his foot. Lily pushed her stomach out so that she looked suddenly seven months pregnant and he went sheepishly away.

'He's got a Mr North listed. Would that be your boss?' She sounded pleased at her own efficiency.

'That's him. He's terrible. He'd forget his own funeral if I wasn't there to remind him.' They both laughed at the stupidity of powerful men who couldn't exist without intelligent secretaries behind them. 'Thanks a million. What time is it supposed to be?'

'Twelve-forty-five.'

'I'll pour him into a taxi. Byeee.'

Lily had fifteen minutes to get there from Oxford Circus. The taxi driver said he could do it in twenty. And he did: going through only two red lights and one no-entry sign.

The mews beside the building was empty of cars except for a black shiny Jaguar with a chauffeur dozing in the front under a copy of the *Sun*. Behind him, standing together in front of an attractive building in the Tesco Village style of architecture – all pitched roofs, gable ends and little clock towers – were three people: a natty little chap who looked as though he should be working in Harrods' gents' outfitter section, Judith herself and a taller powerfully built man in a cashmere coat. It had to be Barry North. Lily kicked herself for not having thought of bringing a camera to record the best thing of all – Judith was hanging on to Barry North's arm with all the possessiveness of a jealous mistress.

Lily turned quietly away from the scene and slipped off to her waiting taxi. With a taxi-driver like hers, she could still get the two-thirty train.

By the time she got off at Bidchester and picked up her car from the car park, Lily still hadn't decided what to do about what she'd seen. Should she tell her mother, or Jonathan? But what if Jonathan were involved too? That would break Charlotte's heart. And how could she go up to her brother and suggest his wife was having an affair? Especially when she had no hard evidence for the accusation. Without photographs or any other evidence it would simply be her word against theirs. North would claim the site was for one of his other businesses and implied nothing sinister for Victoriana. Somehow she had to prove it.

In Darcombe she stopped at the village shop for milk and bread, still uncertain what to do. To her immense relief she bumped into Evie, who was outside the shop, swearing at the stamp machine.

'Bloody thing!' The late afternoon sun glinted on Evie's gloriously unnatural hair and her purple leisure suit threw into relief the subtle russets and olives of Darcombe's more conventional inhabitants. 'That was all the money I brought. It knew it. I swear that machine knew it!' She waved the letter at it as though it had an electronic eye concealed behind its sedate Victorian exterior.

'Evie, thank God, I need your advice.'

'A swift half in the pub?' suggested Evie.

Lily shook her head. 'Somewhere private. Down by the river.'

Safely away from inquisitive ears, they walked along the riverbank and Lily told her aunt what she'd seen, and her suspicions about Judith and Barry North.

'The bitch!' Evie shouted. 'And your mother thinks the sun shines out of her pastel-coloured arse!'

'What do you think we should do? If Ma knew North was planning to move Victoriana to London, surely she wouldn't sell?'

'But can we prove that building's for Victoriana? Judith's as slippery as an eel on heat.'

They came to a stile. Overcome by sudden exhaustion, Lily flopped down on to it. Evie joined her, her eyes alight with concern.

'This has all been awful for you, Lily love. You're doing brilliantly you know.'

'It isn't that. Evie, I'm pregnant and I don't know what the hell to do.'

Evie felt her breath trapped in her chest. Was history pre-destined to repeat itself? She pulled herself back to the present. 'You poor girl. You don't need this, do you?'

The warmth of her aunt's unquestioning sympathy almost made Lily lose control. 'Oh, God, I feel so completely confused. A year ago I thought I wanted a baby, but the circumstances were so different.'

Evie stroked her hair. 'You could still go ahead if you wanted. You're your own woman. No one would tell you never to darken their door again.'

Lily hesitated, thinking of the beginning of life inside her, struggling to put into words something she'd never even admitted to herself. 'That's not the problem.' The anguish in her niece's voice wrenched at Evie. '*I'm* the problem. I don't know if I could love it, that's what's so dreadful.' Lily's voice rang with the pain of years of hope that hadn't been fulfilled. 'The trouble is, I don't love myself, so how could I love someone else?'

Evie listened, her heart breaking. *She* knew why Lily felt like this: because she'd never felt loved by the one person who ought to have loved her; the person who should have always been there to catch her from her falls and urge her on to flights of joy and achievement; the person whose love should have been unconditional and strong. Christ, Charlotte, she thought bitterly, sometimes I hate you for what you've done to Lily.

The urge to hold her niece, and love her, and tell her the truth, was almost overwhelming. Lily was like the daughter she'd never had. If Lily had been hers, how different things would have been. If *they* had been her parents, Lily would be proud and strong and happy. Evie would have made sure of it.

She could listen no longer. It was time to act, to stop this sad legacy being passed from mother to daughter. Charlotte might not admit it, but her life had been blighted too. If she had been able to love and value Lily she would be congratulating her now instead of selling the company to which her daughter had contributed so much.

She hugged Lily one last time. 'Lily, love, I've got to run. There's someone I need to talk to pretty urgently.'

Sadness flowed through Lily at her aunt's sudden departure. She'd somehow hoped for more from Evie. She saw that she'd begun to treat her aunt almost as a Wise Woman, someone with superhuman qualities of perception and sympathy, a seer in hand-dyed silk. The reality was that Evie had faced sadness of her own, attested to by her three failed marriages. Maybe Evie was no wiser than anyone else.

Lily forced herself to forget about her own personal crisis and think about the future of the company instead. The board meeting was next week and she had to prove that Victoriana had overcome its problems. She decided to ring Clive Green at First Venture to tell him the good news that they could make their payment after all. If she could also talk Sam into accepting part-settlement of his debt they might just be able to pull through.

'First Venture Finance,' greeted a brisk voice. 'Whom would you like to speak to?'

For a crazy instant she thought of saying Paul Allan and telling him everything, but how could she when she was so unsure of how she felt about him?

'Clive Green, please. This is Miss Lily Brandon.'

The brisk voice returned. 'I'm very sorry, Miss Brandon, but Mr Green says he's only authorized to deal with Mrs Charlotte Brandon or Mrs Judith Brandon. Perhaps you could get one of them to call?'

Lily swore colourfully. How dare he do this to her?

When Evie found Charlotte, she was leaning on the wooden frame of the pergola Edward had constructed for her, looking at her favourite view of rolling Dorset downs. Evie could smell the bonfire Edward was busy making at the far end of the garden. Edward's project was almost finished now, and the love he had poured into it was reflected from every clipped hedge and each perfectly placed stone urn, tumbling with geraniums. Had he been using it though, Evie wondered, as a means of opting out of reality? Lily had needed him and he could have stood up to Charlotte more than he had.

This place, with its mellow golden stone, its tasteful interiors and its rolling acres might be the English dream, but it had been built on the foundations of too much deception for Evie's taste.

Charlotte turned as though she'd almost been expecting the visit. 'You look unusually stern. Not bad news from home?'

'A bit nearer than that. Charlotte, I've got something to say that you're not going to want to hear.'

Charlotte sat down in a teak garden chair, lowering herself into it stiffly, Evie noted with a touch of surprise. She had recovered from the heart attack but she was getting old.

324

Such a thing seemed impossible. For all her faults Charlotte had always had the energy and determination of a woman half her age.

Evie was equally dogged when she wanted to be. 'It's time to tell Lily the truth, Charlotte.'

Charlotte made no pretence of misunderstanding. 'Don't be ridiculous. This is my life and I'll run it as I choose.'

'But that's just the point. It *isn't* just your life. It's Lily's too.' She held her sister's gaze, wondering how she would take the next revelation. 'And now there's another life at stake. She's pregnant, Charlotte, and she's considering an abortion because she can't be sure she'll love it.'

Charlotte felt the tight fingers of jealousy grip her and squeeze her heart painfully. Lily had confided this precious information in Evie but not in her – and yet she knew why. Evie had given her niece an easy affection, had offered a closeness that she herself had felt incapable of. Regret bit into her, sharp and wounding.

'A new life, Charlotte. An innocent human being who might never be born because of you. Do you want to have that on your conscience?'

'For God's sake, Evie, don't be so melodramatic. If Lily decides not to go ahead with this baby, that's her affair, not ours.'

'Except that the reason she fears she can't love it is because you never loved her. Isn't she entitled to know why?'

Charlotte glanced at Edward contentedly making his bonfire. Wouldn't more lives be threatened by the truth than by silence? 'Truth isn't always the god it's made out to be.' There was an air of tired inevitability in her sister's expression that Evie hadn't seen before. 'It can just as easily be a destroyer.'

'I don't accept that. Truth can be survived and built on, painfully perhaps, I agree.' She reached her hand across the table to her sister in a rare gesture of physical appeal.

'Haven't you sometimes longed to hold Lily and explain things to her?'

Charlotte considered the hand reached out towards her and touched it briefly. 'Of course I have. But I can't. It would be the end of everything I've worked for. And can you be so sure she'd thank me if I did?'

'You don't know her very well, do you? She's as strong as you are, in her way. Please, Charlotte, give her a chance of happiness.'

'I'm sorry, Eve, but I've made my decision and I'm holding to it.' She gathered the embroidery she'd been doing before Evie's arrival and headed back for the house, feeling older than she'd ever felt before.

Evie watched her walk, proud and erect, back to the bed she had made and would continue to lie in. Edward, she saw, was watching Charlotte too, as though she were some remote stranger. Did Evie have the right to play God with the lives of those nearest to her? Lily's face, pale and exhausted by fighting a battle she didn't really understand, imprinted itself between the two of them. Evie thought of the embryonic life buried deep inside her niece, the life that could so easily be sluiced out, and decided that she did.

She crept upstairs to Edward's study. She could hear him pottering in the garden still and the strains of Mozart started up from the kitchen, confirming that Charlotte was preparing one of her elaborate meals. Evie felt like storming in and tearing up her copy of Elizabeth David. Charlotte's calmness when everything was falling around her infuriated Evie beyond measure.

On the mantelpiece of Edward's study a clock ticked, a glass covering revealing all its intricate workings. Evie hesitated for a moment, watching him out of the window. His world might be destroyed by her actions, but she was angry with Edward too. He had failed to protect Lily. Besides, his

life was winding down, as her own was. The future belonged to those who still had it to live. She might, on the
other hand, be taking away his past, and that was a cruel
thing to do. But cruelty was sometimes a necessary evil.

The clock rang the hour, reminding her of why she'd
come in here. It would be barely seven a.m. in Australia, but
Leo Orson had the kind of lifestyle where day and night had
less significance than they did for most people. He might,
Evie knew, be setting up deals via fax and modem, or snor-
kelling under empty blue skies on the Great Barrier Reef,
with instructions not to be disturbed by anyone. She hoped
he had recovered from his illness and, even more, that she
was doing the right thing in calling him.

Even now, thirty-five years after she'd fallen in love with
him, the thought of hearing Leo's voice filled her with joy
and terror, as though she were a young girl again, waiting
breathlessly for his call. Evie wasn't given to regret but it
seeped into her today as she waited for a voice to answer
her call. Three marriages, two sons, a busy, successful life –
but the void left by Leo still gaped.

She knew her action could go horribly wrong, and that
she might cause more pain than she cured, but nothing in
life was safe and predictable. You could be driving along
one moment, and the next a lorry jack-knifed in front of you
and it was the end. Some risks had to be taken. If everything
went wrong she just hoped she wasn't the person driving
the lorry at the time.

After twelve rings an answering machine took over, the
voice anonymous and efficient, not even his voice. But then
Leo's time was worth too much to waste on answering machines. She left her message with precision, hoping she had
conveyed the urgency she felt.

It was in the lap of the Gods and the international tele-
communications network as to what happened next, or
whether he would even get the message in time. There was,

however, someone nearer and a lot more accessible she could try meanwhile. Lily would kill her, but she somehow liked the sound of Paul Allan. She had a feeling he would help them.

Chapter 25

Every customer in the Palm Court of the Waldorf Hotel was watching them. The immaculately business-suited young man and the outrageous older woman, in her large hat pinned back with an art deco brooch, made an intriguing change from the usual clientèle of Japanese tourists, grey executives and suburban couples out on their wedding anniversaries. The waitresses had already taken a bet as to whether they were having an affair and would have been deeply disappointed to learn that their conversation was entirely about business.

'I got in touch with you because Lily and I think there's something about this offer from North's Mail Order that stinks to high heaven.'

Instant concern was reflected in Paul's Italianate eyes. 'What makes you say that?' Clive Green had told him only the barest details of the offer.

'We think Lily's sister-in-law, Judith Brandon, may be involved. She's been trying to undermine Lily for months.' Evie noticed with satisfaction that Paul flinched at every mention of Lily's name.

'And you don't think that's simply family rivalry?'

'Unless you call sabotaging our entire press launch family

rivalry. We reckon Judith and North are planning to close down Victoriana and move some vestige of it to Richmond, probably shedding most of the jobs in the process. Judith loathes Dorset.'

Paul thought of the Mill and the unique atmosphere there, how ideal it had all seemed, living and working in one place. 'How sure are you about all this?'

'Pretty sure, but we can't prove it. Lily saw Judith and North looking round the offices in Richmond, but they haven't admitted that it's for Victoriana. The estate agent, on the other hand, strongly hints that it is.'

'So there's nothing hard to go on, then?'

'Hang on, there is one thing. Sam Wilson, the boss of S. J. Wilson's, the supplier who's been threatening to bankrupt them, implied to Lily that Barry North was behind it. Look, Paul, the board meeting to decide whether to sell is coming up fast. If you care about Lily you'll help us. She's already given up her acting career; if she loses Victoriana too, God knows if she'll recover.'

Paul Allen felt the power of Evie's personality beaming across the table at him. Lily had always spoken well of her and she clearly had Lily's interests at heart. If they were right, and North and Judith were sabotaging Victoriana, how much did Clive know about it? He'd always been thick with North. The thought struck him that it had been he who handed Victoriana over, like a trussed turkey, into Clive Green's care. He hadn't been much of a friend to Lily.

'How is she?' They both knew who he meant.

'Not that great at the moment.' Evie noted the concern in his voice and was within a second of telling him why, but Lily would never forgive her and there were limits even to her capacity to interfere. 'I expect it's the stress of all this happening.'

Paul was on the point of asking whether Lily was still with Ben, but couldn't face the pain of hearing about it. He

330

wrenched his mind back to business. It was practical help she needed from him now. 'I'll see what I can find out. Have you got a number I can ring or should I call Lily direct if I come up with anything?'

A tiered tower loaded with tiny sandwiches, buttered scones and tiny chocolate eclairs arrived, temporarily distracting Evie. 'Did you order the Earl Grey, madam?' asked the waitress.

'Can't stand the stuff. Stinks of bergamot oil. Mine's the British Rail variety, three teabags and a teaspoon of water . . . Are you in love with Lily?'

Paul choked quietly on his scented Earl Grey. 'I've never met anyone like her certainly.' In fact, the pain of losing her was still as raw as ever, but he didn't see why he should tell a complete stranger that, even if she was Lily's aunt.

'And you never will. You gave up too easily; you should have stormed in and told her.' Having cut a swathe through the sandwiches, Evie had moved on to the scones. 'That's what's wrong with this country. No one ever says what they bloody well mean.'

'Does she even know you've asked for my help?'

Evie looked him in the eye. 'I'll tell her when you discover something useful.'

The nerve of the woman charmed Paul. She'd asked for his help and was already complaining he was moving too slowly. 'In that case, I'd better get right on the case,' he laughed. 'Look after her, won't you? She always spoke so well of you – as if she almost wished you were her mother. This offer from North's must be very hard for her.'

Evie bit into her éclair and tried to hide the tear that threatened to fall into her delicate cup of pure tannin. Useless emotion wouldn't help anyone. All the same, Lily would be mad if she threw this one away. Unlike most Englishmen, he seemed actually capable of feeling. 'It's tough all right, but not as tough as it'll be if Charlotte sells to this shit North.'

'Then we'd better not let her, had we?'

Evie grinned. 'That's more like it. You may get a call from a friend of mine, Leo Orson, the other shareholder in Victoriana. He's a very powerful man these days. If we tell him anything he'll help us if he can, but he's a hard chap to get hold of. I just hope we find him in time.'

In the cab on the way back to his office, Paul felt more cheerful than he had for months. Lily might not want to see him, but at least he was getting the chance to help her. He'd start with a little research into the relationship between Clive Green and North's Mail Order. What he needed was a chance to look through Clive's papers without being interrupted by Clive himself. What would be sure to tempt Clive out of his office?

It was already six when Paul rang and asked Clive to join him at the Trading Floor to celebrate some good news. Paul knew he wouldn't be able to resist the killer combination of free drink and the hint that Paul might be stealing a step above him on the career ladder.

Paul waited until he heard Clive leave. He had twenty minutes, maybe half an hour, before Clive would get restless, perhaps longer if anyone else bought him a drink.

Paul's heart sank at the sight of Clive's office. It was strewn with styrofoam cups of cold coffee, unread documents, unanswered correspondence and company reports that were probably already out of date. If he had a filing system it was nowhere in evidence. The cabinets appeared to be used simply as a combination minibar and chest of drawers for Clive's grimy squash kit. There was nothing else there.

Paul began methodically working through it all, his palms sweating with the knowledge that if he was caught, it would be the end of his career. First Venture wouldn't sanction snoopers, no matter how honourable their intentions.

Fifteen minutes later he'd got nowhere and then had a minor scare when someone emerged from the next-door office. Thank God they didn't put a head round.

He looked at his watch again. Jesus, he'd already been twenty minutes. Then he noticed Clive's lap-top computer sitting in the middle of his desk. Why hadn't he tried that first? He sat down and whizzed through the files, hoping desperately for something saying Vict or BN for Barry North, but there was nothing. Paul swore. He wouldn't get a second chance like this. And then he saw it: a folder on the screen marked Con. His heart racing, he accessed it.

It was indeed confidential. Under NMO for North's Mail Order it contained all the correspondence and a detailed report on the strategy North was adopting to acquire Victoriana. With a quick glance behind him, Paul printed out three copies.

Back in his office, his pulse still thundering in his ears, he found a fax waiting for him on his desk. It was from Leo Orson, announcing his imminent arrival in London and a request that Paul come and meet him. At least he'd have something to show him, but they'd have to move fast. If Leo Orson was so rich and powerful, maybe he could get someone to keep an eye on Barry North and Judith Brandon's movements.

Light-headed with relief, Paul headed off to meet Clive at the wine bar. He'd have to see if, after six glasses of free champagne, he could squeeze anything more out of him, the scumbag.

Lily took one look at the blinding light flooding through her high, arched windows and put her head back under the pillow. The sickness was beginning to pass but this morning she felt something less physical and harder to control – the beginnings of panic. The board meeting was approaching fast and she'd spent the whole day yesterday tearing up blind alleys. Mr Nutley of King, Flitch and Montague had declined to speak to her when she'd called to try and winkle out some more evidence about Duke's Reach. Then she'd tried the landlords who owned the offices, but it had turned out to be a faceless property company based in Jersey.

The only spark in the darkness was that Sam Wilson had agreed to accept part payment of the debt, but to her intense disappointment he'd refused to be drawn any further on Barry North. What infuriated and depressed her was that she was even more certain about some sort of deal between Judith and North, but she still hadn't got a shred of hard evidence.

Lily made herself a pot of fresh ground coffee in an attempt to cheer herself up and opened a magazine. A photograph of a mother nuzzling her small daughter made her heart close up with pain and uncertainty. Was the baby inside her a boy or a girl? She pushed the image from her mind. Until she was sure she was going ahead with the pregnancy she couldn't afford to think like that.

Maybe she'd go and look for Evie. Evie always cheered you up – but she had been behaving very oddly lately: smug and pleased with herself, as though she were hugging a party invitation, to which only she had been invited. It struck Lily that Evie was up to something, though God alone knew what. Since they only had two more days, any miracle would be welcome.

Connie couldn't remember such intensity of misery in her life. The whole carefully-built structure of her existence, which had seemed secure to the point of boredom, had collapsed beneath her. Jeremy was home, but refusing to talk to her; her role on the catalogue was finished; Connie had none of the props which she now saw she had depended on, rather than being suffocated by.

Her most irrational reaction was to Euan. She somehow

blamed him for tempting her, even though it had been her own decision every step of the way. The very independence and spontaneity he had represented now seemed to make him an empty and selfish person.

All she could think of was how to get Gavin back. She couldn't believe he would seriously fall in love with Terri, big buxom Terri, who had always seemed a joke between them. Connie saw with a shiver of self-disgust that she was not only jealous but also angry, because he'd chosen to console himself with someone who was large and frumpy, an unfitting rival.

'But why are you splitting up?' Tara kept asking her mother, bleak and uncomprehending, like a dog kicked by the owner it loves. 'You're not even unhappy. Bags of my friends have parents who're unhappier than you.'

'You don't know everything about Dad and me, darling,' Connie tried not to convey her own distress. 'This isn't out of the blue like you think. It's been hovering for months.'

'It's that photographer, isn't it? He was sniffing round you as if you were on heat, right from the start.'

Connie hung her head. How had she ever imagined she would be allowed to have an affair without her family noticing the difference in her. She must have been blinded by lust to think such a thing remotely possible. Even so, she was stung by Tara's need to reduce everything to basics.

'That's enough, Tara. It won't help. I didn't mean to put the family at risk.'

'What *did* you expect then? That Dad would meekly accept it? You don't think much of him, do you? I hate you, Mum. Jeremy's upstairs with his arm in stitches and Dad's God knows where. All because of you! I'm going to Roz's.'

Connie said nothing. It would probably be best if Tara did go to her friend's. There was no point trying to reason with her. Maybe it wasn't even fair to try and get your children to see your point of view. They were hurting so much they needed someone to blame, and she was the person who most deserved it. She just had to be adult enough to live with it.

The door banged angrily behind Tara. Worried that it might have woken Jeremy, Connie decided to check his room.

He was still sleeping among his REM posters, his hero, Michael Stipe, suspended over his bed like a guardian angel in grunge. In sleep Jeremy looked extraordinarily beautiful, almost like Chatterton in the famous portrait, his long hair framing his face. Pain and regret bit into Connie again. Would she have damaged his psyche, long after his physical scars had healed?

She baulked, suddenly angry that once you had children your life was no longer your own. But then having children at all was an act of narcissism. You gave birth to them because you wanted to fulfil your biological destiny, you weren't doing them a favour. Maybe for that you owed them a lasting debt.

A noise on the floor below startled her. Not a burglar! That would be too much. Braver in adversity than she would ever be had all this not happened, Connie strode down to the middle floor.

Gavin was standing in his dressing room, surrounded by cricketing photos and the trophies of his boyhood, packing clothes. He looked up when Connie burst in, then went on silently stuffing shirts into the case. For a crazy moment Connie almost asked him if he had any washing, before she recalled that his washing was no longer any concern of hers.

'I ran out of clothes,' he explained, trying not to look at her.

'I thought maybe you'd come back. Gavin, I'm so sorry.'

'Leave it, Con. I don't want your fucking apologies.'

'No.'

'How're the kids?'

'Angry with me.'

'Yes. Well.' She knew he had every right to scream and shout and be even angrier, but it wasn't his way.

'It wasn't deliberate. I didn't mean to hurt you all.'

'Things never are deliberate, though, are they? But there's still a choice. A moment where you can do one thing or the other. You chose to have an affair.'

Connie felt the fight drain out of her. 'Are you staying away permanently?'

Gavin went on packing his case, not answering. Then he looked up at the wife he'd thought he'd known and anger tore at him. 'My business is on its knees, my son's ripped his arm open, my wife's been having an affair, what the hell have I got to come back to?'

He picked up his suitcase and flung it across the room. For a moment Connie thought it was going to hit her. Instead it crashed into his dressing table knocking over silver-topped bottles of cologne and shattering the glass of their wedding photograph. Connie watched, horrified. Gavin had always been the gentlest of personalities. 'Please Gavin, I wish I could take the last few months back. I love you all.'

His eyes locked on to hers, stripping her away to try and get at the truth. 'Do you?' His voice held the slightest nuance of tenderness and her heart leapt.

Into the weighted silence the phone cut the air like a car alarm on a peaceful country road. Connie ignored it, but it continued to ring. Eventually it was Gavin who picked it up. His face closed in on itself at the sound of the male voice on the other end.

'It's for you.' His gaze nailed her to the spot. 'He says it's urgent.'

She grabbed the phone and told Euan she would call him later. By the time she'd persuaded him to get off the line, Gavin had gone.

Connie threw herself on the bed face downwards. She

was sure there had been something in Gavin's expression, tenderness as well as anger. She was convinced of it, but how could she get him to acknowledge it and forgive her? She'd read countless articles about what to do if your husband had an affair, but not what to do if *you* had. She knew she had to do something or she'd go mad.

She wrote a note to Jeremy, explaining that she'd had to go out, then grabbed a sleeping bag and ran to the car. She wasn't the type to force entry into Terri's house and demand Gavin come back with her. But she could spend the night outside their window. Maybe that would convince Gavin she was more sorry than she could find words for.

Terri's house was in a small estate in Bidchester that aspired to being executive homes but were several sizes too small. She couldn't imagine Gavin living behind those ruched frilly blinds. He'd always liked big rooms and large dramatic artworks. Terri probably collected porcelain dogs.

She felt curtains twitch all down the street as she parked outside the front of the house. Someone would probably summon a posse from the Neighbourhood Watch if she made any trouble. But Connie wasn't going to make any trouble. She was just going to sit tight.

It was Terri who noticed the car outside and she screamed. 'She's out there, Gavin, right at the bottom of the drive. She must be mad.' Gavin came over to the window. Connie's pale face stared up at him. She looked about sixteen.

'I'll go down and talk to her.' He pulled on a sweater and jogging trousers and picked his way through the crowded decor. Connie was right about the porcelain animals.

To his horror the car wasn't even locked. He got in. 'You must go home, Con, this is madness. You can't stay out here all night.'

Connie smiled faintly. 'Don't worry I'm not going to lob a

338

brick through the picture window. I just wanted to show I was prepared to fight for you. Pathetic, isn't it?'

He touched her cheek with a finger. 'Okay, message received, but this isn't the ideal place to talk. I'll ring you tomorrow. I promise.'

Upstairs, Terri watched mournfully. At eleven stone she couldn't do the waif and stray act like Connie. She sighed with relief when the car door opened and Gavin stepped out. Across the road her nosy neighbour watched the proceedings with open glee. Gavin saw the old woman at the window and bowed low as if on stage. Annoyed at being caught out, she snapped her curtains together.

The next day was agony for Connie. She didn't leave the phone for five minutes and jumped out of her skin each time it rang. When Lily called she even sounded irritated with her for taking up the phone line and was astounded when Lily reminded her about the board meeting. 'Tomorrow? It can't be! Since Gavin left I've been right out of it. I'm sorry, Lily, I'm no use, am I? I should be threatening to pull out Judith's false nails until she tells us the truth, instead of pining ludicrously by the phone.'

'That was good,' Lily said. 'You actually made a joke.'

'No I didn't. That was a hundred per cent serious.'

'No word from Gav then?'

'He promised to ring today. That's why I was grouchy about you taking up the line.'

'I'd better get off then. Good luck with Gavin. See you tomorrow.'

'Absolutely.' Connie couldn't even think about tomorrow. She couldn't even think beyond Gavin not ringing her.

'By the way,' Lily asked finally. 'Any idea what Evie's up to?'

'Why?'

'She's going around beaming like the Good Witch of the West.'

'Maybe she's got a scheme to save Victoriana.'

'I do hope not. Last time she had one of those, you took your clothes off and ended up losing your husband.'

'Anyway,' Connie argued, ignoring her last comment, 'surely doing something's better than waiting for the blow to fall?' It was advice she might take herself. There would just be time to go round to the shop and look for Gavin. After all, tomorrow, if she was at the Board Meeting, he wouldn't be able to find her.

Connie drove into Bidchester and just as she was parking outside One World, Margot emerged. Connie dodged back behind the car. Margot looked furtively around her, then disappeared down the street.

Connie couldn't resist the opportunity.

The door wasn't locked. The shop was looking better since she'd last visited it. The goods on offer seemed new and interesting, rather than the sad, faded selection that had been there before. One dramatic new feature caught her eye. A vast red chenille curtain cordoned off the opening into the store-room. Connie pulled it back. Some of the stock had been pushed aside to make room for a small day-bed. On top of it was the suitcase Gavin had taken with him when he walked out.

Connie's breath stopped in her chest. He must have moved out of Terri's. A noise behind her made her turn. Margot must be back.

'I'm afraid we're just closing,' said Gavin's voice, as he clicked the latch.

'That's all right,' Connie replied from behind the curtain. 'I don't think I'm going to find what I was looking for anyway.' It was a calculated risk, but at least she had his attention.

'What's that?'

'The life I used to have, before I mucked it all up.'

Gavin's eyes behind the gold-rimmed glasses were wary.

His hair flopped down in front of them and he flicked it back. She found she wanted to reach out and do it for him, and to brush the fluff off the lapel of his jacket – such stupid nurturing little gestures.

It struck Connie that this was exactly where she'd gone wrong in their marriage. She'd maintained him so efficiently that she'd stopped desiring him. Now she wanted him again. Her infidelity had somehow brushed the dust off their marriage. It had left pain instead, but pain didn't kill desire in the way that familiarity did. The heartbreaker was that he didn't seem to feel the same way.

'Please come back.' Connie's voice was hoarse with pain. 'It wasn't just Euan that came between us. I stopped considering you and what you wanted in all the excitement over the catalogue. I won't do it again. I'll take over the shop. It'll be like it was before.'

'I don't want it to be like it was before.' Suddenly he was angrier than she'd ever seen him. 'You were bored with our marriage. I don't want to take away your independence! I just want to be part of your life, a part that matters.'

She held out her hand to him. 'You are, Gavin. You're the centre. Without you, none of it makes sense. I can see that now.'

Gavin turned away. 'I can't just forgive and forget. It's gone too deep.'

'I know.'

'Are you sure you're not choosing hearth and home because it's safer?' His voice was harsh with anger and hurt pride. 'You've had your shot of passion and now it's to be slippers by the fire and boring sex with your husband?'

'Yes, I'm sure, I'm absolutely sure.' She pulled his face close to hers and kissed him hard on the lips.

At first he tried to turn away, but she could feel him hardening in spite of himself. His hand slipped inside her shirt, caressing the nipple. Connie sighed in genuine pleasure.

He looked into her eyes, his own still distant with distrust. She knew this might not really be forgiveness, just the excitement of the moment, that even after this he might still hate her, but she was prepared to take a chance.

'I love you, Gavin, whether you come back to me or not.'

There was a loud knocking on the door and Margot's voice shouted indignantly that her handbag was locked inside.

'Go on.' Connie did up her blouse, nuzzling his ear. 'I can't be responsible for Margot spending the night on the street as well as screwing up our marriage.'

Gavin pulled back the curtain a little and went to open the door.

'Thank goodness you're there, Mr Wade,' Margot bumbled. 'I just nipped to the shops for a packet of biscuits because my sister's coming round tonight and you know how that Mrs Jenkins in the Post Office chats on.'

Gavin knew that it was far more likely to be Margot who chatted on.

'A funny thing, though, Mr Wade. She says Mrs Wade's car was parked outside on the double yellow line and it's just been towed away to the car pound.'

At this a muffled giggle came from behind the red curtain, causing Margot to blush redder than the ruby chenille. She knew men went off the rails a bit when their marriages broke down, but this was too much. Floozies in the storeroom. Maybe it was time she retired after all. She stared at the curtain as though the sheer power of her disapproval might shrivel it up and expose the trollop behind it to public gaze. One shoe, she noticed, was sticking out from under it, a beige casual with a fringed tie, very like one of Mrs Wade's.

In a flash of insight akin to Archimedes and the bathwater, Margot made the connection. 'I'd better get along home now.' Margot's face was lit up by a sudden and indecent grin, then, realizing that her analysis of the situation might be premature, she picked up her bag and made for the door, looking carefully ahead. Her features twitching with the effort of suppressing her glee, she closed the door and went off to tell her sister how Mr and Mrs Wade had finally seen sense and that maybe now they'd stop being so bloody miserable and get on with saving their business.

Evie plucked the head off a gaudy red dahlia and sniffed it. It was a careless act but then she'd never liked dahlias. The scent was indeed pungent and evocative, but it simply reminded her of all the things she hated about the coming of English autumn and winter. The smell of woodsmoke and the gleeful way total strangers pointed out that nights were fair drawing in filled Evie with gloom. She was suddenly angry with England and with what seemed the inevitability of tomorrow. Leo had let her down. She had had no word from him. Perhaps he'd never even got her message.

But most of all she was angry with Charlotte.

Evie had crossed the world all those years ago to get away from Charlotte – Charlotte with her style, and her steely determination, and her laughing, clever group of friends who were so artistic, so witty, so enamoured of Charlotte that they had followed her and Edward from London and settled in Dorset. Evie had found them terrifying and utterly seductive. She had sat quietly, pretending to read a book, while they drank bottle after bottle of red wine and argued about novels and paintings, architecture and design, their conversation peppered with words she didn't understand, like Bauhaus and Biedermeier. They had all made things, but only from natural fabrics, of course, using techniques and patterns drawn from ethnic cultures in bright outlandish colours. They had believed, they said, in winding their lives and their work into one seamless pattern.

Evie had thought it was all nonsense, the product of over-education, but she was also honest enough to know that she envied Charlotte, and that London would not be far enough to go to slough off this envy. Several continents was about the right distance.

Australia suited her. She loved its extremity, its honesty and lack of pretension, the fact that its people didn't forever look over their shoulders at the past but were more intent on the present and the future. She loved the women especially. The men were harder. They tended to group at the periphery.

And then Leo had arrived there, as eager as she was to make a new life and, although she knew he had been a friend of Charlotte's, Evie had found his charm and energy irresistible. At this distance Charlotte no longer seemed a threat.

About that, of course, she had been wrong.

Leo had seemed to share her impatience with the past. His home was in Australia now and he wanted to open his arms to its opportunities. He had that rare blend of being both artistic and entrepreneurial. That first winter they did everything together: swam, picnicked, laughed at how freezing it must be in Dorset. Leo's red-gold hair lightened as his skin deepened, pointing up the fierce yellow brown of his eyes. He stopped looking British and the Australians loved him for his lack of airs and graces.

But not as much as Evie loved him. In her, he evoked a passion of such intensity that it hurt. Leo seemed too glorious, too much like the gift that she'd longed for, so that she treated every day as though it were their last. She knew from the start that her passion wasn't reciprocated, but she didn't expect it to be. Men like Leo didn't fall hopelessly in love with large-framed, freckly, slightly clumsy girls like her.

Evie, however, had begun to hope, to believe that

spending so much time with her had to mean *something*. Perhaps it might have done, if Charlotte hadn't chosen that of all moments to accept an invitation to Sydney for a business conference. It was all-expenses paid and deeply flattering, of course. Victoriana, new and exciting, had been in all the papers and the organizers wanted Charlotte to share her secret. Leo, a friend and shareholder, had to be there too of course.

But he didn't have to fall in love with her.

It was only later that Evie realized he'd always been in love with Charlotte, that loving her had been part of his motivation for going to Australia. The irony of that had tasted bitter indeed to Evie. Charlotte must have known. She could so easily have refused the invitation. She must have guessed what would happen.

Charlotte always protested that she hadn't, that she had seen Leo simply as a friend until that moment, when he had taken them to a tiny remote island for the weekend, and she had fallen in love too. It had been a tragedy for Charlotte as well in the end. She had loved him with the crazy intensity of an amateur on a high wire, in a way, Evie knew, she had never loved Edward. Every new day was an act of daring. She had never seen her sister like that. Strong-minded, rigid Charlotte, who at home had always draped herself in a stylish camouflage of greys and indigos, had discovered her body and its hidden beauty.

Evie's heart was breaking and yet there they were, the three of them, in one of the most beautiful places Evie had ever seen. She began to hope that perhaps it was simply the setting, but back in Sydney their love still flared as bright.

After two weeks they had to decide. Charlotte's stay had been intended only as a matter of days, and she had stretched it to its limit. In the end she went.

Despite her jealousy, Evie even felt sorry for her. Her friends might have believed in Bohemian promiscuity but

Charlotte had always had such a clear-eyed view of the world. She wanted it to be decent, honest and simple. And Charlotte had never in her life been troubled by doubt. Now all her certainties were in pieces at her feet.

On the day Charlotte left, she asked Evie to take Leo away somewhere so that he couldn't see her leave, because she couldn't face the pain of parting. And Leo had never forgiven Evie for it. Had Charlotte known how much she was asking?

Evie tore the dahlia into pieces. Maybe people were better off without that kind of love. Charlotte had chosen Edward and her child and made a great success of her life. Evie had tried three times to find a man to match Leo and each time failed. Yet she hadn't been unhappy. She had two sons who had proved fertile and many grandchildren who loved her and whom she entertained with all the outrageousness she had developed in later life. It hadn't been a bad life. You might say that it had all worked out perfectly well – apart from Lily.

Lily had been the fly in the ointment, the lump in the bed, the permanent itch for Charlotte. Evie had kept her distance because she couldn't face the layers of deceit, the life built on a lie. But Charlotte could. Trust Charlotte.

And now Evie had decided to intervene because she saw what it would do to Lily to lose Victoriana, and with it that precious self-esteem she had earned over the last year. So she had turned to Leo – but Leo hadn't come. Perhaps – the thought made her shiver in the warm evening – Leo didn't want to know. After thirty-five years of building another life, Leo was entitled to want to leave things to lie.

Evie turned back for the house in a swish of silk that sounded like the rustle of dead leaves. It was unfair, she knew, but she was disappointed in Leo Orson.

Charlotte dipped back behind the heavy curtain before her

sister could notice her. Evie was up to something. She was sure of that much. Charlotte sighed, an uncharacteristic gesture. Was she right to sell Victoriana? A sudden pain darted across her chest, momentarily crippling her. They had started again, those pains. At first she had assumed it was the stress: the fear that Victoriana would go bankrupt, that she would be humiliated, that they would lose everything. Lately, it had seemed to her that perhaps it was because she had buried so much that her chest was hurting, that the body was insisting on an acknowledgement that the spirit had resisted.

Would it have been better if she had told the truth? She had chosen not to for the sake of the survival of the family, and yet, subconsciously, she'd blamed Lily, as though it were Lily's fault that she had to make this terrible sacrifice, not Charlotte's own. She had held it against Lily and Lily's personality had reinforced her instincts. She was always so difficult and rebellious. When she grew up, she had insisted on being an actress, with the awful wandering life that entailed; there had been the promiscuity and the awful publicity when her relationships went wrong. Despite all that, there was the supreme irony that Edward loved her best of all the children.

Charlotte reached for her pills. She hated introspection as she hated weakness. She also hated indecision, but since this business started, the fears and doubts had begun to seep under her defences like wet rot attacking timber, making her both weak and indecisive. I have to resolve this, she warned herself, I have to stop the rot.

She steadied herself against one of the posts of her half-tester bed. They had found this, run-down and neglected, its oak frame whitened by damp, in the barn belonging to one of their farming neighbours. It had taken Charlotte weeks of sanding and treating and staining to restore it. She had been pregnant with Lily, and that and the demands of the burgeoning Victoriana had taken her mind off what she was actually doing. Once the restoration was finished she had made the curtains for it herself, in a Liberty print of peacock feathers, ignoring her outraged cleaning woman who insisted that it meant the evil eye. Then in a rashly childish gesture she had carved a heart on the inner side of one of the wooden joints where no one but she would ever see it.

Feverishly Charlotte scrabbled at the bedclothes and pulled the heavy mattress back. It was there still.

'Charlotte, what on earth are you doing?' For a moment she had to shake her head and remind herself that it was not Leo's voice but Edward's.

'I lost my glasses,' Charlotte insisted, roughly pulling up the bedclothes again.

Edward watched her in consternation. Perhaps it was the strain of tomorrow's meeting. 'You're already wearing them.'

Charlotte's hand flew up to her face, but she continued to sit. 'How ridiculous of me.'

'Charlotte . . .' Edward tried to put an arm around her shoulders, but her body stiffened and withdrew from him. 'We really ought to talk about tomorrow.'

'I see no reason for that. You must vote as you think fit. The company's yours as well as mine.'

Edward's voice hardened. 'We both know that isn't true. It's your company and always has been. I've never felt I really counted in it.'

Charlotte felt as though a freezing draught of air had chilled her, like walking into air-conditioning when you were already wet and cold. 'I didn't know you felt like that.'

She thought he was going to elaborate, but he didn't. 'I think I'll sleep in the spare room tonight. We both need a decent rest.'

Charlotte sank back on to the huge oak bed. It felt horribly empty – like her life had started to do.

Chapter 26

Lily woke early, as she always did when she was nervous, but today she was starving and longed for the taste of frying bacon. Stress always made her hungry. While others sipped black coffee and bit their nails, Lily longed for calories and carbohydrate.

To take her mind off the ordeal ahead she dressed with great care – forget the sedate, corporate image, an occasion like this called for the real, undiluted essence of Lily Brandon. She sorted through her wardrobe until she found what she was looking for: the crushed velvet mulberry trouser suit that made her feel like Marc Bolan, if he'd been a foot taller and changed sex. She'd had enough of dressing for other people.

As a final gesture she dosed herself liberally in Paloma Picasso, not a perfume for the shy and retiring, and applied her dark red lipstick. She was as ready as she was ever going to be.

Everyone at Victoriana knew about the board meeting, that much was obvious. There had been no official announcement to the staff, yet the tension was apparent round every corner. Lily realized she was walking around the building as though she were saying goodbye, trying to memorize the place in which she'd spent the last year. She'd already gazed at the exterior: the way the Mill had claimed for itself the most enfolding, sheltered spot in the valley; the willows outside it drooping gracefully into the slow-flowing stream; the weathered flint of the two barns with their rusty, lichen-covered tiles, swooping down on one side in what local builders called a cat slide roof. Inside, the place hummed with activity. It was as though every staff member was forgetting the future by working twice as hard today.

Lily couldn't believe that after tomorrow all this might belong to someone else, might even close down and fall into dereliction as North's waited a brief interval then moved what remained of the operation to Richmond.

Inside the larger of the barn conversions the sun streamed in through the huge glass windows where only a couple of weeks ago June, Evie, Shauna and she had sat, laughing and waiting with the other girls for the response to the Special Offer that they'd hoped would save the company, or at least buy them more time to sort out its problems. There had been a wonderful atmosphere that day, almost like pulling together in wartime. They were a terrific bunch and Lily knew they'd enjoyed working for her.

There had been, it now struck her, a different mood during the time she'd run Victoriana from her mother's era. Charlotte had run the company on respect. She demanded it and her employees gave it. Lily had aimed for something subtler, a kind of comradeship which lightened the mood and made working hours rewarding and fun, even when they were exhausting.

At the sight of Lily, June abandoned her post and ran towards her clutching a wad of photographs.

'Lily, look, Shauna's had her baby!'

And there it was, a pale little scrap with a tuft of bright red hair sticking out of the scruffy hospital blanket, its mouth open in a lusty roar. 'The darling!' She leafed through the photographs until she came across one of Shauna herself, looking like she'd been run over by a bus, but deliriously happy.

Lily thought of Shauna in the delivery ward with no proud partner to hold her hand and reassure her that she was doing brilliantly. 'Was her mother there for the birth?' She hoped someone was.

June grinned. 'She told her mother to stay at home, she didn't want fag ash in the formula. She'd rather have Billy with her.'

'Her *brother*? But he's only seventeen!'

'I know,' June winked at her, 'but he's very big for his age and built to match. Shauna says he's a threat to every un-married woman under eighty in the country. She thought that if he saw where it all ends it might make him watch where he put it in future.'

'And did it work?'

'Apparently. He's abandoning bonking in bus shelters and going to take up youth work.'

What an amazing girl Shauna was. If she could brave her family and have a baby without support, why couldn't Lily? Connie would be supportive, of course, and her father, but what about Charlotte? Would she turn a frosty gaze on the child? Lily closed her eyes and tried to imagine her mother's whole-hearted congratulations. It was no good. Instead she remembered how disapproving her mother had been of Shauna's pregnancy. How would she react when she discovered her own daughter's?

'Is it a boy or a girl?'

'A girl. Oh, goodness, I forgot. She wants to know if you'd mind if she called it Lily.'

For a moment Lily's eyes threatened to blur Shauna's photos. At least there would be one good thing to come out of her time at Victoriana.

*

Charlotte had hoped that Edward might have softened over-night. They hadn't spent a night apart in years and the expe-rience had robbed her of her usual confidence. The protec-tive cloak Edward threw over her had never been under-stood by those who simply saw her as the dominant one. But there was no sign of any change of heart.

They drove silently to Victoriana. Charlotte stared out at the landscape she loved so much. Soon the ploughed fields would be mole-brown and empty, the colour of faded velvet, their surfaces dotted with broken stones.

Edward's voice cut into the silence, sharper than one of the flint arrowheads sometimes found in those fields. 'Are you happy now that you're finally defeating Lily?' He'd been awake half the night worrying about the effect to-day's outcome would have on her. 'Even if it means selling Victoriana to an asset-stripper?'

'Don't be ridiculous.' Charlotte tried to shake off the leth-argy which was threatening to envelop her. 'North is not an asset-stripper. He's promised to keep as many jobs as he can. He's the one who can ensure Victoriana's future. We were within five minutes of going bankrupt, for God's sake. If you didn't worship Lily so much you'd see that.'

'And if you didn't resent her so much you'd see what this is doing to her. It can't be worth it.' His hands tightened on the wheel. 'If you sell, Charlotte, I'm not sure about our future together.'

'Are you telling me, I can't count on your support?'

They were just turning into Victoriana's driveway. Edward slammed the car to a stop outside the front en-trance, making the receptionist look up in surprise. Mr Brandon was usually such a calm driver. 'I think I'm telling you rather more than that, Charlotte.'

The receptionist held open the door for Charlotte and stood back proudly. The reception area looked more like a funeral parlour at Harvest Festival. There were bunches of flowers everywhere, some in large vases, some in jam jars. There was even a bunch of Michaelmas daises in a decorated Perrier bottle.

'Where on earth did they all come from?' asked Charlotte.

'The staff brought them – a sort of good luck offering, I think. You don't mind, do you, Mrs Brandon?' she asked, suddenly nervous. Then she smiled over Charlotte's shoulder at Lily who had just made an entrance, wearing some curious outfit that appeared to be made from an Odeon cinema's reject curtains.

She likes Lily, Charlotte thought, startled, and she's frightened of me. Once I would have been pleased about that.

'Hello, Ma. Are any of the others here yet?' There was a chilly distance in Lily's voice Charlotte had never noticed before.

The girl on reception answered her. 'You're the first. Do you want to go up? Shall I ask them to bring the coffee?'

She directed her question at Lily, but it was Charlotte who answered it. 'That would be lovely. Thank you.' It irritated her that the girl glanced to Lily for confirmation.

The run of good weather had deserted them and today was gloomy. It struck Lily as a bad omen. Sunshine reflecting on polished wood floors and light flooding through huge windows had become as much a part of her picture of Victoriana as the comradeship of the people working there.

Before the meeting started, she slipped up to her office for her notes. A huge and hideous card in the shape of a horseshoe, signed by everyone in the company from Brian in the warehouse to the canteen ladies, waited for her on her desk. Lily bit her lip, trying not to give in to the tears that were threatening to undermine her. In small and inconsequential ways this place had become the centre of her life. The past year came back to her as a series of moments strung together like gems on a necklace: that first day with

George when he'd said she had a quick brain for figures; Connie and the catalogue, the Bathsheba look that had attracted so much attention; Shauna and her baby; the growing sense that she was competent and talented. On the wall beside her she'd framed the ad featuring Connie in the camisole.

Where was Connie, come to think of it? Lily took a deep breath and went down to join the others.

Outside the boardroom Evie – who was attending the meeting by special invitation – beckoned vigorously, a lighthouse of encouragement in a sea of gloom. 'Come on, Lily girl, get your pecker up. We're all relying on you to talk her highness out of selling.' Evie's enormous earrings reminded Lily of satellite dishes with jellyfishes marooned on them. They clattered cheerily against her silver aboriginal necklace every time she moved.

'Thanks, Evie, I'll do my best.'

There was still no sign of Connie.

'I'll wait for her,' Lily offered, ushering Evie into the boardroom where the others were already seated.

'Where on earth is Connie?' asked Charlotte irritably. Now that it had come to it, she wanted to get the whole thing over as quickly as possible. In the tense silence that followed they could hear excited voices shout encouragement and good luck to Lily as she waited in the corridor.

'Listen to that,' Judith commented to her husband, 'anyone would think she was Joan of bloody Arc.'

When Connie finally arrived no one could have missed her entrance. She was wearing an ivory silk suit and a grin that stretched halfway to Bidchester.

'My God,' Evie mouthed to Lily, 'you don't think the angel Gabriel has come down upon her?'

'No,' Connie whispered back, 'only my husband.'

'Shall we finally get started then?' Charlotte demanded.

She would have made a good headmistress, thought Evie,

remembering her own, a grey-haired old lady who showed her pupils the kindness and understanding of Mrs Squiers. But Charlotte certainly knew how to hold the attention. Even the motes of dust suspended in the air seemed stiller when she spoke. An end-of-season fly stopped its buzzing and settled. Ranged round the Heal's walnut table, vast and in the style of the Arts and Crafts movement, everyone leaned forward in their seats.

'As you know,' Charlotte continued, 'North's Mail Order has offered to buy the company. It is not as substantial an offer as we might have wanted' – Judith caught her husband's eye in a conspiracy of infuriating smugness – 'but that is hardly surprising, given the circumstances. Victoriana, as you all know, has had serious financial problems, resulting in one of our suppliers very nearly taking out bankruptcy proceedings against us. The financial report is in front of you. This is an extraordinarily hard decision for us all, but I have to say that I've studied all the information available and I have to recommend selling to North's.'

As everyone round the table knew, Charlotte could not sell without the support of one other shareholder. Unconsciously they glanced at Edward, but he waved them on, almost as if he had no strong view either way. Lily slumped. She'd been hoping so much for her father's support. Perhaps, in the end, he was too much in her mother's shadow after all.

Lily stood up. She had to persuade them not to sell the company that had taken a year of her life, and which she believed passionately had a brilliant future.

'As the person responsible for all these financial problems I'd like to put my case for holding on to Victoriana.' Everyone except Judith was watching her. 'Of course it's been a difficult year. I made mistakes; but I learned from those mistakes and even turned one of them – the overs we had of the silk camisole – into an advantage. The financial situation has improved dramatically. Thanks to the Special Offer we can repay First Venture and Wilson's have already accepted part payment for their cloth.'

Lily saw Judith glance at Charlotte – so she hadn't known that the crisis was over. Now was the moment to go on the attack. 'The design, the marketing, the catalogue, are all coming together brilliantly and we're drawing in younger buyers. This isn't the time to sell Victoriana. It might even be the time to expand. It's a company with a fantastic past and an even more amazing future, providing we just adapt to the times.'

'Perhaps Victoriana should get the Queen's Award for Industry,' Judith suggested nastily, 'instead of going bankrupt and losing a hundred and fifty people their jobs. At least North's would save some of those.'

Lily could hardly believe the nerve of the woman.

'If North's is so intent on saving jobs locally,' she demanded angrily, 'then why have you and Barry North been looking at a new HQ for Victoriana in Richmond?'

For a second Judith looked panicked. Jonathan's head swivelled comically towards hers. Clearly this had come as a complete surprise.

Judith leaned over and patted him. 'Duke's Reach, you mean?' She recovered herself swiftly and sounded convincingly incredulous: 'That's for one of North's other companies. How could it possibly be for Victoriana?' She smiled at Lily, as though they were playing some elaborate game and Judith knew she had the winning hand. 'It's in Richmond and Victoriana's based down here.'

Lily bit back her disappointment. She'd used her best card and Judith had topped it.

'I think you'd better apologize to Judith for that unpleasant suggestion,' Charlotte said coolly.

'There's no need,' Judith dismissed. 'Lily's been under a lot of strain lately. Steering a company from success to near-bankruptcy in less than a year can't make you feel too good about yourself.'

Under other circumstances, Lily decided, she would like to have slapped her sister-in-law. Don't crumble, she told herself, that's what she wants.

Why doesn't Edward speak up for her? Evie thought angrily. He gave her the responsibility now he's letting her carry the can instead of standing by her.

'The only real way to save jobs,' Judith carried on relentlessly, 'is to have a secure company like North's behind you. That's why I'm convinced we should sell.'

'Absolutely,' echoed Jonathan. He had obviously decided to accept his wife's explanation about the HQ being for someone else. 'Look,' he began, in what he hoped were jovial tones, 'Why don't we stop for coffee now . . .'

Lily began to lose heart. Her father clearly wasn't even going to bother to defend her. Perhaps he was just going to vote with Charlotte and get back to his garden.

'Does anyone else have anything to add?' asked Charlotte.

Jonathan stood up and Edward followed him, but coffee, it transpired, was not uppermost in Edward's mind.

'What surprises me,' he said, leaning on the table and addressing them almost with condescension, 'is that with so many business minds assembled, and this includes you, Charlotte, none of you seem to be able to tell cash-flow problems from long-term viability.' Jonathan sat down again. 'Lily has had cash-flow problems, and believe me, I blame myself for not helping her sort them out. I thought it would be good for her to stand on her own feet, but she was too inexperienced. As she says, she's learned a lot since then – and Victoriana's long-term growth prospects, according to George, are very healthy indeed.' Blissful relief flooded through Lily. He was not only defending her personally but acknowledging her business capacities as well. 'I would, contrary to the prevailing mood of this meeting, like to congratulate you, Lily, for a job well done.'

Lily glowed as though a shaft of sunshine had beamed down on her. He still believed in her. He was proud of her. He didn't think she'd wrecked Victoriana.

Evie clapped loudly, and Connie joined in too, but Edward wasn't quite finished. 'The final thing I have to say is that I am opposing this sale, not just because I believe in Victoriana's future but because Barry North is a shit. And if you sell to a shit then don't be surprised if he behaves like one. Now, as Jonathan clearly wishes, I suggest we have a break before coming to a decision.'

Lily got up from the table after the others, her pride in herself leaking away at the sight of her parents' hostility to one another, and at the general mood of resigned inevitability. It was as though the vote had already taken place and they had lost. Charlotte clearly hadn't changed her mind, neither had Jonathan. Even with her father, Connie and herself opposing the sale it could still go through.

Coffee and biscuits were laid out but Lily, for once, had lost her appetite. She just wanted it to finish so that she could pick up the pieces of her life.

They were about to sit down again when George beckoned discreetly to Lily and Evie. 'We've just had a phone call from Paul Allan at First Venture.' Lily caught her breath. What was Paul doing phoning out of the blue? 'He says to tell Eve that Leo Orson is on his way.'

'Evie,' Lily demanded, a splinter of insight penetrating her mind, 'what exactly is going on?'

'Ah,' Evie said joyously, 'Paul Allan and I have got a little surprise for you. He's been doing some digging into Barry North's activities.' She had no idea what Leo Orson and Paul had found out. She just hoped that whatever it was, it would be enough to change Charlotte's mind.

Chapter 27

Lily slipped unobtrusively down to Victoriana's front entrance. The company's familiar wine-coloured vans with their black lettering were filling up with deliveries. A family of ducks hopped out of the stream and approached her, hoping for someone's lunchtime sandwiches. It was a peaceful scene, but Lily felt anything but peaceful. Her mind was racing. What had Leo Orson, someone she only knew as a name on Victoriana's letter-head, managed to find out? And how on earth was Paul involved in all this?

A black cab turned into their drive, as incongruous in this rural backwater as a London bus, its diesel engine sputtering through the quiet morning air. Her heart lurched at the thought that Paul might be in it but only one person was sitting in the back, chatting to the driver. Surely to God he hadn't driven all the way from London in a taxi?

The passenger climbed out, a tanned and fit man in his sixties with an expensive haircut and wearing a pale pink cashmere sweater and immaculate slacks. On first glance he looked like one of the international rich who had started out for Harrods and somehow taken a wrong turn and ended up in Dorset. Then Lily looked at him more closely. He was smiling faintly, his warm brown eyes holding hers. They

359

had a mesmeric quality, those eyes, so that she couldn't look away. He was reaching out his hand to her.

'You must be Lily.' His grip was firm and he showed no sign of letting go of her, yet there was no hint of familiarity nor of flirtation. Lily stood rooted, feeling as though an electric charge of confidence was being pumped through her.

Leo finally released her and Lily felt an unaccountable jolt of disappointment, as if she'd been cut off from a powerful energy source. 'How far have they got with the meeting?' he asked.

'We were about to vote on the sale.'

Leo smiled. 'Thanks to your friend Paul, we should be able to open a few eyes on that score. Shall we go up?'

Outside the boardroom Lily put her finger to her lips. Her mind was racing with all the different possibilities, but she knew instinctively she could trust Leo. 'If we're going to do this, let's give them their money's worth. You stay here until I introduce you.'

'For goodness sake, Evie,' Charlotte was demanding angrily, 'where on earth has Lily got to?'

'Shall I go and look for her?' offered Connie, just as the boardroom doors opened and Lily reappeared.

'Really, Lily,' carped Charlotte, 'we've all been waiting for ten minutes to have the vote.'

Lily was unrepentant. 'We may have to hold the vote. There's been rather an important development.'

Judith's perfectly made-up eyes fastened themselves on Lily's. There was something about Lily's manner she didn't like. Lily had the kind of suppressed excitement of someone who's in possession of bad news before anyone else.

'What development?' demanded Charlotte.

'We have an unexpected guest.'

'For heaven's sake, Lily, this is a private meeting. We

don't want any more guests,' – she glanced irritably at Evie – 'unexpected or otherwise.'

'What about if they happen to be shareholders in the company.'

Charlotte felt the blood draining from her face as Leo Orson walked out of her past and into the room. 'Leo!' she whispered. 'My God, is it really you?'

He stood for a beat of a second with his eyes locked into hers then turned to the rest of the gathering and introduced himself.

At the sight of him panic took hold of Judith. Then, after doing a swift mental calculation, she calmed down. Leo Orson might have come half way across the world to vote, but it would make no difference. He only owned 9 per cent of the shares to Jonathan's 10 per cent. They could still out-vote him.

'Since you're here' – Charlotte was recovering herself now, but her voice still shook at the edges as though she were suffering from shock – 'we might as well get on with voting. Or would you like us to recap on the offer first?'

'No thanks.' Leo was disconcertingly calm. 'I know all I want to know about the offer – but *you* might like to read this document before you go ahead and make up your minds. It's pretty hot stuff I assure you.' He distributed copies round the table.

Judith picked up the four-page document in front of her and scanned it. A freezing gut-wrenching horror paralysed her. It was a report written by Clive Green, outlining plans for firing every local employee, moving the whole operation to Duke's Reach and cancelling all contracts with their British suppliers in favour of cheaper ones in the Far East.

Judith's immediate temptation was to deny all knowledge of it. There seemed to be no evidence that she was implicated. If she insisted strongly enough they would have to believe her. It was just a question of chutzpah and she had plenty of that.

Then she saw her husband's expression. It was filled with loathing. 'How very cosy,' Jonathan's tone hissed with malice. 'So you were going to run it all for him, were you? Was that before or after the divorce?' He looked as though he might skip the matrimonial proceedings and go straight for a *crime passionnel*.

'What on earth are you on about, Jonathan?' Judith opened her blue eyes in apparent innocence.

'Look at who the memo's copied to,' he suggested unpleasantly.

That stupid creep Green had included Judith's name at the end under the title managing director designate.

Charlotte read the piece of paper through twice. Her first thought was: how on earth has Leo laid hands on this damning information? And then its significance hit her. Judith – the daughter-in-law she'd trusted and admired for her style and her toughness; who'd reminded Charlotte of herself; whom she'd even wished was running the company instead of Lily – had all the time been planning to join North in his massacre of all her most cherished ideals. 'Well, Judith?' Charlotte demanded finally. 'What duplicitous answer are you going to come up with to all this?'

Judith decided this wasn't the moment for pretence. The deal had fallen through anyway, and probably her boring marriage with it. She reached down, picked up her small neat bag, slipped her gold-plated pen in it and closed it with a dismissive snap. She'd had enough of the bloody Brandons. 'You're living in the past, Charlotte. Victoriana could be a goldmine if you didn't run it like a charity. Lily's no better. She may have introduced computers but she's got the same ludicrous attitudes as you. Business isn't about employee welfare, it's about making money.'

'Lily and I happen to believe it's possible to achieve both.' Lily felt a quickening of pleasure at her mother's words. It was an acknowledgment, however slight, of what Lily had done. 'You probably wouldn't understand that.' Charlotte could see that Judith was about to take the initiative and walk out, so she got in first. 'I think you should go now, Judith, or we might have to consult the lawyers about all of this.'

Judith summoned all the dignity her small, neat body could muster and walked calmly from the room. Jonathan stared angrily ahead, studiously ignoring her.

'I take it that after this we all intend to turn down the offer from North's Mail Order?' There was the merest suggestion of wry humour in Charlotte's question.

Her eyes rested momentarily on Leo, as if she were about to say more, but instead she gathered up her papers and started towards the door. At the last moment she turned. 'Thank you, Leo, for coming to our rescue.' Her voice held such intensity that Lily glanced from one to the other. 'You saved me from making a terrible mistake.'

The room fell silent as though no one wanted to interrupt them. Then Charlotte seemed to remember where she was. 'Are you coming, Edward?'

Edward made no move to leave.

In the end it was Evie who took her arm and led her out. Once they were outside the room, Lily noticed, Charlotte lost her stiffbacked bearing and began to lean heavily against her sister.

Jonathan remained at the table. Without the dreadful Judith he looked like a jowly ownerless dog. My God, thought Lily, I bet if North won't have her, he'll take her back in the end.

Charlotte let Evie drive her home without protesting, and even agreed to sit with a rug over her knees and be fed camomile tea. 'Can't stand the muck,' Evie confided, handing it to her, 'but people say it calms you down.'

'It was you who brought him here, wasn't it?'

'I had to stop you selling. Lily knew Judith was in bed with North but she couldn't prove it. I thought he was the one person you might listen to. And it worked.'

'Why didn't Lily tell me her suspicions herself?'

Evie hesitated. 'She didn't think you'd believe her. She knew Judith would deny it, and that you'd accept every word she said. You always thought everything Judith did was right, didn't you, Charlotte?'

Charlotte seemed to crumple and sink down in her chair. 'I can't believe how wrong I was about Judith. All my life I've trusted my instincts and she was simply deceiving me.'

Evie sat on a footstool and took her sister's cold hand in hers. 'What about how wrong you were about Lily? It was she who really saved Victoriana. She found out about the plans to move and that Sam Wilson was being leant on.'

Charlotte tried to take her hand away but Evie hung on to it. 'She's talented and brave and determined and she loves you more than anyone else on this earth, Charlotte. Doesn't that kind of love deserve to be returned?'

Charlotte seemed to shrink up like an old woman. 'I don't know whether I can.'

For the first time in her life, Evie actually felt sorry for her sister. 'Charlotte, surely it's time to face the truth? You've had to sit on your emotions for so long you can't feel anything for anyone any more – not just Lily, but for Edward, or Jonathan, or even Connie. You've turned yourself into a dry well, and it's been your loss as well as theirs. Giving love isn't a weakness, it's a strength.' Charlotte looked away. 'If she gets rid of this baby because she's frightened of not loving it, how will you feel? Another wasted life on your conscience, Charlotte. Yours, Lily's and now this baby's. I think you owe her an explanation for why you haven't loved her.'

Charlotte stared into the fire. 'It's a terrible risk. What about Edward? It will hurt him so much.'

'Life is a terrible risk. She's not happy, Charlotte.'

'I need to talk to Leo first.'

'I know. I asked him to follow us.'

The clanging of the doorbell sounded to Charlotte like a death sentence. Her first temptation was to run away, to leave things as they had been, but that would be the coward's way out and Charlotte, for all her faults, was no coward.

As she waited for him to come into the room, she forced herself to be Charlotte Brandon, grande dame, founder of Victoriana and darling of the press.

'Hello, Charlotte.' She had forgotten his eyes, that fierce yellow-brown, so like Lily's, half laughing at her, still. And she had forgotten the electricity, the sense of danger and possibility that his presence had always evoked in her. 'As calm and queenly as ever, I see.'

Charlotte almost laughed. Her emotions were racing, whirling wildly through her like a sandstorm. 'I wanted to thank you properly for what you've done.'

He nodded dismissively, still holding her eyes with his. 'Think nothing of it, Charlotte. I wouldn't want you to make a mistake about something so important that you'd regret it for the rest of your life, now would I?'

He hasn't forgiven her then, thought Evie, watching them both. Leo had always been like this, light and teasing about those things that mattered to him most. She knew they had both forgotten her presence. It was just as it had always been: as if they were the only two people in the room or, indeed, on the planet.

'How are you?' Charlotte asked eventually. 'Evie says you've been ill.'

'You too.' Leo stood up and stared into the fire for a moment. 'I want to tell her, Charlotte.'

'That's your prerogative. I can't stop you.'

'You could deny it, say I'm some madman.' The look in her eyes told him that she wouldn't do so, that such a betrayal of their love wouldn't be possible for her.

'Leo.' She had to ask him the question she was asking herself. 'How can you be sure it won't damage her?'

'I can't.' Leo had always been truthful. 'But Evie says she's never been able to settle down, she's always searching for something. It could be me.'

The thought of all she had to lose crowded into Charlotte's mind: whatever love Lily had for her, Edward, the life she'd built. But that life was crumbling anyway. Charlotte saw Lily's unhappy face, the yearning for love that Charlotte had never been able to give. Perhaps knowing the truth about Leo would help her after all.

'Tell her then.'

The excitement in Leo's face made him seem like a young man again.

She watched from the long drawing-room window as he ran out to his car, and knew she must go and find Edward to warn him. It was time she told him too, but he still didn't seem to be back from the meeting. 'Where's Edward got to? Surely he's not still at Victoriana?'

Evie came and sat on the arm of her chair. 'He's gone, Charlotte. He asked Connie to tell you.' A thud of pain hammered into Charlotte's chest. 'He says he needs some time to think.'

Charlotte stared ahead of her. 'I've lost them both. Finding out will destroy Edward. And Lily will never forgive me for not telling her Leo's her real father. This is the end for me.'

She silently reached up and took her sister's hand in hers. Evie held on to it, fighting back her own tears, as if trying to pull Charlotte out of the icy waters that threatened to engulf her. No easy words of comfort came to Evie. All she could do was stay and wait.

Together they sat watching the darkness fall over the house and landscape Charlotte loved so much, waiting for the blow to fall.

A leaf fell off the huge oak outside Lily's window, then another tumbled in the late afternoon sunshine. She sat on her low window seat in the eaves, looking out at her special view, but it gave her none of her usual feeling of pleasure. On her desk there was a long list of calls to return, and she knew a start must be made on the new season's catalogue. Instead a powerful feeling of anti-climax gripped her. She had no idea whether her mother intended to stay on or not. After the meeting she'd longed for some recognition from Charlotte of the work she'd done for Victoriana, but there had been nothing. Maybe her mother wasn't as grateful as all that, when the truth came out about North and Judith's intentions, after all.

Lily stared out of the window again, remembering the other decision she had to make. By some extraordinary process of nature she had already started to think in terms of we. The primitive desire to have something of her own to care for ran deep in her, stronger than her fears that she might not be able to love it.

The announcement of Leo Orson's arrival cheered her hugely. She knew so little about this man, yet he seemed to have run like a skein through her parents' life, and now he'd saved Victoriana. She'd even suspected that Evie might once have been in love with him. She couldn't wait to get to know him.

When he walked in, she knew at once why women found him so fascinating. In spite of his understated air of wealth there was something of the buccaneer about Leo Orson, a sense that anything was possible, that he didn't fit into the narrow confines of society but made his own rules. Where her own father was the rescuer, Leo was the pirate who carried you off in the first place.

'Lily,' he said simply, reaching out and taking her hand. 'I've heard so much about you.'

Lily laughed. 'And I've heard far too little about you. All I know is that you saved Victoriana.'

'It was only worth saving because you'd done such a good job laying the groundwork. Besides, I didn't do the real work. It was your friend Paul. He took a big risk for you, exposing a colleague. Companies don't like employees investigating each other, even when it's called for. He's a charming man. Clever too.'

Lily deftly steered the conversation away. She still didn't know what she felt about Paul. It was true he'd helped save Victoriana, but then so he should seeing as he'd handed it over to someone who'd turned out to be in Barry North's pocket. She glanced down at her still-flat belly. Sooner or later she was going to have to make a decision about whether to tell him.

'I want to hear everything about you,' Lily insisted, 'right from the very beginning.'

'It's a long story.'

'Let's go for a walk and you can tell me it. Then I can show you how beautiful it is here – how stupid of me, you used to live here, didn't you?'

They walked for an hour through the slanting evening light with Leo explaining to her about his life as an impresario and Lily making him laugh with her tales of the theatre and being a thorn in the side of pompous directors. She was, Leo decided, exactly the kind of daughter he would have wanted.

'So, what are you going to do now?' he asked gently, as they turned back towards Victoriana.

'That rather depends on Ma. I don't know whether she intends coming back.'

'It must have been hard, having Charlotte for a mother.'

Lily's eyes darted to his. He sounded as though he understood. 'Yes. But fortunately I also had Pa. He's a wonderful antidote.' The affection in Lily's tones stabbed at Leo. It had clearly been Edward, more than Charlotte, who'd provided the stability in Lily's sometimes shaky world.

Leo's motives were struck by an unwelcome shaft of honesty. He saw that his real reason for rescuing Victoriana, and in coming here today, hadn't been love, as he had convinced himself, but selfishness. He had wanted Lily to love him, to lend his life a meaning beyond money and material success. Now he could see that any revelation might simply destroy her. It was Charlotte, not he, who held the key to Lily's happiness. He couldn't tell her after all.

But he couldn't let her go either. If she were to come and live with him, surely he could find ways of giving her the love and confidence she lacked. He stopped just before they reached the Mill and took her hand again. 'Come and work for me.' His voice was low and intense with emotion. 'With your acting background you'd be perfect. I've put on some wonderful plays, with names from all over the world. You hate directors. Why not direct yourself?'

Lily suddenly had a blissful vision of herself back in the world of acting, but calling the shots this time. There'd been so many times she'd watched some talentless fool and felt she could do better herself. Leo Orson was actually offering her the chance to try.

'But what about Victoriana?'

Leo committed a small act of selfishness. 'Charlotte has done nothing but interfere, you say. Let her run it – or perhaps Connie.'

Lily was shocked at how tempting she found the prospect he was offering her. She'd had so little thanks from her

369

mother for the last year. It could be a clean slate, whatever decision she came to about the baby.

'I'm leaving the day after tomorrow. Why don't you make up your mind by then?' Ignobly, Leo pressed home his advantage. 'Sometimes it's better to follow your instincts and take a risk.'

Chapter 28

Charlotte didn't know how long she'd been standing at the open window, staring out, when Lily's car drew up. Time had frozen for her. She knew she was cold, and that it had got dark, and that there was still no sign of Edward, but that was all.

She scanned Lily's face for a sign of anger and loathing at Leo's revelation, but Lily seemed just the same. Happier, perhaps, more energetic, but there was no hint of the furious anger Charlotte dreaded.

'What on earth are you doing there, Ma?' Lily's voice held only concern at her mother's distraught appearance. The drawing room was the same as it always was, elegant and stylish with an arrangement of lilies on the low table between the two sofas, their heady scent filling the whole room. It was her mother who was different. She'd never seen Charlotte like this, her hair dishevelled, freezing, an almost despairing look in her eyes.

Lily led her to the sofa and sat her down, then closed the window.

Charlotte screwed up her courage. 'Did Leo Orson find you?' She almost put up her arm to ward off the blow.

'Yes, he did.' Lily's manner seemed as relaxed as ever. 'He's a fascinating character, isn't he?'

Charlotte's head shot up at the question. Leo couldn't have told her after all.

'Actually it was to do with meeting Leo Orson that I came to see you. He's asked me to go and work for him.'

Charlotte's heart helter-skeltered wildly. 'In Australia?'

'Yes. As a director.'

He hadn't told her. He must have lost his nerve at the last moment, or maybe he had decided it wasn't fair. Charlotte felt like a prisoner facing the firing squad who is told she can take off her blindfold. Whatever the reason, she had been given another chance. And this time she wasn't going to throw it away.

'Don't worry, I'm not going.' Relief flooded through Charlotte, she couldn't bear to lose Lily now. 'His offer made me think though. It's time I left Victoriana. Connie could run it for you, she's very able.'

'No, Lily!' Lily had rarely heard such passion from her controlled and dignified mother. 'I've been thinking too. I've been wrong about so many things. About Judith. About you. Edward was right. I did want you to fail. It's shameful to admit it, but I didn't want to believe that anyone but me could run Victoriana.'

Lily held her breath. Her mother was actually apologizing to her.

'Stay, Lily. Stay and run Victoriana. Please.'

These were the words Lily had hoped for so many times and yet they had come too late. Even after all this time, Victoriana still felt like her mother's company.

'No, Ma, I don't think so . . .'

'That's a pity,' Charlotte's eyes held the ghost of a smile, 'because I'm making over my entire shareholding to you.'

'But Victoriana's everything to you!' She was about to add: more even than your husband or your family.

'Not any more. I saw how the people who work there treat you. They did things for me because they were frightened. They did them for you because they wanted to please you, to give you their best. You *are* Victoriana now, not me. I don't expect you to forgive me after all I've done, but do it for them. Don't let them all down. They love you, Lily, and so do I.'

Charlotte opened her arms and Lily ran into them, kneeling at her mother's feet and holding her, all her childhood yearning spilling over into tears of joy that fell into her mother's soft woollen lap.

In the fading darkness they stayed locked together, neither wanting to let go and break the magic.

In the end it was Charlotte who spoke. 'Have you decided what to do about the baby? I'll give you all the support I can, if you want to go ahead.'

'How did you know?' Lily asked.

'Evie told me.' There was a trace of hurt behind the love at being excluded from such important news.

'I should have told you myself but I know what you think of unmarried mothers.'

'Not if they're my own daughter.' Lily could hear the smile of self-mockery in her voice as she stroked Lily's long hair. 'Evie says you're frightened of not loving it. You will, you know. You're brave and talented and loving. You'll be a wonderful mother. Far better than me, thank God, but I do intend to be a wonderful grandmother.' She realized the old Charlotte was emerging again, trying to run other people's lives. 'That is,' she added sheepishly, 'if you do decide to go ahead and have it. Have you told the father yet?'

'Not yet.' Lily thought of Paul and how he would take the news. She had a strange but compelling feeling that he might be entirely delighted.

'Tell him. Secrets are dangerous. I know.'

Across the room, hidden by Charlotte's ancient aspidistra,

Evie was eavesdropping for the last time. There was a humility in her sister's tone she'd never heard before. Charlotte had finally learned that she could be wrong.

Evie brushed away a tear. Had she been right to come halfway across the world and throw her oar into her sister's life with such dramatic consequences?

On the whole she thought she had. Soon it would be time to make the journey home. But before she left there was one last act that had been crying out for her attention. An hour ago she'd telephoned Paul Allan and invited him to join them so they could thank him.

'Lily,' she called softly. 'Could you take the car and go into Bidchester? A friend of mine is arriving from London and I'd hate it if there was no one there to meet him at the station.'

Lily's head lifted from its new home on her mother's knee. She knew that tone only too well.

Aunt Evie was interfering again.

THE END

SIGNET

By the same author

SCENES FROM THE SEX WAR

'Maeve Haran is the new star chronicler of the contemporary scene . . . you feel real regret when her novel ends' – *Annabel*

Allegra Boyd, warm and beautiful, has always been there for chat-show host Matt and their two daughters. Rather like an old sofa. And with the girls growing up and Matt deep in his dazzling career, Ally begins to feel just about as noticeable.

So Ally decides it's *her* turn now. To her amazement she lands a daytime TV slot as an agony aunt and her star begins to soar, bringing with it fame and glamour – not to mention the temptation of up-and-coming Danny Wilde – just as Matt's is starting to wane. But can Matt cope with his wife's success or is Ally's bid for a little independence about to go horribly wrong?

By the same author

IT TAKES TWO

Hotshot lawyer Tess Brien and her ad-man husband Stephen know that a good marriage is hard to keep. They should. Enough of their friends' relationships are crumbling around them. But theirs is a happy home, a secure base for their two lively teenagers.

But when Stephen suddenly gives up his job, leaving a stressed and angry Tess to pick up the bills, and another woman seems determined to have Stephen at any cost, distrust and disruption threaten to destroy their idyllic home ...

'Maeve Haran has a feel for the substantial concerns of her readers ... which is why she has become required reading for modern romantics' – *The Times*

also published:

Having It All